Praise for Jane Moore's *Fourplay*

"Hilarious cynicism about relationships will appeal to anyone who's ever lost in love. As therapeutic for heartbreak as a voodoo doll!" —*Glamour*

"Jane Moore's novel is a feel-good read, which sparkles with her trademark funny one-liners." —*Elle*

"Moore's endearing exuberance and sense of humor are seductive while the male cast and sex scenes are . . . good fun." —*Sunday Times* (London)

"A hilarious and assured modern-day Jane Austen romp." —*GQ*

"A slickly plotted, sassy tale [that] takes a look at the highs and lows of being newly single." —*Cosmopolitan*

"A fairy tale for grown-ups." —*Marie Claire*

"A lighthearted read that might make you yearn for your days as a single woman!" —*Family Circle*

"*Fourplay*'s like a deliciously gossipy session with your girl-friends—it's compulsive."

—Cathy Kelly, author of
What She Wants and *Someone Like You*

Also by Jane Moore

Fourplay

Broadway Books

New York

The Ex Files

a novel

Jane Moore

PRINTED IN THE UNITED STATES OF AMERICA

BROADWAY BOOKS and its logo, a letter B bisected on the diagonal, are trademarks of Random House, Inc.

Visit our website at www.broadwaybooks.com

First edition published 2004

Book design by Dana Leigh Treglia

Library of Congress Cataloging-in-Publication Data

Moore, Jane, 1962 May 17–
The Ex Files : a novel / Jane Moore.
p.   cm.
I. Title

PR6113.O557E9 2004
813'.6—dc22
2003056054

ISBN 0-7679-1602-6

1   3   5   7   9   10   8   6   4   2

For my husband, Gary

The Ex Files

He booted open the bedroom door with his bare foot, then removed her slip-dress in one swift motion as she raised her arms. Now wearing nothing more than a G-string, Faye yielded as he pushed her against the wall and continued the kissing session that had started on the living-room sofa just five minutes earlier.

While she fumbled with his shirt buttons, he saved time by undoing his belt and fly, then kicked off his trousers, which fell in a crumpled heap on the floor. Maneuvering her towards the bed, he pushed her backwards so that she plunged into the duck-down duvet. The movement jolted the bedside table, and a framed photograph of a middle-aged woman crashed to the floor. Standing over her, he stared into her eyes, a crooked smile on his lips, then slowly pulled off the G-string. He dangled it on the end of his finger, then tossed it aside.

Damn, he's sexy, she thought, as he lowered himself towards her, never taking his gaze from hers. She fully expected him to be a "Monopoly" lover, a term she and her friends had coined for men who selfishly moved straight to "Go," so her breath caught as he started to slow-kiss his way down her body from just beneath her breasts.

Unlike the inept performances of the stamp lickers she and her friends also complained about, this one knew *exactly* what he was doing.

She closed her eyes to savor the sensation, then snapped them open again. Initially she'd wanted nothing more than to have sex with this man, but the reality of knowing that it was about to happen suddenly brought her to her senses. What on earth was she *doing*?

It had been easy, as flirtation always was. A couple of meaningful stares across a crowded cattle market—or do they call them wine bars?—followed by a couple of slow lip-lickings. Within minutes of her friend Susie's departure to catch the last train, he was at Faye's side.

"May I buy you a drink?" He smiled.

"I already have one, thanks." She held up the remnants of a glass of white wine.

"In that case, as we're being pedantic, may I buy you *another*?"

Normally, having established a man's interest, Faye would have brushed him off and headed home, but tonight she had found herself nodding. "OK."

She encountered gorgeous men all the time in her job as a model, but there was something mesmerizing about this one. He had dark hair, blue eyes, and a well-toned body, but he also had an X factor that intrigued her. Flecks of gray were starting to appear just above his ears, but it suited him. He was confident and, judging by his Gucci shirt and Ralph Lauren loafers, not short of a bob or two.

"Are you drinking alone?" she said, craning to see if anyone was behind him.

"Yep. Just fancied a quick one." He waved his beer in front of her. "But it turned into several."

"Are you from around here?" She couldn't believe she was asking such humdrum questions, but his confidence and maturity unnerved her.

"No." He didn't elaborate. "You?"

"Just round the corner." She felt her neck flush as she said it.

For the next half-hour, they were engrossed in conversation, never taking their eyes off each other until Faye felt a hand on her shoulder. It was the bar manager, gesturing behind him where chairs were being stacked on the tables.

"I'll walk you home," he said, in a tone that suggested he wasn't going to take no for an answer.

"Thanks." Curiously, she felt protected rather than threatened.

During the short walk, she had vowed she would say goodbye on the doorstep, but when they arrived at her front door she felt compelled to spend more time with him.

"Coffee?" she had asked. "And, no, that's not a euphemism."

"Damn." He clicked his fingers in mock frustration. "But can I have wine instead?"

The bottle of Chablis they shared had been her undoing.

Now she was studying him as, hair flopping into his face, he concentrated on the task in hand. She still felt attracted to him, but her desire for him had been outweighed by pangs of guilt about her uncharacteristic sluttishness. Yes, he was gorgeous, sexy, funny, and interesting, but he was also a complete stranger and she just didn't *do* that sort of thing.

"Look, if you don't mind, I'd rather we didn't go all the way," she said. She put her hands on his shoulders and eased him away.

A fleeting look of surprise crossed his face before he fell beside her, wiping a bead of sweat from his forehead. She grabbed a corner of the duvet and draped it over her naked body. Then she reached into her handbag and pulled out a pack of Marlboro Lights. The small chrome clock on the bedside table read 12:10 a.m.

Propping herself up on one elbow, she glanced at him lying next to her, then he suddenly caught her eye. Embarrassed, she blew smoke towards his face, then giggled to show it was a joke.

"Your bedroom habits could do with a little work." He frowned.

"Look, I don't mean to be rude, and I'm really sorry, but this doesn't seem like such a good idea after all, and I have to be up horribly early. So if you don't mind, I'll call you a cab," she said.

He raised his eyebrows. A small twitch started in his cheek, and his blue eyes turned darker as his pupils expanded. After a few moments, his expression softened and he stroked the side of her face gently. "Why don't I stay a little longer?" he murmured.

Faye was tempted to let him, but she felt deflated and angry with herself for allowing a wine-bar flirtation to develop so far. Now that the effect of the wine had worn off, she realized she knew nothing about this man. He could be a psychotic killer, yet she'd brought him back to her flat without anyone else knowing. How reckless, she thought. How desperate. How unbelievably stupid.

Her mind went into overdrive. She had no plans for Sunday, so her mutilated body might not be found until late next week when maybe her best friend, Adam, or her mother would have made several calls and be wondering where she was. Or perhaps the woman downstairs would eventually notice the smell.

She took another drag of her cigarette and tried to calm

herself. Psychotic killers didn't go to wine bars for a casual drink . . . did they?

She gave a cavernous yawn, fatigue creeping up on her, and ground out the cigarette. "As I said, I'd really rather you left." She looked apologetic.

Flopping onto his back, he lay there motionless. For a moment, she thought he was going to be difficult. She couldn't believe it: so many of her female friends had whined that men couldn't wait to leave straight after a sexual encounter, yet this one wanted to stay. It testified to the "treat 'em mean, keep 'em keen" philosophy, but Faye didn't want him keen. She just wanted him out.

He sat up suddenly and swung his tanned, muscular legs out of bed. "Well, at least make me some coffee first. I'll get dressed and follow you down." He picked up his white cotton boxer shorts that were partially tucked inside a leg of his trousers.

Faye was relieved that now an end was in sight to this cheap little episode. "OK." She smiled. "I'll get the cab to come in about ten minutes." She grabbed her white cotton robe from the end of the bed and headed out of the door.

Downstairs, she crashed about opening cupboards and throwing coffee into a mug bearing the words "caffeine queen." Then she rang her local cab firm and asked them to send a car immediately.

"Where to?" asked the dispatcher.

"Um, no idea," said Faye. "The passenger will tell you." She hung up and poured boiling water into the mug.

"Hi." He appeared fully dressed in the kitchen doorway, his suit jacket slung over his arm. He looked disheveled but still gorgeous. "What was your name again?"

She held up a teaspoon. "Milk and sugar?"

"That's an unusual name." He grinned.

Through the beginnings of a headache, she vaguely remembered that *his* name was something like "Toby" She was pleased he'd forgotten hers. "Let's just keep it as a mysterious encounter," she said.

He looked at her quizzically, then shook his head. "No sugar, just a splash of milk, thanks." He made a small sighing noise. "So, are you in the habit of picking up strange men in bars and bringing them home?"

"No, absolutely not," she said firmly, walking across to the doorway and handing him the mug. As he took it, his hand touched hers and she felt the flutter of butterflies. "It was completely out of character and I won't be doing it again."

"I see. That disappointing, was I?" He took a sip of coffee and peered at her over the rim of the mug.

She wrinkled her nose. "That's really not the issue here."

"So what is?"

"Sorry?"

"The issue," he said. "What is it?"

"There isn't one. We saw, we conquered, we almost came . . . then I changed my mind. Simple as that. I'm sorry." She looked at her watch and folded her arms, attempting to indicate that the subject was closed.

"Oh, please don't apologize, the pleasure was all mine." He looked at her curiously. "You're unusual, do you know that?"

"You mean I behave like a man?" she replied. "You're probably right, but it doesn't make me a bad person." She just wanted to go upstairs and crawl back into bed . . . alone.

"I didn't say it did. In fact, it's quite refreshing. It's better than being asked to go and choose curtains together."

She laughed a little and looked at him. He was smiling broadly, and she noticed he had a small gap between his front teeth.

In clothes, his broad shoulders and height were accentuated and she wondered whether he'd done any modeling. In the wine bar, he'd brushed aside her question about his job, describing himself as "a glorified salesman." Now, she was dying to ask him to elaborate, but refrained in case it was construed as interest in seeing him again.

There was the faint sound of a cab pulling up outside, followed by the honk of its horn—always a joy for the neighbors at that time in the morning.

"That'll be your cab." She hoped the relief on her face wasn't too obvious.

"Thanks, Sherlock." He grabbed his briefcase, drained his mug, and put it on the kitchen table. "I have a strong feeling the answer is going to be no, but I'll ask anyway. Any chance of seeing you again?"

Faye looked up at him and shook her head. "I doubt it," she said. "I'm getting married next weekend."

Friday, June 28
2 p.m.

"That Michael Caine film with the Minis keeps popping into my head," said Brian, his eyes squeezed shut.

"I think you'll find it was set in Italy, and it was actually a *coach* that ended up hanging over the cliff. We're in France and this is a Fiat Cinquecento." Mark was grim-faced as he negotiated the twists and turns up the side of the mountain overlooking the town of Céret. They were on their way to the tiny village of Montferrier, a quaint but unremarkable place.

"Couldn't you just have got married at city hall like normal people?" Brian was looking distinctly green, his cheek pressed against the half-open window. "A quick ceremony, a couple of pigs-in-blankets, then off to the pub. Much more civilized."

"And I was wondering why some girl hasn't snapped you up," said Mark sarcastically, his eyes never leaving the road. "I'm afraid I didn't have much say in it, mate. Faye has pretty much organized the whole thing. All I have to do is turn up."

"If we don't plummet to our deaths first."

"What?" Mark grimaced as the road became even steeper and narrower.

"Nothing."

They lapsed into silence, Mark concentrating on the road, his friend on keeping his breakfast down. He wasn't great at traveling in cars at the best of times, but Mark had assured him it was mostly flat from the airport to the village. He'd neglected to mention the road up to the hotel, which looked dangerously as if they'd soon need a sherpa.

"There it is!" Mark pointed, then thought better of it and clamped his hand back on the wheel. The château was clearly visible through the trees, its roof highlighted by the afternoon sunshine. "Another ten minutes and we'll be there."

Brian opened his eyes, but was still clutching the sides of his seat. "Can you make it sooner?"

"God, now I've seen it, I'm nervous." Mark's eyes were shining. "It suddenly seems so real . . ." He turned to look at his friend. "I'm getting *married*. Isn't that exciting?"

"I'm at fever pitch, mate." Brian's voice was flat with nausea.

As Mark negotiated a tricky bend, a donkey pulling a cart came into view. It was being led by a man who looked in no hurry to be anywhere. "This could take a little longer than I thought." He ran a hand through his floppy brown hair and sighed. There was no way he could get past the cart: he would just have to fall in behind and crawl along.

Brian evidently preferred this sedate pace. He fumbled in the pocket of his gaudy Hawaiian shirt, pulled out a pack of cigarettes and lit one. He exhaled smoke out of the window, then screwed up his eyes as some floated back into his face. "I still can't believe you're having separate rooms tonight, particularly as you'll be seeing each other at dinner."

Mark shrugged. "Faye wanted to keep a bit of the traditional stuff. She didn't want me to see her dress before the ceremony tomorrow either."

Brian looked surprised. "She doesn't strike me as the traditional type."

"I know what you mean." Mark fiddled with the car radio to see if he could pick up any local stations. "I guess most women like to be a little old-fashioned on their wedding day."

Euro-pop filled the car and Brian let out a low wail. "Turn that shit off. This whole country has van Gogh's ear for music."

Mark laughed. He'd asked Brian to be best man partly because he was a never-ending source of gags and one-liners, but he'd made him swear to keep his speech clean for the benefit of the parents and aged aunts. "How's the speech going?" he asked.

"Not bad." Brian stubbed out the cigarette. "I've had a few thoughts, and I'll add to them when I've met more of your guests at dinner tonight."

"There's enough material there to fill an entire comedy festival, particularly my aunt Ethel. She's the only person I know with Tourette's." He grinned as a memory popped into his head. "She once told our local vicar he was a twat, although she claimed later she meant to say twit."

"Fantastic!" Brian slapped his palm against the dashboard. "I *insist* on sitting next to her."

As they edged round another corner, the donkey-cart veered through a small gateway at the side of the road.

"Thank God for that," muttered Mark, and rammed the gearstick into second. He grinned. "I can't wait to see Faye."

"That's nice to hear. I hope I'll feel like that about someone one day."

"You will," said Mark, firmly. "If I can meet and marry someone like Faye, so can you. You've just got to keep looking."

Brian seemed doubtful. "She's too high maintenance for me. I need someone normal."

"You make her sound like an alien with two heads. Anyway, your version of high maintenance is a woman who complains if you forget her birthday or spend all day in the pub."

Brian slapped his chest in mock hurt. "How little you know me."

"I know you better than anyone, and you just don't make enough effort with women."

"Yes, but there's effort, and there's *effort*." He stretched his arms behind his head. "You like the drama of life with Faye, but I'd prefer someone more low-key. Like Jenna, for example."

The corners of Mark's mouth turned down. "Jenna's lovely, and I'm really looking forward to seeing her tonight. But only as a friend." He looked at Brian, who was putting on his sneakers. "What I love about Faye," he continued, "is that every day is different."

"You mean every day is a pain in the arse," said Brian. He went back to staring out of the window.

Brian lifted up the lid of his school desk for protection, and lowered his head behind it. "Psssst!"

Mark snapped out of his daydream and turned to look at him. "What?" he whispered, so that the geography teacher wouldn't hear.

"Did you . . . you know?" Brian formed a circle with the thumb and forefinger of one hand and used his other forefinger to make a thrusting motion through it.

"No," Mark replied glumly. "Not even close." He thought about sex a lot. On a good day, it distracted him maybe twenty times; on a bad one, it could be up to sixty. His main problem was that he wasn't getting it. Worse, he'd never had it. Catastrophically, Brian had.

He didn't reckon that Brian was better-looking than he was, or that he was brighter or wittier—no, they were pretty well matched in those areas. The inequality in their sexual experience was down to the fact that Brian had bought—to put it kindly—the *free-spirited* Hannah Foley a snowcone at the local package store and been rewarded with perfunctory sex in a disused shed at the local park.

But Mark was dating Jenna Davis. She was "a nice girl," and didn't do that sort of thing. Her father was a bank manager who had recently been transferred to Southampton from Norwich, so she had only joined Mark's secondary school at the start of the 10th grade. As a new girl, her arrival had prompted a fleeting interest from several of the boys, who always got short shrift from their wised-up female schoolmates. But she had got on with her work, giving them no encouragement. Finally they had got the message.

About a month after she had started, Mark had sat opposite her in the library one day and struck up a conversation about the Second World War, swiftly followed by a track-by-track analysis of the latest Nirvana album.

He hadn't really noticed Jenna before that but, to his surprise, he found himself suggesting they make a Saturday trip together to Woolworth's to check out the charts and new releases and she agreed. The outing marked the start of their relationship.

Then, Mark's sexual urges had been distant rumblings. Now, six months later and with his sixteenth birthday behind him, it was all he could do to keep from pawing at her every chance he had.

Brian's gauche mime was referring to the previous night,

when Mark and Jenna had stayed in alone at her parents' house. Halfway through a bottle of cheap but effective Thunderbird wine, he had made his move and, tantalizingly, he hoped, kissed her neck.

"Hmmm, that's nice," she murmured, moving closer, her hand rubbing his knee. She was wearing a loose blouse and he had caught a glimpse of her bra. Slowly, he tugged her blouse out of her waistband, his hand creeping up the hitherto forbidden flesh. "I do love you, Mark," she whispered, planting small kisses on his upper and lower lips.

Reaching her left breast his hand rested on the erect nipple.

She shot backwards as if she had been stung and pulled her blouse back into place. "What are you doing?"

"Sorry," he said hurriedly. "I thought you wouldn't mind."

"Whatever gave you that idea?" She frowned, as if disappointed in him.

Mark had masked his frustration well, even telling Jenna that he respected her for turning him down, but inwardly he was desperate.

Jenna was pretty, in a natural way, and undeniably a lovely girl. Mark preferred her to some of the brassier, more boisterous girls at school, and enjoyed her company. But she wouldn't go all the way, which threw him into a daily dilemma.

"Just dump her and date someone who will," said Brian, with his trademark sensitivity. "What's she waiting for? Bloody marriage?"

"What are you waiting for? Bloody marriage?" Mark parroted to Jenna a few days later, after she'd yet again slapped his hot little hand away from her breast.

She looked hurt. "We don't have to have sex just because we can," she said quietly. "I want to wait until I'm ready."

"And when will that be?" he snapped, and conjured up an image of his beloved Southampton soccer team in an attempt to make his erection subside.

"Your voice sounds funny," she replied, looking hurt. "Why are you so angry with me for wanting the time to be right? I thought you respected me for that."

As ever when she was upset, Mark apologized, enveloped her in a cuddle, and assured her that, yes, she was right to take her time and that everything would work out just fine. It pained him to think he'd hurt her, but he was increasingly frustrated in this sexless relationship and finding it harder than ever to disguise it.

Several months later, and now past his seventeenth birthday, Mark's hands had progressed across Jenna's body with the stealth of Hitler across Europe. But, much to Brian's amusement, he was still technically a virgin. "You've only done it once yourself," he retaliated, after yet another of his friend's unsubtle gibes.

"Ah, but the one-eyed man rules in the kingdom of the blind," said Brian, amiably. "Or, in this case, the kingdom of the one-eyed trouser snake."

It was true. In Mark's mind, Brian's experience gave him carte blanche to lord it over his friend at every available opportunity—and it grated.

Jenna now allowed him to fondle her breasts and, on a couple of occasions after one white wine spritzer too many, she had allowed his hands to roam down her waistband. But she had still refused his pleas to go all the way, and had recoiled in horror when he had produced a condom from his jeans pocket one night when her parents were at the movies.

"Oh, I see. You thought I was a sure thing for tonight, did you?" Her bottom lip was trembling. "You had it all planned on a stupid little checklist. Parents at the movies, empty house, take a condom."

Mark sighed. "No, Jenna, it wasn't. If you want the truth, I've been carrying this condom for weeks, probably months, in the vain hope you might make love with me. In fact, it's probably rotted by now . . . much like this relationship."

His remark hung in the air between them, an admission he had been holding back for some time.

"Do you really mean that?" Her voice was small.

Mark cleared his throat. "No, it hasn't rotted . . . wrong words." He took her hand. "But I *do* think we need a break from each other, time to think about what we want."

It was standard drivel taken straight from some soap opera he'd watched the previous week. Mark already knew what he wanted: sex. And he wasn't getting it.

"How long?" Jenna's face was crumpled with distress.

"Let's just see," he said softly. The ball was firmly in his court and he didn't want to throw it back too soon. "Time will tell."

A man with a mission, he had approached Hannah Foley between classes, even before Jenna's tear-stained pillow had dried out. "Fancy a night out?" he asked nonchalantly.

Hannah, chewing gum, looked him up and down. "Where?"

"I thought we could have dinner at the Harvester."

"Oooh, get you," she said. "All right, then."

Over steak and chips, she had bored him stiff with her encyclopedic knowledge of the life and death of the Doors' Jim Morrison, while he stared down her ample cleavage and imagined the delights cupped within. At one point, she removed a clumpy black shoe and placed her bare foot between his legs, massaging his groin under the table. Mark thought he might pass out with sheer ecstasy.

Later, tense with anticipation, he placed an arm round her shoulders and walked her home via the school playing fields. Pulling her towards the shadowy safety of some nearby bushes, he started a kiss of some ferocity. Within seconds, his hand was inside her blouse, the other lifting her skirt, and when he felt no slap to his face, there was no stopping him.

There, on the playing field where he'd scored a good few rugby tries, he dropped his trousers, wrestled on a condom, and kissed his virginity goodbye.

"Bloody hell, it only cost me a snowcone to get my leg over," said Brian, when a glowing Mark had told him the next day. "Trust you to fork out for a three-course meal with wine. I hope the steak wasn't fillet."

Actually it had been, but Mark didn't care. He was walking tall, his chest puffed out with pride that he had become—in his own eyes, at least—a man. The relief was overwhelming.

He had been brought up to respect women and treat them well, so he had asked Hannah for another date, anxious that she shouldn't feel cheapened by what might have been a one-night stand. This time there was no fillet steak, just a stroll down to the local recreation ground and a shared bottle of lukewarm beer stolen from his parents' cellar.

"D'ya wan' another shag, then?" said Hannah, as they passed the beer bottle between them, and Mark realized she probably didn't trouble herself with feeling cheap. Now that he'd lost his virginity, his interest in Hannah had waned. But he didn't want to upset her by rejecting her offer. So to make himself feel better about it, he fumbled around with her one more time, *then* never called her again.

Since their decision to take time out and think about their relationship, he and Jenna had seen each other several times for a drink and a chat but little had been resolved. Occasionally Jenna looked wistful, but Mark pretended not to notice. The last thing he wanted was endless hand-wringing heart-to-hearts that ended with her saying, "I'm not ready for sex." He assumed that when she was ready she would tell him so. Until then, it was best to keep it platonic and fun.

All three passed their finals and were headed into their senior year, and they spent a pleasant summer together.

When September arrived, they had enjoyed a surfeit of good times and were ready to throw themselves into schoolwork.

Since he was a small child, Mark had wanted to become a chef with his own restaurant. His parents were wealthy: his father had invented a compact, cost-effective air-conditioning system aimed at small businesses. The idea had been taken up by a major company, which paid him a small percentage of the value of each system it sold; when it took off overseas, his parents had been rolling in cash.

Mark had told them of his restaurant dream, but they had never offered to help him out and he'd never dared to ask them outright for backing. They were traditional parents, and Mark knew they wanted him to get a university degree, like his brother, Tony, who was ten years older and worked for a major investment firm in London.

So he'd toed the family line, spent the next year studying hard for his A levels, and applied to several universities to study English.

Although Mark and Jenna were still apart on the day the results were to be pinned on the school noticeboard, they agreed to meet up with Brian to face the music together.

"Yes! Fucking yes!" Brian punched the air and danced around the corridor.

Mark's eyes scanned the list until he found "Hawkins, M: English, A, geography, B, general science, B." "Oh, my God!" he spluttered. "I've done it. I'm going to Birmingham!" He joined Brian in a victory dance.

Several seconds passed before they realized that Jenna was motionless.

"Jen?" Mark put his hand on her shoulder and turned her to face him.

A tear was rolling down her cheek. "I've only passed one," she whispered. "I'm not coming with you."

"I won't go, if you like," Mark had said, as he and Jenna sat nursing their coffee in the local Burger King later that night, "Maybe it's the perfect excuse I need to get a job in a restaurant and work my way up." He knew she'd never try to stop him going to Birmingham, but he had to offer.

"Don't be silly," she replied. "I'm not sure I'm the university type so I'm not that bothered."

Mark wrinkled his nose. "What went wrong? It's unlike you to fail."

"No idea. I thought I'd prepared well, but I guess my mind was on other things."

Mark knew she was probably alluding to their fragmented relationship, but guilt stopped him saying so. He changed the subject. "How did your mum and dad react?" he asked. He didn't mention that his parents had cracked open some vintage champagne to celebrate his results.

"They were fine about it—they knew I'd tried my best. That's all they've ever asked me to do."

"So, what now?"

Jenna brightened. "You know I've always loved doing people's hair? Well, I'm going to see if I can get an apprenticeship in a salon round here." She gestured out of the window. "Who knows? One day I might even open my own place."

"I could open my restaurant next door." He smiled.

Whether from genuine love or the thought of Mark leaving for university in a couple of months' time, they shared a long, tender kiss across the Formica table and picked up where they had left off.

As he walked her home, his arm protectively round her shoulders, Jenna mentioned that her parents were away next weekend, and she would be alone. "I'm ready to make love." She nuzzled the back of his neck. "If you still want to . . ."

Unsure of what their future now held, Mark thought it would probably be wiser to leave things as they were. But he knew what it had taken for her to suggest it, so rejecting her was not an option. That Saturday night, clutching a bottle of wine for courage, Mark rang the doorbell.

"Hello." She put her arms round him and kissed his cheek. She was wearing a light touch of mascara and lipstick and her long brown hair was loosely curled, softly framing her face. He thought he had never seen her look so lovely. "Come in." She led him into the living room, scene of his former frustration, with its lace curtains, floral sofa, and the picture of the stern-looking woman over the fireplace.

The wine, abandoned on a side table, wasn't needed. Propelled by a mixture of nerves and excitement, they began to kiss immediately in the middle of the room.

"Lie down on the floor," Mark murmured, taking a cushion from the sofa and placing it under her head. He kissed her tenderly until he felt her relax.

"I'm glad to see you've brought that condom with you." Looking apprehensive, she smiled.

Afterwards, they lay quietly for several minutes while he stroked her hair, occasionally burying his face in it and inhaling the heady scent of Jenna mixed with apple shampoo. "How do you feel?" he said eventually. Of course, what he meant was "How good was I?"

"It was well worth waiting for," she murmured.

His backside was starting to go numb on the hard floor, so he shifted. "Come on, let's go to bed." He stood up, took her hand and led her towards the stairs.

In her bed, he held Jenna in his arms until her breathing steadied and he knew she'd fallen asleep. Mark stared at the ceiling. He had released the years of frustration, but he couldn't relax. His mind was racing with thoughts of university and what his future might hold.

The big dilemma was whether his plans included Jenna.

Friday, June 28
2:05 p.m.

Adam removed his pink Chanel sunglasses with all the high drama of a spaghetti-western star and eye-balled her. "But *why*?" he asked again.

"Why not?" Faye took a defiant glug of the house champagne she'd ordered from room service. "Men can have a last fling before they get married and no one questions it."

"Not strictly true, darling, but I'll let that sweeping generalization pass for now. Supposing that *was* the case, it still doesn't explain why *you* would want to behave in that way. The last time I looked you didn't have a dangly bit between your legs."

During an arduous journey of flight delays and a French cab driver who had been even more irritable than the norm, Faye had told Adam about the previous weekend's "night of shame"—as he was now calling it. Now they were reclining on the vast mahogany four-poster bed in the château's honeymoon suite and indulging in what they loved best: a good, analytical gossip—although Faye had to admit that she preferred it to be about other people than herself.

Adam, her best friend—who described himself as "Homo sapiens, homeopathic, and homosexual"—had clearly been torn between reveling in this outrageous piece of news and reproving her. He had chosen the latter and had now been lecturing her for fifteen minutes.

"Don't get all sanctimonious on me." She stretched her left leg across the lavishly embroidered bedcover. "You lot are terrible at staying faithful."

Adam put a hand on his heart and assumed a wounded expression. "If by 'you lot' you mean the gay community, then you're wrong," he said. "We are perfectly capable of staying faithful in long, rewarding relationships. It's only when we're unhappy that we seek love elsewhere."

Faye made a face. " 'Seek love elsewhere,' " she mimicked, in an infomercial voice, and they both burst out laughing.

"Oh, all right, then, I meant shag around. But the sentiment's the same." He removed the olive from his martini and bit into it. "I just don't understand why you'd want to do something like that when you're about to get married. I mean, what's the point?"

"I told you." She pouted. "I'd had a bit to drink, he was handsome, and, if we absolutely *must* analyze it, I suppose I was panicking about getting married. But I didn't go all the way."

Adam shook his head. "I meant, what's the point in getting married?"

It was an uncomfortable question, which Faye felt too weary to answer. She wasn't sure she even had an answer, so she used the age-old tactic favored by politicians: she dodged it. "Anyway, what Mark doesn't know won't hurt him."

"But it hurts the *relationship*," said Adam emphatically. "It's the same thing."

Faye looked at him incredulously. "You sound like a bloody therapist."

"My sweet, that's what you need. There's—something—missing—in—there." He tapped the side of her head as he said each word.

"Maybe." She turned down the corners of her mouth. "But it's true that *if* a man has one last fling, it's seen as a rite of passage before he becomes manacled to his wife and supposedly loses his freedom . . . I hate that imagery, by the way. But you're saying that *women* aren't allowed to do it."

Adam lobbed his olive pit into the bin. "I don't think either gender screw around if they're serious about something, but it's a scientific fact that some men can have a one-night stand without it affecting a serious relationship while women can't. They're different." When in doubt, he always used the "scientific fact" argument, fictional or otherwise.

"But are we naturally different?" she asked. "Or are we just brought up to think and behave in a way that suits men?"

He made a face. "This is all getting very deep. All I'm basically saying is, I hope you're doing the right thing."

Faye stood up to pour herself more champagne. "Of course I am. Once I'm married to Mark, I'll be faithful, I promise." She placed her fingers against her temple in the Brownie salute. "Besides, if it makes you feel any better to hear it, I hate myself for my little indiscretion. It was a cheap thing to do and I wouldn't want to repeat it."

Adam stretched, pulled down his T-shirt, which bore a sequined heart on the front, and leaped up from the bed. He went to gaze out of the mullioned window that led onto an ancient stone balcony. "God, this place is beautiful."

She walked across to stand next to him, and they were silent for a few minutes, absorbing the stunning Provençal scenery, lush after an unusually rain-soaked winter and early spring.

Faye had stayed at Château Montferrier for a magazine fashion shoot a couple of years previously and fallen in love with the place. A few kilometers outside Grasse, it was perched on the side of a hill and had once belonged to an aristocratic family who, through lack of funds, had allowed it to fall into disrepair. Just before the new millennium had dawned, they had moved to a smaller estate, and sold it to an exclusive hotel chain. A few million had restored it to much more than its former glory.

After years of living with the constant noise of London, Faye relished the silence, punctuated only by bird calls or the occasional sound of car tires on the gravel drive. From the moment she had arrived there on her modeling assignment, she had felt the stresses and strains of everyday life ebb away to be replaced by a relaxed serenity. She'd always vowed that, when she met the right man, she would be married there.

Now here she was, just a day away from pledging her future to Mark Hawkins, a fantastic but struggling chef, and all-round wonderful man. "Let's see if my dress has survived the journey," she said, keen to get into the spirit of the occasion. She walked across to the mirrored wardrobes that lined one side of the room and opened a door.

There, protected by a vinyl cover, was the dress she and Adam had spent weeks choosing and perfecting for her big day. It was made from snow-white chiffon, with a scoop neck, sheer sleeves and a long, bias-cut skirt. Adam described it as "classic."

She rummaged around underneath it, and pulled out a small cardboard box with "Jenny Wick" embossed on top: the hand-made crystal tiara she'd bought for an extra touch of glamour. "All present and correct." She peered inside the wardrobe and checked the box that contained the dainty Kurt Geiger sandals. "Shall I risk asking the staff to steam the dress?"

"Definitely." Adam nodded. "It creases so easily." He returned to the bed and fell back onto the silk-tasseled cushions placed along the headboard. "Have you thought any more about your hair?"

"I just want to look like me, really. So many people have some boring updo for their wedding day, and I always think it looks rather staid."

"True." He smiled affectionately. "Besides, those trophy-cup ears of yours are best kept hidden."

"Have you ever thought of getting a job with the diplomatic corps?" She poked out her tongue. "Thought not."

She opened the suitcase perched on the end of the bed, and pulled out a pair of seamless beige panties and a sheer white bra with clear plastic straps. "It's all very well wearing sexy underwear on your wedding day, but with most fitted dresses it's impossible." She sighed. "I can only wear these passion-killers under mine. Anything else would show through."

She looked at Adam, but he didn't seem to be listening. He was staring into the distance, deep in thought. Then he spoke: "Are you absolutely positive you're in love with Mark?"

Faye made a face. She'd thought that the conversation had moved on. "Yes, of course."

"Good."

"But I must say," she continued, "it's hard to believe that anyone can stay interested in the same person all their life."

Adam pursed his lips. "Coming from any woman, I'd find that remark sad, but from a woman who's getting married tomorrow, it's seriously worrying."

Faye walked over to him, took his hand and squeezed it. "Don't worry. Just be happy for me . . . Pretty please?"

"I'll try."

She dropped his hand and gave him a full-beam smile. "That's the spirit. I want you to be fun, not to rain on my parade."

"Sorry. It's just that I'll always tell you the truth, however brutal."

Faye knew that Adam's impeccable sense of style would be invaluable on her wedding day, but she wished he'd left his disarming honesty behind. She recalled getting a dose of it the first time they'd met . . .

Pausing outside the giant metal doors leading to the warehouse, Faye took a few deep breaths. She was nervous about this assignment with *Couture* magazine, a glossy trend bible considered to be the upmarket brand leader and, consequently, run by phenomenal snobs who could pick and choose from the best the fashion world had to offer.

Her modeling break had come when, according to press reports, one of the "supermodels" on her agency's books had suffered "a particularly debilitating case of food poisoning," otherwise known as a tricky Ecstasy tablet.

Faye had been drafted as an eleventh-hour replacement and it was the first time she'd posed for *Couture*. While she was undoubtedly a very pretty girl, she didn't have the extra something that placed her on the most-wanted list. Her long sandy hair, green eyes, and smattering of freckles were too Californian and healthy in an era when waif chic and urchin cuts were the hot look, but Faye made a comfortable living from posing for mid-market magazines.

She walked into the tiny reception area, and stopped in front of a desk made from corrugated iron. Above it was a lurid painting of two dogs mating. "Hello, I'm here to see Adam Sissons," she said to the receptionist, a sullen girl with four or five hoops through her nose. She was reading a copy of *Bizarre* magazine.

The girl punched numbers into a phone. "Adam, someone for you." She looked at Faye. "Name?"

"Faye Parker."

"Faye Parker," she echoed, then put down the phone. "Studio Five," she said, gestured behind her, and returned to her magazine.

At first, Faye couldn't see a soul as she wandered through the door marked "5." Then she heard a lavatory flush and a man walked out of a small door to her right. "Sorry, nature called," he trilled. With his closely shaved head and well-toned torso trying to escape his tight white T-shirt with "All this *and* brains" written on the front, he was an eye-catching figure. "I'm Adam."

Faye shook his hand, and followed him round a corner to where various trendy types were rushing around like worker bees.

"Put this on." Adam lobbed a flimsy black dress in her direction.

She held it against her. "I'm sure you know best," she purred, lowering her eyelids and trying to look coy, "but black drains me." She pointed at a nearby clothes rack. "Could I wear that gorgeous stripy thing instead?"

"Nope." His voice was clipped. "You're not slim enough for that. Black will hide those lumps and bumps."

As he strutted back to the clothes rack, Faye stood stock still, feeling as if she'd instantaneously ballooned to the size of the Michelin Man. She hadn't been expecting such an important assignment, so she hadn't been watching her weight very closely, but lumpy? Hardly.

She had started attending yoga classes recently, but after two or three weeks she had started missing sessions if something better came up. Eventually she had fallen so far behind the rest of the class she had given up.

"If God had wanted me to touch my toes, he'd have put them on my knees," she'd muttered to the instructor, during one particularly strenuous session.

"And by the way," Adam shouted over his shoulder while hurling the stripy number at some raven-haired, chalk-skinned pipe-cleaner, whose diet clearly consisted of cigarettes, vodka, and Advil, "it's useless trying to flirt with me. I'm gay."

Fortunately, Faye's mutinous expression fitted in rather nicely with the current trend favoring miserable models, but Adam pushed her so far back in the pictures that only her head and shoulders could be seen behind the four others. As someone who was used to being the center of attention on photo shoots, she found the whole experience uncomfortable and humbling, particularly when he left her out of the last picture altogether.

Faye returned to where she'd left her clothes, and fumbled with the buttons of her jeans. Tears of frustration pricked her eyes.

Adam walked over to her. "Are you upset?" He kept his voice low.

"No." Faye was aware she didn't sound convincing.

"It's nothing personal," he said. "It's just that you're different from the other three and I wanted a uniform look for the last shot."

"Whatever," she replied, and kicked herself inwardly for sounding so standoffish.

His face was set. "It's my job to criticize," he said calmly. "If I didn't, the fashion shoots would look like shit." He bent down and gathered up a couple of Polaroids that had fallen on to the floor. "The magazine's reputation is based on being the best, and you don't get to the top by worrying about hurting people's feelings. You also don't get it by booking lazy models who take their looks and figure for granted."

Faye's face blazed with humiliation. "As you know, it was a last-minute booking," she muttered.

"Not the point," he said, and blew a kiss to one of the departing models. "You have a fantastic face and, with a little more effort on your part, I'd book you all the time. But you need to watch those hips. They have to be slimmer to cope with this season's tailored looks. Sorry, but that's the brutal truth."

"No one else complains," she said stiffly. "I get plenty of work, thank you very much."

Adam sighed. "Well, if you're happy being the darling of the supermarket catalogues . . . If I were you, I'd go on a diet, dear. When your knees become fatter than your legs, start eating again." He swiveled on his glittered Cuban heel and walked off to where the photographer and his assistant were deep in conversation.

Faye was left gasping like a fish out of water, struck dumb. What galled her was that deep down inside, she knew that every word he'd said had been true. A total stranger had skewered her with pinpoint accuracy and it wounded. Grabbing her handbag from under the clothes rack, she walked out without uttering another word to him or anyone else.

Two weeks went by. Then a booker from her agency rang in a state of high excitement to say that Adam had been in touch and wanted her to call him. "Maybe it's a *Couture* cover," the woman gushed.

"More likely the 'before' picture for a cosmetic surgery article," Faye gulped to herself when she'd put the phone down.

Of course, if he'd been a heterosexual man possibly asking for a date, Faye would have waited several days before calling him, but as he was gay and in charge of booking models for the country's most prestigious magazine, she rang him immediately. "Hi, is that Adam? It's Faye Parker, the woman with the childbearing hips."

He laughed. "Sorry about that. On reflection, I was rather harsh."

"I think they call it being cruel to be kind," she replied. "What did you want to speak to me about?"

"Mainly to apologize, but also to see if you fancied doing another small job with me. It's nothing to do with *Couture*, it's for a friend of mine who runs an ad agency. They need a model who looks good in a sarong."

"Ah, the good old hip-covering sarong. Perfect for me." She smiled to herself. "When and where?"

It had been the start of a beautiful friendship.

They were standing in the château's spectacular hall, with its mahogany wall paneling and ceiling frescos of plump clouds and even plumper cherubs. Directly in front of the vast oak entrance door, a marble staircase lined with oil paintings of past French monarchs curled upstairs, and a small visitors' book lay on a Louis XIV bureau.

"Ohmigod, this is to die for!" squealed Adam, finding a wrought-iron handle secured to the paneling. He pushed it down and a concealed door swung open into the library. "Ooh, I'm like Alice in Wonderland!" he said, placing a glittery Skecher on the threshold.

Faye was about to follow him when she glanced back and saw her mother struggling through the front door with a battered suitcase. A frustrated-looking porter was following, trying to wrestle it from her grasp.

"No, no, leave it, thanks. I'll take it to the room myself," said Alice firmly, using the loud, staccato voice she adopted with all foreigners.

"Hello, Mother." Faye strolled over and planted a kiss on her hot pink cheek. "Why don't you let him help you?" She nodded towards the porter.

Alice shook her head. "They only want money for it, dear. It's not worth the bother. I'll have it up there myself in no time."

"This is a five-star hotel." Faye's heart sank at the thought of an entire weekend of her mother's little ways. "And it has a strict no-tipping policy."

Alice pushed ancient sunglasses to the top of her head and wiped her forehead with the crisp cotton handkerchief she had pulled out of her sleeve. "Nothing is free in life, dear. You should know that by now." She made a small tutting noise as if her daughter's imagined naiveté had disappointed her.

"Alice! How lovely to see you!" Adam had emerged from the library and was bearing down on them, arms outstretched. If Alice was surprised to be given a bear hug by someone she'd met only twice, she didn't show it. "Good trip?" he asked.

Faye winced. She knew what was coming: her mother had spent three weeks planning her journey with military precision, and was only too eager to relate the details.

"Not really," said Alice. "First of all, the train to Dover was two hours late—no, ninety-eight minutes to be precise—then the ferry crossing was rather choppy . . ."

Faye wandered to the front desk and left them to it. When she returned five minutes later, her mother's room key in her hand, Adam's expression suggested he was gradually decomposing.

". . . but it turned out the local bus only went as far as the bottom of the hill, so I've had to walk the last two miles in that heat."

"Mum! Why didn't you just get a cab up here? You know I'd have given you the money," Faye demanded.

Alice looked at her as if she'd just stepped off the banana boat. "Darling, the minute those cab drivers know you're a stranger in their country, they automatically double the fare and then short-change you. It's a fact."

Faye couldn't be bothered to argue. "Come on, I've got your key and Adam will carry your bag. *He* won't want paying."

Back in her room, Faye patted Adam's leg with one hand and poured champagne, into his empty martini glass with the other. "Now then," she said, "no more dreary talk. Let's have some fun."

He gave her a warm smile. "It's a deal." Knocking back a mouthful of champagne, he winced as some of it dribbled down his chin. "I'll tell you what. Why don't you fill me in on who's staying here as well as us? I want all the dirt." He plumped up a cushion and stuck it behind his head. "I feel like I'm on one of those murder mystery weekends."

Faye laughed. "Considering the cast there could well be a few dead bodies by the end of it, and my mother might be the first if she does any more journey anecdotes."

"It's the exes I'm interested in," said Adam, who seemed to be salivating at the thought. "I can't *belieeeeeve* they're coming!" He rubbed his hands with undisguised glee. "Only you could dream up that one."

"It was Mark's idea, actually. He's still quite chummy with a couple of his ex-girlfriends and wanted to invite them, so I felt I should do likewise." She grinned mischievously. "Trouble is, I had to track them down first."

Adam screeched with laughter. "You are priceless! Nothing like making your wedding day a meaningful one with just close friends."

"I'm just making sure things start on an equal footing, that's all." She pouted.

He looked unconvinced. "I couldn't believe it when you rang and said you wanted me to get Nat's new number for you. He's such an arsehole, although a bloody gorgeous one."

"At least you'll have him to ogle at if you get bored."

"True. I still can't believe you've invited him, though, especially after all the terrible things you said about him."

Faye frowned. Over the two years that she had known Adam, she had discovered that gay menfriends were significantly different from their female equivalents. When you pour out your heart, soul, or post-relationship vitriol to another woman, an unspoken etiquette has it that if you end up back with or even marrying the man in question, the lurid details of what you said in distress are not mentioned again. Not so with a gay man. If she said something derogatory about anyone who'd upset her—another model, perhaps, or casual acquaintance—Adam would always remind her of it if he ever saw her being friendly to them.

She decided to move on. "My other invited ex is Rich . . . I've told you about him before."

Adam drained his glass and placed it on the bedside table. "You did, but I didn't pay much attention because I didn't think I'd ever meet him."

A few weeks ago inviting exes had seemed such a good idea, but now Faye felt mildly nauseous. "It's going to be a rather stressful couple of days," she mused.

"Oh, I don't know. It sounds intriguing to me. Take a bride and groom, several relatives, four exes, mix with alcohol, and stand well back. Boom." Adam flung his arms wide.

Pouring the last of the champagne into Faye's glass, he waved the bottle at her. "Let's order another and you can refresh my memory about Rich."

Faye handed the gruff, middle-aged man a leaflet entitled "Art Attack, 1997" and flashed him her special megawatt smile. "Do come again, sir."

The second his back turned, the smile vanished like ice on a radiator. "Christ, how much longer?" She let out a long sigh.

The woman opposite glanced at her watch. "Only another five minutes, thank God."

Faye fixed her smile back in place as a couple of teenage boys halfheartedly took copies of the leaflet. She was standing at the exit of Chelsea Town Hall, shivering in a wind that was too cold for May, and handing out flyers to people leaving an exhibition of "modern art" that included a montage of spaghetti thrown against a canvas, a broken television with "Unplugged" painted across it, and what resembled an old dog blanket folded on a small white podium. "What a load of crap." She jerked her head in the direction of the hall. "If I vomited onto a canvas and called it 'I'm sick of life,' some artsy-fartsy fool would probably buy it."

"Do it. Sounds a great idea."

Faye turned to see a youngish man standing beside her, his hand outstretched. Without thinking, she shook it. "Actually, I wanted a leaflet," he grinned, "but pleased to meet you anyway. I'm Rich."

"Lucky you. I'm incredibly poor—which probably explains why I'm doing this." She was about to tell him her name, when a cough from her leafleting companion interrupted her. "Time's up," she said. "I'm off. See you tomorrow." She stuffed her remaining leaflets into a carrier bag, gave a cursory wave, and left.

Faye stooped to pick up her handbag. When she straightened up, Rich was still beside her. He looked apprehensive. "As you're the best work of art in here, I was wondering if you fancied a quick coffee with me?" he said.

"God, that's a cheesy line." Faye hooked her bag strap over her shoulder. She took a closer look at him, sizing him up.

He was quite tall, a little over six feet, she guessed, and had a fairly average face made distinctive by pale green eyes with thick dark lashes. His clothes were a bit dull but under them his physique looked honed and fit.

"No, I won't have a coffee, thanks . . ." she watched his face drop ". . . but I'll have a glass of wine. Come on. My name's Faye."

Five minutes later they were sitting in a side-street pub that stank of last night's revelry. The once cream ceiling was covered in the nicotine of ages, and the walls were plastered with old newspapers from the 1960s and 1970s, the occasional dog-eared theater program and fading photographs of not-very-famous people who had popped in for a drink over the years. It was 6 p.m. and they were the only people in there.

"So," Rich placed a glass of white wine in front of her and took a swig of lager, "is life as a leaflet distributor rewarding?"

"Oh, yes," she said. "It's what I've always wanted to do, ever since I was a little girl. I took an A level in leaflet distribution, and here I am today."

He raised an eyebrow. "And now the real story?"

"It's mind-numbingly boring and I hate it, but in the absence of any modeling work, my agency occasionally sends me to be a promotions girl and smile sweetly at people." She gave him a well-practiced false smile to illustrate.

"Well, it worked on me," said Rich. "I'm not sure about your mate, though. I think her smile needs a little work. She looked like she had indigestion."

"Can't have. She never eats." Faye lit a cigarette and took a closer look at his smooth blemish-free face. She put him in his early twenties. "What do you do?" she asked, blowing smoke to the right of him. "Apart from hang around dodgy art exhibitions chatting up nice, innocent girls like me."

"I'm a Formula One racing driver." He drank some more lager.

"Ah." She grinned. "Well, while we're being so honest with each other, I'm actually a supermodel-turned-actress who's re-searching my role as a leaflet distributor in Spielberg's next block-buster." She looked at him questioningly. "And the reality is?"

"I'm a van driver," he said sheepishly.

"Just like Postman Pat," she teased.

"Not quite. I deliver flowers. I'd just brought some for the woman who runs that exhibition. I saw you on the way in and thought I'd take a chance on the way out." He rubbed his right eye. "It's a stopgap while I wait to hear if I've got into the police force."

They sat chatting for another hour, during which Rich told her all about his long-standing fascination with fighting crime. It had stemmed from his childhood passion for *Starsky and Hutch* and *Hill Street Blues*. "It looked so exciting, much better than sit-ting behind a desk," he said. He explained that his father, Roger, had been a solicitor specializing in real estate. He was so wedded to his job that he had often worked weekends and had taken Rich with him, which had convinced him that an office job wasn't for him. His father followed the same route to work every morning, sat behind the same desk, talked to the same people and performed the same tasks. Familiarity was the glue that held his life together, but to Rich it was akin to being buried alive.

But his father had been an overpowering man who had for-bidden his son to pursue a career in the police force: "It's dan-gerous and underpaid," he had said. So like all too many others, Rich had found himself pursuing his father's dreams rather than his own. He studied law at London University, and received a de-gree.

"But I'm glad I did it." He smiled briefly at Faye, then his face became serious. "Three months after I finished, Dad died in a road accident on holiday in Spain. But at least he knew I'd got my degree . . ." He tailed off. "He was so proud of me," he added.

"I'm so sorry," murmured Faye. "Is your mother still alive?"

"Oh, yes. It took her a couple of years to get over his death, but she seems to be coping now. I moved back home to help her through it."

"I live with my mother too. It has its bonuses, but it also has huge drawbacks."

"I'll say. Only this morning mine asked if I was wearing a vest when I left the house. She said, 'Careful, or you'll—' "

" '—get a chill,' " interrupted Faye, and they both burst out laughing. "Do you like working as a van driver?"

"It's OK, but I hope not to be doing it much longer. I had my interview for the force last week, and I think it went well."

"I'll keep my fingers crossed for you." She glanced at her watch. "Look, I'd better head off now. I'm meeting some friends for dinner and need to go home to change first."

"I'm so sorry. I've been rambling on and on about myself, and we haven't got round to talking about you and how you got into modeling."

She rolled her eyes. "God, it even bores me to think about it!"

"Nonsense. I want to hear every fascinating detail. Can we do this again?" He looked at her expectantly.

For a moment Faye thought about it. She couldn't say he'd rung her bell, but neither had he irritated her. There was no other man on the horizon, so that made him worth seeing again, even if it was just as a pleasant diversion until someone else came along.

"OK." She took a pen from her handbag and scribbled her number on the back of his hand. "Call me."

She rang the doorbell and took a step back to study the outside of the house, bathed in September sunshine. It had suburban sitcom written all over it, with garages to one side, a neat little cobbled driveway, and a front garden whose borders had evidently been trimmed with nail scissors. A hanging basket swayed gently over the porch, and a hand-painted sign saying "Tintagel" was secured to one side of the glossy red door. Faye saw movement behind the glass and smoothed her skirt.

A middle-aged woman with curly, salt-and-pepper hair and floury hands opened the door. She wiped her fingers on her striped apron and smiled. "Hello, you must be Faye."

Faye shook her hand. "And you must be Rich's mother."

"Call me Marjorie. Come in."

Faye wiped her feet dutifully on the pristine mat, and followed her into the hallway. Its walls were lined with pictures of Rich from boy to man, his graduation photographs prominent among them. The brown shag-pile carpet bore stripes of a freshly mown lawn, a clear sign that Marjorie had been busy with the vacuum. "What a lovely house," she said, straight from the what-to-say-to-mothers handbook.

"Thank you, dear. I struggle a bit since Roger died, but Rich helps when he can." She led Faye into the long, narrow living room, partitioned by wooden double doors that had been flung open. It was decorated in a rather overpowering, green Regency stripe, and the two-seater sofa had been pushed back against the wall. A picture of a man who Faye presumed was Roger sat on top of the television. He looked about forty, with slicked-back brown hair and a pencil mustache.

Adjacent to his photograph, there was an old-fashioned fireplace with several cubbyholes. Each one housed the national doll of a different county.

Around ten people were gathered in the room, chatting quietly with drinks in their hands. Rich was leaning on the sideboard, next to a photograph of himself aged around seven, with neatly combed hair and wearing a school uniform. "Ah, you're here!" He leaned between the two men he was talking to and gave her a kiss on each cheek. "This is Brett, and this is Greg. They both started police training this week too."

"Hello." Faye shook their hands.

Brett looked like Mr. Potato Head. He had small beady eyes, a bulbous nose, and a bushy mustache that might have been glued on. But Greg was something else: blond, with narrow green eyes, he looked like a big cat that might pounce at any moment. Faye perked up at the thought of an afternoon's harmless flirting and she gave him her best leaflet-dispensing smile.

Rich was a kind and occasionally witty man, but the bottom line was that, increasingly, Faye had been finding him rather dull. It had taken just two weeks for him to say he loved her and three months later, she still hadn't returned the compliment. He also made no secret of what he wanted in the future.

"I'd like to get married and have children" he'd said, over cocktails one night, around six weeks after their first meeting.

"What, now?" quipped Faye, taken aback by the speed of his declaration.

"Ha-ha." He made a face at her. "I just think it's something you have to be honest about at the start of a relationship because the other person might not feel the same way."

I don't, thought Faye. "I haven't thought about it," she said truthfully. "I'm only twenty-three and there's a million things I want to do before settling down."

"Oh. Like what?"

"Like go to Pompeii, Machu Picchu, swim with dolphins . . ."

"Can't you do that with someone you love?"

"I suppose so. It was the children bit I was referring to, really. I can't see a toddler wanting to traipse round looking at lava-covered corpses." She smiled reassuringly at him.

The rest of the evening had passed in a less than jolly atmosphere, with Faye talking brightly about her day and Rich bor-

dering on a sulk. She knew he had been upset by her lack of enthusiasm for settling down, but she didn't believe in lying simply
to make others feel better.

For many women, Rich would have been the perfect man. He
was straightforward, lovable, and unafraid to show his emotions.
Also, as he already had a law degree he would probably rise
quickly to a senior post in the police force. But Faye liked a
chase, and she liked a challenging relationship. Rich's uncomplicated, loving nature meant that he presented no challenge and
that there would be no chase.

Since the marriage-and-children conversation, Faye had
known she would have to end the relationship. It was only a matter of time before it stopped being lighthearted fun and Rich began to pressure her for commitment. She had avoided meeting
his mother until now, because, as far as Faye was concerned, an
introduction to parents was one step away from choosing a wash-
ing machine together.

The night she'd planned to deliver the "it's not you, it's me; I
don't deserve you" speech, they had arranged to meet in his local
pub. That way, she felt she could say her piece, then leave him to
find someone he knew to have a drink with. She'd got there first
and found a secluded banquette in the far corner, away from the
bar and an irritatingly intrusive slot machine that kept beeping
and flashing.

Five minutes later he'd turned up, grinning from ear to ear
and waving a letter to say he'd been accepted into the police
force.

Faye could be pretty determined, but realized swiftly that
now wasn't the time to speak her mind and pop his balloon. Instead she'd treated him to dinner and a bottle of champagne in
the local curry house and said absolutely nothing about breaking
off their relationship. Then he'd mentioned the celebratory party
at his mother's house and she'd felt it would be unkind as well as
churlish not to attend.

Now, the tigerlike Greg was casting an approving eye in her direction. "What made you want to become a boy-in-blue?" she asked him.

While he wittered on about wanting to help the community, Faye adopted an expression that suggested she was hanging on his every word, but in fact she'd tuned out. She never ceased to be amazed by the stream of bestselling self-help books on how to get a man. As far as she was concerned, it was easy. As Helena Rubenstein had once said, "There are no ugly women, only lazy ones," and Faye made sure she always looked her best.

That was step one.

Step two: pretend you're endlessly fascinated by him.

Step three: don't talk about yourself too much and maintain an air of mystery.

Step four, when the relationship has developed a little: give a great blow job.

Men fascinated her, and Faye liked to think she understood them. According to her law, they could be quickly and accurately compartmentalized.

Rich was Mr. Nice Guy, a simple soul who decided he liked a woman and stuck with her. He would never stray unless he was pushed into it.

Greg was a tart, pure and simple. It was written all over his face. Any woman with an ounce of self-respect would avoid him like the plague: he would turn even the most relaxed girlfriend into a jealous paranoiac. He and Rich would probably become great friends through training together, but Faye knew that if she gave him the come-on, he'd choose the woman he'd only just met over loyalty to his colleague. Of the two, she'd choose Rich every time.

She was just about to make her excuses and mingle elsewhere when Marjorie did the job for her. "Would you excuse us?" she said to Greg, took Faye's arm and led her to a couple of empty chairs at the side of the room.

Faye's heart sank. She had resolved to finish with Rich in the next few days, so the last thing she wanted was to get chummy with his mother.

"Do you mind if we sit down?" said Marjorie. "My back isn't what it was." She winced as she lowered herself into a chair. "Now, tell me all about yourself. Rich says you're a model. How exciting!"

Faye shrugged. "Not much to tell, really. I do a bit of magazine work from time to time—you know, mail order catalogues, that sort of thing."

"He talks about you a lot." Her eyes were twinkling. "I would say he's very taken with you."

"Really?" Faye felt a thump of dread in her chest. "It's still early days, nothing too serious."

"Nonsense. I shouldn't tell you this," she whispered conspiratorially, "but he's thinking of buying you a special something with his first pay check."

Oh, God, thought Faye, please don't let it be an engagement ring. "How sweet of him."

Marjorie sighed. "It's nice to see him finally meet someone who interests him. The last girl was a disaster."

"Oh?" Rich had mentioned someone called Sarah and that they'd drifted apart. "I thought they parted on friendly terms?"

"Goodness me, no," exclaimed Marjorie. "They were together for three years and she was desperate to get married, but he didn't want to. In the end, he came clean and said he didn't think she was the one for him. She was devastated, poor love."

It was right there, sitting on two wicker chairs in Rich's mother's living room, that Faye realized you couldn't help whom you fell in love with. Equally, you couldn't make yourself love someone.

Here she was, about to finish her relationship with a man, who was really keen on her, and had recently dumped a woman who'd been really keen on him. She decided to stop beating herself up over it.

"It's been lovely meeting you," she said, "but I'm afraid I've got to go." Smiling, she stood up.

She found Rich in the kitchen, talking with a horse-faced woman about the Criminal Justice Bill. "Gotta go. Call you later," she said, and backed out into the hallway before he could stop her.

As she turned the front-door handle, she heard someone walk into the hall behind her. "Here." It was Greg. He pressed a piece of paper into her hand. "That's my number."

Raising her eyebrows, but saying nothing, she stepped out into the blinding afternoon sunshine and the door closed. She let out a small sigh. "Men," she murmured, setting off down the road.

A few yards farther on, she screwed the piece of paper into a tiny ball and threw it into the trash can.

Friday, June 28
2:35 p.m.

Kate got out of the cab and stood looking at the château while Ted paid the driver. She let out a low whistle. "My god, this must be costing a fortune. Either the bride and groom's careers have taken off bigtime, or the wealthy parents have dug deep."

Ted dropped their suitcases and wagged a finger at her. "Now, now, we agreed we weren't going to be Miss Rude this weekend, didn't we?" he said. "You have to think positive to get through this. Breathe deeply and let's go get 'em."

One Saturday morning a couple of months ago, Kate had wandered bleary-eyed into her hallway and picked up the mail. There was a *Reader's Digest* subscription offer, a leaflet from a local estate agent saying that "Mrs. M" wanted to buy a house in her road, and one interesting-looking envelope that clearly contained an invitation. She opened it after she had thrown a tea bag into a mug and flicked the kettle on.

As she pulled out the card, the names "Faye Parker" and "Mark Hawkins" leaped out at her, then, "You are invited to celebrate the marriage of . . ."

"Oh, my god," she exclaimed. She sat down at the kitchen table and studied the silver-edged card. The elaborate black inscription informed guests that the wedding would be held in France over the weekend of June 29 and 30 "Kate plus one" was written in black pen in the top right-hand corner.

A map of the area around the hotel was tucked inside the envelope with details of flights, and a note that informed her she was one of a select number of guests invited to stay in the hotel where the wedding would take place.

A tight knot formed in her throat as she picked up the phone and rang Liz, a work colleague with whom she'd become friendly since the breakup with Mark. "Is it OK to go to your ex-boyfriend's wedding?" she said, not bothering to introduce herself.

"If you're over him and able to handle it, it's a very mature, reasonable thing to do," Liz replied. "However, if you're going to stand at the back of the church shrieking, 'It should have been me,' then perhaps it's better to skip it."

"Oh, I'm so over him," Kate reassured her. Still, it had jolted her to the core to receive the invitation out of the blue.

After he'd walked out on her, Kate had resisted all Mark's attempts to be friends. She knew that the fastest way to get over him was to go cold turkey and, eventually, he'd given up calling. But after about a year, he'd rung to wish her a happy birthday and they had shared a long conversation in which he told her about his new job as a restaurant chef, and she told him she'd been made features editor of a diet magazine.

After putting the phone down, she had sat for several minutes in her kitchen, mulling over how she felt about him. The answer: that she could tolerate some kind of friendship. Since then, they'd caught up on each other's news from time to time and enjoyed a little of the jokey banter that had once endeared them to each other.

During one chat, Mark had mentioned he had a new girlfriend called Faye, and that she was a model. But Kate didn't ask questions: she still hadn't been ready for that.

The Saturday the wedding invitation had arrived, Kate steeled herself to call Mark's mobile. She just hoped he wasn't in bed with *her*.

"Hello?" The background noise sounded like traffic.

"Hi, it's Kate. Are you OK to talk?"

"Hi!" He was overeffusive, as people are when they're nervous. "Yes, it's fine. I'm on my way to work, waiting for the bus."

"I'm just ringing to say congratulations."

"Oh, yes, thanks!" The overeffusiveness again. "Can you come?"

"Yes, but that's hardly the point." She struggled not to sound shrill. "Why didn't you tell me?"

For a few seconds he was silent. Then, "Yeah, sorry about that. I chickened out."

"Why?" Kate had the faint hope he was about to say he'd made a terrible mistake in proposing to Faye and that it was *her* he truly wanted.

"Because of what happened between us, I suppose. We never resolved anything, so the thought of calling to say I'm getting married . . ."

Thud. The glimmer of hope had bottomed out. "Well, that's all history now," she said flatly, then made a conscious effort to brighten her tone: "I'm very happy for you."

"Thanks," he said. "That means a lot. So shall I add you to my yes list?"

"Yep. Plus Ted."

"Who's Ted?"

"Are you the guest police?" she teased, anxious to keep the conversation light.

"Well, it *is* my wedding."

"Yes, I know, and you sent me an invite with "plus one" written on it. As I don't know anyone of that name, I'm bringing a bloke called Ted."

"Is he a boyfriend?"

"None of your business."

"Kate . . ." he said wearily.

"OK, OK. Yes, he is. It's early days, though."

"I gathered that much, particularly as you haven't got round to telling me about him."

"This from a man who didn't tell me he was getting married!" she chided him gently.

"Touché."

Afterwards, Kate had spent the rest of the day trying to work out how she felt about the news. At the back of her mind there had always been the faint hope that she and Mark might reunite. Now the possibility was gone forever, and there was no denying that she felt slightly nauseous.

When she'd stepped out of the cab in France, the nausea had developed into a feeling of sickness in the pit of her stomach. She was here to watch Mark marry another woman.

Another car pulling up behind them jolted her out of her reverie. She turned, and her throat tightened.

It was Mark and Brian.

"Fucking hell. That's it, I'm staying here for good." Brian fell towards her as he caught his foot on the doorsill. "I can't face that journey again, especially downhill." He planted a kiss on Kate's cheek.

"A pleasure . . . as always." She beamed. "This is Ted."

"Hello, mate." Brian extended a hand. "And you are?"

"My boyfriend," said Kate quickly, annoyed that Mark hadn't deemed it important enough to tell Brian on their journey. Consequently she greeted him with a scowl as he emerged from the boot of his car with a large case and a garment bag. "Hi," she said flatly.

But his broad smile disarmed her. "I'm so glad you made it!" He dropped the bags and stretched out his arms towards her.

Perhaps he assumed I'd duck out, she thought, and said, "I wouldn't have missed it for the world." Taking both of his hands, she planted a sisterly kiss on his right cheek. The familiar smell of his Issey Miyake aftershave gave her butterflies.

"And you must be Ted." Mark dropped Kate's hands. "I've heard so much about you."

Kate resisted the temptation to look surprised at this blatantly untrue statement. "Yes, sorry, I should have introduced you both. Ted, this is Mark."

"Congratulations, and it's lovely to meet you," said Ted, smiling broadly. He had a pleasant face, with brown eyes and a clear complexion most women would envy. There were blond streaks in his mousy brown hair.

"Congratulations to you too," Mark replied.

Ted looked baffled. "Sorry?"

"You're a very lucky man." He nodded towards Kate.

She resisted the urge to grab his jugular and hiss, "So were you once." Instead she laughed, and said, "He is indeed," kissing Ted full on the lips.

"Where did you meet?"

Now it was Kate's turn to look startled. She hadn't expected Mark to probe any further, and was faintly irritated that he had. He was clearly betting on the fact that she wouldn't say "mind your own business," in front of Ted.

"I'm a photographer on the magazine," said Ted. "We spend a lot of time together doing those makeovers where we use bulldog clips to hide the excess skin of someone who's lost loads of weight . . . just months before they put it all on again."

Mark winced. "What a lovely thought. How long have you been together?"

Annoyed by his persistent questions about her private life when he had steadfastly failed to fill her in on the details of his own, Kate decided that enough was enough. "As I said, it's early days." She gave Mark and Brian a quick smile, then looped her arm through Ted's. "Come on, lover boy, let's find our room."

Ted smiled sheepishly at them. "See you at dinner."

They left their luggage for the porter to deal with, and climbed the steps that led up to the front door. As she pushed Ted into the château ahead of her, Kate shot a quick glance over her shoulder.

Brian was following them in, but Mark was standing stock still, staring out over the valley. He seemed deep in thought.

Mark crunched the gear stick into third and pressed the accelerator pedal to the floor. The car belched, then, after a terrifying nanosecond of inaction, lurched forward and edged into the access road for Birmingham's notoriously tricky Spaghetti Junction.

"Is this bloody roller skate going to make it?" said Brian, his face ashen.

"Shall we take your car instead, then?" said Mark sarcastically.

Brian looked wounded. "I'll have you know I've got a Ferrari. Somewhere."

Mark's ancient Citroen 2CV had been a gift from his parents. They could have bought him a top-of-the-line sports car, but they'd brought up their boys to appreciate the value of money and had compromised with the 2CV. It made it easier for Mark to travel home at weekends to see them and, of course, Jenna, and he'd made the trip several times since starting university.

Brian often finagled a lift. His contribution to the car's up-keep had been to buy two bumper stickers that read "Honk if you love peace and quiet," and "Pardon my driving. I'm reloading."

Initially both boys had felt homesick, but as the weeks wore on and their social life in Birmingham kicked in, they showed less enthusiasm for making the arduous journey home. This weekend, to his shame, Mark had called Jenna to say the car had a flat tire and he wouldn't be coming. "Besides, I could probably do with getting some studying done," he had added guiltily.

Now he was driving his car, with four perfectly inflated tires, for a night out with Brian.

They shared a stinky apartment with two other blokes from the university, and it was on a main road that led to the labyrinthine junction around which the car was now hiccuping.

Cheap but not very cheerful, the flat was a seventies shrine, with brown-and-cream swirly wallpaper, polystyrene ceiling tiles, and a grimy avocado bathroom suite. The carpets were virtually threadbare and covered with unidentifiable stains left over the years by previous occupants.

They had a weekly kitty for food, and each had an allocated night on which to cook a meal for the others. Monday was Brian's toad-in-the-hole, Tuesday was Mark's chili con carne, Wednesday was Shane's penne arabbiata, and Thursday was Steve's lasagne and chips. At the weekends, they suited themselves before returning to the same menu the following week. Their student allowances didn't stretch far, so a lot of nights out were spent in the university's subsidized bar. Tonight was no exception.

As he locked the car, Mark felt a slight pang of guilt as he thought of Jenna sitting at home with her parents. But it soon evaporated as he walked in to the vibrant mix of loud music and animated conversation.

Mark was good looking, with a touch of Mel Gibson about him, but Brian was more Mel Brooks. His droll sense of humor meant he enjoyed moderate success with women, until they got to know him and realized what an unadulterated slob he was. "I was such an ugly kid that when I played in the sandbox the cat kept covering me up," he once said to Mark. "My parents clearly felt the same way—my bath toys were the toaster and a radio."

After making the inevitable decision to collect the car in the morning, Mark and Brian sank a couple of pints in swift succession. Then, for Brian's benefit, they edged towards a group of girls in the corner.

"Anyone sitting here?" slurred Brian, pointing to two low chairs with huge tufts of foam rubber protruding from them.

"Yes, you are," said a girl, whose acne gave her face the look of a join-the-dots puzzle. In the sober light of day, she was what they'd have described as "a ten-pinter"—the amount they had to consume before they'd consider it.

But Brian's beer goggles clearly portrayed her as a great beauty. Licking his finger, he pressed it against her blouse. "Let's get you out of those wet clothes."

Five minutes later, he was snogging her face off while Mark stared disconsolately into space. He wished suddenly that he had made the trip home. I could be enjoying a video and a cuddle right now, he thought ruefully. Instead, I'm stuck with the unedifying spectacle of Brian's tongue disappearing down some girl's throat.

"Hello, do you need rescuing?"

The female voice snapped him out of his self-pitying stupor. "Uh, sorry?"

"Do you want some company? It looks like your friend's abandoned you—if not in body, then certainly in spirit."

Mark caught only half of what she'd said, but it took him all of five seconds to see that she was very attractive, with an elfin face and short brown hair in an urchin cut. A vision of his hands running through it flashed into his mind. "Sit down." He reached out and pulled over a chair. "Can I get you a drink?"

"Ooh, a rich student," she said, her eyes mocking him. "Yes, please. A double gin with diet tonic, please."

Mark was down to his last fiver, so he used Brian's old tried-and-tested trick of pretending he hadn't heard what she said and returning with two halves of lager.

Ten minutes later, he'd discovered that her name was Kate Evans, she came from Manchester and was in her first year of media studies. He also discovered that he had developed selective-memory syndrome: he conveniently forgot that he had a girlfriend, and asked her out on a date the following week.

"I'd love to go out with you," she said, pressing her face against his, "but, in the meantime, let's go back to your place."

After years spent trying to overcome Jenna's resistance, Mark could barely believe that this gorgeous woman was offering herself on a plate. No angst, no meaningful talks, just a no-nonsense let's-shag approach to life. He thought he'd died and gone to heaven.

Propelled by sheer lust and a crippling erection, he borrowed ten quid from Brian, and hailed a cab to whisk Kate back to the apartment.

There, Mark discovered great sex. After the first frenzied session, they slowed down for a second go, and then Kate fell into a deep sleep. But Mark lay in the darkness and wondered what the hell he was going to do. Torn between feeling horribly guilty about Jenna and ecstatic at having bedded a woman he found irresistibly attractive, he spent most of the night staring at her.

At 7 a.m. he gave up on sleep and crept into the kitchen for a glass of water. There he encountered a green-faced Brian sitting at the table. Above his head were the handwritten "House Rules" he'd pinned there when they first moved in.

- It is OK to cry during videos if (a) a heroic dog dies to save his master or (b) Sharon Stone unbuttons her blouse.
- Never fight naked, unless you're in prison.
- Always offer condolences if your girlfriend's cat dies, even if it was you who secretly threw it into the ceiling fan.
- Friends don't let friends wear Speedos. Ever.
- Under no circumstances may two men share an umbrella.

"When did the bloody mystery taxi arrive?" Brian muttered.

"Sorry?"

"The mystery taxi that arrived this morning, whisked away the fabulous beauty I pulled last night, and replaced her with the armadillo that's currently snoring in my bed." He shuddered. "She's the only woman to have appeared live on *Spitting Image*."

Mark laughed. "True, she wasn't a great looker. But you know what they say, beauty is in the eye of the beer-holder."

"I vaguely remember thinking she had great tits," said Brian, "but it turned out to be one of those zeppelin bras, impressive from the outside but fuck all within."

"Well, if you think you've got problems, listen to this," said Mark. "There's a girl in my bed . . . and it's not Jenna."

"Who's Jenna?" Kate was standing in the doorway. She scratched her head, making her hair stand on end.

"Oh . . . she's um, just a friend," Mark had flushed bright red.

"Really." Kate's expression left him in no doubt that she didn't believe a word and was thoroughly pissed off. "Well, I only do monogamy, so if you can handle that then give me a call."

She picked a pen out of the clutter on the table, and scribbled a number on Mark's arm. "If not, go to hell." She hooked a finger under the denim jacket she'd thrown onto a chair the night before and walked out.

Seconds later she popped her head back round the door and looked at Brian. "And you'll be pleased to know that *my* zeppelins are all my own." She disappeared.

Mark and Brian stared silently at each other, not daring to speak in case she was still in the next room. Eventually, Brian pulled a face and stood up. "I'm off," he said. "Do me a favor. Go into my room and tell the snoring warthog I've gone out or something. I'll call you in a couple of hours to check it's safe to come back."

And that was the end of Brian's meaningful relationship.

But Mark's evening with Kate was definitely something he wanted to repeat. He transferred her number from his arm to a piece of paper, then gave himself a couple of days to think things through.

"Hello, it's Mark."

"Oh, hi. Have you finished with your girlfriend yet?"

Mark was taken aback by the speed with which she had cut to the nitty-gritty. "Er, not as such, no." He faltered.

"Why are you calling, then? I'm not interested in emotional tangles. They bore me."

"I just wanted to say that the relationship is on its last legs and I really want to see you again."

She paused for a couple of beats. "Well, as I said, I only do monogamy, so when those tired old legs have crossed the finishing line, do get back in touch."

There was a click and Mark realized she had hung up. He placed the receiver back on the cradle and stared into space. He was desperate to see Kate, but he now knew he had to sort out the Jenna situation first.

The following weekend he drove, Brian-less, to Southampton. Whatever excuse he gave, it wouldn't be easy and he felt nauseous even thinking about it. Worse, when he arrived at her parents' house, Jenna jumped excitedly into the car and told him she had a surprise for him. Directing him to a mansion block about a mile from the city center, she got out and waved a set of keys. "I decided I wanted a bit more freedom so I've rented my own flat. It also means we get lots more time on our own."

That night, Mark couldn't bring himself to broach the subject of separation. Instead, he made sure his visit was platonic, claiming that exhaustion and stress meant he wasn't interested in sex. He didn't want to take advantage of Jenna, and, anyway, in his heart he was already moving on.

The next weekend, Jenna had bought him a cashmere sweater, then cooked a wonderful meal in her new flat. Again, he chickened out of telling her, playing the too-stressed card to avoid sex.

Fortunately, Jenna finally took the initiative herself and a long Dear Mark letter arrived on the following Wednesday morning. She wrote that she had sensed an increasing distance between them since his departure for university and that one of them had to address it. She suggested they take a month's break then call each other to discuss whether it was worth carrying on: "Otherwise we'll never get on with our lives."

Mark spent what he saw as a respectable day moping, then picked up the phone to call Kate.

"It's over," he said, and in his mind, it already was. As he saw it, the month's break was a cooling-off period before he called Jenna and told her that her instincts had been right; they were better off as friends.

In the meantime, he threw himself headfirst into a life of heated, idealistic debates and passionate sex with the feisty, opinionated Kate.

At first, Brian felt aggrieved that this new woman was encroaching on quality curry-and-football time, but it soon became clear that Kate was as close to an OK-with-your-mates girlfriend as it was possible for a woman to be, without actually being a man herself.

She had a great sense of humor, and even enjoyed watching soccer in a darkened room that smelled of last night's cigarettes and lager. Better still, she didn't seem to mind when Brian dragged Mark off on a boys-only drinking session.

Life was good, for a while.

Friday, June 28
3 p.m.

Woozy from too much lunchtime champagne, Adam had slunk off for an afternoon nap. Faye contemplated doing the same, but as she always woke up grumpy after a daytime snooze she decided against it. Instead, she locked her door and went to her mother's room.

Like most parents, Alice could drive her to distraction with her "little ways," but the older Faye became, the more clearly she understood how much her mother had sacrificed to give her a happy, secure upbringing.

She tapped on the door marked "6." Seconds later

Alice opened it, looking flustered. Her usually neat white bobbed hair was sticking out at one side and her brown eyes were perplexed. "Oh, hello, dear. I'm glad you're here. I can't seem to operate my radio."

Her mother was of the radio generation and, when she wasn't watching soaps, she had Radio Four playing all day in the background.

"You won't get Radio Four here, you know," said Faye, peering at the digital radio next to the bed.

"Yes, I assumed that. But what about the World Service?"

After a minute or two, pressing "mode" and "search," Faye cracked it, and a posh English voice was talking about the Middle East crisis.

"That'll do nicely." Alice beamed. "Just turn it down a bit." She walked across to her suitcase and started to unpack.

"What are you wearing for the wedding?" said Faye casually, flicking through the hotel's amenity book.

"I'm glad you asked that." Alice lifted a floral dress out of the suitcase and held it up. "This." She laid it on the bed. "I wanted to ask your opinion before we came out to France, but I didn't have a chance."

Alice had rung Faye several times to ask if they could meet up to discuss outfits, but Faye had been so busy with her own preparations that she'd only managed it once. She felt guilty.

"I'm so sorry, Mum, but it looks like you made the right choice anyway." If she'd met up with her mother beforehand, Faye would probably have persuaded her to wear something plain but she wasn't going to say so now.

"I also have a couple of things in here for you," said Alice, rummaging down the side of the case. She pulled out a little box and handed it to Faye. "It's something old."

Faye opened it to find a dainty silver pendant in the shape of a heart. The chain was exquisitely fine. "It's beautiful," she murmured.

"It was your grandmother's. It was the only thing she left me. Your auntie Clara got everything else."

Faye fastened it round her neck and looked at herself in the mirror. "In that case, I'll just borrow it for the ceremony."

"No, I want you to have it. I don't feel sentimental about Mother. My life began on the day she died," said Alice matter-of-factly.

Faye enveloped her in a hug.

"What was that for?" She looked surprised.

"For being a wonderful mum, despite having a lousy one of your own."

Her mother smiled. "You don't know how much it means to hear you say that." Her face brightened. "Now, then, have you got something borrowed and something blue? Obviously, your dress can be the new bit."

Faye pointed to a large aquamarine ring on her right hand, a present to herself after a particularly lucrative modeling job a couple of years ago. "This is the blue, and Adam has loaned me a pair of his earrings to wear."

"Adam? Earrings?"

"Yep. He has one pierced ear, but often has to buy earrings he likes in pairs."

"Is it hygienic?"

"Mum!" Faye laughed. "He hasn't got any diseases."

Alice looked dubious. "But isn't he . . . you know?"

"Gay? Yes, he is." She raised her eyes heavenward. "And, no, it's not contagious. And he doesn't have AIDS either."

It was at times like this when the chasm between Faye and her mother was at its widest. Although Alice was only in her late forties, her sheltered life had given her the mindset and demeanor of someone much older. Describing her once to a friend, Faye had likened her to "a vicar's wife," serene and kind but old-fashioned.

"Well, I hope you know what you're doing," said Alice,

returning to her unpacking. She placed the latest John Grisham novel on her bedside table.

Faye decided to change the subject. "There are lots of lovely walks around here," she said, knowing how her mother loved to ramble—in every sense of the word.

"Yes, I thought I might explore a bit in the morning, maybe after breakfast. Fancy it?"

Faye knew that *The Good Daughter's Guide* would advise her to say yes, but she just couldn't face it. Long walks weren't her forte. "I haven't any suitable shoes with me," she lied, "and I suspect I'll be in a bit of a tizz in the morning, making sure everything is going according to plan."

"Are you nervous?" Alice zipped up her now empty suitcase and looked straight at her.

Thrown by the question, Faye stumbled: "Er . . . no . . . not exactly. Apprehensive, maybe."

"What's the difference?" Alice's tone was light, not antagonistic.

"Um . . . I suppose apprehension is more something you feel when you want everything to run smoothly." She frowned, editing her words as she went along. "Nerves would mean you were worried about the decision to marry in the first place."

"And you're not?"

"Not what?"

"Worried about the decision."

"No. Not at all. Quite the contrary, in fact."

"Good." Alice took a hairbrush from her toilet bag and ran it through her fine hair. Several loose strands fell to the floor.

"Why do you ask?" Faye said.

"No reason. It's just that people always say you get last-minute nerves on your wedding day . . . not that I'd know."

Faye felt herself relax. "Yes, they do," she said. "I suppose it *is* a bit nerve-racking, having to make a decision you're supposed to stick to for the rest of your life." She looked across at her mother for a reaction. There wasn't one, but she could tell that Alice was listening intently. "I mean," continued Faye, "it's a bit like being asked to choose the car you'll drive forever, or the house you'll live in forever."

Alice pursed her lips. "I know what you're saying, but at least in this day and age you can get out of marriages easily if you feel you've made a mistake."

"Yes, but that's not the point, is it? I'm marrying Mark tomorrow on the basis that we'll be together forever. Otherwise, why bother?"

The question hung in the air between them, a conundrum to which neither woman had the solution.

Faye sighed, puncturing the silence. "Best not to think about things too deeply, or I *will* get nervous." She stood up. "I'm going to go and check that everything's in place for dinner tonight."

Alice stifled a yawn, and sat down on a hard-backed chair near the window. "Who's coming?"

"Well, apart from you, Mark's parents, Auntie Ethel, and a couple of Mark's other relatives, there's Adam, Mark's best man, Brian, a couple of Mark's exes, and a couple of mine."

Alice raised her eyebrows. "Any exes I know?"

"There's Rich," said Faye. "You remember, the policeman . . . He dropped me home once and came in for a cup of tea."

Alice frowned as she dredged through her memory. Then her expression changed to recognition. "Ah, yes. A very nice boy. And who's the other?"

"Nat, a male model. You never met him."

"Why not?"

"He's not really your type. He's rather . . . How shall I put this? Colorful." Faye winced as she said it.

"Well, now I'm intrigued. I can't wait to meet him."

"Believe me," muttered Faye. "You can."

Lolling around on a bright-red, lip-shaped sofa, Faye glanced at her watch for the umpteenth time. It was two o'clock and the photo shoot for the Christmas 1999 edition of *Elle* had been due to start an hour ago.

"Where *is* he?" she asked the flustered fashion editor, who was clutching a clipboard as if her life depended on it. "Has anyone tried ringing him?"

"We have to go through his agency, we're not allowed to contact him direct," said the girl, looking as if she might cry. "They said he's five minutes away."

"From where, New Zealand?" said Faye. She stood up and stretched. "I hope he's worth it when he gets here."

"Oh, Nat's a fantastic model," said the girl, dreamy now. "He always looks brilliant in pictures."

"It helps to turn up, though, doesn't it?" said Faye, and realized that her sarcasm was lost on a woman who was clearly depriving a village somewhere of its idiot. She walked across to the window, which overlooked the litter-infested canal to the rear of the studios. Two swans were trying valiantly to cleave a path through the discarded cardboard boxes, drink cans, and occasional item of clothing.

It was two years since she'd ended it with Rich and, apart from a couple of non-starters, she hadn't been in a relationship since. Now she was tired of being alone.

Her job meant she was invited to the opening of every door in town, but Faye longed for the normality of staying in with a boyfriend and ordering pizza. But not just any boyfriend: she wanted someone to whom she was attracted and who stimulated her mentally. Sadly, Rich hadn't fitted into either of those categories. He'd taken it pretty well, though, considering he'd professed undying love to her.

Faye had used the age-old get-out clause often favored by those who wish to cushion the blow. She told him she needed a break to think things over. "It's not you, it's me," she'd said, quoting from the well-worn script of gentle brush-offs. "I'm just not ready for a serious relationship. I need time to think."

His brown eyes softening with sadness, Rich had resembled a spaniel whose bone had been taken away. But all he had said was, "Let me know when you've decided what you want."

Faye knew already, of course, but she'd left it four weeks before she wrote to him saying she thought it better that they parted for good.

I don't know what I want, and you're too good and kind a man for me to drag down with my indecision and inability to commit. You're a wonderful person, Rich, and I know you'll find someone who's perfect for you. Someone loving and uncomplicated who'll give you the care and attention you deserve. Sadly, I'm incapable of that right now.

She believed what she'd written, but she wondered whether she would always be incapable of commitment. Married friends had said, "You'll know when you meet the right man," but Faye hadn't come close yet. She had met men to whom she was sexually attracted, and she had met two or three, like Rich, who were pleasant enough to date for a while. But a man she wanted to marry, have children and sit on the porch with in old age? She couldn't imagine it.

Her thoughts were interrupted by a door slamming, then a loud voice. "Sorry I'm late. Let's get this show on the road."

She turned to see Nat Finch fling his leather jacket onto a chair and plant a kiss full on the lips of the awestruck fashion editor. He was even more devastatingly handsome in the flesh than in his photographs.

About six foot three, he had shoulder-length dark brown hair, swept back from his face in a sexily unkempt style. With the chiseled jaw of a romance novel hero, he cut an imposing figure. Trouble was, he clearly knew it.

As he moved round the room, he charmed, cajoled, and complimented every man and woman in it, until his late arrival had been forgotten. Then he turned the headlights on Faye. "Yowza! You've really come up trumps with this one!" He took Faye's arm and swiveled round to show the fashion editor he was talking to her. "She's a beauty."

Faye slapped away his hand. "I'm not a bloody exhibit," she snapped. "And where the hell do you think you've been? You've kept us all waiting an hour."

The fashion editor paled and disappeared into a changing room. For a fleeting moment, even Nat looked thrown. But he quickly recovered. "Ooh, a feisty one!"

Faye scowled. "Christ, it's d'Artagnan. Any minute now, you'll be slapping your leg and jumping on your horse." She took a step back and pretended to study him further. "Still, it explains the hair."

He held out his hand. "Hi, I'm Nat. Remember my name, you'll be screaming it later." He was grinning from ear to ear, enjoying winding her up.

She did not take the hand, but allowed herself a small smile, then turned her back on him and walked to the photographer. "Ready? I'm sure we all have lives we'd like to get on with."

The shoot was for the catalogue of a new Italian designer who specialized in men's clothes. Nat was every designer's darling and had appeared in high-profile campaigns for Gucci, Armani, and Ralph Lauren. Faye had been booked as his appendage, but found it hard to achieve the required look of adoration.

"Look at him as if you think he's the most wonderful man you've ever met," said the photographer, peering at a Polaroid to check the lighting.

"I'm a model, not an Oscar-winning actress," she muttered.

"You're funny. I like that," said Nat.

"Two hours, three outfits, and several rolls of film later, the photographer announced it was "in the bag."

"Thanks." Faye beamed, keen to ingratiate herself with the team and thereby ensure future bookings. She rushed off to change.

Throwing her outfit over a hat rack in the corner of the cubicle, she stood in her bra and pants and began to wipe away the thick layers of foundation and eye shadow that had transformed her into a smoky-eyed siren. Sensing someone behind her she twisted round to see Nat leaning nonchalantly against the door frame. He was staring openly at her breasts. "You look great in the Polaroids." He held up three.

"Thanks." She extended her leg and nudged the door so that it closed gently in his face. She pulled on her shirt rapidly in case he reappeared, and smiled to herself. Nat was arrogant, but she nevertheless found him disturbingly attractive. Unlike many of the "pretty" male models she'd worked with, he had an appealing rugged look and "get into my bed right now" eyes. He was also a bit of a bad boy, a type she usually avoided, but her Siberian love life made it difficult to resist.

When she'd dressed and combed the sticky mousse out of her hair, she went back into the studio. Nat was nowhere to be seen and the assistants had returned to their usual stance of sniffing and slouching. They barely looked up as she bade them goodbye.

Outside, the sun was shining but it was a crisp, blustery day. Faye pulled her fake-fur coat tightly around her and set off for the tube station. As she turned out of the side street in which the studio was located, she heard a car horn. She ignored it, but when it became more persistent, she turned.

Nat was driving an eye-catching Aston Martin in British racing green and wearing a baseball hat with "69" on the front. "Hello again," he shouted, above the engine noise. "Fancy a lift?"

"No, thanks." She was desperate to hop in. "I'm going on the tube."

He switched off the engine. "Where do you live?"

"In a house." She meant it as a quip, but it had come out more firmly than she had intended.

His brow furrowed. "Are you always so unfriendly?"

She pursed her lips, but her eyes held a friendly twinkle. "Only to men who keep me waiting for over an hour."

"Yeah, sorry about that. I had a couple of things to sort out. Come on, hop in. I don't bite, you know."

Faye mulled over the options. She could struggle home on the overcrowded, dirty tube, or she could let this strikingly handsome man take her in his impressive car. Tricky one.

"OK," she said, and opened the door. "But it's south of the river."

"Don't worry, I've got my passport in the glove compartment." He grinned and locked her seatbelt. She squinted in the low afternoon sunshine, and he put his hand into the car's side pocket, then handed her a pair of pink-tinted sunglasses.

"I'm sure your girlfriend will be thrilled to know her belongings are being shared around," said Faye, pushing them up the bridge of her nose.

"I haven't got a girlfriend. They belong to my sister."

During the stop-start journey through the rush hour traffic, Faye learned that he was twenty-eight and originally from Tunbridge Wells in Kent, where his parents still lived. His sister was twenty-five and worked as a makeup artist for Granada Television.

Nat owned a one-bedroom flat in the heart of Covent Garden, but wasn't there much because of all the traveling to modeling assignments. He was signed to the hugely powerful Guru agency, and there was little doubt that he earned ten times as much as Faye. The car confirmed it.

As they drove along the main road through East Sheen, Faye directed him to her mother's house and thanked him for taking such a lengthy diversion. He shrugged. "I did it because I fancy you."

Faye was unsure how to react, then threw back her head and laughed. "Well, you're certainly straightforward."

They pulled into her mother's road and she gestured for him to pull up outside number thirty.

He killed the engine and smiled. "So, how about it, then?"

"How about what?"

"You and me getting it on."

"How very Marvin Gaye," she said mockingly, and rummaged in her handbag for her door keys. She looked straight at him. "It takes more than a lift home to win me over."

"How about dinner, then?" he said, his eyes playing strippoker with her. "I do fancy you, but you make me laugh too. It would be nice to do something away from work."

Faye stepped out of the car and smoothed down her coat. As far as she was concerned, she could say no for reasons of dignity, then spend days convincing herself she had done the right thing, or she could say yes and go on a date with a man she found uncommonly sexy.

Dignity doesn't keep you warm at night, she thought. "OK, dinner." She handed him one of the business cards she'd had printed on a machine at King's Cross railway station.

He took it. "Great. I'm off on a calendar shoot for a fortnight from tomorrow, but I'll call as soon as I get back."

Faye suspected he'd forget all about her.

In the event, it was four weeks before he got round to calling, and Faye had all but given up on him. When he did, he was disarmingly apologetic, blaming his workload for the delay.

Their first date had been dinner at the Ivy, London's most prestigious restaurant where the celebrity head-count was always high. Impressively, Nat had secured a table at short notice, always an indicator of someone's current social standing. Faye was introduced to a stream of people who came over to say hello, and she had to admit it was a dazzlingly fun evening.

Nat's specialist subject was himself, but he was occasionally witty, mesmerizingly handsome, and paid the bill without flinching.

He made a lame attempt to get her back to his flat, but when she said no, he ordered a cab on his account to deliver her home.

The second date had been to the cinema where, at Faye's insistence, they'd gone to see the latest hip foreign film with subtitles. As it reached its tear-jerking climax, Faye turned to gauge Nat's reaction and found he was fast asleep. Afterwards she'd gone straight home.

On their third date, she could tell there was something on Nat's mind, and had a pretty good idea what it was. Clearly he wasn't used to women resisting his obvious charms for long.

"Is there any chance of us having a shag tonight?" he said, as they ate their appetizer in a quiet Italian restaurant in Soho. A woman at a nearby table choked on her asparagus.

Faye raised an eyebrow. "Possibly. If you're a good boy." She licked a blob of butter provocatively from her forefinger.

Nat put his elbows on the table and leaned towards her: "Sorry, no can do. I intend to be a very bad boy indeed."

Faye could feel his knee pressed hard against her leg and felt lightheaded with lust. She knew that if they didn't have sex tonight, it would all be over. Nat wasn't the kind of man who respected a woman for holding out: he would simply shrug his shoulders and find someone with less willpower.

Besides, Faye found herself increasingly annoyed by the self-help books so eagerly consumed by her girlfriends. *How to Find a Man. How to Keep a Man. How to Get Back Your Man.* They were all full of dating "rules," the most irritating being the one that specified how many dates to go on before you had sex. Faye never had sex on a first date, but after that her decision was based on the man involved and no "expert" was going to change that. She had noticed there were no such rules for single men. They were happy to sleep with whomever they wished, whenever they wished, without any ensuing hand-wringing or guilt.

"I think," she whispered, so that the asparagus woman wouldn't hear, "we should have our main course and go back to your place for dessert."

Half an hour later they were walking into the foyer of Nat's minimalist apartment building directly opposite the Covent Garden piazza. "Good evening, Mr. Finch." The concierge tilted his head at Faye. "Madam."

"Good evening." She wondered how many women he'd seen Nat coming and going with. She stepped into the lift.

The second the doors closed, Nat pressed her against the chrome wall with such force that she couldn't have escaped if she'd wanted to, but luckily she didn't. By the time they reached the fourth floor, his hand was inside her blouse and things were becoming heated. When the doors opened, the floor was empty, sparing Faye's blushes as she hastily rearranged her bra.

Nat grabbed her hand and dragged her along the corridor to a door marked "45" where he stopped and fumbled for his keys.

As he opened the door he nuzzled her ear and whispered, "I'm going to fuck you senseless."

Three hours later, her senses were still intact, but she had to admit he was an impressive and relatively unselfish lover. Her skin still tingling, she lay back and studied his bedroom. It was starkly male, with gray walls and a glass-brick partition separating it from the en-suite bathroom. The bed was king-size, with surprisingly tasteful white linen sheets and a black fake-fur throw placed along the foot. Hanging above it was a giant photograph of Nat, taken from the previous season's Gucci campaign. Lying next to her now in a disheveled heap, she had to admit he was even more luscious in the naked flesh.

He opened his eyes and caught her looking at him. "You can't believe your luck, can you?" he joked.

"On the contrary . . ." Faye yawned. "I feel very under-whelmed by the whole experience."

He propped himself up on one elbow. "I like your sarcasm. I'm used to women fawning all over me."

"Really?" Faye adopted a surprised expression. She threw back the sheet, swung her feet out of bed and on to the cold wood floor.

"The call of nature?" he asked.

"Nope. The call of home. I've got heaps to do." She walked around the room, picking up her clothes.

He looked at his watch. "But it's four in the morning." He patted the bed. "Come on, hop back in and I'll persuade you to stay."

"Sorry, no can do," she said. "I've got a lot to do tomorrow, so I need to get home. Can you order me a cab, please?"

In truth, there was nothing she'd rather do than leap back into bed for another passionate session: this man's sheer animal magnetism almost overwhelmed her. But if there was one thing Faye had learned about men like Nat, it was not to look too eager in the early stages. She wasn't sure if she'd hear from him again, but her seeming reluctance to stay might heighten her chances. She believed that there was no such thing as an across-the-board bastard. It all depended on what you let them get away with. One woman's bastard was another woman's puppy dog.

It was the same with her. Certain men brought out her worst side, not because they deserved it but because they let her get away with too much. She had every faith that, out there some-where, was her match: a man who would bring out the best in her while letting her know that he wouldn't tolerate any bad be-havior. It was all about finding and maintaining a delicate bal-ance of power.

She knew that any relationship with Nat wouldn't progress

past shallow fun, but it would be enjoyable while it lasted. Nothing more.

As she washed her face in the bathroom, she heard him order a cab, again on his account. At least he's not tightfisted, she thought.

Walking back into the bedroom, she collected her handbag from the bedside table and turned to face him. He was lying with his hands behind his head, looking utterly edible. "I'll go and engage your concierge in scintillating conversation until the cab arrives," she said. "Thanks for ordering it."

"No problem. Least I could do." He showed no sign of saying anything else.

"Right, then, see ya," she said, and left. God, she thought, I sounded like someone from a bad soap opera. But she had been determined not to have any eggy moments in which she waited for him to suggest another date. He had her number, so he could call if he wanted to. If.

Ten days later, Faye was contemplating another night of watching reruns with her mother. She had resolved to start saving hard to buy a passport out of there, if only for a tiny studio flat in central London. Smearing a piece of toast with low-fat margarine, she walked into the sitting room where Alice was already engrossed by the television and sank onto the sofa beside her. The phone rang. She picked up the hands-free unit, got up, and wandered out of the room.

"Hello?"

"Hi, it's me."

Faye knew instantly who it was, but she wasn't going to give him the satisfaction of instant recognition. "Sorry, who's 'me'?"

He let out a mildly impatient sigh. "Nat."

"Oh, hi," she said casually. Annoyingly her heart rate had increased. "How are things?"

"Good," he enthused. "I'm rushed off my feet with work or I'd have called sooner."

"Don't worry. I've been horribly busy myself." If you can count handing out free chocolates at the Ideal Home Exhibition, she thought ruefully.

"Great!" He sounded genuinely enthusiastic. "What campaigns have you done?"

"Oh, this and that," she said. "To be honest, I find all that kind of thing horribly boring to talk about."

"Yeah, me too," he said unconvincingly. "Look, the reason I was calling was to find out whether you want to come to the première of a new film with me tomorrow night."

"Which one?"

"No idea. My agent just thought it would be good for me to be seen at it."

What a Philistine, she thought. But a sexy one. "Yes, why not?"

The première of Martin Scorsese's latest film was the first of several high-profile dates between Faye and Nat who, thanks to the latter's status, found themselves appearing in several newspapers diary columns over the next couple of months.

For Faye, the media attention was a novelty, and she was under no illusion that anyone would be interested in her if she wasn't hanging off Nat's arm. But it certainly boosted her own career: the catalogue and magazine jobs flooded in. Most important, she'd got her eleventh-hour chance to do the shoot with the hugely influential *Couture* magazine, where she'd met Adam.

The pattern of her and Nat's dates was always the same: he'd send a car for her, they'd meet in the foyer of his flat, then walk round to whatever film première or launch party they were to attend that evening. Afterwards, they'd return to his flat for some mind-blowing sex. Occasionally, she'd stay all night, and a couple of times they had even strolled round to a local café for coffee and croissants while they read the papers in virtual silence.

To her, the mundane things couples did together were as important as the exciting ones, if not more so. It was easy to get on with Nat while they were pitching up at crowded social events and drinking the free alcohol, but she knew the test would be a quiet country weekend with him, or staying in with a video.

Outside the bedroom, she found him increasingly dull. His conversation rarely veered away from either himself or his beloved Fulham Football Club, and his interest in her life was microscopic. It was clear he'd got used to people making an effort for him because of his looks, but he rarely bothered to return the compliment.

For a while it suited Faye that their "relationship" amounted to hanging out in noisy places, then returning home to exchange grunts in bed, but eventually, against her better judgment, she found herself wondering whether *she* could be the one to change him.

Faye felt that one of womankind's greatest weaknesses was the desire to be loved, irrespective of how suitable the man was. And, try though she might, she was no exception.

Like everyone, she had her insecurities, which manifested themselves in a desire to be so witty, interesting, and *different* from all the others that no boyfriend could bear to be without her. A psychologist might say that this was rooted in having been abandoned by her father before she was born, but Faye had never booked a therapy session to find out.

In a bid to put their relationship on a more normal footing, she'd invited Nat for dinner at a restaurant to meet Adam and he made it quite clear that the only reason he would come was her friend's influential position at *Couture*.

The evening had been an unmitigated disaster, particularly because Nat had turned up an hour and a half late. If Faye and Adam had planned to spend the evening on their own, they'd have enjoyed it, but as it was, they kept consulting their watches and glancing at the door every time it opened. Being late without calling was typical of someone so self-centered: Nat couldn't make an impression with his personality, so he placed his own indelible stamp on the evening by keeping people waiting.

"I hope he's worth it when he gets here," muttered Adam, starting on his second bread roll, "though if he's like most male models I know, I doubt it."

Nat hadn't bucked the trend and proved himself to be every bit as disappointing as Adam had thought. The icing on the cake was when he told a story about a gay male model and used the term "booty bandit."

Afterwards, two weeks passed in which Faye didn't see or hear from him. Pride prevented her calling him, although on several occasions she had been just moments from doing so.

She scoured the daily diary columns for any clues to his whereabouts, willing his absence to be attributed to a long modeling assignment abroad. Even then, she knew it would have been easy for him to call and let her know. Several times, she contemplated the idea that he might be unfaithful, but as they'd never really discussed the status or permanency of their relationship, she was unsure whether he even thought of her as a girlfriend.

It was unusual for Faye to feel so emotionally wobbly, but she put it down to the uncertainty of the situation rather than any depth of feeling for Nat.

As the silence edged into a third week, he called out of the blue to invite her to a launch party for the new album by the latest girl band, Minx. They followed their usual routine, and ended up at Nat's flat where he made up for his lack of conversational skills with particularly passionate sex.

Glancing through the papers, the next day, she saw that a picture of them arriving at the party had made Nigel Dempster in the *Daily Mail* as well as the Londoner's Diary in the *Evening*

Standard. Consequently another handful of modeling jobs came in via her agency.

Soaking in the bath one night, while her mother watched television downstairs, Faye mulled over her relationship with Nat. Although she wasn't sure of the depth of its future, she felt optimistic enough to try to crank it up a notch. Perhaps I'll suggest a weekend away, she mused, or maybe spend a Saturday and Sunday at his place and see how we get on.

The next morning, she got up early and headed off to a catalogue shoot in north London, making a mental note to call him that evening.

Grabbing a bite of lunch between outfits, she picked up a copy of that morning's *Standard.* She took a bite of her brie and tomato baguette, and flicked idly through the pages, speed reading the headlines. As she turned to page twelve, a lump of bread stuck to the roof of her mouth and her jaw dropped.

There, in front of her, was a picture of Nat arm in arm with a stunning redhead. The caption read; "Top male model Nat Finch out on the town last night with rising film star Jade Brogan."

And that was how she found out it was over between them.

Friday, June 28
3:10 p.m.

Tony Hawkins stood in the reception area, studying the ornate ceiling, while an anxious Mark collected his room key from the desk.

Tony hadn't asked him to do it, but he had an air of authority that made others feel the urge to jump through hoops for him. From the Clint Eastwood less-is-more school of thought, he was proof that what you *didn't* say proved more effective than what you did.

A ruthless businessman, Tony had sat many times at a conference table saying nothing, merely raising an eyebrow here or pursing his lips there. His silence had troubled many into hastily offering more than they had intended in a deal, but it never bothered him. He could say nothing for as long as it took to get what he wanted.

The heartfelt hug he'd just shared with Mark on the hotel steps had been the first in nearly two years, and Tony was surprised by the deep feeling it had stirred in him. He was very fond of his younger brother.

Since he'd moved to New York, they'd kept in touch with occasional emails, but Mark had been so tied up with his new job that he'd resisted Tony's offers to pay for him to visit. In his turn, Tony had been too busy in New York to come home.

He'd first gone there to work for a bank, but was now chairman of Jam, the biggest sportswear manufacturer in the world. It was fashion-victim clothing and he wouldn't be seen dead in it, but he had been employed for his business acumen and had singlehandedly turned the company's fortunes from loss to brand leader.

It had taken him three weeks of sixteen-hour days to clear enough space in his hectic schedule to make the trip to Europe, but he was glad he had. New York was a vibrant, cutting-edge place to live, but it was also uptight and snobbish. You had to live in the right area, have the right friends, wear the right clothes, and go to the gym with monotonous regularity. Otherwise you didn't fit in. And if you were seen hanging around the city on any weekend between April and November, you were considered the lowest of the low by those who migrated to the Hamptons every Thursday after lunch.

Tony believed that Europeans had nothing to prove in the culture or lifestyle stakes, so they were much more relaxed and went with the social flow. He was ten years older than Mark, who'd been their parents' little "surprise" when they'd all but given up hope of conceiving any more children, and his younger brother was the spitting image of their father, Derek, with his open face, hazel eyes and shock of pale brown hair. Tony took after their mother, Jean: with dark brown hair—her natural color—and royal blue eyes; and he had also inherited her thinner, foxier face. Most striking of all, he was six foot three to Mark's five eleven.

Because of the age difference, their relationship had always been that of mentor and pupil, and he was protective of his younger brother. Their differing personalities also meant that forthright Tony had unwittingly dominated the more malleable Mark for most of his life. It wasn't until some distance separated them that Mark had been able to develop more independence and make his own decisions in life.

But despite becoming more his own man, Mark had still balked at the idea of telling Tony about his forthcoming marriage. Although his brother had known he was dating, he hadn't asked many questions about Faye, preferring in their brief conversations or emails to discuss their parents and Mark's struggling career.

But Mark knew that once the girlfriend became a prospective wife, Tony wouldn't be able to resist asking all sorts of questions aimed at finding out whether his younger brother was making the right decision.

Sure enough, when he received a long email containing the news, Tony had called immediately. However, instead of casting doubt, he had been thrilled and told a surprised Mark exactly that, adding that he couldn't wait to meet his future sister-in-law.

Later that night, though, his natural pessimism had kicked in, particularly because Mark and Faye had only been dating for a year. Rather than express any doubts to his brother, he had decided to consult the oracle.

"Hi, Mum, great news about Mark," he said, during a call that he had timed not to clash with their favorite television show.

"Yes, isn't it?" Her response seemed muted for a woman who was desperate for one of her sons to tie the knot.

"You don't sound keen."

She cleared her throat. "Oh, it's not that I don't like her—in fact, she seems a lovely girl. It's just that she and Mark are like chalk and cheese. She's the cheese, and I suspect she'll go off quickly, if you get my drift."

The comment had intrigued him, and he wondered what he would think of Faye when they met, whether he would approve.

That was Tony's main problem: his arrogance. Or, at least, that's what so many of his ex-girlfriends had told him, particularly the ones he'd dumped. His favorite observation had come from a woman he'd dated casually for a couple of months before deciding she was too flaky.

"You'll never find another woman like me," she'd pouted.

"Thank God for that," he'd muttered beneath his breath, before ushering her out of the door.

Mark interrupted Tony's silent reminiscences. "Here's your key, and there were some faxes and a couple of envelopes for you too." He handed them over. "You can leave New York, but you can never escape work, eh?"

"That's for sure." Tony grimaced. "I can assure you that most of it will be in the trash in a few minutes' time."

"You go up, the porter will follow with your luggage."

"Thanks, bruv." Tony gave him another hug. "It's so good to see you. You look great by the way."

"That's love for you!" Mark's whole face lit up. "I can't wait to introduce you to Faye. You won't believe what a lucky man I am."

That depends, thought Tony, but—as always in a sensitive situation—he stayed quiet. He wanted to equip himself with the full facts before passing judgment, so he just smiled encouragingly. "When am I going to meet her?"

Mark flushed. "Well, as a nod to tradition, we're not sharing a room tonight, so I won't be seeing her until dinner, and I doubt you will either." He took a step back and studied his brother. "If you make dinner, of course, I'd forgotten you'll probably be jet-lagged."

Tony shook his head. "Nope. I flew to London last weekend,

but I didn't want Mum and Dad to know, and I knew you'd be up to your eyes with all this . . ." he made a sweeping gesture with his arm ". . . so I didn't bother calling to try to meet up."

"Oh." Mark looked nonplussed. "Was it a business trip?" His voice was barely audible.

Tony looked around him, checking for anyone in earshot. "It was Melissa business."

Mark's expression slowly changed to one of understanding. "Crikey. No wonder you wanted to keep it quiet from the Groans, he said, using their pet name for their parents.

"Precisely. The last thing I wanted was Mother weeping all over me at your wedding." He grinned suddenly. "Unless it's tears of happiness at seeing you get hitched, of course."

"So what's the state of play, then?"

Tony's face clouded. "Well, after all these years of us both avoiding the issue, she finally asked for a divorce." He held up the envelopes Mark had handed him. "I suspect one of these is the decree nisi."

"Sorry, mate. It must be tough for you to come to my wedding just as your marriage is ending."

"Not at all." Tony shrugged. "These days, I barely think about her. I saw her in the solicitor's office a couple of days ago, and she felt like a stranger to me."

⁂

As an eight-year-old, Mark had seen Tony's girlfriends come and go with bemusement. At fifteen, he'd watched enviously as twenty-five-year-old Tony moved to London, started to earn more, and occasionally came home for Sunday lunch with a succession of women who wouldn't have looked out of place on the cover of *Vogue*. None had ever enjoyed a repeat visit, until a twenty-three-year-old makeup artist called Melissa arrived on the scene.

From the moment Tony first brought her home, Mark had been transfixed by her beauty. She was exquisite, just like a porcelain doll that might snap in the wrong hands. Her jet-black hair was cut into a short bob that drew attention to her large green eyes, and she spoke softly with a slightly high-pitched tone, like that of a small child.

To the gauche, inexperienced Mark, she was the embodiment of femininity, and he wanted to wrap her in cotton wool and look after her. Luckily, she also seemed to have this effect on Tony, who lavished attention and gifts on her with equal measure.

Jean adored Melissa because she was quiet, unassuming, and clearly devoted to Tony.

"We'll never have any trouble with her," she said to Derek, after the first visit. After the second she could barely contain her excitement as she predicted they'd just met their future daughter-in-law.

She was right.

Six months later, Tony had brought Melissa home again to announce their engagement. The wedding, held at Chelsea Town Hall followed by a reception at the Waldorf, had been a networker's dream combination of the fashion and business worlds. Tony and Melissa were one of the hottest couples in town, and before long they had bought into the dream of big-house-in-the-country with a London pied-à-terre.

Melissa went part-time, taking on only London-based assignments so that she and Tony could see more of each other. Two years later, they seemed more in love than ever. Then, one summer weekend in 1998 when Mark and Kate were visiting Southampton from London, Jean and Derek got a call to say Tony was on his way.

Jean could barely contain her excitement: "He wouldn't tell me on the phone, but I have a strong suspicion Melissa might be pregnant! We could be grandparents by next year!"

Later that night when Tony walked in, Mark knew immediately that something was painfully wrong. His brother's face was alabaster white, and his eyes were shot with red thread-veins of sleep deprivation. He looked so devastated that even Jean remained silent.

"There's no easy way to say this . . ." Tony stared down at the wedding ring he was twisting. "Melissa and I are going our separate ways."

Mark, his parents, and Kate sat still, looking like experienced poker players, their faces devoid of emotion.

A sob broke the silence. "What do you mean?" Jean had asked the question so many do when told bad news, as if, somehow, they'll be told second time round that it's all been a misunderstanding.

"It's over, Mum," he said quietly. "She's left me."

"Why, son?" Derek had his arm round the now inconsolable Jean, but remained calm.

Tony sat down at the kitchen table and rubbed his eyes. "It's been a long time coming, but I guess I ignored the signs."

Mark glanced at Kate and cleared his throat. "Is there . . ." he faltered, ". . . someone else?"

"Yes." His brother's voice was hard. "Apparently, he doesn't work the hours I do and gives her more love and attention."

"Who is he?" inquired Derek.

"Some bloke from our local gym. Turns out he was teaching her a bit more than just Pilates." He couldn't hide the bitterness in his voice.

"The little cow." Jean had stopped crying and found the strength to speak. "Does she think that the lovely houses, cars, and designer clothes all grow on trees? Someone's got to work hard to pay for it all."

Tony patted her hand. "I know you mean well, Mum, but I probably do spend more time at work than I should. It's a terrible habit and it's certainly not good for a marriage."

"Oh, so it's *your* fault she's run off with another man, is it?" Jean asked incredulously.

Tony sighed. "No, Mum, of course not. That's her doing." He massaged the bridge of his nose with a forefinger. "But I do accept that I neglected her emotionally. She tried to warn me several times, and I just kept right on working, working, working . . ." He petered out and stared at the table.

They all lapsed into silence.

Then Mark spoke. "Where is she now?"

"At the flat in London, packing her things. She's going to rent a room with a girlfriend for a while."

Several hours later, when Jean and Derek had gone to bed and Kate was luxuriating in the bath, Mark and Tony had adjourned to their father's study for a brandy.

"How did you find out Melissa was seeing someone else?" Mark asked, as he lit his brother's cigarette.

"Strictly between ourselves?"

Mark nodded. "Absolutely."

Tony stretched his legs in front of him, leaned back and stared up at the ceiling. "You get a hunch about these things. Mine came when I got home earlier than usual one day and she arrived back from the gym wearing makeup."

"That was unusual?"

"Correct. She never wore makeup to the gym, so I made the assumption she was doing it to impress someone there." He tapped his cigarette on the ashtray.

"Then what?"

Tony took a drag and narrowed his eyes against the smoke as he exhaled. "I went to work as usual, then took the afternoon off and turned up at the gym unannounced."

Mark's eyes widened, but he said nothing.

"They were in the bar, holding hands" he said flatly.

"Is that it?"

"It was enough," said Tony. "They sprang apart when they

saw me, and as soon as we got home she confessed everything . . . said she was in love with him . . ." His voice trailed off.

Mark grasped his brother's forearm and squeezed it. "I'm so sorry . . . I really thought you two were for keeps. "He let go and sat back. "Are you sure there's no way you can get it back on track?"

Tony gave him a thin smile. "Nope. I did suggest that. I said I'd try to forgive and forget . . . but she insisted it was over."

For the next half-hour, the two of them sat in the half-light, Tony shedding silent tears and Mark consoling him with the occasional hug.

It was the first time he'd seen his brother cry.

Friday, June 28
3:12 p.m.

⚛

"Have Mum and Dad arrived yet?" said Tony, in a valiant attempt to change the subject from his imminent divorce.

Mark looked relieved to move on too. "No. They're not due for another couple of hours because Mum wanted to stop off at some scenic village or other. But Kate's here."

"*Your* Kate?" Tony's surprise was undisguised.

"Well, not mine anymore, but yes, that one." Mark looked awkward. "I know it seems a little strange, but both Faye and I have invited a couple of our exes to the wedding. Jenna's coming too."

Tony threw back his head and roared with laughter. "Bloody hell, you like to live dangerously, don't you? I'd never let my exes anywhere near each other. They might swap notes."

"It'll be fine." Mark looked less than certain of this. "Kate's brought her new boyfriend with her and Jenna would never cause trouble."

Idly tossing his room key in the air and catching it again, Tony looked at his watch. "Right! A bit of a nap, I think. I'm feeling a little jaded from the past few days."

"Well, if we don't see you at dinner, I'll understand," Mark told him.

"Miss dinner?" Tony looked horrified. "Are you mad? With all those exes in attendance, I'm sure it's going to be the best night I've ever had."

Soon after eight, resplendent in his shiny aquamarine suit, Adam was first down to the library for the predinner drinks. He propped his elbow on the ornate fireplace, looked up at the oil painting of a doleful King Charles spaniel hanging above it, and waited.

The room felt steeped in history, with its mahogany-paneled walls and uneven parquet flooring, worn away from hundreds of years of use. Its freshly painted white ceiling was squared off by ornate cornicing, and the leaded windows looked out over the rear gardens.

"Champagne, sir?" A waiter appeared with a bottle of Krug and, not for the first time that day, Adam wondered how much it was all costing.

Faye had told him that Mark's parents were bearing most of the expense as their present to the "happy couple," but it wasn't so much the amount that worried him as the waste on a marriage he was convinced wouldn't last.

Adam had only known Faye for a couple of years, but they had spent an inordinate amount of time together, and he probably knew her better than anyone else. They were similar in character, both attention-seeking, equipped with an acerbic wit and a perilously low boredom threshold.

He knew that the novelty of the wedding was holding Faye's interest for the time being, her own little piece of theater in which she was the central character. But once the limelight had faded and everyone left the château to carry on with their lives, Adam thought that she would tire of Mark. It might be weeks, months, or even a year, but he was certain it would happen.

Adam might not have been an expert on women as lovers, but in Faye he recognized his own mother. She, too, had been a feisty, compelling woman. His father was a pleasant man who had let her make all the decisions, purely because he was easygoing. Eventually, she had perceived this as weakness and became frustrated by it. They were now just good friends, happier apart.

As a child, Adam had watched all this at close hand, and he thought the same pattern might develop between Faye and Mark. She needed someone to give her a verbal slap every now and then, to let her know loud and clear that she couldn't get away with shabby behavior. But Mark wasn't that man. He was too laid-back, not to mention smitten.

But it was Adam's heartfelt belief that there *was* a man out there who could find the right balance with Faye, and whom she in turn would make happy.

"Mark's too nice, too much of a Romeo for you," he had said to her one day.

"You'd do, but you're too much of a homo," she replied, and blew him a kiss.

"Homosexuality is God's way of ensuring that the truly gifted aren't burdened with children," he'd retorted.

Adam smiled now as he remembered the exchange. He sipped his champagne and hoped that his prophecy of doom would turn out to be wrong. He dearly wanted Faye to find long-lasting happiness.

Just as he was wondering if he'd got the wrong time for the predinner drinks, the door opened and a stunningly handsome perma-tanned man walked in. Hanging on his arm was a full-size Barbie doll, with inch-thick foundation and blond hair extensions. She was wearing leopard-skin trousers with a plunging lace corset that made her waist look no bigger than a Cheerio.

Adam smiled thinly. "Hi, Nat."

"Hello, mate . . . Alan, isn't it?" Nat shook his hand.

"Adam, actually," he muttered, through gritted teeth. Nat might be a bit of an arse, he thought, but he looked incredibly stylish in a black Comme de Garçon suit with a crisp white shirt underneath. "And you are?" He extended a hand towards the blonde, who was flashing her best Colgate smile at him.

"McLaren," she rasped, in a voice that could cut glass.

"Sorry?"

"That's me name. McLaren. It's a sort of stage name, really."

"Yeah, it means she's sleek and extremely racy." Nat clutched a large chunk of her backside and squeezed hard, causing her to squeal with delight.

"What's your real name?" said Adam, unable to take his eyes from this apparition before him. She was camp heaven.

"Elizabeth. Boring, innit?"

"On the contrary, it's rather classic . . . Champagne?" Adam gestured to the waiter for two glasses. He was anxious to ply McLaren with as much drink as possible, then stand back and watch the entertainment. He had every confidence she'd be a one-woman circus. "So what do you do to earn an honest crust?" he asked, taking a glass of champagne from the waiter's tray and passing it to her.

"I'm a glamor model—but I only do soft porn, not the butcher's-shop-window stuff."

"How reassuring." Boy, was she going to liven things up

around here. "I work for *Couture* magazine." Adam lingered on the last two words and waited for her to look impressed.

"Oh." She looked at him blankly.

An awkward silence descended, broken by the arrival of Alice in a marquee-sized stripy dress that showed off her broad hips. Her hair was much curlier on one side than the other, which gave the impression that she'd left her room in a hurry. "Oh dear, am I late?" She looked anxious.

"No, you timed your arrival perfectly," said Adam. He sneaked a sideways look at Nat whose hand was roaming up McLaren's thigh. "I could do with some extra company."

Hot on her heels came Jean and Derek, who greeted Alice with a peck on each cheek. Faye had told Adam her mother and Mark's parents had only met once before, when Jean and Derek had been in London for the weekend.

"And how do you know Faye and Mark?" said Jean, shaking Nat's hand.

"Faye and I used to hang out," he said, with a wink.

"Sorry?" Jean looked a little distressed, thrown by this loud, uncouth man.

"It means they went out together, dear," murmured Derek, smiling uncertainly at Nat.

Jean, in a pale-blue Louis Feraud suit, put on her best Hyacinth Bucket expression. "Ah, yes, this silly business of inviting exes to the wedding. Quite ridiculous, if you ask me. If you don't like each other enough to stay together, it defeats me why you stay friends afterwards."

Nat nodded, and a generously gelled strand of hair flopped over his eye. "I'm as surprised as you that I was invited, particularly as I hadn't heard from Faye for months. I think she only rustled me up because Mark was inviting a couple of *his* exes."

Adam scowled at Nat for this indiscretion, but he had returned to staring down McLaren's cavernous cleavage and didn't notice.

Jean gave a "what's a mother to do" sigh. "Kate just seemed to dump poor Mark out of the blue, after all those years together. It's astonishing he wants her here," she said, to no one in particular. "But I can understand why he asked poor Jenna. Such a darling girl. She was his first girlfriend, you know."

"Really?" Nat couldn't have sounded more uninterested if he'd tried, but Jean plowed on regardless.

"Yes, they were at school together and she absolutely adored him. Then he went off to university and met Kate. Simple as that. Poor Jenna was heartbroken."

Just as Adam was wondering whether Jean ever referred to her son's first love without the prefix "poor," a slightly built girl made her way into the room. She was wearing a button front floral dress, and her pale brown hair was clipped back on either side of her pale face. She personified the style that had nearly put Laura Ashley out of business.

"Ah, there she is! How are you, dear?" said Jean, in a tone that suggested there had recently been a death in Jenna's family.

"Fine thanks, Mrs. Hawkins." She smiled. "How are you?"

"Oh, struggling along in a cruel world, dear, you know how it is," said Jean dramatically. "This wedding has taken *sooo* much organizing and I'm exhausted."

Adam looked at Jean and felt that, far from being exhausted, there was plenty of hot air in her yet. He also noticed that Jenna looked uncomfortable in her presence and decided to rescue her.

"Hi, I'm Adam," he said, and smiled. "I'm a friend of Faye's. Can I get you a drink?"

"Just an orange juice, thanks."

"Orange juice?" Adam was horrified at the thought of one of the exes remaining sober. That didn't fit into his entertainment plans at all. "What nonsense! I mean, it's not as if any of us are driving, is it? You *must* have a glass of champagne."

Jenna flinched. "OK. It's just that I don't usually drink much."

"Don't worry." Adam put an arm round her shoulders and

squeezed. "I'll look after you." He handed her a full glass and tapped his own against it. "To Faye and Mark."

"Yes, absolutely," she said, taking a small sip and screwing up her eyes.

"So, you were Mark's childhood sweetheart?" Adam didn't believe in wasting time when he was on a mission to gossip.

"Well, I was his first girlfriend, if that's what you mean."

"How long were you together?" He gestured for her to sit down on one of two red velvet armchairs to their right.

Jenna smoothed her dress under her. "Um, a couple of years, about three in all." She looked wistful. "It was all a long time ago."

"Yes, but I don't think we ever forget our first love, do we?" Adam sighed ostentatiously. "Mine was a bloke called Doug. Ooh, the thought of those strong hairy forearms still makes me go weak at the knees."

Jenna looked perplexed, and it dawned on Adam that, despite the aquamarine suit, it hadn't crossed her mind that he was gay.

"Trouble was, he was an agoraphobic homosexual, which made it rather hard for him to come out of the closet." He tittered at his joke, but Jenna's face remained blank. He gestured to the waiter to top up their glasses. This one was going to take some defrosting.

"Do you have a boyfriend now?" she asked seriously.

He made a scoffing noise. "Darling, it's been so long I'm thinking of joining a monastery. At least there'll be some single men in it!"

She laughed, and Adam noticed how pretty it made her look. She had distinctive dark green eyes that would have benefited from a smidgen of makeup to enhance them, and her skin had the blemish-free glow of someone who rarely ventured into the sunshine. "Do *you* have a boyfriend?" he asked her.

"No. I dated someone for a while, but it ended about six months ago. Southampton isn't exactly awash with eligible men."

Adam raised his eyebrows. "Believe me, dear, if it was, *I'd* be living there. What do you do?"

"I'm a hairdresser."

"Why don't you move to London? There are hundreds of hairdressing salons." He was thinking of the suburbs, but didn't say so. "If you like, I could have a little ring round for you, see what's going."

"Thanks, but no thanks. I've thought about it, but I don't know anyone there except Mark, and he's got his own life now. I can't imagine Faye would want me hanging around them."

"Oh, I'm sure she wouldn't mind," said Adam, lying through his teeth to make Jenna feel better. "She's very easygoing about things like that."

Jenna didn't disguise her surprise at this remark. "Where is she, by the way?"

"Oh, she's always late." Adam made a dismissive gesture with his hand. "Her ancestors arrived on the *Juneflower*." Someone tapped his shoulder and he turned to find Derek behind him.

"Hello, I've just come over to say hello to Jenna," he said. "You look lovely, dear." He jerked his head to the other side of the room where the rest of the guests had gathered. "Come on, I'll introduce you to everyone."

8:40 p.m.

✳

The antique phone in Faye's room rang shrilly.

"Where are you?" It was Adam. "Everyone's asking."

Faye had been ready for a good fifteen minutes, but she was determined to be the last down to ensure a full audience for her grand entrance. She was the star of the show and she wanted to make sure no one was left in any doubt about that.

She smoothed down the skirt of her black Chanel shift dress and took one last look in the ornate gold-framed mirror that hung inside the wardrobe door. She had always favored a chic, understated style, and tonight was no exception. Her only jewelry was her engagement ring, and a simple string of Asprey and Garrard pearls, bought for her by Nat in a rare flash of thoughtfulness. Her black shoes had kitten heels, carefully chosen so she wouldn't tower over her husband-to-be.

"Go get 'em, gal," she said aloud, grabbing her clutch bag and heading for the lift. On her way down, she checked her hair in the chrome wall and tried to ignore the butterflies in her stomach. After months of preparation, there were no longer any minor chores to distract her from the main event. This was it. The wedding weekend had arrived. Tomorrow, at just after five o'clock, she would be Mrs. Hawkins. She wasn't sure if the butterflies were of excitement or apprehension.

Outside the library she took a couple of calming deep breaths, then pushed open the double doors and stood still, smiling towards the throng. To her mild annoyance, everyone carried on talking.

At last Mark caught sight of her. "Darling!" He rushed over and grabbed her hands. "You look fantastic!"

"Thank you." She beamed, and allowed him to lead her across the room to their guests.

"Hey, everyone," shouted Mark, and clapped his hands for attention. "The bride-to-be is here!"

All the guests stopped their conversations and gave a ripple of applause laced with a few "oohs" and "aahs" at Faye's appearance.

Her smile fixed in place, she scanned the room and identified most of them. She'd never met Jenna or Kate, but recognized them from pictures in Mark's photograph albums. Jenna had changed very little, her hair still long and brown. Kate wore the same short style, but had applied a few lighter streaks to the front. In the way that women do, she assessed Jenna as plain, but with enormous potential for improvement, while Kate was prettier, a natural-looking girl of the type that boys always fancied most at school. She looked fresh and radiant, in a pink, strappy dress and dainty sequinned shoes. Faye also noted that while Jenna was clapping enthusiastically, Kate's hands were at her sides and she wore a thin apology for a smile.

"Jenna, darling, lovely to meet you!" deciding to reward her for her magnanimity, Faye enveloped her in a limp, rather showy hug.

If Jenna was surprised at the display of sisterly love, she didn't show it. "You look absolutely beautiful," she whispered, clearly embarrassed at being the center of attention.

"So do you!" Faye gushed, which wasn't strictly true: Jenna's floral dress swamped her slim figure. Then she extended her hand to Kate. "Lovely to meet you too."

"Hello, Faye." Kate's tone was noncommittal. "Congratulations."

"Thank you." Faye smiled at her, then turned to Mark. "Darling, would you find me a glass of champagne, please?" Mark wandered off in the direction of the waiter, and she turned back to Jenna and Kate.

"So!" she said brightly. "It's so great you could both make it."

"Glad to be here." Kate gave a quick smile.

"Yes, it's lovely to see Mark looking so happy," said Jenna, glancing at him across the room.

Faye had arrived with certain preconceptions about Jenna and Kate, formed from what Mark had said about them. Kate, with her cool demeanor, pretty much fitted the bill, but Jenna was a surprise. Faye had expected her to be less friendly because she had assumed her to be still in love with Mark. However, Jenna seemed genuinely pleased for them both.

Mark reappeared. "Here you go." He handed a glass to her and grinned. "I can't tell you how weird it feels to see my future wife chatting to two of my ex-girlfriends."

"Be afraid—be *very* afraid," laughed Faye. "We've been swapping notes and the wedding's off."

"Great, now I can get *really* pissed." He gave her a peck on the cheek.

Faye saw an almost indiscernible look of mild derision cross Kate's face.

"Is your brother here, darling?" she said, linking one arm through Mark's and waving at her mother with her free hand.

Mark frowned. "No." He scanned the room to check. "He's been flying round all over the place so I suspect he's fallen asleep. I'll give him a buzz in a minute, chase him up."

"We'd better circulate a bit," said Faye, and smiled at Jenna and Kate. "Catch you later."

As they turned away, she and Mark came face-to-face with Nat. It was tricky, but Faye managed to contain her shock at the vision standing next to him.

"Hello, bridey," said Nat, and gave her a dry kiss on the cheek. "This is McLaren."

"Hello, I've heard *soooo* much about you," the girl squawked, and pumped Faye's hand with such enthusiasm that her corseted breasts jiggled alarmingly. "And congratulations on getting married."

"Thanks, lovely to see you here."

As Nat started to tell a story about their journey, Faye discreetly studied McLaren close-up. She was actually very pretty, but the effect was lost under the heavy orange makeup she'd caked on to her face. The telltale lumps and bumps on her skin told Faye that it had been smothered in foundation for too many years, but she had beautiful, catlike green eyes and impressively high cheekbones. Her stunning figure would have needed little air-brushing to make the front of *Loaded* magazine.

She was blatantly sexual, and Faye came to the conclusion that she was undoubtedly an ideal woman for Nat. It wasn't that he was cold, simply that he showed his affection for women through sex, and McLaren looked the type to be happy with that.

Mark's voice interrupted her thoughts. "Darling, we should mingle a bit. There's still a lot of people to say hello to."

The château had thirty rooms, and the guests invited to stay included family, a few close friends, and the exes. Faye's family consisted of Alice, Auntie Clara, and a couple of distant cousins, but Mark's was larger, with Jean and Derek's brothers and sisters and their partners, plus Great-Auntie Ethel. Work colleagues and other friends were staying elsewhere and arriving for the ceremony on the day.

"Hello, Auntie Ethel," said Mark, tugging Faye towards a white-haired, elderly woman sitting near the door. "This is Faye."

"Oooh, she's lovely," the old lady said, her small eyes screwing up as she smiled. Her red, button-front dress gaped slightly to reveal a glimpse of voluminous bra. "Mind you, dear, I'd have had him if I were twenty years younger." She jerked her head at Mark.

"Sorry?" said Faye, confused.

"Yes, you did hear her correctly," Mark murmured. "She likes to shock, particularly when my rather censorious mother is in earshot."

"Ah, I see." Faye grinned and shook Auntie Ethel's hand. "Lovely to meet you. Are you having a nice time so far?"

Auntie Ethel's papery mouth turned down at the corners. "My pillows are too hard and French food always gives me terrible wind," she said.

"Well, we can get your pillows changed, but I'm not sure about the food," Mark said. He turned to Faye with a twinkle in his eye. "Is there a McDonald's near here?"

Before she could reply, Auntie Ethel had chimed in: "That reminds me, I could do my song later," she said, and started to hum "Old McDonald Had a Farm."

"I don't think so." An anxious-looking Jean had appeared at Mark's side.

"If she wants to, that's fine," interjected Faye, anxious to make a good first impression on her future husband's eccentric relative.

Mark turned to her and lowered his voice. "It's called 'The Cocaine Song' and she simply uses the tune of 'Old McDonald,' doing a sniff-sniff here, and a sniff-sniff there."

Faye burst out laughing. "It's an absolute *must* for after dinner. I shall introduce it personally."

Jean looked as though she were about to pass out. "Please, no." She looked beseechingly at her son.

Mark gave her a wink. "Don't worry, Mum, there's so much going on, it'll probably be forgotten."

"Aha!" Jean caught his arm. "It looks like Tony's joined us. Let's go and say hello."

Faye followed her eyes to a far corner where a tall man was standing with his back to the room, chatting with Derek and Alice. She and Mark picked their way through the guests until they were standing right behind him.

"And here's the happy couple!" chirruped Alice.

Mark placed a hand on his brother's shoulder. "Tony, this is Faye."

At that moment, Derek leaned across her and gave her a fatherly kiss on each cheek. "Lovely to see you, dear."

As he moved aside, Faye was still smiling broadly as she looked up into the face of Mark's brother.

It was as if someone had punched her, sharp and hard, in the sternum. She struggled to appear calm as she felt panic rise in the pit of her stomach and threaten to explode from her chest.

It was the man from the wine bar, whose face had been buried in her naked neither regions just seven days before.

"Tony, this is Faye," said Mark, beaming from ear to ear. He took a step back. "Isn't she gorgeous?"

Just a couple of seconds passed as they stood there, frozen, with all eyes on them. To Faye, it felt like hours, weeks, months.

Her mind was racing with memories of her behavior with this man, and of the implications it might have for her wedding weekend.

He was stony-faced. To outsiders, he probably seemed cold, but Faye could see the shock in his eyes.

Then, his rigid expression melted into one of seeming congeniality. "A pleasure," he muttered. There was that achingly sexy smile again, although this time it was certainly forced.

It took Faye a couple of seconds to realize that his hand was extended towards her. Unsure what else to do, she took it. "Hello." She noticed that his handshake was almost limp with reluctance.

"So . . ." the word hung in the air ". . . you're marrying my brother."

Jean, Derek, Alice, and Mark all smiled as he said it, assuming they were watching the start of a wonderful brother and sister-in-law relationship. But Faye knew it was a loaded remark, and that the ammunition behind it might be deadly to her future.

"Yes, that's right." She kept her smile in place, but her cheeks were stinging with humiliation. "It's wonderful to meet you. Mark has told me so much about you." Clichés were all she could muster right now.

"Likewise." His voice was clipped. "In fact, I feel I know you extremely well already."

The panic had now become full-blown nausea as the reality of the situation sank in. She had almost slept with another man the weekend before her wedding, and now it turned out that he had been her fiancé's brother. Things couldn't *be* any worse.

An awkward silence descended as the five stood in a circle, the others evidently expecting Faye and Tony to chat. But he was silent and Faye felt far too nervous to risk any further conversation, in case it prompted him to spill the beans. All she could think about was moving away.

Eventually Mark broke the lull. "Well, it's dinner in a few minutes, so I hope you're all hungry."

"Oooh, yes," chorused Jean and Derek. Tony said nothing.

Seeing her chance, Faye grabbed it with both hands. "I'm sorry to be rude, but I have to find the loo before we sit down." She gave them all a weak smile. "Will you excuse me?"

With her head down, she rushed through the guests to the double doors, anxious not to get into conversation. She had to go somewhere private and quiet—she needed time to think.

Five minutes ago she'd been relaxed and happy, looking forward to her big day. Now she felt breathless and claustrophobic, as if the walls were closing in.

9 p.m.

Just as the clock above the ornate mantelpiece chimed nine times, a waiter appeared at the doors that led through to the dining room. "Dinner is served."

Faye, having composed herself after a brief spell in the loo, walked back across the room to Mark. "Hello, darling." She smiled, studying his face for any sign that he'd been delivered a bombshell in her absence, but there was none.

She noticed her hands were shaking and interlinked them behind her back. All she wanted was for Mark to envelop her in a hug and tell her everything would be all right. But as he didn't know that everything was going horribly wrong, why would he?

"Shall we?" he said, crooking his elbow for her to hold.

They led the way into the dining room, which was decked out in blue and gold, with a vast table centerpiece made from candles and lilies. Each place was laid with ornate silver, crystal glasses, and a card with each guest's name on it, indicating where they should sit. The ceiling lighting was muted, and opaque tea-lights gave the room a subdued, cozily intimate feel.

Faye had spent hours, if not days, agonizing over where to place people, and especially over who should sit next to her: she wanted some fun on the night before her wedding. Trouble was, there were plenty of bores and not enough witty raconteurs. In the end, she'd settled on Adam to her left and Derek to her right; she found Mark's father slightly dull but tolerable.

Mark was at the other end of the table, with the safe sandwich of Jean to his left and Alice to his right. She had made damn sure he was nowhere near Kate.

As he was an unknown quantity, Faye had placed Tony between Jenna and Alice, but after mulling over the matter in the ladies', she had a better idea. She wanted to talk to him privately, and perhaps a noisy dinner table would be the perfect place to do it without arousing suspicion.

Striking a teaspoon against her champagne glass, she waited a few seconds until everyone was looking in her direction.

"Last minute reshuffle, folks," she trilled. "Tony, you swap places with Derek and come and sit next to me." She patted the back of the chair next to her. "It'll give me a chance to get to know my future brother-in-law a little better."

She gave him the full benefit of her best 120-watt smile, but he glowered at her, his mouth set. The same mouth that had pressed her against the bedroom wall the previous weekend.

Derek stood up and started to walk round the table, but Tony held up his hand. "No, thanks, I'll stay here," he said crisply. "Jenna and I have a lot to talk about."

The room fell silent. Everyone looked down the table towards Faye, but she didn't say a word, struggling once again to control the panic she could feel building inside.

Tony cleared his throat. "In fact, why don't you sit there, Mark?" he said, looking across at his brother. "It'll give you a chance to get to know the bride better." He gave him a grin, as if to indicate he was kidding but it was obvious he meant every word.

Mark knew from their brief email exchanges that his brother thought the marriage a little hasty, but he was furious with Tony for making his feelings known so publicly on the day before the ceremony.

"Good idea." He laughed falsely, anxious to avoid a scene, and hoped that his apparent joviality might make everyone else at the table interpret Tony's remark as a joke. A couple evidently did, and felt confident enough to emit a snigger, most noticeably Kate.

Mark moved round to sit next to Faye and the others started to talk among themselves, confident the show was over. "What's his problem?" he whispered in her ear.

"Oh, ignore him darling. He's just being silly." She looked down the table to see Tony in deep conversation with Jenna, seemingly untroubled by the upset he'd caused.

"I expect you're right. Let's forget about it." Mark nuzzled her neck. "Anyway, no one would be deliberately horrible to someone as gorgeous as you."

Faye leaned away from him. She felt irritated, which was so much more dangerous than just plain annoyed. "Utter rubbish, but sweet of you to say so," she said, and flashed a smile at Derek, who was waving at her from his new location. "But one thing's for sure, nothing's going to ruin our wedding weekend." The thump of her heart in her chest belied her words.

"That's the spirit, darling," said Mark, relief etched on his face.

"So come on then, what have you done to upset big brother?" It was Adam, sitting to her left.

She hadn't decided when or if she was going to tell Adam, but it wasn't going to be now. "No idea." She jerked her head at Mark who was now chatting to McLaren on his other side. "And he can't shed any light on it either. It was probably just a joke."

"Oooh, no, there's a definite friction there. Perhaps he fancies you."

Her face burned as she shook her head. She needed to throw Adam off the scent. "No, I know when a man fancies me, and when he doesn't." She picked up her wineglass and clinked it against his. "Anyway, let's not talk about him anymore. As guests go, I wish he would."

By ten the dinner party was in full swing and the loud buzz of lively conversation dominated the room. They had already enjoyed a starter of asparagus tips with hollandaise sauce, and a main course of lamb noisettes with vegetables julienne. Faye had asked the staff to hold back the dessert for half an hour so that everyone could relax and chat.

For most of the meal she had steadfastly avoided looking in Tony's direction, but at one point she had stolen a glance and found him staring straight back at her. She felt as if she had been jolted by a cattle prod and the nausea of uncertainty welled again. Like two children indulging in a staring competition, each was too stubborn to be the first to look away. He even picked up his glass and drank without shifting his gaze. As Faye stared back unblinkingly, she found herself wondering how two brothers could be so unalike.

"You OK?" The hand on her shoulder made her start. She swiveled her head away from Tony to find Mark smiling at her. "You were miles away."

"I know." She rubbed her forehead. "I'm just a little tired, that's all."

During the break between courses, guests took the opportunity to mingle and, spotting Jenna's empty seat next to Tony, Kate stood, picked up her glass, and walked round the table to talk to him.

When Jenna returned from the loo, she experienced a flutter of panic as she saw that her chair had been occupied. Without fuss, she slipped quietly into the vacant seat between Rich and Ted. She had started the evening terrified at the thought of spending one minute, let alone an entire weekend, with these alarmingly sophisticated people, but since she'd been placed next to Tony at dinner, her nerves had eased up.

Although Tony had left home by the time she and Mark were dating, she had met him on several occasions at family dinners and over Christmas—he had been working in London at the time rather than New York. He'd always been charming to her, and tonight was no exception. When he was talking to you, Tony could make you feel as if you were the only person in the room. But now she felt socially adrift again. She didn't know Rich or Ted, and wished Kate had stayed where she was.

"Hi, I'm Rich." The man to her left extended his hand and gave her a pleasant smile.

"Jenna."

"Nice to meet another crucial component of the freak show." He grinned.

"Sorry?" She was lost.

"The exes. You're one of the groom's, aren't you?"

"Oh, yes." She laughed nervously. "I am indeed."

"Well, I'm one of the bride's, so we're in this together. White wine?" He waited for her to nod, then filled her glass.

Jenna had now sunk three glasses of champagne and two of wine. She was quite lightheaded, but had to admit she liked the feeling. Unusually, she even felt slightly flirtatious. "How did you and Faye meet?" she asked.

Rich gave a little chuckle, which accentuated his dimples. "I think what you mean is, how do Faye and I have anything in common?"

Jenna blushed until her cheeks matched the pink roses on her dress. She *had* been wondering why this seemingly pleasant and uncomplicated man had been drawn to Faye, but she would not have dared say so.

"It's OK." He ground out his cigarette in the ashtray. "I often wonder about that. In retrospect, I was probably an experiment in Faye's life. A short-lived one."

"An experiment?"

"To see how long her low boredom threshold could cope with an ordinary bloke." He sighed.

"How long did it last?" Jenna couldn't believe she was asking such personal questions.

"Oh, about three months, give or take a couple of weeks to account for Faye's walkouts." He raised his eyes heavenward.

"Yes, she does seem quite feisty," said Jenna carefully. "In full flow I suspect she could be terrifying."

They lapsed into silence for a moment. Then Rich jerked his head at Mark. "He seems a really nice guy."

"Yes, he is," she said warmly, "one of the best."

"You seem very fond of him."

"I am. We've known each other since the fifth year at school. My parents had just moved to the area and I didn't know anyone, but Mark looked after me."

Rich looked surprised. "Oh, you two go that far back, do you? I thought you were a fleeting ex like me, one who's been dragged out of the woodwork after years in the wilderness."

Jenna giggled: the alcohol was mellowing her usual aversion

to gossip. "I am in a way, although we've stayed in touch over the past couple of years. I think Kate and I have been invited because Mark regards us as friends."

"You mean, rather than as tit-for-tat against Faye, like myself and Nat up there?" Rich gestured to Nat, who was using his tongue to extract a Bendick's bitter mint from McLaren's cleavage.

Jenna was about to deny thinking any such thing, but Rich went on, "It's true. I was surprised to get an invitation, partcularly as Faye and I only have patchy contact, these days. We speak a couple of times a year and she sends me a Christmas card, but that's about it."

"So why did you come?"

"That freak-show factor I mentioned earlier, I guess." He pursed his lips. "I wanted to meet the man who has captured her heart." He clutched at his chest melodramatically.

"And?" She looked at him expectantly.

"And from what I've seen so far . . . Mark seems like a really nice guy."

"And totally not in control of her." Jenna smiled knowingly.

"Don't get me wrong. Faye's lovely most of the time, but there's a deep-rooted insecurity that makes her pretty high maintenance." He took a swig of wine. "I'm no psychiatrist, but I would hazard a guess that it has something to do with her father walking out before she was born."

Jenna frowned. "I didn't know that." She took a tiny sip of her drink. "I remember seeing an edition of *Trisha* once about people who had been abandoned by parents. Some expert said it's common for them to want to be in the driving seat of future relationships, so they feel it's something they can control."

"Eureka! There you have it." He grinned and topped up her glass.

"In which case," Jenna continued, "Mark may be right for her because he's secure and clearly adores her. She can't be in any doubt of it."

"No, but it's not as simple as that. She needs someone whom she adores in equal measure, to give him a bit of bargaining power when she plays up."

Jenna looked at him blankly, then burst out laughing. "I'm afraid you've lost me."

Rich made a snorting noise. "Ah, fuck it. What do we care anyway? More drink!" He knocked back the contents of his glass and refilled it. "What's the scoop with you and Mark now?"

"Nothing much. We're friends, that's all. I occasionally see him when he comes home to visit his parents, but that's about it."

"Why did you break up? Or is it too personal?"

"No," she reassured him. "He went to university and I didn't."

"And . . . putting two and two together here . . ." Rich narrowed his eyes and looked across the table ". . . I presume he met Kate."

She smiled. "Well done, Columbo. Another case solved."

"God, I'll bet you were really pissed off," he said, with masterly understatement.

"Heartbroken would be a better description." She sighed. "But I'm over it now."

"Anyone since?"

"I would hope so! It's been several years after all. No one serious though."

They were jolted from their chat by Derek banging his empty coffee cup on the table. "Ssssh, everyone," he shouted. "I just want to say a few words before we all get too pissed."

"Derek, really!" Jean looked as if she was sucking a particularly bitter lemon.

"I know the wedding speeches aren't until tomorrow afternoon," Derek plowed on, "but I just wanted to propose a toast to our hosts for this evening, the bride- and groom-in-waiting, Faye and Mark!"

"Hear! hear!" everyone chorused, over the noise of chairs scraping on the wood floor as they got to their feet.

Only Tony remained seated. Once the noise had stopped and everyone had noticed, he got to his feet with the speed and enthusiasm of a man approaching a noose.

Derek waited for him. "Congratulations!" he said, raising his glass towards Faye and Mark, and everyone followed suit except Tony, who again remained motionless.

After a pause, he raised his empty glass. "And I'd like to propose a toast to absent friends . . . namely the wine waiter."

Brian let out a loud laugh, and a couple of others tittered, clearly unsure how to react. Faye remained poker-faced.

Derek leaned forward to pick up a bottle of wine from the ice bucket in front of him, walked round the table to where Tony was sitting, and cuffed him playfully round the ear. "Some people are just too grand to look after themselves," he said, and filled his son's glass. A few seconds later, the buzz of conversation started again, and Faye relaxed as attention drifted away from her. "He's trying to make out we're stingy," she whispered to Mark, her eyes filled with tears.

"No, he's not," Mark said soothingly. "It's just his warped sense of humor."

Her expression changed from hurt to mild annoyance. "You can't excuse *all* barbed remarks as jokes."

"Why would he want to be deliberately nasty at our wedding? He's my brother, for God's sake," Mark reminded her.

Faye took a swig of her wine and looked down the table. I know why he's playing up, she thought. All I have to do is find out how far he's going to take it.

11 p.m.

Mark stood up and was surprised by how unsteady he felt. "They would like us to adj—adj—go to the library for coffee," he stuttered, "where there will also be lots more wine for anyone who wants it." He looked pointedly at Tony, who was grinning from ear to ear.

The guests trooped through and Mark stayed behind to marshal any stragglers. Eventually only he and Brian were left.

"You OK?" asked Brian. "You look a bit harassed."

"I never realized weddings could be quite so stressful."

"Well, at least it's the one and only time you'll have to do it."

"I hope you're right," said Mark ruefully. "I'm rather wishing we'd just buggered off on our own to the Elvis chapel in Las Vegas."

"What? And deprive your best friend of seeing the spectacle of so many exes and egos under one roof?" Brian lurched, and steadied himself by holding on to the table. "Shame on you."

"Ha bloody ha. Come on," He jerked his head towards the library. "It's round two."

"Ah, there you are, darling!" Jean descended on them in a waft of White Linen. "I'm just off to powder my nose."

"You didn't tell me your mother had a coke habit." Brian grinned.

Mark scowled at him, but Jean's mind was evidently on other matters. "I've just been having a lovely chat with poor Jenna," she said. "Such a darling girl, so obliging." She floated off in the direction of the lavatories, with Brian following.

"What she means is, so malleable and so willing to do whatever Jean wants." Kate had appeared at Mark's side.

"Unlike you, you mean."

"Oh, I don't know." She looked wistful. "Jean and I didn't particularly get on at first, but I like to think we had a grudging respect for each other by the end."

Mark nodded slowly "She was gutted when we split up."

"I know," she said matter-of-factly. "She wrote and told me."

He looked stunned. "My mother wrote to you?"

"Yep."

"Why didn't you tell me?"

"It seemed irrelevant. It was hardly going to change anything between you and me." She put her hands on her hips. "Oh, hi, Mark. Kate here. Your mum reckons we should get back together, so do pop round later."

He stuck out his tongue. "What did it say?"

She frowned. "Does it matter? It was all a long time ago."

"I'd still like to know."

Kate surveyed the room. "She seemed to be laboring under the misapprehension that I had dumped you."

"Really?" Mark did his best to look surprised.

She shook her head slowly. "You know, if you ever decide to give up cooking, you'd make a great actor."

He grinned apologetically. "Well, perhaps I did mislead her a bit. But it wasn't strictly untrue. I *did* want the relationship to carry on after I'd moved out, and you wouldn't hear of it."

"Hmmm, what a convenient perspective. Anyway, judging by her letter, your mother clearly fell for it."

"Was she terribly harsh?"

"She basically said I'd lost the best thing that had ever happened to me and that my stupidity knew no bounds."

"Ouch. Sorry about that."

"She was partially right. I *had* lost the best thing that had ever happened to me. But it was *your* stupidity that knew no bounds."

"Mea culpa." He held up his hands. "We had a great few years, though." He nudged her playfully, and her champagne splashed over the side of her glass.

"Christ, all those years." Kate looked wistful then wrinkled her nose. "What a waste."

"Is that how you see it? A waste?"

"Well, six of my prime years were spent with someone I had no future with, so yes, I'd call it a waste. It's like putting all your money into a bank account for that long, only to find you don't get any interest at the end of it." She folded her arms and stared at him pointedly.

"You see our relationship like a *bank account*?"

"One that's closed, yes."

"Well, you're the one who closed it," he muttered, anxious now that no one should hear their charged conversation.

"Bollocks," said Kate loudly. She apparently didn't give a

damn *who* heard. "You're not talking to your mother now. I know what *really* happened."

They glared at each other until a voice broke into their battle. "Hello there. What are you two talking about?" It was Derek.

"Long-term investments," said Kate, quick as a flash.

He nodded approval. "Oh, very wise." It didn't seem to strike him that this was an odd subject for his son to be discussing with an ex-girlfriend on the night before his marriage to someone else. "It's something to which we should all give serious consideration."

"I couldn't agree more," said Kate emphatically.

"Kate!" It was Ted, trailing Alice in his wake. "I've been looking for you. Alice was just telling me all about her journey here." He crossed his eyes.

"Oh?" Kate turned away from Mark and Derek to smile at Alice.

"Yes, proper little Attila the Hun she is," said Ted. "Land and sea to get here."

"Didn't you fly?" said Kate, opening the floodgates to tedium once again.

"No, dear, that's far too expensive. I got the train to . . ." Alice was off again, but Kate didn't care. Although all the right expressions came to her face, her mind was elsewhere, whirring with the ins and outs of the conversation she'd just had with Mark. When Alice closed her eyes to try to remember a bus number, Kate took the opportunity to glance over her shoulder.

He was still standing with his father, who was in the middle of a long story too, by the look of it. As she was about to turn back, Mark gave her a wistful smile.

As Mark's last year at university drew to a close, reality set in. With a 2:2, commonly known as "a drinker's degree," under his belt, he faced the sobering prospect of having to decide what he wanted to do with his life.

Brian was sorted: he had already started at Chester to do a one-year CPE course in law, and Kate was determined to break into journalism. Using the scattershot approach, she had written dozens of letters to London-based magazines, and eventually landed a job as junior feature writer on a diet magazine.

By September, she and Mark had moved into a rented studio flat on the wrong side of Kilburn in north London.

Mark had decided he wanted to pursue his dream of becoming a chef and had made two unsuccessful applications, but got lucky with the third: he was taken on as a trainee chef at a restaurant in Wandsworth, south London.

The hours were torturous and he was treated very much as the junior, but he adored it. He thrived in the highly charged atmosphere, and absorbed every little bit of information he could. At home, he practiced on the two-plate Baby Belling cooker. He had never felt so content, but he was scared witless of telling his parents about his job.

"They won't be pleased," he said to Kate one night. "They think I'm applying to banks in the City."

"Oh, for fuck's sake," she snapped. "It's about time you stood up to your mother and stopped her trying to make you into another Tony. You're your own person, stop being such a scaredy-cat."

He knew she was right. All his life he had lived in the shadow of Tony's towering achievements. "Tsk, why can't you be more like Tony?" was his mother's battle cry as, yet again, she made it clear she was disappointed by something Mark had or hadn't done. Over the years it had undeniably taken a toll on his confidence.

Spurred on by Kate's scaredy-cat remark, Mark went alone to Southampton to tell his parents that he had no intention of following Tony into banking. He offered to help his mother with dinner and was peeling potatoes while his father sat reading the local paper at the kitchen table, when he broached the subject.

"By the way, you two," he said, with as much cheer as he could muster, "I've got a job."

"That's fantastic, son!" Derek laid down the paper. "Which bank?"

Mark refrained from answering as Jean enveloped him in a congratulatory hug. Then he said, "Don't get too excited. It's nothing to do with banking."

"Oh." Derek looked disappointed, then gave his son an encouraging smile. "So what is it, then?"

Mark looked at his parents' expectant faces and swallowed hard. "I've just started as a trainee chef."

The silence was deafening. Jean looked at Derek as though her world had just caved in.

"Do you mean to tell me," his father's tone was low and measured, "that you've completed three years at university to take on a job you could have got straight out of school?"

Mark raised his eyebrows. "You could look at it like that, I suppose, but I choose to see university as a positive experience that makes me better equipped to deal with the pressures of the restaurant business." He wasn't sure what he'd just said, but it sounded good.

Clearly Derek didn't view it like that. "What pressures, Mark?" His voice was harder. "Is it whether to put beef or lamb on the dinner menu? Or whether to order more Chablis than chardonnay?"

"There's no need to be sarcastic, Dad." Mark was seething at his father's dismissive tone, although he remained calm. "Just because I don't want to follow in Tony's footsteps doesn't make me a failure."

Jean touched his forearm. "Of course you're not a failure, darling. It's just that we wanted so much more for you than sweating in a kitchen all year round for peanuts. It's a tough profession."

"I know that, Mum. Grant me some intelligence. I haven't gone into it lightly."

"So why have you gone into it?" Derek's tone was softer, but his expression was still tense.

"Because it's what I want to do. It's what I've *always* wanted to do, but I was just too scared to tell you. Little wonder, considering your reaction."

"So you only went to university to please us?" said Derek.

"Sort of, yes. But in retrospect I'm really glad I did. I wouldn't have missed it for the world."

As his parents began grudgingly to ask more questions, Mark told them it was a small but prestigious restaurant in south London, known for its excellent French cuisine. The plan was for him to do a year learning the basics, then attend one of the famous chefs' Cordon Bleu courses part-time, juggling it with his job.

The next morning, he set off back to London with a lighter heart. He knew he'd disappointed them, but at least he no longer had to live a lie.

The downside of Mark's having "come out" was that he felt even more obliged to make an unqualified success of the path he had chosen.

After eighteen months in the job, his tenacity and dedication paid off and his boss moved him from lunches to dinners, but this meant that he and Kate became "grumpy shits that pass in the night," as she put it. Her hours at the magazine were nine to six, while his were five to midnight. She had every weekend off, he had Sundays. After an exhausted Mark had enjoyed a lie in, they had one afternoon a week in which to cram their relationship. Inevitably, their conversations became stilted, as if an aged aunt had asked them to recap on the week they'd had. Their feelings on important matters had to be aired on Sunday, or held over until the next, and were inevitably stifled or forgotten.

Their social lives went separate ways, with Kate often going out to product launches or dinner with friends, while Mark sometimes hung around the restaurant for after-hours drinks just to wind down.

Soon, Sunday became argument day and the gulf between them widened. Kate would complain that he didn't show enough interest in her job, and Mark would retort that he was too "bloody exhausted" to think of anything but sleep. It went on for a year, until one particular Sunday in August.

They were sitting at the kitchen table having yet another row because Kate had just discovered he hadn't managed to get time off to attend her magazine's annual summer ball. "I told you ages ago to take the night off," she snapped. "I can't believe you've let me down like this."

Mark sighed wearily. "I'm sorry, but I'm still pretty junior and I don't call the shots. I put the request in, but they came back yesterday and said no."

"I might as well be single," muttered Kate. She poured herself some more coffee from the filter jug.

Mark waited for her to put the potential weapon down. He'd been mulling over their problems for some time, and had hatched a plan he thought might alleviate the situation. This was the perfect opportunity to bring it up. "This isn't working, is it?" he said softly.

She nodded. "You're damned right it isn't."

"In which case, I have a solution."

"Oh?" Her expression was mocking.

Feeling the faint tickle of nerves in his chest, he paused.

"Brian's new job is in Croydon . . . and I thought I might rent a flat with him."

Kate blinked a few times, clearly absorbing what he'd said. Then her face crumpled, the bravado gone. "Have you been planning this behind my back?"

In fact, Mark had been telling Brian for some time that he and Kate weren't getting on. So when Brian suggested sharing a flat, he'd given it some serious thought and concluded it was probably a good idea for a short while at least. "No, no," he said hastily. "Not at all. He suggested it the other day and I thought it might be a good idea. You know, give us some space."

Kate shook her head slowly in disbelief. "What utter rubbish. Christ, Mark, you must think I'm really stupid." She stared at him defiantly, but he didn't respond. "So when are you going? This afternoon?" she asked sarcastically, tapping her watch.

He decided honesty was the best policy. "It won't be until the end of next week," he said quietly. "But if you want me to go before then, I can find temporary accommodation."

"If *I* want you to go before then?" she spluttered, a solitary tear running down her cheek. "Mark, I don't want you to go at all. I thought this was forever."

"Kate, I'm not saying it's over, just that we should live separately for a while because we seem to be arguing so much."

She looked at him as if he'd taken leave of his senses. "And when will we be seeing each other, Mark? Between midnight and two a.m. on Wednesdays and maybe a couple of hours on Sunday afternoons—provided, of course, the bus from Croydon runs on time?"

They fell into a sullen silence, which was punctured by a distant car alarm. Mark picked up a ballpoint pen and started drawing glasses on a magazine cover picture of Jude Law.

Wiping her eyes, Kate cleared her throat. "I'm not one for ultimatums, as you know, but I just don't think this is a healthy way to deal with a bad patch. You're running away from me, which doesn't solve anything. If you move out of here to live with Brian, it's over. I don't want half measures."

They went to sleep that night, two people in the same five-square-foot bed, without touching. Mark knew the ball was firmly in his court, and slept barely a wink.

In the morning, as Kate got ready for work, he pretended to be asleep. When he heard the front door click, he got up, made himself a cup of coffee, and sat down at the kitchen table to write a letter.

Dear Kate,

We both know we haven't been getting on for some time now, and I put it down purely to our circumstances.

We are both working long hours, trying to get a foothold in our respective professions, and it means we have little time for each other. Added to that, we live in a very cramped space and seem to be getting on each other's nerves. That's why I thought it would be better for me to move out for a while, to give us some space from each other. I felt it would be a bonus to regard it almost as dating again, seeing each other as a treat, rather than late at night or early in the morning when we are both feeling tetchy. I felt that if I changed our circum-stances for a while, then the pressure would be off and we could slowly get things back on track. Yet you seem to think this is a bad idea, that I am somehow running away from our problems. That was never my intention.

The last thing on my mind was for us to finish. I love you very much and thought we had a future together, but I still feel strongly that we would benefit from living separately for a while. If you don't feel the same, then obviously it's your right to say so.

Tonight I am going to check into a B&B until the other

*flat is ready, basically because I don't want either of us to suf-
fer several days of tension.*

    *Please, please reconsider what you said, as I would like us
to continue going out together.*

    *I will call you in a couple of days when you've had time to
think, and see whether you have changed your mind.*

All my love, Mark XX

He knew he had twisted things and made it look as though any
split would be all her doing, but he genuinely wanted to carry on
with the relationship. He just couldn't stand the close-quarters
arguing anymore, and longed for the simplicity of life with
Brian.

    He left the note on the table, went into the bedroom, and
started to pack.

In terms of cleanliness and location, it was certainly a comedown
from the studio flat Mark had shared with Kate. But he preferred
it because there were no more arguments or disapproving looks,
just a best mate who never judged or criticized him and who
could talk about the four-four-two formation long into the
night. Male heaven.

    In an ideal world, Mark would have lived with Brian and car-
ried on dating Kate, just as he'd done at university. But she had
stuck to her decision that if he moved out it was over for good.

    Mark found a B & B quite easily and had left it three days be-
fore he plucked up the courage to call Kate at home one evening.
After a stilted conversation in which he inquired several times if
she was OK and she answered, "Fine," stiffly, he had suggested
they meet for dinner.

    "What for?" she said tersely.

"To talk things over."

"What's to say? Are you coming back to live here?"

"No, Kate. But I don't understand why we can't go on seeing each other."

"You don't understand much at all, Mark, do you?" Her voice was cold. "You feel you can't live with me, and I don't see the point of going back to the beginning again and dating. All that means is that you want to get laid without any commitment." She made a small sobbing noise. "I'm not interested in being your friend. You've broken my heart, and the easiest way for me to get over it is to have no contact with you. So, if you care about me at all, you'll leave me alone." The phone went dead.

Mark had felt sick for several days, wondering if he'd done the right thing. He'd thought Kate would come round to his way of thinking, and it was a huge shock when she didn't. They had shared so much over the past few years that he felt lost without her.

Three months later, when he was rewarded with a small promotion at work, it took all his strength not to pick up the phone and tell her. He wanted to hear her tell him how much he deserved it, how it was just the beginning of the dizzy heights he was going to scale. Instead, he told Brian.

"That's amazing, mate," Brian said, his eyes fixed on the television.

Mark went to his room for a self-indulgent cry. Life just wasn't the same without her, but he knew he didn't want to move back in with Kate. Not yet, anyway.

As only men can, he and Brian had spoken about his split from Kate just once, when the shattered relationship had been referred to fleetingly in football terms. "I always thought you two were playing the long game, mate," said Brian, after Mark had relayed an old story that involved Kate, as most of his anecdotes did.

"So did I. But I think we both took our eye off the ball."

Mark sighed. "We just started to argue about everything. She even had a go at me for that old cliché of leaving the loo seat up."

"I get round that one by pissing in the washbasin." Brian sniffed.

Exhausted by that emotionally draining exchange, they had avoided the subject of relationships after that.

Initially, Mark had missed Kate acutely. He ached to hear her voice, but most of all he missed holding her in the middle of the night.

As the months passed by, the pain dulled, but she was never far from his mind.

Friday, June 28
11:05 p.m.

In the ladies' loo Faye leaned over the washbasin and studied her reflection in the mirror. It was one of those brightly lit ones, great for putting on makeup, but appalling for highlighting even the slightest facial blemish.

Absentmindedly applying lip gloss, she was absorbed in thoughts of Tony and finding the right time to talk to him. When they had all gone back into the library, he'd been engrossed in conversation with his father.

Faye had dealt with some tricky situations in her time, but this was the king of them all. She was getting married in just over fifteen hours' time and her mind was on constant spin cycle, whirring with this possibility and that.

"Tony, about last weekend," she murmured to her reflection. "It shouldn't change anything . . ."

No, she thought. That's too bossy. A man like him will want to feel that *he* decides whether it will change anything.

"What are you going to do about last weekend?" No, that put the ball too firmly in his court . . . "We need to talk about last weekend . . ." Better, but still just the tip of the iceberg. "Duh!" She slapped her palm against her forehead. How could she have been so recklessly stupid.

She came to the conclusion that the best way to handle it was to instigate a discussion, then go with the flow. Worryingly, everything rested on what Tony did with the information he had and, judging by his behavior so far this evening, he wasn't giving her the benefit of the doubt.

The best she could hope for was that, once she got a chance to talk to him and explain herself, he'd recognize she was a nice person and perfectly able to make his brother happy. The only gaping hole in this scenario was that she hadn't worked out her explanation of last weekend's behavior.

Smoothing her hair, whispered, "Chin up, girl," and stepped out into the corridor.

"Oh!" She collided with Nat, who was on his way into the gents'.

"Aha, I was hoping we'd get a chance for a chat," he said.

"Save your breath. You'll need it later to blow up your date." She had quite liked McLaren, but she couldn't resist having a dig at him via her.

He grinned. "You always did make me laugh. I like that." Then, before she could object, he grabbed her by the elbow and streered her into a small locker room farther down the corridor. He used his foot to close the door behind them. "You look sensational, by the way," he said, holding her by the arms and looking her up and down.

"Thanks," said Faye, flatly. "Now what do you want? I have guests to look after."

"OK, I'll get straight to the point." He looked earnest. "What are you doing marrying *him*?"

She scowled. "Because he's a fantastic person, and I love him."

Nat rolled his head from side to side in a gesture of impatience. "Yeah, yeah, whatever. But I'm telling you, he's not the man for you."

"Oh, *you're* telling me, are you?" said Faye derisively. "And since when have you been the expert on *any* relationship, let alone mine?"

"I just know what you're like. I was expecting a grown-up, someone a little tougher."

"Mark is a kind, lovely man who I intend to marry tomorrow."

"Kind and lovely?" he repeated scathingly. "We all know that's what women *say* they want when they're answering magazine surveys, but in reality they want someone who gives them a hard time occasionally."

"Like you, you mean? Someone who only calls when they want sex?"

He let out a low whistle. "Ooooh, I never knew I bothered you so much."

"You didn't," she said huffily. "You were about as important to me as that splash of wine on your lapel." She pointed to the offending stain.

"Come on," he murmured, moving closer. "You missed me as much as I missed you."

"You missed me?" She was genuinely surprised.

"Yeah."

"How much?" Faye felt nothing for Nat, but she was intrigued nonetheless. Like most people, her vanity got the better of her from time to time.

"For me, quite a lot. I'm used to moving on quickly after something breaks up, but I kept thinking about you."

"You did?" Her resolve melted a little. "In what way?"

"The others didn't make me laugh like you did, and they let me get away with too much. You always pulled me up."

"Anything else?" Faye was looking for something more romantic, something to compensate her for the humiliation she'd felt when it ended, a validation that *she* had meant more than all the others.

Nat thought. "Yeah, there was one other thing that made me realize you'd had quite an effect on me."

"Yes?" Her face lit up.

"Whenever I banged one out, I thought of you."

The smile vanished. "What an honor" she said sarcastically.

"It is," he agreed seriously. As he saw it, he'd just paid her a huge compliment.

"Look," she sighed, "I must be getting back."

"Just a minute, I haven't finished what I was saying." He looked earnest again. "Mark's not right for you, Faye. I've been watching you with him all night"

"I'm flattered, really I am," she said, "but there's nothing you can say to convince me I'm making a mistake."

She opened the door, but as she was about to walk out, he grabbed her arm and pulled her back towards him. "You and I were good together," he murmured, "and I see you're still wearing the necklace I bought you." He tried to nuzzle her neck.

"Don't flatter yourself," she muttered. "I like it, that's all." Sexually, she conceded privately, they *had* been good together, and even now she found his proximity unnerving.

But when it came to a meeting of minds, Nat's hadn't shown up.

Faye tilted her head away and stifled a yawn. "Look, I've met

Mr. Right, and you seem to have met your perfect woman. She doesn't say much, she hangs on your every word, *and* she has enormous breasts."

"Yeah, McLaren does have a couple of very fine points, but she's not you." He moved in closer still, his hand traveling down to her waist and stroking the area just under her left breast. "We really had something."

Faye was about to slap away his hand, when a small movement caught her eye. As Nat attempted to nuzzle her neck again, she stood ramrod straight and her blood ran cold.

There, standing in the doorway looking straight at them, was Tony. "I hope I'm not interrupting anything." His face was like stone. "I was looking for the men's room."

"Second door on the left, mate, just down the corridor," said Nat, clearly unfazed by the situation.

"It has a picture of a man on the door," said Faye pointedly, her face blazing with a mixture of guilt and embarrassment. "I think you'll find you've walked straight past it."

"Silly me." He gave her an icy smile and disappeared.

The moment he'd gone, Faye slapped away Nat's hand and stepped backwards as if she was retreating from a nasty pavement turd. "Get away from me, you moron," she spat. "That was Mark's brother."

Nat shrugged. "So? Big deal, what's he going to do?"

"That's just my problem," she muttered, as she stepped out into the empty corridor. "I don't know."

11:15 p.m.

Faye turned left at the end of the corridor and found a door that led into the gardens. She walked outside, lit a cigarette, and spent five minutes gathering herself. It was a pleasant, balmy night, with all the stars clearly visible, boding well for tomorrow's all-important weather. Her mind cast ahead to the ceremony and she imagined how she would look as she walked across the lawns to her waiting guests.

Then her locker-room liaison with Nat popped back into her head and spoiled it all. She replayed Tony's disgusted face in her mind's eye, and her spirits sank. She now had a major damage-control exercise on her hands.

Any explanation she might have come up with to justify her behavior last weekend was now null and void, her sluttishness compounded by being found in a compromising pose with an ex-boyfriend. However innocent it had been on her part, she knew it looked bad. Really bad. Grinding out her cigarette with her stiletto heel, she leaned against the wall and did a few of the deep-breathing exercises she'd learned at yoga classes. She knew she had to find Tony and explain herself, and she wanted to keep calm while she did so.

When she returned to the library, he was locked in conversation with Adam and didn't even glance up. Trying to ignore her heart's pounding, she sauntered over to them. "Hi, sweetie," said Adam, putting his arm round the small of her back and pulling her close. "Where have you been?"

"Just catching up with an old friend," she said, and glanced at Tony's face for a reaction. There wasn't one.

"Tony's just telling me about life in New York," said Adam, clearly oblivious of any tension. "It sounds like a queen's dream."

But Faye wasn't listening. All she could think about was getting rid of Adam and cornering Tony for the private conversation she hoped might keep her wedding weekend on track. "Why don't you go and get some more to drink?" she said pleasantly.

"I'm fine, thanks." Adam held up his nearly full wineglass.

"Well, I'm *not*," she persisted, waving her empty hands at him. "So would you *please* get me a drink."

"I'll get it," said Tony. He wandered to the other side of the room where a waiter was filling Jean's glass.

"Look, you idiot," muttered Faye as soon as he was out of earshot, "will you *please* make yourself scarce? You're supposed to be on my side."

Adam inspected his nails nonchalantly. "As you well know,

darling, I can easily turn in the face of such a gorgeous man. He *is* utterly edible."

She scowled. "He's also utterly straight, so forget it."

"You never know," said Adam, with the eternal optimism displayed by so many gay men towards a handsome heterosexual. "He might not have met the right man yet."

But Faye didn't have time for his whimsical meanderings. "Quick, before he comes back," she said urgently, squeezing his arm to get his full attention. "There's something I need to discuss with him in private."

"About what?" He looked intrigued.

"Something *private*," Faye persisted.

He pulled a wounded face. "Darling, you know you can say anything in front of me."

"Certainly. It's just your big mouth afterwards that worries me." She gripped his arm urgently. "When he comes back, you're going to pretend there's someone across the room you're desperate to talk to."

"Here?" Adam looked aghast. "God knows, I'd be struggling."

"I don't care. Just as long as you *get lost*," she muttered, smiling with gritted teeth as Tony approached.

"A glass of wine for *madam*," he said. He handed it to her, then rapidly looked bored, casting his eyes around the room. He was displaying the body language of someone who was about to walk off.

Faye widened her eyes at Adam, who was steadfastly refusing to look in her direction.

"Something wrong?" Tony was now looking straight at her.

"Sorry?"

"You were making a strange face."

"No. I just thought I had something in my eye," she said. While her eyes held Tony's, her foot pressed down hard on Adam's shoe.

"Ouch!" Her supposed best friend started to hop on the spot.

"You OK?" Tony asked him, apparently faintly amused.

"Fine, thanks," said Adam, stiffly. He straightened his back. "Anyway, I *must* go and find your mother, Faye. Apparently she had a fascinating journey here and I want to hear all about it . . . again." He delivered the sentence in a staccato fashion that left everyone present in no doubt that he'd been ordered to make his excuses.

"Right," said Tony, noncommittally. "Now that you've got rid of him, what is it?"

"We need to talk."

"I know," he said brusquely. "That's why I came to find you out there." He jerked his head in the direction of the door that led to the corridor.

Faye lowerd her voice. "That wasn't what it looked like."

"Wasn't it?" he said dismissively.

"I was coming out of the loo and bumped straight into Nat. He pushed me in there."

"Pushed you?" he said. "I can't imagine anyone pushing *you* around."

Faye was irritated by this, but deliberately softened her expression. "He shoved me in before I had time to gather my senses."

"What for?"

"Sorry?" She was bewildered.

"What for?" he repeated impatiently. "*Why* did he push you in there?"

"Well . . ." She paused, a humble look on her face. "This is going to sound very bigheaded, but he just wanted to tell me he still had feelings for me."

"You're right, it does sound bigheaded." Tony flicked a piece of lint from his jacket sleeve. "It also sounds like a load of rubbish. Having spent five minutes in the man's company, I can tell you he's incapable of any feelings except in his penis. Judging from where his hand was, perhaps that's what he was referring to."

"His hand was on my waist," she muttered.

"Didn't look like that to me," said Tony, with an "I'd like to believe you but I don't" sigh.

"Well, it's the truth. Take it or leave it." She was overcome with the urge to slap him. "Anyway, that's hardly the issue, is it?"

"At last you've got something right." He touched her elbow and her arm erupted in goose pimples. "Come over here, away from any potential eavesdroppers." He guided her towards a low wooden bench on the other side of the room, overlooked by an oil painting of a ferocious-looking elderly woman, wearing a marquee-sized taffeta gown and a lace bonnet.

He gestured to Faye to sit down, and lowered himself next to her. "There is no way you can marry my brother tomorrow," he said firmly.

Taken aback by his directness, Faye said the first thing that came into her head: "Why?" Her throat contracted.

He looked at her incredulously. "*Why*? Are you serious? OK, I'll remind you. Last weekend, I went to a wine bar, picked up a woman, and went back to her place where we almost had sex. The following weekend, I pitch up for my brother's wedding and discover she's the woman he's marrying. Have I missed anything?"

Tears pricked in the corners of Faye's eyes, but she held herself together. "You don't understand . . ." she whispered. "You don't know me."

"I don't have to know you," he said. "I know your sort and that's enough." His face was deadly serious.

Faye, sprang to her feet, her eyes blazing. "My sort?" she exclaimed. "Just who the fuck do you think you are?"

"Sit down," he hissed, and surveyed the room to see if anyone had noticed. "You're not dealing with the little league now. Have some bloody dignity."

Stung, Faye found herself doing as he said. She sat down, blinking furiously to stop herself weeping with shame and frustration.

Tony's voice softened. "OK, so if I *knew* you, what would convince me that you should go ahead and marry Mark?"

"I love him," she said petulantly, refusing to look him in the eye.

"No, you don't," he said matter-of-factly. "You're very fond of him, I can see that, but it's not enough to sustain a marriage— not a modern one anyway."

"So, Mr. Expert, if I don't love him, why on earth would I be marrying him?" she said triumphantly.

"Not entirely sure," he said. "All I know is that you and I were stark naked in your bedroom last weekend, and I'm not the man you claim to be in love with."

Faye glowered at him, rendered speechless by the knowledge that there was nothing she could say to justify her outrageous actions.

"Maybe the money has something to do with it," he suggested.

"Money?" Faye was baffled.

"Both Mark and I will inherit a lot when our parents die."

Her mouth froze open in disbelief. Then she let out a sarcastic snort. "I see. Now I'm a gold digger, am I?"

"You tell me," he replied.

Faye knew that a show of indignant rage was not the way to win with this man. She scanned the room for his parents and spotted them talking to Alice in front of the fireplace. She nodded in their direction. "Neither of them look unwell," she said. "In fact, I would say there's a good twenty or thirty years in them yet."

Tony raised his eyebrows. "So?"

"So, do you seriously think I would marry someone for the faint promise of some cash when I'm in my fifties? Besides, I earn good money of my own, thanks."

"Knowing them, they'll offload quite a bit in our direction before then. I mean, let's face it, they paid for all this." He gestured round the room.

"We didn't ask them to, they offered," Faye said. "I would have been happy with warm wine and cold vol-au-vents at the local city hall, but Mark wanted to do something proper for your mum to enjoy. Apparently, *you* didn't involve them in your wedding."

"Point taken." He took a mouthful of wine. "OK, I was clearly wide of the mark by assuming you're marrying for money, so why, then?"

She sighed impatiently. "As I said, call me old-fashioned, but I love him."

"No. That's not it." He looked at her thoughtfully. "Maybe you just love the idea of getting married and any old bloke will do." He stopped and fiddled with his plain silver cufflink. "Something like that, anyway."

"Utter bollocks," she said.

"Oh, very ladylike." Tony looked at his watch, a sixties-style Tag Heuer as favored by Steve McQueen. "Look, I'm sure you're a lovely girl and all that, and one day you'll make someone very happy . . ." he scratched the side of his face ". . . but it's not going to be my brother. This has got disaster written all over it."

Faye nodded dramatically, as if she'd just cracked the Enigma code. "I get it. All this talk of status and money, it's got nothing to do with whether Mark and I are suited, it's just that you don't think I'm good enough to join your precious family."

He frowned. "No, on the contrary, it's almost worth the marriage just to see you deal with Mother. I suspect she's finally met her match." He paused. "No, you're just not in love with Mark, simple as that. If you were, you'd never have taken me home with you. Marry him and you'll ruin his life . . . for a few years anyway. Not to mention your own."

"What are you? A Grim-Reaper-o-gram?"

Tony laughed reluctantly.

They sat looking across the room to where the other guests were still drinking and chatting. Then Faye said, "Tony, I understand your reservations, truly I do . . . but I love Mark and I promise I'll make him happy."

"I suggest you think very carefully about what I've said. Sleep on it, even. Forget the expense, there'll be a lot less long-term damage if you pull out now."

"I won't change my mind."

A flash of annoyance crossed his face, but he rapidly composed himself. "In that case, I have to warn you that my objection to this marriage will go up a gear tomorrow. I'm not going to stand idly by and watch my brother marry a woman who couldn't even get to the wedding day before being unfaithful."

Tears welled in Faye's eyes. He was frightening her. "Why do you hate me so much?" she whispered.

"I don't," he said emphatically. "On the contrary, I find you fascinating and really quite likeable, despite all that's happened."

"Yet you still want to destroy me?"

He stood up, smoothed down his jacket. "It's nothing personal, Faye, just a case of those living by the sword getting wounded by those who don't. It's purely based on your unsuitability for my brother. Now . . . we really must get back to the throng or they'll wonder what's going on."

He started to walk away, then looked back over his shoulder. "Believe me, you'll eventually be thankful you didn't go through with it."

Mark and Brian's rented flat was above a post office in Croydon, with triple-glazing to block out the constant hum of traffic on the main road outside.

The dark, narrow staircase led into their regrettably dark,

narrow living quarters, the windows covered in the grime of constant exhaust emissions. They had made a few attempts to brighten the place up, with an Ikea psychedelic lampshade here, a few brightly colored cushions there, and some posters that marked the new millennium they'd celebrated just eight months earlier, but it still felt stuffy and somber.

In the two years they'd lived there, they had rapidly established a routine of eating endless curries, watching football, and talking bollocks long into the night.

With Mark working all hours in the restaurant and Brian coming home with piles of paperwork on humdrum cases no one else wanted, neither of them had much of a social life, but they didn't care. Money was tight and they had each other to talk to if they wanted company. If they didn't, they retired to their rooms and did their own thing.

Recently Mark had "enjoyed" a one-night stand with a waitress who worked at the restaurant, but Brian's sex life remained woefully nonexistent.

"I regard my sex life much like a game of bridge," he said to Mark one night. "I may not have a good partner, but I've got a very strong hand."

One August night, forty minutes after he had ventured out to get take-out, Mark barged through the front door with a greasy brown-paper bag in his hand.

Brian was in his customary horizontal position in front of the television, watching some trendy discussion show for which the producers had evidently forgotten to book anyone with an opinion. He didn't even bother to look up.

"I've just met the woman I'm going to marry," said Mark, placing the bag on the floor. He went into the kitchen to get forks and plates, and returned a few seconds later.

Flicking through the TV channels, Brian attempted to sit up. "Sorry, mate," he yawned, "I could have sworn you just said something about marriage."

"That's because I did." Mark flicked the top of a Red Stripe lager and passed it to him.

Now Brian was wide awake. "Hello? You only went to get take-out and you've come back with a wife?" Mark had never expressed such named emotion during his four years with Kate.

"I'm serious," Mark said "I'm not letting this one go. She's a really striking blonde. I've got her phone number and I'm taking her out for a drink next week."

Brian, somewhat stunned, fell silent. Then he said. "So hang on, let's rewind. She was in the takeout place?"

"Nope." He took a swig of his drink. "The food was going to take twenty minutes, so I popped into Jay's wine bar. She was in there."

"And in just twenty minutes, you, Mr. Two Left Feet, managed to chat up what I presume is a gorgeous blonde?"

"She's amazingly beautiful," said Mark dreamily.

"So, forgive me, dear friend, but what on earth does she see in you?"

"I don't know, but she was standing at the bar on her own when I walked in, and it seemed like fate."

Brian pretended to vomit. "Are you sure she's not a hooker and you're not going to find yourself with a bill for dinner plus extras?"

Mark rolled his eyes. "When did you become so cynical about love?"

Brian took a bite of his Peshwari naan. "Around the same time I found out that that girl in Liberty's nightclub had a penis."

Mark laughed. "God, yes. I'd forgotten that. Well, I can assure you she doesn't have a penis and she's not a hooker. She was waiting for her friend."

"And in the meantime she just happened to slip you her number?"

"No, I asked her for it. I figured I had nothing to lose. She could only say no."

"But she didn't."

"No." Mark held up a piece of paper he'd dug out of his jeans pocket. "Faye Parker," he said. "It looks from the code that she lives in town."

Brian might well have been half joking, but Mark had to admit to himself that he, too, hadn't been able to believe that such an attractive woman could be interested in him. Faye was in another league. She had sandy blond hair, feathered around her face, a smattering of freckles, and sage-green eyes. The overall effect was Californian and, more important to the gender led by its groin, very sexy.

Mark had spotted her the minute he walked into Jay's. She had been sitting on a high stool, trying to turn the page of a broadsheet newspaper with a giant antitheft pole attached.

"Nightmare, aren't they?" he had said, and smoothed the page for her.

"I'll say. I don't know why they bother with them," she said, using her elbow to press it down.

Mark was pleased that she'd stopped reading and was looking straight at him. "Can I get you a drink?" He couldn't believe he'd come out with it so casually.

She was still gazing at him. "Thanks," she said slowly. "White wine spritzer, please."

Mark caught the sullen barman's eye and ordered the spritzer with a beer for himself.

"What kind?" said Laughing Boy.

Mark turned to her. "Um, any preference about the wine?"

"The wine's house," said the barman, in a bored monotone. "I meant what kind of beer?"

"What is there?" Mark looked around for beer taps, but there weren't any.

With a sigh of such force that Mark felt the man's breath on his face, the barman raised his arm to a blackboard above his head. "Becks, Michelob, Sapporo, Miller Lite, Budweiser . . ."

"Bud's fine, thanks," said Mark, flashing an uneasy smile at Faye.

"Normal or Czechoslovakian?"

"He'll have normal." It was her. "And as your delivery has been so utterly charming, there won't be a tip with it."

As the barman crashed noisily around getting their drinks, she made the wanker sign behind his back. "I don't know why such grumpy people are drawn to jobs that require them to deal with the general public," she said.

"Maybe they weren't grumpy at first, and dealing with the public made them that way. I'm Mark, by the way."

Their drinks were plunked angrily in front of them and she chinked her glass against Mark's bottle. "Cheers. I'm Faye."

"So, Faye, of all the bars in all the world, what brought you to mine?" Mark winced inwardly at the corniness of his remark, but she didn't seem bothered by it.

"I'm supposed to be meeting someone for a drink, but even though he's been working just round the corner all day he's late."

Mark's spirits fell, but it was as if she'd read his mind. "He's gay, and it always takes him forever to get ready. His bathroom looks like a Clarins showroom," she said, and sipped her drink.

Gay. That's good, thought Mark, whose spirits and another part of him rose slightly. He was still in with a chance, although it was a faint one because time was short. He decided to be bold. "Look, I only popped in for a quick drink while they were getting my takeout ready next door. I'd abandon it, but I have a pathetic flatmate who'd shrivel and die in his armchair if I didn't turn up to feed and water him from time to time . . . I was wondering . . ."

"You go," she interrupted. "It's been lovely to meet you, and thanks again for the drink."

Mark stood rooted to the spot, struck dumb by indecision. He wanted to ask her out, but knew this wasn't the school disco or a university bar. This was a frighteningly sophisticated woman who might throw back her head and laugh at his suggestion of a date.

The rules of modern dating were confusing to even the most experienced men. To Mark and Brian, or Tweedledum and Tweedledumber as Kate had nicknamed them, modern London women were a minefield. On the other hand, he thought, she might just say yes. Either way, he had nothing to lose but his pride, and that had always been of microscopic proportions anyway.

"As I was saying," he continued, "I was wondering if you'd like to go out for a drink . . . other than the one we've just had."

There, he'd said it. Now he felt both expectant and exposed.

She took another sip of her spritzer. "Yes, I'd like that."

Mark's stomach churned with childish delight and a broad grin spread across his face.

"Great!" He took a pen from his inside pocket and handed it to her, then glanced up to check Mr. Happy wasn't watching as he tore off a corner piece of the newspaper. "I'll give you a call."

Friday, June 28
11:25 p.m.

Mark looked across the room and saw Faye and Tony sitting together, deep in conversation. Their expressions seemed friendly enough and he studied his bride-to-be for a few moments as she chatted to his brother.

There was a wall light directly above her head, illuminating her blond hair so that it looked like a halo. Her slim arms were faintly tanned, and she was wrinkling her freckled nose at something Tony was saying. God, she's beautiful, thought Mark.

"Penny for them?" It was Jenna.

"Not very interesting, I'm afraid," he said apologetically. "I was just feeling thankful that Faye and Tony seem to be getting on now." He indicated where they were sitting. "They didn't get off to a very good start."

Jenna followed his gaze. "There seemed to be a lot of tension between them at dinner," she said. "Has that happened before?"

"This weekend is the first time they've met."

"Really?" She looked surprised. "I assumed he'd taken a dislike to her at earlier meetings."

"Nope," said Mark, thoughtful. "But I'm not sure it's dislike. I think they're just two strong characters battling for supremacy."

"Blimey." Jenna giggled. "It sounds like *Star Wars*." She held out her hand and rotated it as if she was brandishing a light saber. "May the force be with you."

Mark noted that she was drunk, but not incoherently so. Her cheeks were flushed and her hair was falling around her face. Dishevelment suited her.

"He can be quite intimidating, though," she said.

"Who?" Mark had lost the plot.

"Tony."

"Can he?" Mark was puzzled. "Did you ever feel that?"

Jenna's brows knitted; clearly she was waiting for her fuddled brain to absorb the question and come up with an answer. "No." She shook her head. "Because we were both so young, I don't think he took either of us terribly seriously. But there's no doubt he still intimidates you. I watched you with him earlier."

Mark resisted the urge to look surprised at Jenna's transformation into someone who spoke her mind. "I wouldn't say he intimidates me," he said, "but I do care about what he thinks."

"So what does he think about all this?" she said, making a sweeping gesture with her arm.

Mark looked at the new, forthright Jenna curiously. "I think he probably disapproves of me marrying Faye, although I'm not sure why. I suspect he thinks we're not suited."

She said nothing.

"I take your silence to mean he has a point." Mark's voice had a slight edge. "And what, in the eyes of Jenna, Tony, and anyone else who cares to air an opinion, makes us unsuited?"

Jenna's face crumpled, her newfound confidence short-lived. "I'm so sorry. You're absolutely right, it's none of my business. You should marry whomever you want to marry."

Mark's expression softened. "No, *I'm* sorry," he said gently. "I shouldn't have snapped at you like that. It's just that Tony's disapproval has got to me."

"Tony isn't everyone," said Jenna.

"It's not just him. Brian reckons we're not suited and, judging from what you've just said, so do you too. That's three people before I've even *asked* anyone else's opinion."

She patted his hand. "It's your life and I don't even know her, so who am I to judge? Ignore me, I've had a bit too much to drink anyway."

"I like you even more when you're pissed." He ruffled her hair. "Alcohol gets rid of your inhibitions." He caught the arm of a passing waiter and asked him to fill their glasses. "Anyway, how's life with you?"

It had been several months since Mark had seen Jenna, but they had spoken on the phone once or twice.

"How's life with me?" she repeated. "Well, pretty much the same, really. I split up from that mechanic I was seeing."

"Dave, wasn't it?"

"I'm amazed you remember his name."

"Well, all I can say is, I hope you got your car fixed before you ended it."

"No, sadly the relationship went wrong first, then the car a few days later. I thought about trying to patch things up, but decided it would be a bit transparent!"

They were silent until Mark coughed nervously. "By the way, I'm not sure I ever apologized to you."

"For what?" she asked uncomfortably, staring at her feet.

"The way I ended our relationship."

"Funny, I could have sworn I ended it." The way she spoke suggested that they both knew the truth.

"I was cowardly," continued Mark. "I should have talked to you about it, but instead I withdrew and hoped you'd notice something was wrong."

Jenna took a sip of wine. "Hey, no big deal. Maybe we'd do things differently in retrospect, but we were both pretty young. You do whatever you feel is right at the time."

"That's no excuse for bad behavior."

"You sound like your mother."

"Oh, God." He groaned. "You know how to wound a man."

She placed a hand on his forearm. "If you really want to know, I *was* devastated for a while, but I'm fine now." She brightened. "More importantly, I'm thrilled to bits that you've found someone you want to share the rest of your life with. Truly I am."

Mark studied her face for some indication that she meant what she had said. Her expression suggested she did, and he knew from the past that she wasn't one to say something for effect. "Thanks," he whispered.

"Now let's stop talking about the past. You're getting married tomorrow." She said it with the false cheeriness of someone telling you that you'd only lost one of your legs after the accident, not both.

They surveyed the cast of characters before them for a while. Eventually Mark turned back to her. "Do you truly think I'm doing the right thing?"

A small muscle twitched in Jenna's cheek. "In getting married or in marrying Faye?" she asked.

"Both."

"I don't think I'm the right person to answer that question." Her face was impassive.

He straightened his back and took a deep breath. He was suddenly determined to gain Jenna's perspective on the marriage.

"You've known me longer than pretty much anyone else, so I reckon you're the perfect person to answer it."

"OK, let me rephrase it," she said, her voice low and deliberate. "I don't think it's fair of you to ask me that question."

He saw suddenly that there were tears in her eyes.

With the modeling jobs small but coming in steadily, Faye managed to buy a one-bedroom flat in a new warehouse development called Millennium Heights in the Clerkenwell area of London. It hadn't quite up-and-come yet, but a few trendy restaurants and bars were opening and it was handy for the center of town where most of her assignments took her.

Two days after her wine-bar rendezvous, she was sitting at the kitchen table reading about a local hero in the newspaper when the phone rang.

"Hello, it's Mark. We met in Jay's wine bar."

How different from Nat's first call—"Hi, it's me"—she thought. She liked Mark's lack of ego. "Hello," she said. "How lovely to hear from you." And she meant it.

He'd drifted into her thoughts several times over the past couple of days. After the shallow, sex-obsessed months with Nat, she was drawn to Mark's warmth. He seemed pleasant and uncomplicated, and those qualities appealed to her right now. She just hoped that, unlike Rich, he had that extra something that would keep her interested.

Now she was going to find out.

Their first date was in a busy central-London wine bar where they had to shout above the noise. Encouragingly, he made her laugh several times and spent a lot of time asking questions about her life—which Nat had rarely attempted.

"I really enjoyed this evening," he said, as they walked arm in arm to the taxi rank.

"So did I."

He looked slightly apprehensive, then asked "Do you think you could bear to see me again?"

She placed her forefinger on her chin. "Hmmm, let's see. Oh, go on then, why not?"

"Great! I'll call you tomorrow when I've checked the restaurant schedule, and we'll arrange something."

He saw her into a black cab, leaned in, and gave her a peck on the cheek. "Till next time, then."

It turned out that "next time" was the high-profile launch of a new bar to which Faye had been invited. She wondered how Mark would react to the celebrities and glitterati who would be milling around.

To her relief, he seemed remarkably laid-back and chatted amiably to anyone she introduced him to. More important, he had the good manners to keep checking that she was OK. Nat had always abandoned her at social events until it was time to go home for sex.

Because of the antisocial hours they both worked, they fell into a pattern of seeing each other once or twice a week. Often Faye would take a couple of her model friends to Mark's restaurant for dinner. That way, she got to see a bit of him as he popped in and out of the kitchens, and she knew her friends' presence added a touch of much-needed glamor to the place, which pleased François, the restaurant owner.

Six months after they met, Mark called her in a state of high excitement. "I've been made head chef!" he said, clearly on a high.

"Darling, that's fantastic! One step closer to running your own business," said Faye, anxious to sound encouraging. In fact, she was wondering how his new job would encroach on what little time they already had together.

"Listen," said Mark, "I haven't been to see Mum and Dad in

a while, so I thought I might go this weekend before I start the new job, and tell them about it. You might like to come too."

Given her usual reluctance to do the parent thing, Faye surprised herself by saying she would.

To celebrate putting his foot on the next rung of the career ladder, Mark decided to treat them to a half-decent journey. Instead of bumping and rattling to Southampton in the 2CV, he hired a brand new Citroën Xantia with a sunroof. As it was bright and sunny when he arrived to collect Faye, they cranked it open to let some air into the car.

"They're really looking forward to meeting you," Mark said. "My mother will probably ask you which university you went to, but ignore her. It's her stock question."

Faye leaned back against the headrest. She didn't speak for several minutes, just enjoying the sun on her face.

She hadn't given much thought to Mark's parents so far, but now that she was on her way to meet them, she imagined what they might be like. In her head, she pictured a pebble-dashed semi with a neat garden and a highly polished middle-of-the-line saloon car parked on the front driveway. Jean and Derek would be an ordinary, charming, suburban couple who had worked hard to bring up two decent sons and were now enjoying their retirement. Soon, her thoughts gave way to sleep.

A couple of hours later, she was woken by Mark shaking her shoulder gently. "Darling, we're here."

She opened her eyes, blinked a few times, and focused on their surroundings. Mark was fumbling in the passenger glovebox, and pulled out a small remote control. He aimed it at the electronic gates that loomed in front of them. They cranked open and he edged the car on to the gravel drive that curled into the distance. Faye was confused by the splendor. It crossed her mind that his parents might live in the lodge or some other cottage in the grounds.

"Welcome to County Coldair," said Mark, in a mock-Irish accent.

"What are you on about?"

"That's what my brother and I call it. It was bought from the proceeds of air-conditioning machines."

The driveway curled round to reveal a vast Georgian house, of the style usually drawn by children. It was almost square, with an imposing front door slap-bang in the center and even a wisp of smoke from one of the four chimneys.

Faye was speechless. She had had no idea that Mark came from such a wealthy background. He had never mentioned it, and his whole demeanor was that of a nice, ordinary, middle-class boy. That he'd never boasted about his parents' wealth pushed him up even further in her estimation.

She soon discovered that Jean and Derek were the antithesis of what she'd imagined. Jean looked younger than her sixty-two years, with dyed, ash-blond hair cut into a neat bob that went up at the back. She was tall and slim, with an elegance that screamed money, wearing a pair of tailored black trousers with a gray cashmere sweater, and a single string of pearls round her neck. Derek was in a brown tweed suit, with an open-necked shirt and silk cravat. He was gray and balding, but his face seemed virtually unwrinkled.

Faye noticed that the best Wedgwood china had come out for her visit. Either that, or they used it all the time, which was even more impressive. They also had good taste in wine. "It's so lovely to meet you," said Jean, holding out her glass by way of a toast. "Mark has told us lots about you."

Her smile seemed genuine, and Faye relaxed a little. "Lovely to meet you too." She sipped from her glass.

"Mark says you're a model," said Derek. "What kind?"

"I mostly do fashion stuff for women's magazines or mail order catalogues. Nothing too fancy."

"So, what happens afterwards?" asked Jean. "You know, when

you . . ." She waved her hand as if to indicate she needed help in finishing the sentence.

"When I get too old?" said Faye, helpfully. "I don't know, really."

Jean cleared her throat. One hand was fiddling with her pearls. "Do you have anything to fall back on, like a university degree?"

Faye looked across at Mark who gave here a subtle smile. "No, I didn't go to university," she said. "It wasn't my thing."

"Oh, I see." Jean looked disappointed. She'd always dreamed of an *educated* woman for her younger son. "Mind you, Mark went to university, then didn't make use of his degree."

Mark tapped a finger on the table. "Ah, now, about that. I've been promoted."

"That's great, son." Derek smiled, but Faye noticed it didn't reach his eyes.

"I'm now head chef, which means more money. It'll look great on my CV."

Derek still looked unconvinced. "Well done." He held up his glass. "To Mark's success."

They raised their glasses and chorused, "Success."

"And to both of you and the future," said Jean, looking from Mark to Faye expectantly.

Mark had felt from the outset that Faye was "the one," although, of course, he neglected to say this on their first date in case she thought he was a Looney Tunes obsessive who might start hanging around her house and writing her letters in green ink.

He'd never felt like this before about anyone or anything, not even his cherished match program from the 1966 World Cup final. She popped into his head hundreds of times a day, and each time he felt a chemical release that warmed his entire body.

"It's a crush, that's all," said Brian, after one of Mark's tedious monologues on the wonders of Faye. "You fancy her rotten and you're having great sex."

Mark sighed. "You just don't get it, do you?"

"What, sex?" said Brian, facetiously. "You're damn right I'm not getting it. In fact, I'm thinking of hanging a 'condemned' sign on the end of my knob."

"No, I mean you don't get the fact that this is it for me. I can't imagine my life without her."

Brian yawned, not bothering to cover his mouth. "I'm sure you felt like that about Kate once."

"Yes, I did, or I thought I did. But this is different."

Brian made it no secret that he regarded Faye as extremely high maintenance. But, then, his version of a high-maintenance woman was one who would complain if he wanted to spend Valentine's night watching reruns of old cup finals.

On the few occasions Faye had stayed at the flat, she had castigated them both for living in such slovenly conditions, and he'd seen the way she could wrap Mark round her little finger with a cutesy smile or a spot of well-timed petulance.

"She manipulates you all the time," he said one night, a few months after she'd first arrived on the scene.

Mark stared at him. "No, she doesn't. I do things for her because I want to."

"Yeah, right." Brian scratched his crotch. "You're not yourself when you're with her, you act differently. You never seem relaxed."

"That's crap."

"No, it isn't."

"Yes, it is. Give me an example."

Brian paused, then looked triumphant. "You were never like that with Kate. You behaved the same way with her as you do with me."

"Well, maybe that's why the relationship went wrong. Perhaps you shouldn't behave the same way with your girlfriend as you do with your best mate."

"Bull. You should be yourself at all times." To illustrate his point, Brian lifted one buttock and emitted a gentle fart.

Mark winced. "Suddenly it becomes crystal clear why you don't have a girlfriend."

"I wouldn't want one if I couldn't be myself with her."

They sat in sullen silence, watching the flickering image on the muted TV in front of them.

"Anyway," said Mark, breaking the lull, "you'd better get used to the idea of us being together . . ."

Brian raised his eyebrows. "Oh, yeah. Together forever, are you?"

"I hope so." Mark took a deep breath. "I'm thinking of asking her to marry me."

Brian picked up the remote control and switched off the television—a sure sign that he was taking the matter seriously. "Wow," he said flatly. "Now that really is grown-up stuff." He stood up, went into the kitchen, and came back with two beers. He handed one to Mark. "Isn't it a bit soon?"

"It's been almost eight months. Besides, they always say that when you know you *know*. And I know."

Brian looked at him with undisguised scorn. "That's all right, then. As long as you *know*."

Mark placed his beer on the table and fell into an armchair. "One day you'll feel the same way about someone and you'll know exactly what I mean," he said.

Brian lowered himself into the chair next to his friend. "I'm not being funny, mate," he said, "but what makes you think she'd say yes?"

"Why wouldn't she?"

"Well, it's just that she's very . . . well, you know . . ." he was clearly struggling to find the right word ". . . glamorous."

"What are you trying to say? Mark was annoyed. Too glamorous for little old me, is that what you mean?"

Brian rubbed his eyes. "In a way, yes, that *is* what I'm saying. It's just that she's a jet-setting model and you . . . work in a restaurant."

"Don't make it sound like I'm a bottle washer," said Mark sharply. "I'm head chef. One day I might open my own restaurant." He took a deep breath and exhaled slowly. "But that's not the point."

"It isn't?" Brian looked unconvinced.

"No. The point is that we love each other for who we are not what we do."

"Mate, I wish I could share your optimism about life, I really do. But I think you're taking on a lot more than you can handle."

Mark snorted. "You make her sound like some unruly thoroughbred." He got up in high dudgeon, grabbed his beer, and headed for his bedroom. As he closed the door, he sneaked a quick glance at Brian.

His friend was staring at the floor, slowly shaking his head.

Saturday, June 29
12:10 a.m.

‿✿‿

By midnight, Jean was leaning against the library door, looking decidedly squiffy. A resigned Derek was now holding her by the elbow.

"I'll be fine, let me go." She wrestled her arm from his grasp and attempted to take a couple of steps forward but stumbled and knocked over a small Louis XIV–style table.

Tony was across the room in an instant. "Get her out of here, she's drunk," he muttered at his father.

"I'm trying to. She was just going to say goodnight to Mark."

Tony set the table upright. "Wait here," he said firmly. "I'll bring Muhammad to the mountain." He strode across the room to where Mark was chatting to Kate and Ted.

"Mother's lost the plot," he said. "Get Faye and go and say goodnight to her and Dad. She'll be safer in bed."

Mark put down his glass and wandered off to find Faye.

"We haven't met properly," said Tony, shaking Ted's hand. "I'm Mark's brother."

"I know. Kate's told me all about you."

"Really? That must have taken all of five seconds." Tony patted Kate's shoulder. He was immensely fond of this strong-willed girl and had taken to her from the moment they had met.

Mark had brought her home to Southampton, shortly after starting university. He'd told Jean and Derek some cock-and-bull story about him and Jenna drifting apart, but Tony had suspected Kate was the reason for the breakup. As soon as he met her, he was certain of it.

Kate was everything Jenna wasn't. She was feisty, opinionated, in an idealistic, student way, and had a wicked sense of humor. Tony thought she was perfect for Mark; she brought him out of his suburban, Southampton shell, but did not overpower him. He hadn't spent much time with the pair, but when he had chatted to them, he had thought the balance of the relationship seemed healthy.

So he had been deeply shocked when Jean told him they had separated. It had never crossed his mind that they might—they'd always seemed perfect for each other.

When he'd tried to broach the subject in one of his less frequent calls to Mark, his brother had brushed it off as a mutual decision, brought on by their ever-increasing arguments. Tony hadn't pressed him because he himself was on shaky ground: he had always been resolutely unforthcoming about his own private life, always telling Mark that what people didn't know they couldn't nag you about. He could hardly complain that Mark had clearly taken the advice.

Tonight, fueled by several glasses of wine, he decided to grill Kate for her side of the story. But first he had to get rid of Ted. "So where did you two meet?" he said, looking from Kate to Ted like a Wimbledon spectator.

"Er, at work." Kate was flushed, but Tony couldn't tell whether from embarrassment or drink. "Ted's a photographer on the magazine I work for."

"I see." Tony drummed his fingers on his empty glass, and allowed a silence to drag on and last until he got what he wanted.

After thirty seconds, Ted had read the signs and leapt to his feet. "I need to find the loo," he said and grabbed Tony's glass. "I'll get that filled for you on the way back."

"Thanks." Tony gave him a quick smile, then moved in for the kill. "So?"

"I won't pretend it's not difficult," she said, correctly interpreting his loaded meaning in that one little word. She had always been on his wavelength, he recalled. "But I'm coping."

He raised his eyebrows questioningly. "You don't reckon you'll be standing up during the ceremony, shouting, 'It should have been me'?"

Kate looked sad. "No, I think I'll manage to restrain myself. But you know what? It *should* have been me."

She hung her head slightly, her front teeth scraping back and forth over her bottom lip. Her eyes looked desperately sad.

Tony put a fatherly arm round her shoulders and gave her a squeeze. "What happened between you two? I never got any sense out of Mark about it."

"Tell me what he told you, then I'll give you my version," she said.

"He said you'd started arguing a lot and made a mutual decision to split up."

"Did he?" She pondered this, then wrinkled her forehead. "I go over and over it in my head all the time," she said, then added hastily, "he doesn't know that, though. He thinks I'm totally over it."

Tony made a zipping motion across his mouth: indicating her secret was safe with him.

She blinked rapidly and continued: "In a nutshell, we'd been living together for a while in a horribly small flat, we were both working terrible hours and we started to get on each other's nerves. It happens, doesn't it?"

Tony nodded, but stayed silent.

"We did start to argue a bit more, but I thought nothing of it. In fact, I was building up to suggest that we should consider getting married and having a child in the next couple of years." She drank some of her wine.

"And?"

"Before I could mention it, he came home one day and said that, as we weren't getting on very well, he was going to move into a flat with Brian."

"Didn't you try to talk him out of it?"

"I didn't see the point. After six years together, we'd had a bit of a rough patch and he gave up on us. That told me something." She stared fixedly ahead, her eyes glazed.

"And that was that?"

"Pretty much. He said he wanted us to carry on seeing each other, but I'm an all-or-nothing person and said so. He chose the nothing part by carrying on with his plans to move out." She sniffed. "But at least my ultimatum meant he was able to tell your mother that *I'd* ended it."

"No late-night drunken phone calls where he begged to come back?"

Kate shook her head.

"And no second thoughts on your part? If you'd carried on seeing each other, it might have worked out in the end."

"Maybe, maybe not. I suppose I was hoping he'd miss me so much that he *would* make the drunken phone call and beg to come back. But he never did." She looked across the room to where Mark and Faye were laughing at an animated Adam, who was gesticulating wildly to illustrate whatever story he was telling.

"Then he met *her*. And now here we are, one year later, at their wedding." There were tears in her eyes. "In all the time we were together, he never showed any inclination towards marriage."

Tony didn't blame her for looking and sounding bitter. "You know, it's a funny thing," he said softly, "but sometimes you have to meet someone who's wrong for you to know who's right for you. If anyone dares to *tell* us they think someone's wrong, we think they're interfering and we invariably go ahead and make mistakes."

"Do you think Mark and I were wrong for each other, then?" Kate looked like a little girl who'd been told she couldn't have the dolly she wanted for Christmas.

"I thought you were great together," said Tony reassuringly. "Trouble is, Mark had only been out with Jenna before you, so he hadn't had much experience of women." He paused to see whether Kate wanted to comment on this observation, but she said nothing. "You got on so well most of the time that he probably took it for granted. Then, when you hit a rough patch, he assumed it was *all* going wrong and stupidly bailed out."

Kate was evidently hanging on his every word.

"Then—pow!" Tony smacked his hands together. "He meets a beautiful but difficult woman and mistakes it for a grand passion. He's bowled over by her for all the wrong reasons."

Kate looked dubious. "You're probably right, but it doesn't make me feel any better." Her voice was barely audible.

Tony pursed his lips. "It doesn't thrill me either. But I have an ace up my sleeve."

"Really?" Kate perked up at the whiff of intrigue.

Tony realized he'd said too much and changed the subject. "You know what? It's one of life's iniquities that women are suspicious of men who've been round the block a few times, but the truth is that they're far more likely to settle down because they've done it all and know what they want. It's the inexperienced ones who often end up screwing you around."

"Nice try," Kate said, "but I'm not letting you off that lightly. What was that about an ace?"

"Nothing. The pissed waffle of a man who's now been drinking for . . . ooh . . ." he looked at his watch ". . . too many hours."

Kate evidently wasn't satisfied with that. "Yeah, right. Well, whatever it turns out to be, I hope it bloody works," she muttered.

"Aha! I wondered where he'd got to." Tony pointed to where Ted was clutching two glasses of wine and talking to Brian, having been intercepted on his way back to them. "Quickly, before he comes back, how's it going with you and him?"

Kate grimaced. "Can you keep a secret?"

"Hand on heart," he said solemnly.

Kate pinched his earlobe between finger and thumb, pulled him towards her, and whispered in his ear.

12:15 a.m.

Mark and Faye waved at Derek as he removed Jean from the throng, turned back to each other and burst out laughing.

"I have *never* seen Mum so drunk!" he spluttered. "I'm shocked."

"I'm not." She grinned. "In fact, I think it's a shame she's gone to bed. She could have livened things up a bit."

"Aren't you enjoying yourself?" Concern was etched on Mark's face.

"Yes, I am," she replied, with false brightness, "but I want to get to bed so tomorrow will come sooner."

Mark enveloped her in a cuddle, his arms wrapped around her torso. She buried her face in his neck. He smelled wonderful, a mixture of musk and freshly lit cigarette. She wanted to stay there forever, breathing in the familiar scent and feeling cosseted, but eventually she broke away and took his hand.

"Come on, let's find somewhere to have a quiet moment together." She led him out of the library's main doors and into the empty hallway. A few yards along it, a doorway led to a tiny smoking room painted in dark red, with matching curtains and carpets. Backgammon boards were laid out on a couple of small tables on each side of an ancient three-piece suite in burgundy velvet.

Faye fell into a sofa and dragged Mark down with her. "Ah, that's better," she murmured, nestling into the deep cushions. "I just wanted to get away for a little while."

"Is it driving you mad?" He tucked a strand of hair behind her ear.

"Not mad as such . . . but it's all quite stressful, isn't it?"

"Yes, it is. Much more so than I thought."

"In what way do you find it stressful?" She wondered whether it was for the same reasons as she did.

"Oh, being the constant center of attention, making sure everyone's having a great time, that sort of thing." One arm was pulling her into his chest, the other rested on her knee. "You?"

Faye stared into the empty fireplace. "Pretty much the same. It's exhausting having to talk to everyone all the time. I much prefer going to other people's parties where you can choose who to chat to."

"Mmm. There's nothing like spending a bit of time with relatives to remind you of why you moved away." Mark lay back against the cushions. "But when we've got this out of the way, we'll have two weeks of doing nothing in the Maldives."

"Followed by a lifetime of being able to do stuff like this . . . just curling up on the sofa and watching TV with a takeaway," she said dreamily.

"I've spent the past God knows how long doing that with Brian," he said, "but something tells me I'm going to prefer it with you."

They said nothing for a while, just relishing the peace after an evening of small talk.

Mark broke the tranquillity. "I saw you having a long chat with Tony. What was it about?"

It was an innocent enough inquiry, born of Mark's concern that his fiancée and brother should get on, but to Faye it was the million-dollar question that sent her mind into freefall.

"Um . . . nothing, really," she faltered.

"It was a long time to be talking about nothing," he said, without a trace of confrontation.

Faye sat up, trying to concentrate on what she was about to say. "We just talked about you, and a bit about him. And he asked me about myself, of course."

Mark patted her knee encouragingly. "That's great. So you're friends now?" He looked at her questioningly. "It's just that you were worried he didn't like you."

That's the least of my worries, thought Faye, her insides turning over at the reminder. "No, we're fine now," she said. "Best of buddies."

"Good." Mark pulled her closer to him again. "Because you are my two most favorite people in the world, and I'd hate it if you didn't get on."

Faye closed her eyes and rested her head against his chest, trying to calm herself by concentrating on Mark's steady breathing. She had no idea when, or even if, Tony was going to divulge their secret, but the mere idea of it made her feel dizzy. Not for the first time, she wished that she and Mark had eloped and told everyone the good news on their return.

She felt him shift slightly under her weight. "When we come back from our honeymoon, we'll have to find somewhere to live," he said matter-of-factly.

She nodded, but didn't say anything. They had already discussed the possibility of Mark moving into Faye's flat, but agreed it was too small. Also, Mark felt it was too much her personal space: he wanted them to live somewhere new and mark out their own territory—"piss in the corners," as he put it. Because of their work commitments and planning the wedding, they hadn't had time to start looking. That task had been earmarked for when they returned from abroad; once they'd found somewhere, Brian had said he would start looking for another flatmate.

Mark was stroking her hair, a sensation she had loved since she was a little girl: it soothed her. "Do you feel nervous about tomorrow?" he asked.

There was that question again, and it still took her by surprise. "A bit," she said quietly. "But mainly because I want it to be perfect. Do you?"

"A bit too," he admitted. "But it's only natural."

"Yes," she whispered, "it's only natural." She sat up and smoothed her hair, readying herself to return to their guests. "I do love you, Mark." She took his face in her hands and leaned forward to place a kiss on his forehead.

"I know you do, darling," he said. "I love you too."

They shared a lingering kiss, as her hand caressed the back of his neck and his leg pressed against hers.

If he'd suggested here and now that they run away to Las Vegas then she would probably have done it, pausing only to leave a farewell note at the reception for their guests. Instead, they had to break up their idyll and go back into the mêlée of the library, with its shoal of people and one circling shark.

"Come on, then," she said, "we've guests to entertain."

Together they walked hand in hand towards their destiny.

Mark planned the proposal with military precision. Since meeting Faye, he'd found in himself romantic depths he hadn't known existed—he certainly hadn't tapped them with Jenna or Kate. One night while Faye had slept, he'd wrapped a piece of thread around her finger to get the measurement, and in the past fortnight had spent much of his spare time looking for a suitable ring. He'd eventually blown about two months' wages on an antique diamond solitaire.

"What do you think?" He showed it to Brian just before he left to meet Faye at one of their favorite restaurants, an intimate little French place called La Mer.

Brian peered into the box as if studying a dog turd. "Yes, I can confirm it's a ring," he said, then turned back to the television.

"Thanks for your support, mate." Mark snapped the box shut and glared at him. "I really appreciate it."

Brian muted the volume and sighed. "Look, I'm sorry, but I can't be happy for you about this. It's too soon."

"Says who?"

"Says me. Yes, yes, I know I'm not an expert," he said, as Mark tried to interject, "but even I can see when two people are right for each other . . . and I just don't see that with you and Faye."

"You don't see everything." Mark's expression hardened. "You don't see how she makes me feel inside."

"It's your dick talking, mate," Brian told him ruefully. "She's beautiful, she's got a glamorous job and lots of shaggable friends . . ." He stopped and stared into the distance at the thought. "Sorry, I digressed . . ." He shook his head as if to clear it of such inappropriate thoughts. "She's also got a great sense of humor when she's in the right mood. So, yes, I can see why you're smitten with her. But marriage? You haven't even tried living together yet."

"If she says yes, we won't get married immediately, will we?"

He pursed his lips childishly. "We might get a place together for a while beforehand."

"Well, do that, see how it goes, then think about asking her to marry you."

Mark felt defeated. He knew Brian made sense, but he didn't want to wait that long. "I know it's a big step, but I just can't imagine life without her. I'm scared shitless that it might end, and I want to do anything I can to keep it going."

"If she was right for you, you wouldn't even think of it ending unless you were going through a rough patch. Relationships should feel easy—they shouldn't scare you."

Mark was struck dumb by Brian's sudden interest: he usually steered well clear of conversations about relationships. As if reading his mind, Brian added, "I'm only saying all this because you're my mate and I don't want you to get hurt."

Mark attempted a smile. "Thanks. I know you mean well, but I'll be fine. Really." He stood up and grabbed the ring box from the arm of the chair. "Wish me luck."

"Sorry, mate, but you know me. I can't be hypocritical. As far as I'm concerned, you're about to make the biggest mistake of your life."

Faye arrived early at La Mer because for once her minicab had turned up on time and the traffic was light. She handed her coat to the waiter, settled herself in a dark corner and ordered a bottle of her and Mark's favorite Gavi di Gavi. She had been looking forward to tonight because they hadn't seen much of each other for the past three weeks. Since he had started his new job, Mark had been up to his eyes in work, and Faye had just returned from a weeklong assignment in Spain for a magazine's swimwear feature.

She wanted this evening to be special, not least because her behavior at a recent party had been playing on her mind. It had been held by one of Mark's friends, and he had been keen for her to go, saying he wanted to show her off. He had introduced her to their host, then left them talking while he went to look for drinks and Brian went in search of the loo.

As soon as Mark had disappeared, the host, Ben, wasted no time. "What a fantastic necklace," he said, touching her pendant—and her chest. His hand lingered a little too long for comfort, and Faye took a step back.

"How do you and Mark know each other?" she asked. She already knew, but she couldn't think of anything else to say.

"Oh, I dine at the restaurant regularly," he said airily. "But never mind all that, how did he get to meet a little poppet like you?"

"A little poppet? What planet are you from?"

"Any planet you'd like me to be from," he said lasciviously, moving closer and placing his hands on her hips.

"Oh, get lost." She slapped away his hands and walked out into the corridor.

She was mildly annoyed with Mark for abandoning her to Mr. Octopus, and wished he'd taken her with him to search for the drinks. She peered into the dining room, where about four people were locked in earnest conversation. None was Mark, so she carried on down the corridor towards the kitchen, where she found him, leaning against the table and chatting to a pleasant-looking girl who was on the plump side and had long, brown hair.

Faye noticed he had a paper cup in his hand, full of wine. There was another next to him on the table, which she presumed was hers.

As she approached, he threw back his head and laughed at something the girl had said. Faye pinched his side to get his attention. "I thought you were fetching me a drink. You've been gone ages."

"Have I?" Mark looked baffled, particularly as it had only been a couple of minutes. "Sorry, Rachel was just telling me about something that happened in the restaurant last night. This is Rachel by the way. Rachel, this is Faye."

"Hi." Faye shook Rachel's outstretched hand and turned back to Mark. "Come through to the living room with me, darling."

Mark handed her the cup of wine. "I just want to hear the end of Rachel's story first. You go on, I'll follow in a minute." He turned back to Rachel who took up the story where she'd left off.

In retrospect, Faye saw it had been an innocent enough re-mark, but at the time it had felt like her Achilles heel: disrespect. Temper bubbled inside her and she slammed her wine on to the table, spilling it down Mark's trousers.

"Don't mind me!" she muttered. "Just carry on as if I don't exist!"

Rachel's face betrayed her astonishment and Mark was speechless. Clearly he had no idea of what he'd done wrong, but Faye could not stop herself glaring at him. In the end, embar-rassment forced her to escape the situation she'd created and she headed for the door.

As she reached it, Brian was walking in and she crashed against him. She said nothing, just carried on into the hallway and heard him ask Mark, "What's happened?"

Suspecting Mark might come after her quite quickly, she grabbed her coat from the hallway peg and hurried out of the front door with the speed of a woman who knew she'd behaved appallingly and didn't want to face up to the consequences.

Back home, she had mulled over what had made her lose con-trol. After all, Nat had treated her as little more than an occa-sional shag, and she'd never felt jealous or insecure about him. She decided that it was because she had used Nat in the same way, never expecting any more of the relationship.

But Mark was different. She loved him, he loved her and, consequently, she feared losing him. She consoled herself that her outburst might have been immature and unnecessary, but at least it showed she cared.

The following morning, Mark had called her first thing and apologized. She knew it should have been the other way round, but it would have taken her longer to make the first move.

Faye cringed as she remembered it now, and she cast a glance at the restaurant door, desperate for Mark to arrive. Tonight she wanted to leave him in no doubt that she cared deeply for him. They had only seen each other twice in the past fortnight, both brief meetings, and this dinner was the first time in ages they had been able to meet for a leisurely evening, knowing that neither had to get up in the morning.

Faye, leaned back against the banquette. Studying the menu, she decided that tonight she'd order whatever she wanted rather than worrying about calories. She wasn't fanatical about watching her weight, but she'd become more careful since the modeling work had picked up again.

"Hi, darling!" Mark plonked himself in the chair opposite and leaned across to give her a kiss. "Sorry I'm a tad late, I got talking to Brian."

"Really? You surprise me. His conversations rarely last more than a couple of words."

Mark gave her a wry grin, but said nothing. Faye knew that occasionally her and Brian's spikiness with each other irritated him, but that most of the time he found it amusing.

For the next couple of hours, they caught up on the time they'd spent apart. Faye filled him in on her assignment in Spain, and he brought her up to date on the tiresome restaurant politics that meant he might have to look for another job. He said he felt he was spending too much of his time watching his back and not enough doing the job he loved: cooking. He was also weary of the endless problems caused by the meat or fish man not turning up, staff sickness disrupting the rosters, and François nagging him about the poor number of table bookings midweek.

Halfway down the second bottle of wine, they were both up to date on each other's lives, fleshing out the bones of the many phone conversations they'd shared as a substitute for seeing each other.

When a natural lull came in the conversation, Mark leaned across the table and took her hand. "Darling, I just want to say that, despite all the problems at work, my life is the best it's ever been. And that's because of you."

Faye thought she might cry. "I feel the same way," she said quietly, feeling the effects of alcohol wash over her.

"Good. I can't tell you how much you mean to me, it's frightening sometimes. You excite me, you make me laugh and, of course, I fancy you like mad." He muttered the last bit under his breath.

"But we have our moments, don't we?" Her face was serious. "Mark, I'm so sorry about what happened at the party. I don't know what came over me."

He made a pooh-poohing noise. "Forget it. To be honest, I was rather flattered that you got jealous. I would probably have felt the same way if the tables were turned."

Part of Faye wished he would just say, "Yes, you behaved like a spoiled brat," but she knew it wasn't in his nature.

He leaned closer, clutching her hand more tightly. His other hand was rummaging in his trouser pocket and he pulled out a small box, placing it on the table. As her brain computed what it might be, her stomach turned over. Whether it was through anxiety or pleasure, she was unsure. He stood up, still holding her hand, and moved to the side of the table, where he fell on to one knee.

"Faye darling, I know we've only been seeing each other for eight months, but people always say that you know when you've met the right person. And *I* know." He stared at the floor. Then he looked up at her. "Will you do me the honor of becoming my wife?"

Faye let out a nervous splutter and looked over his shoulder at the other diners, who were all looking at them with smiles on their faces.

Mark's proposal had come out of the blue, and she felt under immense pressure to answer immediately. She would have liked time to weigh it up and give him a considered answer. But with an expectant crowd staring at her, time was not on her side.

"What do you think, darling?" Mark's eyes pleaded with her to rescue him from the embarrassment of kneeling in front of her.

Faye felt a chemical rush of compassion. She was sure she loved Mark, and she knew he would never hurt her, so why not? After all, it wasn't as if he'd sprung the actual *ceremony* on her. She could always change her mind at a later date. Nothing was carved in stone.

"Of course I'll marry you, darling." She leaned forward and wrapped her arms round his neck, closing her eyes momentarily, and she opened them to see the other customers start clapping.

Mark gestured to the maître d' who ducked behind a screen and emerged carrying a bottle of champagne on ice. He placed it on their table and started to wrestle with the cork. "Madam, congratulations. We're all thrilled for you both." He beamed and gestured towards the other staff, some of whom had come from the kitchen for a peep at the happy couple.

"Thanks." Faye gave him a grin. She felt radiant now, glowing in the warmth of being loved so much. Now that she'd agreed to get married, it suddenly felt right.

"To us." Mark clinked his champagne glass against hers. "I'm so delighted you said yes. I wasn't sure if you would."

She raised her eyebrows, her eyes dancing at the thrill of the proposal. "It's a very public place to take such a risk."

He took a sip of his champagne. "I know. But I pulled it off, didn't I?"

Saturday, June 29
12:30 a.m.

⊂ঔৣঔ⌇

Adam was bored. Either this wedding party had to liven up, or he was off to bed to watch the ubiquitous late-night TV movie that involved no plot, unknown actors, and lots of car chases. Leaning against the fireplace, watching the few people left in the library, a smile crept across his face as an entertaining thought crossed his mind. Clapping his hands, he walked unsteadily towards the others. "Come on everyone, round here." He gestured towards the two large sofas positioned in the center of the room, and plonked himself haphazardly into the middle of one. "Let's play a game!" he suggested, as everyone gathered round him.

"What kind of game?" Faye asked suspiciously. "I don't see Monopoly round here."

"Truth or Dare, Consequences—whatever you choose to call it," he said. "It will give us all a chance to get to know each other better." He avoided Faye's furious eyes and looked at the others, trying to canvass support.

"Absolutely not." Faye's voice was firm as she scanned the remaining guests. "It's a ridiculous suggestion." The evening had reached the point at which everyone had drunk too much and she was anxious to see it end.

"No, it isn't. It's a great idea." Tony pulled a chair over to join them. "We could do with livening things up a bit. So far, this evening has made a game of chess look animated."

"Well, I'm off to bed," said Faye, and stood up.

Tony caught her arm. "No, you're not," he said, in a low voice. "As hostess, you should stay and do as your guests wish, not flounce off like a small child who hasn't got her own way."

Shocked into submission, Faye sat down next to Adam. She thought about defying Tony and going to bed anyway, but couldn't muster the strength.

Adam patted the empty sofa cushion on the other side of him. "If any of you haven't got anything nice to say, then come and sit next to me!" he joked.

Auntie Ethel lumbered over, turned her back to the sofa, and launched herself into the space. She was the only member of the older generation to last into the early hours: all the others had slunk off to bed.

"Right!" Adam loved games and was beaming with the thrill of anticipation. "For anyone who doesn't know how to play, we spin this empty wine bottle on the table, and whoever the neck points to has to choose a truth or a dare from the person the bottom end points to. Here goes!"

As the bottle clattered on the wooden surface, everyone leaned forward expectantly. All eyes were on it.

Nat and McLaren were sitting on one sofa alongside Jenna, with Mark on the floor in front of them. Kate and Rich perched on each arm, and Tony sat on a chair to the side. On the other sofa there were Adam, Faye, and Auntie Ethel, with Ted and Brian squatting nearby. With the exception of Faye and Auntie Ethel, everyone was looking the worse for wear, giggling and nudging each other like small children.

The bottle came to a stop with its neck pointing directly at Rich. The bottom was facing Adam. "Oooh," he shrieked. "Troof or dare?"

"Definitely truth. I don't fancy running around the hotel with my pants on my head," Rich said nervously.

"Hmmm, let's see." Adam pressed a finger to his lips and looked up at the ceiling. "OK, I've got it!" He bounced up and down on the sofa. "Have you ever broken the law?"

"Ooh, that's a good one!" Auntie Ethel clapped her hands.

"Um . . ." Rich was clearly stalling for time. "Well, as a policeman, I have to say that I now embrace a blameless life, but when I was a teenager, I stole a pack of cigarettes from my local newsstand."

This dull revelation was greeted with disappointment, but Rich seemed relieved to get his turn over and done with.

"Right." Adam was clearly anxious to move the game on to more interesting confessions. "Rich, it's your turn to spin."

Rich gave the bottle a firm twist. It moved sideways slightly, then stopped in front of McLaren, who giggled hysterically. The end was pointing at Faye. "Truth or dare, McLaren?" she said, her eyes shining at the prospect.

"Truth."

Faye gave the matter some thought. "How long was it before you slept with Nat?"

Jenna let out a drunken snort, and even Mark looked surprised. He took several glugs of his white wine.

Faye regretted asking it and waved her hand in the air. "Sorry, forget I said that. I was just trying to be outrageous. I'll think of something else."

"Don't worry, I'm not shy," said McLaren. She looked at Nat. "Shall I tell them?"

He nodded.

"Half an hour!" she blurted out, her face turning crimson at the memory.

Adam clapped, then burst out laughing so hard he was bent double with his head between his knees. The others tittered nervously at first, then dissolved into drunken hysterics.

Nat rose unsteadily to his feet and punched the air. "I'm irresistible," he cried, and fell back on to the sofa.

Faye was increasingly drawn to McLaren's self-deprecation, and smiled at her. "Half an hour?" she said. "Where were you?"

"At a party." McLaren jerked her head at Nat and gave them all a naughty grin. "He dragged me into the bathroom for a quickie."

"Sounds familiar." It was Tony, deadpan. He was looking straight at Faye. She knew he was referring to her and Nat in the locker room, and her neck burned. She was pleased to see that no one had spotted it.

"Not that I was complaining, mind you," continued McLaren, holding her glass to her lips with one hand and spinning the bottle with the other.

This time it stopped at Faye, with Kate as the challenger. Mark had turned slightly green, whether from too much alcohol or because of what might be asked was unclear. Everyone stared at Faye.

"Dare," she said: she'd rather run round the room naked than give Kate the pleasure of asking her a personal question.

Kate gazed into space, deep in thought, then faced Faye. "Call the wedding off," she said.

Her remark hung in the air and the room was deadly quiet. Adam had gasped and flung his hand over his mouth, while Mark sat frozen, as if he'd been shot.

"Only joking!" laughed Kate. "I wish I'd had a camera to record the look on your faces, though."

Everyone let out a collective giggle of relief, and Mark took several more mouthfuls of white wine. Even Faye managed to smile at Kate's mischievous remark.

"Stand up and sing 'The Funky Chicken,' " said Kate, looking straight at her.

Faye rose to her feet, vowing silently that she would get her own back on Mark's infuriatingly smug ex-girlfriend. Horribly self-conscious, she started to sing the naff lyrics.

"And the motions," Kate interrupted. She moved her elbows up and down to demonstrate.

As she stood there, bent arms flapping at her sides and everyone laughing at her, Faye wanted to curl up in a corner and cover her head. She could pout for a camera, but performing in public made her feel awkward and humiliated.

After one verse, she said, "That's it, no more," and sat down. Through the general murmur of "well done" and "priceless," she could hear a slow handclap. She looked up and Tony's eyes were on hers, a self-satisfied smile playing on his lips. At that moment, her hatred for him was absolute.

Half an hour later, Ted had been made to ask the front desk for condoms. Jenna had performed the dance of the seven veils with cushions, Brian had said the alphabet backwards, and Nat had revealed that he lost his virginity at thirteen to a seventeen-year-old babysitter. To everyone's delight, Auntie Ethel had chosen "dare" and performed her legendary "Cocaine Song." Only Adam had remained untouched by the curse of the bottle. It was now one-thirty and most of them were slurring badly.

"One more, then ish time for bed," said Brian, draining the last of his wine. "As best man, ish my duty to make sure the groom and I don't feel like shit on his wedding day . . ." He glanced at Mark, whose eyes were going in different directions. "Although I think it may be a little late for that." He gestured at Nat to spin the bottle.

Faye went cold. The neck was pointing at her and the end at Tony, who had now swapped places with Kate and was sitting on the sofa. She could have sworn his face lit up. Wary of another funky-chicken episode, she didn't think before answering. "Truth," she said quickly, her face impassive.

Tony looked at her thoughtfully, then at his brother, who was now slumped against the arm of the sofa with his eyes closed. The way his head was lolling suggested he was out for the count.

"Have you ever been unfaithful to Mark?" he asked, in a clear and precise voice that indicated he hadn't been drinking as much as everyone else.

The explosive nature of the question even caused reverberations in Mark's fuddled brain. He opened his eyes and attempted to sit up. Brow furrowed and blinking rapidly, he tried his best to focus on his bride-to-be.

"Of course not," snapped Faye. She prayed Tony wasn't going to choose this moment to reveal their secret.

"Glad to hear it," he said quietly.

Numbed by alcohol, Mark was clearly on a several-second delay. He suddenly sprang to his unsteady feet. "Tony, that's a *terrible* question to ask on the night before our wedding." His fists were clenched at his sides. "Take it back! You are totally out of order."

The room was silent, everyone motionless as they watched for Tony's reaction. He stared straight at Mark, clearly mulling over what he'd said, then raised his arms slowly into the air as a gesture of surrender. "OK, OK, as you wish." He looked at Faye, his eyes dead. "Ignore what I said."

Faye was relieved that the tense moment had passed. Their childish, drunken game had taken a dangerous turn and she just wanted to go to bed and get some much-needed sleep—otherwise she'd be getting married with black bags under her eyes. But the drama wasn't over.

"And apologize," slurred Mark, putting out his hand to steady himself on the arm of the sofa.

"What?" Tony looked at him with disbelief, then irritation. "Leave it, Mark."

"No. Apologize to Faye," Mark repeated. "This is our wedding weekend and you can't ask her something like that. I won't allow it."

"Mark, it's OK . . . really," urged Faye.

Tony stared at the carpet, his hands on his knees. After a few seconds, he stood up. "I apologize," he said stiffly.

"That's OK," she mumbled.

"And now," Tony continued, "if you'll all forgive me, I'm off to bed. I think the evening has reached its natural conclusion." With a nod, he turned on his heel and left the room.

There was a stunned silence. Then Nat got to his feet. "Well, I must congratulate you two on the most entertaining night I've had in ages. If the wedding itself is half as good, then I can't wait. Come on, love." He grabbed McLaren's hand and pulled her up. "Let's go to bed."

"Night, all," tittered McLaren, carrying her bright yellow stilettos in her hand. "See you tomorrow."

After they'd left, the room was silent again. Mark had slumped back on the sofa and it was Faye's turn to stare at the carpet.

Brian coughed. "Right, I'm off too. It's going to be a long old day tomorrow." He offered Auntie Ethel his arm and helped her up. Frank, Ted, Kate, and Jenna all got up, too, and muttered, "Goodnight."

Brian took a couple of paces towards the door, then stopped and turned to point at Mark. "He should go to bed." He looked at Faye. "Do you want me to take him?"

"No, don't worry," she said. "I'll bring him up in a minute."

Then she and Mark were alone, a mass of empty wineglasses scattered around them, the truth or dare bottle on its side on the floor. Faye glanced at her husband-to-be, lolling on the sofa, his eyes glazed. Suddenly she felt depressed. For weeks, she had been planning this wedding weekend down to the last detail. She'd chosen the flowers, the linen, the menu, even the type and color of the name cards. Now her perfect day was in danger of being ruined by her own stupid, irrational behavior with a complete stranger who had turned out to be her future husband's brother. It's like something from *The Jerry Springer Show*, she thought glumly.

"Come on, let's get you to bed," she said, in the direction of Mark's slumped form.

"Huh?" The sound of her voice stirred him from his trance. He sat upright. "Has everyone gone?"

"Yes. It's two o'clock in the morning. Come on." She held out her hand, helped him to stand up, then guided him towards the door and out into the deserted reception area.

As they waited for the ancient lift to crank its way down from the third floor, Mark snuggled his face into her neck and kissed it. "Can I come and stay with you tonight?" He attempted to nibble her earlobe but missed.

Exhausted and deflated, Faye murmured, "No, let's keep things as we planned." She loved Mark dearly, but tonight she just wanted time and space alone to get her head round the evening's events. Pushing him into the lift, she held him up with one hand and pressed the button to the second floor with the other.

When it shuddered to a halt, she held the door open with her leg and rummaged in Mark's jacket pocket for his room key. Pressing it into his hand, she pushed him gently out of the door. "Your room is the third on the right," she whispered. "Goodnight, darling." She kissed his forehead, then stepped back into the lift and hit the button for the third floor.

As the doors closed, she pressed her head against the cool brass panel in front of her.

What had been supposed to be a quiet, civilized dinner for the main guests to get to know each other had turned into a hell that she was glad had ended.

Trouble was, it had only ended for the few hours while they slept. There was still tomorrow, and something told her that things might well get a lot worse.

Saturday, June 29
9 a.m.

Tony unfolded the copy of the *Wall Street Journal* he'd brought from England and spread it out on the table in front of him with a contented sigh. He was alone in the breakfast room, and was keen to eat and leave before he could be cornered.

Tony wasn't a people person. He could turn it on when he had to, at business functions or dinner parties, but away from work he liked his own space and ways of doing things. His morning routine was a cup of tea, followed swiftly by an espresso coffee, two pieces of white toast and marmalade, and a couple of slices of melon to freshen his palate. Anything less and he became jittery.

On his world travels, he'd discovered that several countries had never heard of marmalade so he always took his own. Anything but break the routine. He could happily accommodate another person in his life, but they had to understand that some boundaries were not to be overstepped. Consequently he had once curtailed a burgeoning relationship with a perfectly nice woman because she insisted on taking bites out of his toast.

"Don't," he had said firmly one morning, as they had breakfast at New York's trendy Mercer Hotel. "If you want some I'll order you a portion, but please don't eat mine."

She had carried on doing it, on other occasions too, presumably thinking it was a coquettish love game. To Tony it was irritating, and once he became irritated by someone, it was as though a cancer was spreading through the relationship and, ultimately, destroying it. So he had finished it.

"Why?" she had sobbed.

"Because you keep eating my toast" seemed a little facile, so Tony had sugared the pill and waffled on American-style about not being "in the right place" for a serious relationship.

All his friends teased him that he had a mild form of obsessive-compulsive disorder, or OCD. His New York flat was pristine, all the surfaces bare and polished to reflection perfection by his daily cleaner. As he was there so little, she cleaned surfaces you could already have eaten off, but Tony didn't care. All his CDs were alphabetized, and although his kitchen cupboards weren't used much because he ate out all the time, each harbored rows of jars and tins with all their labels facing forward.

In his two bathrooms, the pure-white towels were folded in regimented lines that made Patrick Bergin, in *Sleeping with the Enemy*, look positively sloppy. His suits, shirts, and ties were all color-coded. "It saves time looking for things," he'd snapped, when his mother had dared to mention it during her one and only visit.

So the thought of a wedding guest pitching up and spoiling his early-morning peace and quiet was too much for him to bear.

"Cooooeeee! Mind if I join you?" It was Alice.

Tony's heart sank without trace as, without waiting for an answer, she sat down in the chair opposite. The weather, he thought. She'll mention the bloody weather.

"It looks like they're going to be lucky with the weather, doesn't it?" said Alice breezily, helping herself to a piece of toast from the little chrome rack at Tony's side.

He folded his newspaper, "Yes, it's very sunny. But, then, it is summer and this is the south of France," he said wearily.

"I know, but you can never take anything for granted these days, not with that globular warming."

"Global."

"Sorry?" Alice looked puzzled.

"It's global warming."

"Oh. Well, whatever it is, I'm glad it's decided to give them a lovely day for it."

With Adam's words ringing in his ears, Tony was sure it was only a matter of time before she talked him through her journey, so he decided to steer her away from the subject and use this un-scheduled breakfast to his fact-gathering advantage. He knew what *he* thought about the forthcoming marriage, but he was curious to find out if there were any misgivings on the part of someone close to the bride.

"So what do you make of Mark and Faye as a couple?" he asked chattily.

Alice stopped chewing her stolen piece of toast and looked thoughtful. "Well, when I first met him, I was quite surprised."

"Really?" Tony kept his voice noncommittal and poured her some tea. "Why's that?"

He sat back and listened as Alice explained that when Faye had called to say she was bringing a boyfriend home, her mind had gone into overdrive. Faye had never brought anyone home before. "I'd always assumed she was ashamed of me," said Alice, without a trace of self-pity. She said she had spent three days re-arranging her ornaments and dusting surfaces that already sparkled from too much attention. "And when I opened the door, I was astonished," she said, scraping a large blob of butter from her toast. "Mark looked so young, not at all what I'd expected."

"Youthful good looks run in our family," joked Tony. "Out of interest, what were you expecting?"

"Oh, I don't know. Someone older, I suppose," she mused. "Definitely a powerful businessman type, someone who loved her but was dominant and looked after her. She'd hate me for saying so, but Faye needs to be looked after."

"Oh?" Tony was surprised, his mind flashing back to the feisty, independent woman he'd experienced so far.

"She gives a good impression of independence, but she's terribly insecure. I did my best bringing her up, but she needed a father figure. She could be very willful."

"She still can be." He made a mental note to ask more about Faye's father later. "How was your first meeting with Mark?"

She told him that during the course of the afternoon she had warmed to him. There was little doubt that he was smitten with Faye, but she felt that her daughter was the one in control, acting as if she didn't have to try because she knew he was eating out of the palm of her hand. "In a way, they reminded me of her and me." She sighed. "I always bent over backwards to please Faye and she ran rings round me. It seemed they were just repeating the pattern."

"Do you still feel that?"

"Not so much, no—although, to be honest, I've not spent much time with them. "She stared out of the window for a moment. "When they left that afternoon, I made a fuss over Mark because I thought it would be the last time I'd see him."

"And here we are at their wedding," said Tony with false brightness.

"Yes, funny, isn't it?" she said, without a trace of humor. "When Faye called to say she was getting married, I was confused enough to ask who the lucky man was!"

Tony couldn't believe how honest she was. It was clear that no one bothered to ask Alice much, so when they did she sang like a canary.

"Faye got very cross with me and said, 'It's Mark, of course!,' and I must have sounded surprised because she asked me why. So I said that he just didn't seem her type." She sipped her tea.

"And what did she say to that?"

"Not much, really."

"Have you broached the subject with her since? A lot of the time, a mum's perspective is the right one you know," said Tony who rarely listened to a word his mother said.

"Try telling that to Faye. She does exactly what she wants, always has. And let's face it, I'm not one to talk when it comes to picking the right men."

He was dying to ask her what she meant, but felt it was a step too far to probe her. He was just about to return to the subject of Faye when she said, "To be honest, I always thought she'd end up with someone like you."

"Me?" He slapped the front of his sky-blue Lacoste shirt and his heart rate increased. Irrationally he wondered if she knew about his and Faye's previous encounter. "Why?" he asked.

"As I said, someone a bit older, who's quite successful and not intimidated by her. She needs handling, if you know what I mean."

"I understand completely," said Tony. "Sadly, I'm not sure Mark's the man to do it."

Alice took another bite of toast. "Bit late now," she mumbled. A large crumb fell from her mouth.

Tony didn't think so, but said nothing. Instead, he topped off her teacup then looked at his watch. "Time is on our side." He smiled. "So tell me more about my sister-in-law-to-be."

Tony had eventually made his excuses when he sensed his conversation with Alice was in danger of veering towards a description of her journey, and headed for his room, opting for the stairs instead of the lift.

He pondered what had been said. Alice might look and sound a bit vague, he thought, but she was as sharp as a tack. She was also entirely genuine, a woman who adored her daughter yet was concerned enough about the suitability of the match to voice her reservations to a virtual stranger. Her first impression of Faye and Mark's relationship seemed to be the right one but, unlike Tony, she was prepared to let them make a mistake.

He looked at his watch. Just five hours to go before the curtain went up on the marital theatrics.

Outside the door marked "18," he paused for a moment, then knocked. He could hear the distant sound of a television, but no one answered. He knocked again, this time with more force.

"Hang on," said a faint voice.

About thirty seconds later, a bleary-eyed Mark opened the door wearing a hotel dressing gown loosely tied at the front. His hair was sticking up in all directions and his eyes resembled poached eggs in blood.

"Oh dear," said Tony, barely disguising a smirk. "Bad night, was it?"

"I feel like shit," said Mark, and gestured for his brother to follow him into the room. "I can't believe I was stupid enough to get a hangover for my wedding day."

"As most blokes end up on Aberdeen railway station with their body in a plaster cast, I'd say you got off lightly." Tony picked up Mark's shirt from the one and only chair and sat down. "I reckon you need a walk."

Mark let out a hollow laugh. "You're kidding, right?"

"No, I'm not. Some fresh air will do you good, young man."

"Christ, you sound like Mum." He groaned, and kneaded his temples. "I'll tell you exactly what will do me good—a massive fry-up to soak up the alcohol and a couple more hours of sleep." He lay back on the bed and stared at the ocher-colored ceiling.

"Nonsense." Tony got up and walked to the door. "I've had a lot more hangovers than you and, believe me, fresh air is the business. I'll be back for you in fifteen minutes. Be ready."

Alice bent down to tie the lace of her walking shoe. She was already several hundred yards away from the hotel, having set out at a brisk pace just after her breakfast with Tony. Their conversation had been troubling her. She had suffered slight misgivings that Faye was marrying the wrong man, but she put it down to a mother's overprotectiveness. Now that she had heard what she assumed to be an objective third party voicing the same fears, she wondered if her instinct had been right. If so, it presented another dilemma: was she going to do anything about it?

The truth was, Faye intimidated her and had done since she was a child. Alice was timid, her daughter was confident; Alice was serene, her daughter temperamental; Alice was almost invisible, her daughter was demanding.

Alice had tried hard to fulfill the role of two parents, providing the much-needed love, stability, and routine in her child's life. But she had forgotten that children also need discipline. She had felt too guilty ever to administer it and, if she was honest with herself, she wasn't sure she was even capable of it.

"You let that child run rings round you," Alice's older sister Clara had chided her one Christmas, when Faye was about four.

"Send her to stay with me for a few weeks and I'll give her some discipline. You need to show her who's boss."

Alice had recoiled from subjecting Faye to the treatment she had received all her life at the hands of her bullying, overpowering sister. Instead, she had sacrificed her own wants and needs at the altar of Faye, who became the center of her universe.

Alice had always been a plain, mousy woman, but she had given birth to a beautiful child who drew endless compliments from shop assistants and passers-by about her blond curls and huge blue eyes. Often, these exchanges were the only adult conversation Alice had for days on end. She lived on benefits and took in sewing jobs for cash, which meant she spent much of her time sitting at home while a preschool Faye either slept or played with toys. It was an insular life, but Alice didn't mind as she found social situations difficult anyway. Faye became her social lubricant, her main point of contact with an outside world that, hitherto, had ignored her as insignificant.

Alice was one of life's worriers, and if she didn't have anything to worry about she worried about that too. Anxiety was the glue that held together her daily existence. By the age of seven, Faye had her mother wrapped round her little finger. She made endless demands for attention, sulked when she didn't get what she wanted, and generally ruled the roost.

In retrospect, Alice knew this hadn't been an ideal situation for a child. She had bred a daughter who went through life doing what she wanted, when she wanted, with little regard for others. But she loved her daughter so much, and felt so guilty about her lack of a father that she capitulated on virtually everything and created a mini monster.

By the age of eleven, Faye had learned how to press all her mother's guilt buttons, an added weapon in her get-what-you-want armory. "When *I* have a child, I'm going to treat them so much better than you treat me," she'd said once, after her mother had refused to buy her some roller skates. Alice wasn't trying to teach her demanding offspring a much-needed lesson, she couldn't afford them: she was a single parent, money was tight, and she simply couldn't afford them. Faye's remark had cut her to the core, particularly because Alice blamed herself that her daughter had never even met her father. It was her fault, she thought, for having allowed herself to get pregnant by such a feckless man.

From the moment David Wood had walked in to the ladies'-wear department of Mason's, the department store where Alice had worked since leaving school, she had been transfixed. Tall, blond, and handsome, he stood out a mile among the drab, unremarkable types Alice had grown used to seeing in the area. She couldn't take her eyes off him as she helped him choose a cashmere sweater as a birthday present for his mother. After he'd left, she had spent much of the afternoon daydreaming about him. But when she got home she gave herself a stern talking-to.

"Who are you kidding?" she said to the mirror. "No man has ever shown an interest in you, let alone someone as charming and good looking as him." This was mainly because Alice had lost none of her ability to blend into life's wallpaper.

Three weeks later, he came in again.

"Hello, did your mother like the sweater?" said Alice, kicking herself inwardly for making it obvious that she remembered him.

"She loved it, thanks."

"Can I help you with anything else?"

He glanced around the shop, presumably to check whether anyone was in earshot. "Actually, yes," he said. "You can come to the cinema with me."

And that was it. He'd taken her to the new Mario Lanza film, then walked her home to her bed-sit. She didn't invite him in, and he didn't ask. He simply gave her a lingering kiss on the lips and asked if he could see her again at the weekend.

Alice had floated into the house, her mind spinning with the heady romance of the evening. As she'd never been out on a date before, the fact that he'd paid for the tickets then walked her home really meant something. Radiating unbridled delight, she practiced saying "Mrs. Alice Wood," to the mirror.

Date two was a little faster in every sense. They met in her local pub and, after one drink, he suggested they go back to her place. He didn't say what for, and she didn't like to ask in case he changed his mind. She was desperate for him to fall in love with her, and naively thought her complicity would make it happen.

As they sat together on her threadbare little sofa, he'd stroked her hair and told her how beautiful she was. Alice had been shown little affection in her life and it felt exquisite. Closing her eyes and leaning against his chest, inhaling his smell and feeling her skin tingle from the gentle caresses that were so alien to her.

After a couple of minutes, his gentleness had accelerated to feverish kissing and fumbling. Alice let him take the lead and went along with what he wanted. It didn't cross her mind to say no: she was desperate not to disappoint him in any way. Now that this handsome, vibrant man had stirred such feelings in her, she didn't want to do anything that might threaten their burgeoning relationship.

After the visits to the cinema and the pub, he never took her out again: their relationship was conducted behind closed doors. David turned up at her bed-sit whenever he felt like it, usually late at night on his way home from the pub, and they would have sex or, as Alice saw it, make love.

She was infatuated with him and spent far too much of her hard-earned money on buying him little treats, on the off-chance that he might pop in to see her. Cigars, cotton handkerchiefs onto which she'd stitched his initials, poetry books, whatever she thought might please him.

When he did turn up, he would mutter, "Thanks," for whatever gift she offered, then instigate sex and leave. Because Alice didn't know any better, this behavior didn't bother her unduly. As far as she was concerned, sexual affection was better than none at all.

She didn't see him for the whole of July, but told herself he must be more busy than usual at his job in the local foundry. She, too, was working hard, and put down her tiredness and nausea to this. When she had to sneak regularly into the store toilets to be sick, she knew she had to see the doctor and get rid of whatever bug she had.

When he told her she was pregnant, her initial shock had soon dissipated to make way for delight. She'd never contemplated a baby, but now it had happened it felt like the most natural thing in the world to go through with it.

Two weeks later she was considering dropping in at the foundry to see David—she'd never had his address—when he knocked at her door late one night. As he lunged for her, she placed her hand against his chest and pushed him away. He looked surprised.

"David," she smiled, "I have some news."

"What?" he mumbled, trying to nuzzle her neck.

"We're going to have a baby."

He stopped nuzzling. "Are you sure?"

"Yes. I've been to the doctor's for a test."

"I see."

"Are you pleased?" She took his hand.

His face had clouded and he was biting his lip. After a few seconds, he snapped out of it and gave her a quick smile. "I'm thrilled." Then he pushed her back on the sofa, made love to her, and got up to leave. He promised to call her at the store the next day to make an arrangement for the coming weekend.

After a couple of weeks had passed, with no word from him, she had walked down to the foundry and asked the foreman where she might find David Wood. He told her Wood had left suddenly just over a week ago, and no one had a forwarding address.

She never heard from him again.

Even now, after all these years, Alice experienced a stab of pain at the memory. The anguish wasn't for herself, she'd got over it years ago, but for Faye. Although her daughter said his absence had never troubled her, Alice was tormented by the idea that every woman should have a loving father by her side when she got married. She had resolved to be the best possible mother on Faye's wedding day, and that meant voicing any doubts was out of the question.

An old muscular pain flared up in her right leg, and she stopped walking, tilting her face towards the morning sun. Looking back over her shoulder she could see the château jutting through the trees.

"Time to head back," she muttered to herself. The return journey would be steeper and more strenuous on her leg.

"Is that you, dear?"

"No, Mum, it's Princess Michael of Kent." Faye dumped her handbag on the chair by the door. Her mother asked her the same question every time, and she was running out of famous names for sarcastic retorts.

She walked into the cramped kitchen where her mother was sitting on a stool at the breakfast bar. She was halfway through the *Evening Standard* crossword, spectacles perched on the end of her nose.

"Hello. Good day?" Alice looked up and smiled.

"Not bad. Not good." It was the same answer she gave most days. "I'm off for a bath." As she walked back down the corridor, she glanced at a framed photograph of her mother holding her when she was just a few months old; Faye was wearing a hideous, hand-knitted turquoise dress with matching bonnet.

For the most part, they got on well, but like most mothers and daughters a little distance was preferable. Living with Alice drove Faye to almost daily distraction. It was the little comments that did it, the ones that mothers can't help making. "Oooh, you're not going out with wet hair, are you, dear?" or "You really shouldn't work so hard, you know."

Faye would simply take a deep breath and mutter, "Mum, give it a rest."

Of course, living with Alice also had major pluses: the home-cooked meals, the clean bedding, the clothes regularly washed and ironed—leaving aside the Prada cashmere sweater Alice had put into the machine, which would now fit a garden gnome.

It was a long way off purgatory, but Faye would still have preferred her own place. Trouble was, she couldn't afford London prices, so Alice's terraced house in East Sheen was her only option. Just a few miles outside central London, she had easy access to her modeling jobs and to a social life in town.

"Faye darling, I really don't think you should be going out like that," stuttered Alice one night, as her fifteen-year-old daughter was going out of the door in knee-high boots and a skirt that just skimmed her bottom.

"Shut up, Mum. You're just an old fuddy-duddy," she'd retorted.

As the door slammed, Alice had realized this was one of the times when she missed having a man about the house. If Faye had had a father, he would have stopped her going out dressed so provocatively.

By sixteen, she'd outgrown her rebellious phase and decided to get a Saturday job in the local Top Shop. She loved clothes, and she got to chat to lots of different people, albeit briefly. It also provided her with a bit more pocket money than the weekly five pounds Alice scraped together.

Two weeks into the job, she was serving at the till when a woman walked up and handed over her business card. She worked for a modeling agency and said she thought Faye had "a certain something."

After lots of heartfelt chats about the importance of a good education, Alice had reluctantly agreed to let her take on the occasional small promotional assignment outside school hours. At first she chaperoned her, but soon Faye was doing so much that it became impossible for Alice to tag along every time. It also meant that she discarded any ideas of taking A levels, preferring to earn money straight away.

By seventeen, she was taking on more lucrative fashion shoots for magazines. Alice was nervous that her daughter was entering such a shallow industry full-time and so young, but the money meant that they didn't have to worry continually about where the next penny was coming from.

However, it also meant Faye had replaced her mother's willing compliance with the sycophancy of makeup artists and photographic assistants who fulfilled her every whim.

Consequently, she still had a lot of growing up to do.

Saturday, June 29
10:20 a.m.

"Feeling any better?" Tony looked at Mark questioningly as they strolled round the symmetrical gardens of the château. Huge topiaries lined the perfectly straight path that stretched in front of them, and in the distance, two rowing boats bobbed on the lake. The sun was just starting to gain strength.

"Marginally," said Mark, although he didn't. He was finishing off the last of a huge bacon baguette he'd ordered from room service. "Although being targeted by Alice on the way out didn't help. She's fretting about everything going smoothly."

"I got collared by her too," said Tony.

"She's terribly sweet," Mark continued, "but I don't think there's enough going on in her life. She worries about the slightest thing."

"I suppose all mothers do on their daughter's wedding day."

"Well, she's got no reason to—Faye and I will be together forever." Mark took the last scrap of bacon out of his sandwich, ate it, and lobbed the bread into a nearby bush.

"Mark—" Tony stopped abruptly as his brother's hand appeared in front of his face.

"If you're going to say something negative, don't. I'm not in the mood." It felt strange standing up to Tony for once, but Mark was determined nothing would spoil the day.

But Tony ignored him. "Some things need to be said, particularly at such a crucial time."

Mark stopped walking and let out an irritable sigh. "Like what, Tony? What exactly *is* it that you'd like to say?" He stuck his hands on his hips. "Let's get it out of the way now so that I can get on with enjoying my day."

Tony put his hand up to shield his eyes from the sun. Unusually, for such a consistently assured man, he looked pensive. He scraped his shoe back and forth on the pathway. "What if you found out something about her that you didn't know?"

"Like what?" Mark said suspiciously.

Tony shrugged. "I don't know." He looked away towards the château. "Just something about her that she hadn't told you, something significant."

"Like what? That she used to be a man?" He pinched the bridge of his nose. "For Chrissakes, where are you going with this? You clearly think you know something about Faye that I don't, so just spit it out and be done with it."

Tony had now scraped a visible rut in the gravel path. He stared into the middle distance over Mark's shoulder. "It's just something I saw last night . . ." He trailed off awkwardly.

Mark's expression changed from irritation to curiosity. "What was it?"

Several seconds passed and Tony said nothing.

"Tony, I asked you what you saw," said Mark, more urgently.

"I was going to the gents' when I . . ." Tony took stock of what he was trying to say. "She was in a little locker room with Nat."

They were still and quiet enough for a bird to land just three feet from them. It flew off as soon as Mark spoke. "And?" His cheeks were flushed and his pupils had dilated. "What were they doing?"

Tony chewed his lip, something he'd done as a child when he felt uncomfortable. "I couldn't hear what they were saying, but he had his hand here." He extended his arm and placed a hand on Mark's ribcage. "She sprang away from him when she saw me."

Mark's face betrayed no emotion. "Is that it?" he asked quietly.

"Sorry?"

"You saw them talking, and he had his hand here." Mark copied the move. "Is that it?"

"I know it doesn't sound like much, but she looked pretty guilty when she saw me. And sneaking off with your ex-boyfriend isn't ideal behavior on the night before your wedding, is it?"

Mark laughed hollowly. "Oh, get real, this isn't the bloody Dark Ages! Men and women are allowed to be friends, you know. Talking to a member of the opposite sex isn't a crime. Not unless you're a jealous paranoiac, anyway, and I'm not."

"True. But she told me he still has feelings for her."

"She told you that?" Mark looked surprised. "Why?"

"Because I asked her what was going on."

"I see." Mark dug his hands deep into his trouser pockets.

"What exactly did she say about these . . . er . . . feelings?" He looked a little less cocksure about his fiancée's "chat" with her ex-boyfriend.

"Dunno." Tony looked uninterested. "She just said he'd dragged her into the locker room to tell her he still had feelings for her."

"Well, there you go!" Mark's face had brightened. "Just because some ex still has feelings for her—and let's face it, what man wouldn't?—doesn't mean she's going to respond. She was just giving him the polite brush-off."

"Hmmm . . ." Tony looked unconvinced. "I wish I could share your charming optimism about life, I really do."

"Well, I don't believe in being suspicious about everything." His face became serious. "Unless there's something else you heard or saw that you're not telling me?"

"Nope, that was pretty much it. But, as I said, irrespective of who took who in there, or who said what, I still don't think it was wise behavior on the part of a woman who's about to get married."

Mark looked straight at him. "But it's not about what *you* think, is it? You're not the one marrying her."

Tony didn't say anything: he simply shrugged in an "it's your life" fashion.

Mark started walking towards the orangery at the bottom of the château gardens. "Is that what all the fuss was about last night? You know, when you asked her if she'd ever been unfaithful to me? You were bloody out of order saying that in front of our guests."

"I know. And I apologized. But Faye didn't look too bothered and I suspect she can be quite volatile. I'm sure she's embarrassed herself enough times with her own behavior."

Mark nodded slowly. "Oh, I get it. You've been talking to Brian, haven't you?"

"Brian?" Tony looked puzzled. "No, I haven't. But, from that, I assume he's witnessed an example of her volatility."

Mark flushed, cross with himself for having opened his mouth too soon. "Yes," he acquiesced. "They don't really get on, but it's only because they're quite similar."

Tony looked at him skeptically. "If you're saying that Brian would describe her as a little temperamental, I'd already worked that out for myself. I've met lots of women like her."

"What's that supposed to mean?"

"Don't get me wrong, I like her. She's sparky, great company, and bloody amazing to look at. But those are her good points. It's the bad ones I'm worried about."

"Everyone has their bad points," said Mark, sullenly. "Even you."

Tony held up his hands in a gesture of surrender. "I'm riddled with them, mate, I know that. But you're not marrying me. Faye's feisty and unpredictable and it takes a certain person to harness that and—"

"Yeah, yeah," Mark cut in irritably. "And I'm not that person. Not according to Tony the bloody oracle anyway."

A hotel maid shuffled past them, her arms stuffed with creased bed linen, and mumbled, "*Bonjour.*"

Tony waited until she was out of earshot before he said, "Take it as a compliment. What I'm saying is that you don't have the necessary tough streak to deal with her."

"What should I do, then? Just give her a good slap every so often?" Mark's tone was heavily sarcastic.

Tony ignored it. "I'm talking about *mental* toughness, as you well know. Faye's like one of those high-maintenance thorough-bred horses who think they call all the shots. You have to play a long, hard game, and while you never truly control them, and vice versa, you at least reach a compromise."

Mark made no attempt to hide his incredulity. "You're comparing dating women to taming horses?" he scoffed. "And there I was thinking you lived in the PC capital of the world."

"Look, forget political correctness Mark," Tony said irritably. "This is your *life* we're talking about. You can be as modern as you like, but relationships are hard enough as it is and if you marry someone whose personality clashes with yours it's going to be disastrous."

"Opposites attract," Mark retorted.

"Indeed they do. They shag each other senseless, wait for the honeymoon period to be over, then split up because they don't get on out of the bedroom. They don't get *married*."

"We don't clash very often, and certainly not dramatically," said Mark.

"That, I suspect, is because you let her get away with any bad behavior. Anything for a quiet life, eh? After a while, your silence will be seen as weakness and she'll end up despising you for it." He lowered his voice. "The only difference between a rut and a grave is the depth."

Mark stared wordlessly ahead, then tilted his face towards the sunshine filtering through the clouds. He showed no sign of responding.

Tony's brow was furrowed in thought. "Even Shakespeare wrote about it," he continued. "*The Taming of the Shrew*—ever read it?"

Mark shook his head, looking glummer by the second.

"No man could get through to Kate until old Petrucchio came along and started dishing out the same treatment to her that she gave to others." Tony looked at Mark to see if he was listening. "It was the only language she understood and before long she fell madly in love with him."

"That's all very fascinating," Mark mumbled, "but two wrongs don't always make a right."

Tony raised his eyes heavenward. "Don't be so bloody idealistic all the time! I'm not suggesting we all have to go through life behaving appallingly to each other, I'm just saying that sometimes you have to be cruel to be kind. You know, show them you won't put up with irrational monstrousness."

"What's to say I don't? You've spent one evening in our company and already you think you're an expert on our relationship?"

Tony stepped into the spectacular orangery, its lavishly decorated ceiling depicting God and the angels, whose wings were picked out in gold leaf. He admired it for a few moments, while he waited for his brother to follow him. A small wooden bench was positioned against the far wall, and Mark strolled over to it and sat down.

Tony moved towards him, but stopped a few paces away. "I don't think I'm an expert," he said, "but I know you inside out and she has a dominant personality."

"And you think I'm a pushover."

"No, I don't think that at all. Kate's feisty and you and she had a great relationship. You rose to any challenge together and you were equals. I just don't get the same feeling about you and Faye. You seem in her thrall, much more acquiescent than you were with Kate."

"Like you and Melissa?"

"What's that supposed to mean?"

"Well, let's face it, she *never* stood up to you. You dominated her. She dressed how you wanted her to, gave up most of her friends to follow you everywhere, and basically worshipped the ground you walked on."

The blood drained from Tony's face and his expression hardened. "You shouldn't speak ill of Melissa, she's got nothing to do with this," he said quietly.

"I wasn't aware I *was* speaking ill of her," Mark replied. "I don't regard being a nice person who's madly in love with their partner as a weakness, but you clearly do."

"My relationship with her is irrelevant."

"Oh I *see*." Mark stood up and walked past him. He stopped a couple of feet away. "You can pass comment on *my* relationship, but yours is strictly off-limits. That's the deal, is it?"

The two brothers faced each other, Mark determined, Tony thoughtful but impassive. After several tense seconds in which neither spoke, Mark glanced at his watch and headed for the door. As he reached it, he stopped and turned back. "Read my lips, Tony. In just under five hours' time, I will be saying, 'I will,' with Faye at my side. If you can't handle that, I suggest you leave now."

He bowed his head, stepped outside, and started to walk back to the hotel.

Saturday, June 29
10:25 a.m.

Faye opened her curtains to let in the morning sun-
light and sat down at the dainty wooden dressing
table to put the finishing touches to her breakfast
makeup. She rarely appeared anywhere in public
without at least one layer of tinted moisturizer, two of
mascara, and a smidgen of clear lip gloss for that "natural" look. When she had started having sexual relationships, it had taken her a while to break the habit
of waking up earlier than her partner and rushing
into the bathroom to beautify herself before he woke.

She was a naturally pretty girl, but for some reason
she felt exposed if any man saw her face as nature

intended. It was only recently that she'd allowed Mark this privilege, and with his typical kindness he'd said she looked barely any different.

Now, as she applied her lip gloss and made one last check in the mirror, she forced herself to smile. "It's your wedding day!" she said to her reflection. But, try as she might to feel euphoric, she felt weary at the prospect. Yet again she found herself wishing that they'd just buggered off abroad and married with the minimum of fuss.

Walking across to the built-in wardrobe, she slid back the door and took another look at her wedding dress, pristine in its plastic casing. In approximately five hours' time, she would be wearing it and walking to meet Mark for the ceremony. Falling back onto an armchair, she stared into the middle distance and thought about what Tony had said the night before: "Maybe you just love the idea of getting married and any old bloke will do."

What if he's right? she thought. *Am* I getting married for the right reasons?

When she stopped to think about it, she had to admit she harbored slight reservations about it, but she had put them down to nerves. Most of her married friends had told her they felt the same way just before their big day. Now, thanks to Tony, her slight reservations were huge nagging doubts.

Did she just love the idea of getting married? She wasn't sure. It was true that the recent marriages of many of her friends had left her feeling a little panicky about the future, and Adam had told her so many times that she was the fickle bitch from hell that she was even beginning to believe it herself. Perhaps she suspected everyone thought that of her, so getting married was her way of telling them they were wrong.

Faye dismissed the idea. No, she loved Mark. She was sure of that. After all, there was nothing about him *not* to love. He was nice looking, kind, romantic, and . . . just a little bit dreary. As that thought popped into her head, Faye let out a small groan. God, she hated being so callous, but she couldn't help herself.

She *did* find Mark a little dull at times, but only at times. And as far as she was concerned, there wasn't a man on the planet who could excite her twenty-four seven. Was there? Her friend Laura claimed that her husband Rory constantly excited her, but as Faye found Laura a teensy bit tedious she put this down to Laura's lower standards. Outside, the hotel staff were milling around, starting to place the chairs for the ceremony. Later, they would decorate the quaint little gazebo with garlands of flowers. The sun was shining, and she guessed that, by now, her mother would be in a state of high anxiety mixed with excitement and Jean would soon be preening herself for her starring role as the groom's mother. All the other family and friends would be looking forward to an afternoon spent drinking free champagne in the blazing sunshine. So why on earth couldn't *she*, the bride, muster up any excitement?

"Mind over matter," she chanted, cross with herself for allowing gloom to descend. That bloody Tony will not be allowed to spoil my day, she thought angrily. For the umpteenth time that morning, she felt a flutter of nerves as she remembered him saying that, today, his aversion to the wedding would go up a gear. What might he do? All she could hope was that it had been the alcohol talking, that in the sober light of day he'd decide to give her the benefit of the doubt. Time would tell.

She ran into the bedroom, gave her hair a quick brush, and went to have breakfast with Adam.

"Pssst, here!"

Faye stood in the middle of the breakfast room, her head swiveling *Exorcist*-style. She could hear Adam, she just couldn't see him.

"Here!"

Out of the corner of her eye, she saw a rustling yucca plant in a small recess to the left of the restaurant, then a glimpse of a neon-pink T-shirt. "Why are you lurking here?" She smiled as she read his T-shirt logo—"DonnaKebab." Normally, Adam loathed fakes or spoofs, but Donna Karan had ignored him once at a fashion party and he'd been wreaking his own small revenge ever since.

"I'm not in the mood for small talk, so I thought I'd hide away," he whispered.

Faye put on a wounded expression. "Those are my dear, dear friends you're talking about." Then she sighed. "I have to say I'm finding this all terribly wearing too. In retrospect, maybe it wasn't such a good idea to invite family and exes all under one roof. We should have just sneaked off to some sunny beach to get married, then come back and surprised everyone."

Adam wiped stray croissant crumbs from his chin. "What? And deprive me of all the fun I'm having? Nonsense! Anyway, the other guests will arrive later and provide some dilution."

Faye took a sip of her black no-sugar tea and refused the sticky pastry he offered her. "Do you think I'm mad to have invited Nat and Rich?"

"My own personal amusement aside, it *is* a little weird, I'll admit." A globule of croissant landed on Faye's chest. "Ooh, sorry, darling . . . I mean, they're not exactly your great friends, are they? You'd lost contact with them both so that should tell you something."

"I know," said Faye, brushing herself with a paper napkin. "I just didn't want to feel left out because bloody Kate and Jenna were here."

"Yes, but Mark's a nicer person than you, darling, so he stays friends with his exes."

"He is nice, isn't he?" said Faye, pleadingly.

"Terrible . . . I mean, terribly." Adam grinned. "I'm sure he'll make someone a lovely husband. Just not you."

"Please don't start. Today of all days, I just want to hear

positive things . . . If only someone would tell that to his bloody brother."

"Hmmm, not keen on you, is he?" He leaned forward conspiratorially. "What was all that about last night, going on about being unfaithful? It was a bit odd, wasn't it? Particularly given what happened last weekend."

Faye spluttered into her tea, then checked around her to make sure no one had heard. Luckily, the breakfast room was empty except for them. "As far as I'm concerned, it never happened," she hissed. "And I wish you'd bloody forget about it too." She was thankful she hadn't told him the bombshell that her one-night stand had been with Tony.

"Sorrreeee!"

She calmed down. "I think he was referring to when he stumbled across Nat and me out by the loos."

"Doing what?"

"Nothing! God, he repulses me now."

"Darling, a prat he may be, but repulsive? He's incredibly sexy . . . until he speaks, of course." He was using a toothpick to clean his nails. "So what *were* you doing?"

"Nat was blathering on about Mark being wrong for me, and he had his hands on my waist. Then I noticed Tony watching us from the doorway."

"What doorway?"

"To the locker room further down the corridor."

"Hang on." Adam shifted in his seat. "You were with Nat in a secretive little side room where he had his hands around your waist? I'm not surprised Tony jumped to conclusions."

Faye narrowed her eyes threateningly. "It was not *secretive* and we were just talking, but Tony already hated me before that so he just saw that he wanted to see."

Adam's face lit up with a realization. "Is that why you were so desperate to get rid of me later on? You wanted to explain yourself?"

"Not explain myself, no. I don't have to explain myself to him. I just wanted to get to the bottom of why he seems so hell-bent on spoiling Mark's and my big day," she said, hoping she sounded convincing.

Adam propped his elbows amid the crumbs. "And?"

Faye shrugged. "He said he had nothing against me personally, but thinks Mark and I are incompatible. He thinks Mark's too nice for me."

"Well, that makes three of us, then," said Adam. "Tony, Nat, and I all think you're marrying the wrong man." He made a loud buzzing noise. "Our survey says . . ."

Her face darkened. "Are you seriously telling me I should call off my wedding because the three wise bloody monkeys think it's not right?" She leaned across and tapped his head. "That peroxide you use has clearly seeped into your brain."

Adam pouted. "Look, Nat's an idiot and Tony hardly knows you, but at least take on board what *I'm* saying. You might surprise me and live happily ever after with Mark, but I very much doubt it." He picked up another croissant and broke off a small piece. "We're not talking Cinderella and Prince Charming here. No disrespect, dear, but you're the Wicked Witch when you want to be."

Faye smiled despite his audacity. "And what's he?"

Adam tutted indulgently. "He's Toto, darling. Sorry, lovely fellow and all that, but too laid-back for you. He'd usually be destined to fawn over you from afar, but for some reason he's got to this stage and can't believe his luck."

"He has had girlfriends before, you know."

"Yes, but no one like you. Don't get me wrong, he's nice looking and he's not bad company, but he just hasn't got the extra something you need to keep you interested."

They fell silent, him chewing his croissant, her licking her fingers and pressing them onto the tablecloth to collect stray crumbs. The breakfast room was still blissfully empty.

"You're wrong, Adam," she said, after a while. "I'm determined to make this work."

"If it was right in the first place, you wouldn't have to," he countered. "It would just tick along nicely by itself."

"When have you *ever* had a relationship that ticked along nicely?"

He looked hurt. "*Moi?* Well, there was Billy."

"Billy!" She dribbled tea into her saucer. "Don't make me laugh!"

Adam and Billy had been an item when he and Faye first met. They had been together for around six months by then, and thrived on arguments, the more dramatic the better. They had one every couple of days, and on the days in between, they were all over each other like a rash. Billy was a social worker and regarded Adam's job as shallow and meaningless. This was the source of many of their conflicts, but they had fallen out over almost anything.

On one occasion Adam had rung Faye at midnight, sobbing hysterically that it was over. He and Billy had been out for dinner, then returned to Adam's flat where a blazing row had broken out over their forthcoming holiday to Australia. As he earned more, Adam had offered to pay the extra so they could stay in a nicer hotel, but Billy had insisted on booking somewhere cheaper and splitting it fifty-fifty. The discussion had developed into a full-scale row about earnings and the validity of their jobs. It had ended with Billy calling Adam "a ruthless Thatcherite" and storming out.

Inevitably, they made up and flew to Australia for gay Mardi Gras, but Adam returned home alone, heartbroken. Billy had taken up with a waiter he'd met in their budget hotel and decided to stay in Australia for as long as he could get away with it.

"Have you heard from him lately?" asked Faye.

Adam made a face. "I haven't seen him since he crawled out of the woodwork that time I told you about. That was about six months ago, and he's rung a couple of times but I haven't bothered calling him back. I'm too old to get back into all that roller-coaster stuff."

Faye laughed. "Listen to you! You sound like an old codger. Believe me, the minute some gorgeous man gives you the eye, you'll get right back on the ride again."

"Maybe you're right; until then, I'd much rather be on my own than with someone who's wrong for me." He looked right at her but she deliberately looked away.

"The benefit of hindsight!" she said pointedly. "If I'd told you that Billy was wrong for you while you were with him, you wouldn't have believed me. You would have carried on until you came to that conclusion yourself."

"So you'll only come to your senses about you and Mark when it's too late to end it without lawyers and divorce and stuff?"

"It won't ever come to that," she said firmly. Desperate to change the somber mood, she clapped her hands. "Right! I'd better go and start the arduous preparation to make myself a radiant bride."

Faye returned to her room, had a quick nap, then enjoyed a long, piping-hot bath. She lay there, trying hard to think happy thoughts about the ceremony, but her mind kept returning to how negative certain people were feeling about it.

Mark was still eternally optimistic, but he seemed to be the only one, except perhaps for her mother. But then she would never mention any misgivings anyway.

At the thought of her fiancé Faye smiled, and it struck her that she was feeling as close to contentment as she imagined she was ever likely to get. Tonight she would be sharing this room with her new husband.

Hauling herself out of the water, she brushed the soap suds from her arms and legs, and wrapped herself in one of the hotel's soft white towels. Over her years as a model, Faye had become adept at doing her own hair and makeup, so her preparations were solitary. Slapping a sea-mud cleansing mask on her face, she planned to leave it there for half an hour before starting the rest of the skin-cleansing process. She had booked a ten-minute session on the hotel's Super Turbo sunbed in an hour's time, then she would return to her room to blow dry her hair and put on makeup.

A faint sound distracted her. Then she heard it again: the doorbell to her suite. "Do not disturb means do not bloody disturb," she muttered, pulling a robe round her and walking out into the sitting room.

"Who is it?" she said, and peered through the peephole. It was Tony. Her stomach lurched. "What is it? I'm in the bath," she lied.

"Let me in. I have something to say." He looked agitated, glancing nervously up and down the corridor.

"It'll have to wait," she said crisply. "I'm about to get ready."

"It won't wait. It has to be *now*."

She flipped back the lock and opened the door. "Come in. This had better be good."

"Are you OK? You look a little green," he said, with a faint smirk.

She remembered the face mask. "Well, funnily enough, I wasn't expecting anyone." She frowned and felt the mud crack. "Sit down, and I'll just go and put some clothes on."

She pushed the bedroom door shut behind her, finished drying herself, scrubbed her face, and threw on a T-shirt and a pair of tracksuit bottoms. Her mind was in overdrive with the possible twists and turns of events that might be about to unfold. Perhaps he's come to say he's prepared to keep quiet about my aberration, she thought, and prayed that was the case.

"Right, you have my undivided attention," she said. She sat in an armchair next to the sofa where he was picking at the edge of a cushion. "I'm intrigued as to what's *so* important that it can't wait until another time."

Tony stopped fiddling with the cushion and looked straight at her. He cleared his throat. "Faye . . . stop this."

Thrown by his directness, she stalled for time. "Stop what?"

He merely looked at her with a "you know better than that" expression. "This self-delusion that everything is all right."

"Look, Tony, I *know* what happened last weekend wasn't an ideal situation, but it's in the past and Mark never needs to know." Her calm tone belied the churning in her chest. "And, let's face it, if it hadn't been you, he never *would* have known."

"I see." His tone was measured. "And that would make it OK to carry on and get married, would it?"

"In my book, yes," she said sullenly.

"Well, in my book it doesn't. Particularly when the main character is my brother."

They stared at each other defiantly for a few seconds, both intransigent in their view that *they* were right. Trouble was, Tony had the moral high ground and Faye knew it.

He sighed. "I've said this so many times I'm starting to bore myself. You were unfaithful to Mark last weekend. You can't marry him." He was studying her intently, watching for her reaction.

She made sure there wasn't one. "We've already discussed this, and I made my position quite clear. I love Mark and I intend to marry him."

His expression hardened. "If picking up a stranger in a seedy bar is normal behavior to you, then fine, I couldn't give a shit. But when you're about to marry my brother, I care deeply about it."

"It wasn't a seedy bar. It was the bloody Pitcher and Piano, for

God's sake." She knew it was irrelevant, but she was damned if she was going to let him paint a scenario that branded her as little more than a hooker.

"Oh, that's all right, then," he said flatly.

Faye had never felt more wretched. She had felt cheap after last weekend's episode, but now a man she barely knew was using it as a means to destroy what was supposed to be the happiest day of her life. "I didn't have sex with you," she said miserably. "If you remember, I thought better of it at the last minute."

"Details, details," he muttered. "Getting naked and inviting a man into your bed constitutes infidelity in my book. I certainly wouldn't want any fiancée of mine behaving like that."

She blushed with shame at the memory. "I agree that even as far as it went, it wasn't the behavior of a woman about to get married. But there were all sorts or reasons for it, and I'm certainly not going to elaborate on them with you . . ." She looked up at him to see if he was annoyed by this, but his face was expressionless, bored almost.

She leaned forward and stared him straight in the eye. "My behavior was reprehensible that night, but what I can't understand is why you would want to ruin the wedding day of the brother you claim to love so much."

This time, she had hit home. "Don't you dare question my feelings for my brother," he said, in a low but firm voice. "I don't give a damn about you, but I want to make sure he marries someone who will make him happy."

"He's a grown man," said Faye, incredulously. "Don't you think he can make his own decisions in life, without big brother wet-nursing him?"

"Obviously not, if this is anything to go by." He swept his hand around the room in a gesture of hopelessness. "He didn't get your measure, did he?"

"And you have?" Faye was seething at this man's bullish arrogance. "You know absolutely nothing about me."

"True, but I feel I'm getting to know you a little bit more as each second passes."

Faye stood up and strode over to the window. The scene outside was tranquil, a stark contrast with the turmoil in her suite. She could see Jean and Derek walking arm in arm down towards the orangery, stopping to share a few words with an old gardener who was trimming the lawn where it met the pathway. "Your parents would be devastated too if the wedding didn't go ahead," she said quietly.

"They'll get over it," he replied dismissively. "Better a short sharp shock now than going ahead with a lavish farce at their expense."

Faye turned to face him. "This is *not* a farce."

Tony stared down at his dark brown loafers, which bore traces of mud.

"What happened, happened," she continued, her heart leaden with misery. "I can't change that. But we *didn't* have sex, and I'll maintain until my dying day that that's because I loved Mark too much to go through with it." She went back to staring out of the window. Jean and Derek had disappeared from view.

Tony was mulling over her remark. "Admirable, I'm sure," he said. "But my brother deserves a woman who loves him so much that she doesn't put herself in that position in the first place."

They fell silent again, the only sound coming from the water tank refilling in the bathroom. Faye stood up and straightened her tracksuit bottoms, which had ridden up to her ankles.

Eventually Tony coughed. "Look, we could go round in circles for hours over the hows and whys of it all, but the simple fact remains that this wedding has to be canceled."

An acidic lump rose in the back of Faye's throat. She swallowed. "Tony, don't do this . . ." she pleaded. Her desperation was such she would happily have got on to her knees and begged. "You can't seriously expect me to call the wedding off at this late stage, after all that's been done?"

"I'm deadly serious," he said, looking exactly that. "I'm sure a lot of people find temptation beckons *after* they're married," he continued, "but you couldn't even get to the wedding day without showing your true colors."

"So what are you expecting me to do?" she said disconsolately.

"Go and tell Mark that the wedding's off," he replied quickly. "I don't care whether you tell him about your appalling lack of self-control, as long as the end result is that we're not all standing there at three o'clock this afternoon, witnessing your marriage."

"And if I don't?" Faye raised her eyes to look at him.

"Then I will stand up and tell all your guests exactly what happened last weekend." He shrugged. "After all, I've got nothing to lose."

For a few seconds, Faye forgot to breathe, such was the shock. In less than two hours, she had been due to get married. Now it was all in ruins. It was almost incomprehensible. "You can't do that," she said weakly.

"Oh, I can," he said briskly. "And, believe me, I will." Tony pulled a cigarette pack out of his pocket. He offered one to Faye, but she shook her head so he lit one for himself.

"Mark will never get over it," she said quietly, a solitary tear running down the side of her nose.

"Yes, he will." Tony's voice was softer now. "Sooner than you think. He may be laid-back, but he's very strong emotionally. Much stronger than me, in fact."

In normal circumstances, Faye would have asked what he meant by that, but she was too consumed by her own drama. She also felt overwhelmed by depression, and exhausted by misery, but deep down she had an almost masochistic urge to try to change Tony's view of her. "I can assure you it was out of character," she mumbled. "I wouldn't normally do that, even if I was single."

Tony ground his cigarette into the small white china ashtray in front of him. "Whatever," he said. "You *did* do it, so you won't be marrying my brother this afternoon. Will you do the honors, or shall I?"

Another tear ran down the side of Faye's nose and plopped onto the corner of the coffee table. "I will." She sniffed. "But you'll have to give me time to steel myself."

Tony looked at his watch. "It's half past one. I doubt you'll have time to speak to Mark and contact all the guests to tell them it's off, so you just deal with him. We'll worry about everyone else later."

Faye felt numb. Tony was talking about the cancellation of her wedding with businesslike brusqueness, as if they were discussing the postponement of a board meeting. "Fine," she whispered. "I'll just wait for my face to calm down, then I'll go and find him."

"Good." Tony stood up and straightened his jacket. "Despite what you might think of me, I'm sorry it had to end like this, you know. More than anything in the world, I want Mark to meet the right girl and be happy."

Faye looked up at him, her eyes dull with misery and defeat. "You mean, *your* version of the right girl for him. That's a tall order."

"That's where you're wrong," he said. "If he was marrying Kate today, I wouldn't be interfering. If he was marrying Jenna, I would probably have told him that *he* would end up hurting *her*."

"Quite the marital expert, aren't you?" she said sarcastically.

He sighed impatiently. "It's just common sense, Faye . . . the same way there's a man out there who will fit you perfectly."

"I'd already found him," she sobbed.

He knelt down and placed his hand on her forearm. "You

know that's not true. If you had, you would never have taken me back to your flat that night." He pulled a tissue out of the box on the table and handed it to her. "When you meet the right man, believe me, it won't even cross your mind to do that." He stood up and brushed down the knees of his trousers. "One day you'll realize I was right to insist on this."

Faye's tears were flowing now, and she used the back of her hand to wipe her face. "Goodbye, Tony." She didn't bother to look up. "I just wish I could say it's been a pleasure."

A few seconds later, she heard the door to the suite open, then click shut. She straightened her back, and took a long, slow look round the room until her eyes rested on Tony's cigarette butt lying in the ashtray.

"You stupid, stupid cow," she mumbled. "You've ruined everything."

Saturday June 29
2 p.m.

"It *has* to be here somewhere," said Brian, pointing the remote control at the television, his finger frantically tapping the change-channel button.

"What?" Mark emerged from the bathroom, toweling his wet hair.

"The porn channel." Brian didn't take his eyes off the screen. "Doesn't every continental hotel have one?"

"This is a classy hotel, mate. You're not in one of your Amsterdam dives now."

The neon symbols moved from eighty-nine to zero, and Brian tossed the remote on to the bed. "All this money on a room and not so much as a naked breast in sight. Still, not that you'll be worrying tonight. You'll have a real pair of your own to play with whenever you fancy it."

"Do you mind?" said Mark, with mock-indignation. "That's my bride you're talking about." He broke into a huge grin. "God, I'm so happy I could bloody burst. I always worried that I'd feel scared on my wedding day, you know, wary of the big commitment or whatever. But I feel absolutely fine—in fact, I'm looking forward to it."

Brian gave him a rueful smile. "Fools rush in. Marry in haste, resent at leisure."

"Oy." Mark gave him a stern look and jabbed a finger at him. "Don't start! You're as bad as bloody Tony, trying to piss on my chips."

"Sorry," said Brian. "I'll keep quiet from now on. Scout's honor."

Mark laughed. "You were expelled from the pack after just a week!"

"I didn't know the peace salute meant holding your two fingers the other way round . . ."

Mark had calmed down after his altercation with Tony. He had returned to his room in a highly agitated state, where Brian tried to mollify him and find out what had happened. As Mark recited the details of what had been said, the expression on Brian's face told him that he probably agreed with Tony, but clearly thought better of saying so. Instead, he'd distracted Mark by ordering two hair-of-the-dog beers on room service and reminding him of their wilder times together.

"God, do you remember that party at Billy Henderson's place?" he said, referring to the night he'd tried to urinate from an upstairs window and leaned a little too far forward.

"Only too well," said Mark, chortling. "I had strategically maneuvered my hand down some girl's blouse and was doing very nicely thank you, when someone came running into the spare room and said you'd really hurt yourself."

"*Hurt* myself?" Brian choked. "A broken collar bone and three cracked ribs! I was fighting for my life, mate."

"I almost came out and finished you off myself for interrupting my little session," he said, with a sigh of lament. "By the time I'd helped load you into the ambulance and gone back indoors, she'd rearranged her clothing and buggered off."

"Such compassion from my dear old friend." Brian flung his hand to his forehead dramatically. Unable to leave the remote alone, he picked it up and started flicking through the channels again. "There must be a decent film we can watch to kill time."

"*Kill time?*" Mark looked at his watch. "I'm getting married in precisely one hour and *you*," he tapped Brian's chest, "are my best man. I suggest you shower and work towards getting your suit on."

Brian hoisted himself up from his horizontal position on the bed and sauntered across to the bathroom. "I'm just going to slip into something less comfortable," he said, and booted the door shut.

Mark went to the wardrobe where his hired gray morning suit was hanging in a polythene wrapper with "Moss Bros." printed on the front. "It's almost time," he whispered, running a finger down the cool plastic.

A loud knock at the door made him start. "Shit!" He went to the door and peered through the spyhole. "Darling!" He flung it open, grinning from ear to ear. "Naughty girl. I'm not supposed to see you before the wed—" He stopped dead as his brain started to compute the image before him.

Faye, her face deathly white and devoid of makeup, was wearing a baggy white T-shirt and blue tracksuit bottoms. Her eyes looked puffy, and her hair was scraped back in an unkempt ponytail.

Mark's heart skipped a beat, and he glanced at his watch. "Shouldn't you be getting ready?"

She looked on the verge of tears. "I need to talk to you," she said and glanced down the corridor. "Can I come in a minute?"

Mark's mind whizzed through several less frightening reasons for Faye's sudden appearance at his door. Perhaps her dress had been torn in transit. Maybe she'd had a row with her mother. He clung on to these lightweight hopes as he stood aside and gestured for her to enter the room.

"Brian's in the shower," he said, "but he should be a little while yet. There's an awful lot of ingrained dirt to remove."

"I'll keep my voice low . . . for a change." She returned his halfhearted smile.

"So, what's the problem?" He felt nauseous with expectation and didn't want to skirt the issue any longer.

She sat down on a hard-backed chair by the window, looking almost terrified. "There's no easy way to say this, really . . ."

"Faye, what is it?" he said. "You're scaring me—no one's hurt, are they?"

"No, it's nothing like that."

Safe in the knowledge no one had died, he allowed himself to look irritable. "Well, what is it, then?"

"I can't marry you."

The punch of her words hit him straight in the stomach. He stared at her, wondering if she was about to break into a "gotcha!" grin. But her expression didn't crack.

"Why not?" It was all he could manage to say.

Tears were pouring down her face now, but she was making no sound. She brushed them away. "I'm so, so sorry, Mark, but I just can't."

"That's not an answer," he said, surprised by how calm he sounded. "I asked you *why*?"

"It just doesn't feel right." She sniffed.

Mark felt a surge of anger, but controlled it. He needed to establish whether this was a redeemable attack of the jitters, or whether this really *was* hell and the wedding was off. "And you couldn't have come to that conclusion *before* we spent all this money and dragged everyone out here?" he said quietly.

"I know! I know!" She leaped up and paced the floor in front of him. "The timing stinks, but I just can't go ahead with it."

"But why now?" He was baffled by the turn of events.

Faye's eyes were etched with the pain she felt at hurting him, and she didn't reply.

"Faye!" Mark's voice was low but angry. "I asked, why now?"

"I don't know," she sobbed. "It just has to be."

Mark blinked very deliberately a few times, then squeezed his eyes shut for a few seconds. He rubbed them vigorously and went over to her. "What's this all about?" He put his hand on her shoulder and gently turned her to face him. "Last night everything was fine, today you're saying you can't go ahead. I don't get it. What's changed in the past few hours?"

She looked devastated, but it was small consolation to him. Inside, he felt the chemical rush of rising panic. His euphoria of half an hour ago was about to switch to a crashing depression from which he might never recover.

"Mark, I love you to bits." She placed the palm of her hand against his cheek. "You are a kind, gentle, sweet man . . . but . . ." She looked lost.

"But you don't want to marry me," he interrupted.

She dropped her hand from his face and looked down at her sneakers. "It's not that I don't *want* to marry you . . . just that I shouldn't."

"*Shouldn't?* What the bloody hell does that mean?"

"I'm not good enough for you."

He put his hand out in front of him in a "stop" gesture.

"Please don't insult my intelligence with the old kind-to-be-cruel tactic," he said.

She shook her head, and her ponytail swung back and forth. "It's not a tactic, it's the truth."

Mark looked at her in disbelief at first, then his expression changed to defiance. "So, come on, then, tell me. Why aren't you good enough for me?"

She looked at him, blinking rapidly as she tried to think of reasons, *any* reason, she could give him, rather than the glaring, ugly truth: "I slept with your brother last weekend." She knew Mark wouldn't let her just walk out of there on the strength of what she'd said so far.

"I'm not nice enough for you," she blurted out, knowing immediately that it sounded pathetic.

"Not *nice* enough?" he said contemptuously. "Is that it?"

"Yes," she said miserably. "I'm too difficult. You deserve someone who appreciates you more."

He looked at her as if she was insane, and she was seized with the urge to tell him the truth. Perhaps he would forgive her and they could go ahead with the ceremony without Tony's threat hanging over their heads. But she knew in her heart of hearts that even if Mark *could* eventually forgive, he wouldn't make that decision in time for the ceremony in just one hour's time.

"Faye." His voice broke into her thoughts. "I don't want anyone else, I want *you*. Is that so hard to understand?"

"No," she whispered sadly. She was desperate to say "I want you too," but knew she couldn't.

Mark's tone softened. "I haven't always been sweetness and light to you," he said. "I always thought mood swings were part and parcel of any relationship."

Faye knew she was losing ground. She had to remain resolute or, if Tony carried out his threat, the afternoon would take an even more dramatic turn than it already had. "Yes, but they were mostly my mood swings, weren't they?" She looked at him imploringly. "It was invariably me being difficult and you trying to placate me."

He frowned. "So, hang on, what are you saying? That if I had retaliated in some way or played the same silly games, we would still be going ahead with the wedding?" His face was twisted with incomprehension. "Am I being jilted simply because I didn't play silly buggers and issue ultimatums?"

Faye sat down on the chair by the window and blew her nose with the tissue Tony had handed to her half an hour earlier. "It's not as simple as that," she sniveled, knowing she was waffling in desperation. She wanted Mark to accept that the wedding was off and not ask any questions, but she knew that was overambitious. She had to say something, even if she didn't mean it. "I'm just saying that our personalities aren't right for each other."

Mark took a couple of seconds to absorb what she'd said, then banged his hand hard against the window frame. The noise made her jump. "For fuck's sake, Faye!" He pointed out of the window. "Those are *our* guests. This is *our* wedding day. And you leave it this long to start talking about personality clashes?" He stared at her. "Do you have any idea how fucking stupid that is?"

They fell into a tense silence, punctuated by the occasional laugh from the guests gathering outside. The sunshine was strong now, bringing a distant lake alive with dancing chips of light.

Eventually, Faye stood up. "I'm so sorry Mark . . . really."

A single tear rolled down Mark's cheek, and he hastily brushed it away. "I'm sorry I met you," he muttered, and looked at her as though she were a stranger.

Seeing the pain on his face was almost too much to bear. In the knowledge that she had caused it, Faye wanted to run and hide from everyone . . . forever. She wanted nothing more than to take him in her arms and tell him everything was going to be all right. But it wasn't, and it was her fault. She wanted to crumple into a heap and sob her heart out, but she knew she had to stay strong, that her tears would be of guilt and self-pity and had no place in this room with Mark.

Paralyzed by a leaden misery, she just stood in the middle of the room and stared at him, blinking rapidly to stop the tears falling.

"The guests are expecting us in just over half an hour, so you'd better go and tell them otherwise. I'll leave it up to you what you say." His voice was cold.

"I'll tell them it's all my fault." Her voice was barely audible.

"Whatever."

She took a step closer to him, but he shrank away from her.

"Mark, I know I've already said this . . . but I'm truly sorry," she said, and stifled a small sob.

"Just go away, Faye," he said wearily, and turned back to the window.

A few seconds later he heard the door to the suite click shut and simultaneously closed his eyes. He relaxed slightly, and massaged the tight knot in his throat.

Saturday, June 29
2:40 p.m.

The string quartet was in full flow as Jean and Derek
edged their way along the second row of chairs on the
lawn.

"Oh, look, there's Norma," said Jean, waving at a
woman several rows back wearing someone's sofa covers. "Oooh, that hysterectomy's aged her." She sat
down next to her husband and began to soak up the
ambience of the grand occasion.

At first, Mark had said he and Faye were going to
foot the bill and it would be a simple ceremony at
a London register office, but Jean had almost wept
with frustration. "Darling! First Tony has a city hall

wedding and refuses to let me get involved in any way, and now you're going to do the same. What's a mother to do? Am I never going to get my big day in church?"

A couple of weeks later, Mark had suggested a compromise. He said they'd had a rethink and would like to get married at a château in France. The trouble was, he'd confessed, they couldn't afford it. Jean and Derek had ended up making them a fifteen-thousand-pound wedding gift to fund the occasion.

Still, thought Jean, as she surveyed the scene before her, it's been worth it. The sky was cloudless, and a faint breeze rippled through the great oak tree that dominated the skyline in front of them. At the base of its vast trunk was the raised platform for the string quartet: three women and one man from the nearby village of Grasse.

Around fifty chairs were set out on either side of a gravel path that led back to the château; it had been sprinkled with petals from Faye's favorite champagne rose. The chairs, which were of a rather heavy mahogany and hard-backed, had been transformed into something more summery with white linen covers, each with a champagne rose tucked in to the lacing at the back. Two five-foot pedestals had been placed to either side of the platform, each bearing an impressive arrangement of roses and lilies, and more flowers surrounded the tiny gazebo where the ceremony was to take place. The flowers alone had cost over two thousand pounds.

Jean sighed with contentment at the thought of the fairy-tale wedding at which she was one of the central figures.

"Mark should be down by now," said Derek, tapping the classic Cartier tank watch Jean had bought him for their first anniversary forty-three years ago.

"There's no sign of Brian either," Jean observed. "I knew he'd be a liability as best man. I can't *think* why Mark didn't ask Tony."

"Well, they've never been that close, have they? I mean, Tony had all but left home when little 'un was growing up." Derek craned his neck to see behind him, and waved at Kate and Ted. "Come to mention it, I can't see Tony either . . ."

"Good grief, look at *this*," hissed Jean, pressing her French-manicured nails into Derek's hand.

McLaren, resplendent in a lime-green Lycra plunge-neck minidress, was walking down the central path. Her six-inch metal spiked stilettos kept piercing the petals. Her hair was piled pineapple-style on top of her head, with a lime-green bow wrapped round it. "Wotcha!" she trilled, stopping next to the row where Jean and Derek were sitting. "Are those two seats free?" She extended a lime-green-painted fingernail towards the empty chairs.

"Sorry, Tony will be sitting there," said Jean, with an expression that suggested there was a bad smell under her nose. She couldn't believe the woman's audacity in trying to sit in the section designated for family of the bride and groom.

"Hi, babes." Nat appeared at McLaren's side, took her buttock in his hand and squeezed it so hard that she let out a little squeal. "This where we're sitting?" He took a step forward.

"Nah. Apparently, one of them is saved for Tony." McLaren fixed Jean with a look that suggested she didn't believe her.

"Can't be." Nat jerked his head backwards. "I've just seen him. He's at the back."

"Really?" Puzzled, Jean turned to see. Sure enough, she could see the top of Tony's head, partially obscured by a woman with frizzy hair. "Derek," she said, "go and tell him we're— Oh, I say!"

Nat and McLaren were shoving their way past her towards the empty seats in their row. As she edged past Derek, McLaren stumbled and her ample cleavage lunged towards him.

A smile spread across Derek's face but it withered rapidly when he saw Jean's murderous expression. She shot him a "wait till I get you home" look, stepped out into the aisle and smoothed down her dress. "I'm going to talk to Tony," she snapped, leaving her handbag on the seat to warn off any further intruders.

Tony's showdown with Faye had left him feeling horribly unsettled, and he couldn't stop thinking about it. If it had been business, he would merely have brushed it aside and moved on to the next task. But this was personal, and he was surprised by how much it had disturbed him.

When he saw his mother bearing down on him, he sighed with such velocity that the feathers stirred on a frightful hat just in front of him.

But luck was on his side. Before she could catch his eye, Jean was waylaid at the halfway stage by Derek's brother, Bob, and his rather portly wife, Kay. Kay's ability never to draw breath during conversation was legendary, and Tony could see that his mother was having difficulty getting away. He seized the perfect opportunity to escape.

It was nearing the wedding hour and the guests were clearly starting to wonder what had happened to the groom and his best man, who should have appeared by now. Their absence told Tony that Faye had delivered the bad news, as she'd promised. He just didn't know what she'd said, which made him feel anxious about bumping into his brother. On top of that, he didn't want any awkward questions from his mother, particularly as he felt that his guilt in the wedding's destruction was written all over his face.

He went into the château's cool, dark entrance hall, stood still for a moment and composed himself. Through an open door to one side, he saw the dining room all laid out for the reception. Hearing voices descending from upstairs, he stepped into the room and closed the door behind him.

There were five round tables of ten settings, all exquisitely laid out with crisp white cloths and silvery cutlery for four courses. Each had a central arrangement of champagne rose heads in shallow glass bowls, surrounded by dainty tea-lights in clear candle-holders. Like the seating outside, all the chairs had white linen covers with a long-stemmed champagne rose tucked into the back.

At the far end of the room there was a clear area, presumably assigned as a dance floor, and to one side was a DJ deck with two large speakers. In the far corner a small table with a round silver base on it stood in readiness for the staff to bring out the wedding cake. Thanks to an effusive description from his mother earlier, Tony knew it was three-tiered and decorated with cream roses.

The room felt eerie, but Tony wasn't sure that this was because of its emptiness or the fact that he knew it was all about to go to waste. He also felt a twinge of guilt that so much money had been spent unnecessarily because of his actions.

"Snap out of it," he muttered angrily to himself. After all, if Faye hadn't been unfaithful in the first place, he wouldn't have confronted her and the wedding would now be going ahead. It was her fault, he assured himself. And, besides, most of the costs had been met by his parents and they could well afford it. The loss of a few thousand pounds couldn't compare with the disastrous consequences of Mark marrying a woman who was totally wrong for him.

He stared at a shaft of light that was pouring into the room and remembered the day when he had married Melissa. A typical London wedding, they had tied the knot in a ceremony at the trendy Chelsea Town Hall, then posed on the steps for their small group of guests and a couple of paparazzi, who were interested in the guests for newspaper gossip-column fodder, to take photos. They had held the champagne-and-sushi reception at the achingly hip Light Bar at the St. Martin's Lane Hotel in Covent Garden, and had left at midnight to have a few hours' sleep beore flying to Bali the next morning.

Everyone who was anyone was there, captains of industry on Tony's side, supermodels and magazine editors from Melissa's circle. It was a networking opportunity rather than a family affair, and consequently he had resisted all attempts by his mother to get involved in the organization. He knew Jean had never forgiven him for this.

Melissa had looked stunning in a Valentino gown made specially for her, and pictures from their wedding made just about every gossip page. For a short while, they were quite a golden couple.

But what did it all mean now? Melissa was seeing someone else, and he was living a shallow life consisting mostly of work with the occasional meaningless fling. Was he really one to judge Faye's behavior?

Again, Tony found himself experiencing more than a twinge of guilt about forcing her to call off the wedding. Having met and spent some time with her, he knew now that his family's money hadn't been an issue. But, up to the point of their showdown, he'd remained convinced that it was an unsuitable match.

Now, standing in the lavishly decorated room, he was having serious doubts about his own judgment. Maybe she *would* have made Mark happy, he thought. After all, no guarantees come with marriage—he and Melissa could vouch for that. He gave it a few moments of thought, then shook himself and told himself to snap out of it. Walking to the door, he opened it just in time to see Faye's back as she stepped outside.

Saturday, June 29
2:55 p.m.

As Faye walked past the guests and made her way to the front, the chatter stopped in a wave as each group laid eyes on her. By the time she got there, the silence was deafening.

She was framed by the wedding gazebo, but this was no bride. Still wearing her T-shirt and tracksuit bottoms, her face was devoid of makeup and it was obvious that she'd been crying. Everyone was looking at her, their faces showing disquiet. The tension was broken by someone's coughing fit.

She waited for it to end, then cleared her throat.

"Hello, all," she said. "I'm afraid there's not going to be a wedding." The clarity of Faye's voice surprised even her.

There was a collective gasp from the guests, then silence again. They looked at her expectantly, evidently anxious for a full explanation.

She took a deep breath and tilted her head towards the sky, eyes closed. She knew that whatever she said now would be reported back to all and sundry, so she wanted to choose her words carefully.

Opening her eyes to face them again, she fixed her gaze on a central point halfway down the aisle. "The reason that I'm standing here and not Mark is that it's all my fault. I just can't go through with it . . ." Now she wanted to sprint away and leave it at that. But she knew it wasn't enough: she had to come up with an explanation, however fictitious.

Her train of thought was broken by loud sobbing, and she scanned the crowd. Jean's head was buried in Derek's shoulder, her hat pushed back to an awkward angle, and her shoulders shaking. Derek reached into his jacket pocket and pulled out a handkerchief.

Faye knew that once the initial humiliation had abated, Jean would be fine. She was a tough, resilient woman who had the added bonus of being surrounded by her husband and sons, always there to make sure she was all right. It was her own mother she was more concerned about, and now she searched for her. Typically Alice was sitting in the third row rather than at the front. She didn't seem to be crying, but she looked shocked, with a deathly white pallor.

The sight of her brought a huge knot to Faye's throat. More than anything, she wanted to be in Alice's cozy living room right now, being cuddled, fed chicken soup, and told that everything was going to be fine.

But she knew that to leave now would be a cop-out. She *had* to carry on, if only for Mark. "Mark is a fantastic, wonderful man . . ." she moved her head from left to right to show that she was addressing them all ". . . and it may sound clichéd, but I just don't think I'm good enough for him."

"Hear! hear!" That was Brian, who had sneaked in and was now sitting at the far left-hand side of the front row.

His comment prompted a few mutterings among the crowd, and Faye saw Tony move like lightning from the back row to his side. He whispered animatedly in his ear, clearly admonishing him for interrupting.

Faye composed herself. "He's absolutely right to say that," she said, nodding towards Brian. "I'm sure a lot of you have had reservations about Mark and me getting married, and a few have even expressed them. But we didn't listen. I suppose we thought we loved each other enough for everything to turn out OK in the end."

By now, Jean's sobbing had reached a crescendo. Derek, a comforting arm around his wife's shoulders, was simply staring ahead, stony-faced. Alongside them, Nat was whispering to McLaren. The smirk on his face told Faye he was finding the disaster incredibly amusing, so she decided not to look in his direction again.

"Sadly, it has taken me until today to realize that I just don't have what it would take to make Mark a good wife, to make him as happy as he deserves to be."

She paused, looking at her sneakers and fighting to hold back tears. She knew that crying would look self-pitying, and if there was one person who wasn't going to garner sympathy today, it was she.

"There's a variety of reasons why I feel I'm incapable of it," she continued, "but I'm not going to make any excuses. As I said, there isn't going to be a wedding. But suffice to say, I still love Mark very much."

She finally picked out Adam, sitting alone and partially obscured by her cousin Marion's large hat. She tried to catch his eye, but he was staring into space.

She gestured towards the château. "The reception is all paid for and ready for you. It'll only go to waste if you don't make use of it, so please do." The knot in the back of her throat was now so tight it was difficult to speak. "Please forgive us if we don't join you."

That was it. She couldn't say anymore. She mouthed, "I'm sorry," at Alice, then stepped out of the gazebo towards a small opening in a tall hedge situated to the side. She knew she should probably stay and face the music, but the sight of an escape route proved too much for her and she darted through it into the vast gardens and woods beyond.

The moment she disappeared, it was as if a hand grenade had been thrown into the crowd. The gentle murmuring of a few seconds ago escalated into excited chatter as they reacted to the drama that had just unfolded before them.

Jean was still slumped on her chair. Her hat had fallen off now and was lying on the floor. She was sobbing quietly while Derek stood by, awkward and surplus to requirements. He looked relieved when he caught Tony's eye and gestured wildly for him to come over.

Tony made his way towards his parents, his heart leaden at the sight of the emotional turmoil around him. "Come on, Mum, no one's died." He placed his hand on his mother's shoulder.

"Tony!" she wailed. "What on earth has happened between them? Can't you sort it out?" Her face was red from crying, and the mascara from her left eye had run into the crevices of her cheek.

"It's their business, Mum. We can't get involved." Little do you know, he thought grimly.

Jean blew her nose and rose unsteadily to her feet. "I must go and find Mark. He'll need me, poor thing."

Tony was unsure how Mark was coping, but one thing he did know: he wouldn't want their mother turning up at his room and making matters even worse. "No." He gently pushed her back into her seat. "I doubt he'll want to see any of us right now."

Jean picked up her hat and placed it on an empty chair. "What *can* have happened?" She sniffled. "They seemed fine last night."

Her remark seemed to break Derek out of his trance. "Yes, they seemed very happy," he agreed. "I can only think that something catastrophic has happened for it all to be called off at the last minute like this." He rubbed his temples. "What a bloody waste of money."

His wife scowled at him. "Trust you to think of your wallet at a time like this. It means nothing compared to our little boy's happiness. I can't bear to think of him sitting up there, feeling rejected and alone." She waved towards the château and looked as though she might burst into tears again.

"Now, now," Tony butted in. "We don't want another marriage falling by the wayside, do we? Let's do some straight thinking."

"Fan-bloody-tastic!" Nat edged around them, grinning from ear to ear. "This is better than television!"

"Shut up," muttered Tony, and squeezed his mother's shoulder reassuringly. "If you can't say anything constructive, don't say anything at all."

"What else is there to say?" Nat plowed on. "Bad-tempered, difficult bird meets nice, slightly boring bloke and it all goes pear-shaped. The only surprise is that it got this far."

"Mark is *not* boring," said Jean indignantly. "He's utterly charming and Faye was right—she's not good enough for him!"

Nat was about to say something else, but Tony took his arm. "Mum, you stay here with Dad. I'm going to see if I can find Mark and I'll report back." He walked off, pulling Nat with him.

A few yards away, he broke free from Tony's grip. "Do you mind?"

"Sorry," said Tony. "It's just that I don't think you're the best person to be around my mother right now, and also I wanted to ask you something."

"Oh?"

Tony glanced around him to check that no one was in earshot. "You know last night when I stumbled across you and Faye in that locker room?"

"Yes . . ."

"Well, what was going on?"

Nat looked at him suspiciously. "Why do you want to know?"

"Because if she was doing something she shouldn't have, it will make my brother feel better about the wedding being off." Tony was thinking on his feet.

Nat shrugged. "Much as it grieves me to say it, there was nothing going on. I told her how much I missed her, tried to get to grips with her, and she wasn't having any of it. In fairness to her, she said she'd met Mr. Right and nothing I could say would convince her otherwise." He jerked his head towards the gazebo. "That's why I'm surprised by what just happened."

"And that's it? Nothing else happened?"

"Nope. A lesser man might think he'd lost his touch, but then she was never a pushover . . ." He was distracted by the sight of McLaren teetering back into view after a visit to the ladies'. "Now if you'll excuse me, I have a large pair of breasts that need attending to . . ."

He walked off, leaving Tony to mull over what he'd said. So, Faye had been telling the truth after all, he thought. It didn't alter the fact that her behavior the previous weekend hadn't been quite so exemplary, but he felt another pang of guilt. She really did seem like a decent woman, and perhaps last weekend *had* been out of character.

Swiveling his head from one side of the gathering to the other, he looked for Brian. He was best man, and Tony felt he should come with him to find and support Mark. But there was no sign of him, and it crossed his mind that he hadn't been seen since his outburst during Faye's speech.

He must be upstairs with Mark, he thought, and headed for the château.

Faye peered out of the lift to check that the coast was clear, then sprinted down the corridor. She opened the door, hung the "Do not disturb" sign on the handle, and slammed it behind her.

After delivering her bombshell to the guests, she had run through the gap in the hedge and into a small copse just behind the gazebo. She was far enough away to remain out of sight, but she could hear the loud buzz of chatter as everyone discussed what they'd just witnessed. She had waited there for a few minutes, then picked her way through the trees to a staff door at the rear of the château.

The last thing she wanted was to bump into anyone and face awkward questions. She knew it was only a matter of time before Adam came to find her, but she wasn't sure she could face even him. She just wanted to sink onto the floor, curl up in a ball, and never face the outside world again.

Walking over to the window and using the curtain as a shield, she peered down to the gazebo to witness the devastation she'd just caused.

Some of the guests were standing in small groups, gesticulating wildly as they discussed what had happened. She could see Nat laughing at something McLaren was whispering in his ear, and assumed it was about her. She didn't blame them: if the boot was on the other foot, no doubt she'd be reveling in the drama too.

Then her breath caught in her throat. There, still sitting motionless on the third row, was her mother. She had her back to the château so Faye couldn't see her expression, but she guessed it wouldn't be one of unbridled joy. She felt sick with remorse and wanted to run back down and drag Alice to her room. But Faye knew she couldn't face any probing questions—or the stares.

She was distracted by a knock at the door. Assuming it would be Adam, her panic subsided slightly. *He* could go and get Alice. Whatever happened, she wanted to scoop up her mother and make sure she was kept away from any more drama.

She peered through the spyhole and felt the hair on the back of her neck stand on end. It was Tony. Without thinking, she opened the door. "What the fuck do you want? Haven't you caused enough trouble already?"

He held up his hands in front of him. "I agree I played my part, but may I humbly suggest that your sleeping with a man who wasn't your fiancé had its own destructive qualities?"

Faye stared at him impassively. "I repeat, what do you want?"

"To talk."

"I have absolutely nothing whatsoever to talk to you about," she said icily. "Our business is done."

"A couple of minutes, that's all." He glanced down the corridor. "Inside, please, I don't want anyone to see me here."

Against her better judgment, Faye found herself standing to one side to let him in. "Make it quick," she snapped. "Besides, shouldn't you be checking on the welfare of your brother rather than bothering me?"

"He's gone."

"Gone? Where?" She was genuinely taken aback by this news.

"I don't know. I went to his room and there was no answer. While I was standing there, a maid came up and told me he and Brian had checked out. Their rental car has gone too."

"Oh." Faye didn't know what else to say. She wasn't sure what she'd expected Mark to do, but bolting without talking to his family hadn't been an option.

Closing the door behind him, Tony turned to face her. He looked awkward. "Look, I just wanted to apologize for—"

"Ruining my life?" She looked at him defiantly.

"No, for ruining your wedding day. Particularly as everyone has traipsed out to France for nothing. It kind of hit home to me when I saw you standing in front of them all." He took a deep breath and exhaled in a long sigh.

Faye gave a mirthless laugh. "Is that it?"

Suddenly Tony looked uncomfortable and stared up at the ornately carved ceiling. "No, that's not it. I was wondering . . . um . . . what you said to Mark."

Her eyes widened. "Of *course.*" She banged the side of her head with her fist. "You're not here to inquire about my welfare at all, are you? You just want to know if I dropped you in it with Mark."

For a moment Faye had allowed herself to think that Tony might be feeling some guilt for the chaos unfolding around them. But no, he was simply interested in whether or not *he* was going to emerge from it smelling fishy. She stared angrily at him, but he didn't say any more, clearly waiting for an answer to his previous question.

"If you must know, I didn't tell him about your involvement." She rubbed her eyes, which were sore and tired from crying. "But not because I wanted to protect *you*. I wanted to protect *him* from the fact that the brother he adores is a tosser who couldn't bear to see him happy."

Tony raised an eyebrow. "Tosser I hold my hands up to," he said, "but there's no way you would have made him happy in the long term."

Faye almost contradicted him, but something stopped her. Instead she crossed the room to the sofa and flopped onto it in a gesture of surrender. "Much as it pains me to say it, I think you're probably right," she said. "When I'd told everyone down there, I ran off into the woods and spent a few minutes watching you all from behind a tree."

"And?"

"And I felt like a huge burden had been lifted from me. I was still upset, but that was because I'd had to hurt Mark." She tucked her legs beneath her. "I think I knew it wasn't right a while ago, but I just buried it and hoped the nagging doubt would go away."

"So I did you a favor."

She realized she'd shown too much vulnerability to the man who had ruined everything. "He's broken-hearted, Tony, and who's to say we wouldn't have made a go of it? He was totally devastated when I told him. I felt like I was pulling the wings off a butterfly."

Tony perched on the arm of the chair next to the sofa. "If you don't mind me saying, that analogy says a great deal about why it would never have worked between you."

She ignored his remark. "I still can't get it out of my head that you would want to do that to your own brother."

He looked mildly annoyed. "I told you, and you've just admitted as much yourself, that it saves him from greater unhappiness later."

"And what makes you such an expert on happiness?" she said scornfully.

"Nothing. But I know a lot about *un*happiness."

"Oh?" Then she remembered. "Are you referring to your ex-wife?"

He was silent for some time, his forefinger scraping against a flake of raised skin on his thumb. "Yes, in that I should never have married her in the first place." He straightened the lamp shade beside him, and a small cloud of dust rose into the air.

Faye made no attempt to disguise her confusion. "I know you've split up, but Mark has always said you were besotted with each other in the early days." She paused. "Melissa, isn't it?"

Tony nodded.

"He also said you were devastated when she left."

"I was, of course I was," he said softly. "She was a fantastic, beautiful person . . ."

Faye threw her hands into the air. "OK, you've lost me."

"She was a fantastic, beautiful woman . . . She just wasn't the woman for me." He stopped and stared into space. Then he said, his voice barely audible, "I loved her, but like you'd love a little sister. I felt totally destroyed when she walked out, but I realized later on that a lot of it was self-pity and guilt."

Faye changed position so that she was facing him. "It's natural to feel self-pity under the circumstances," she said reassuringly, "but she was the one who left, so why the guilt?"

He screwed up his face, clearly uncomfortable with the memory. "Because I treated her so appallingly."

Faye said nothing, hoping he'd expand.

"To use your analogy, she was a butterfly and I pulled her wings off." He stood up, walked to the other side of the room and ran his fingers across a wooden jewelry box on the sideboard.

"How?" she prompted him gently.

"Sorry?"

"How did you pull her wings off?"

He ran a hand through his hair. "There are certain personalities that shouldn't be together, and we were the classic example. I fell in love with her because she was fragile and needed looking after. She appealed to my macho instincts, I suppose. But ultimately I ended up belittling her for it. She brought out my worse side."

Faye gave him a small smile. "And you think I'd end up doing the same to Mark?"

"I know you would."

She toyed with the idea of taking issue with him, but felt overcome by the blindingly obvious. "Maybe." She paused. "I *do* love him, though. He's a wonderful person."

Tony nodded. "He is. In many ways he's a far better man than I'll ever be. He certainly wouldn't treat anyone as badly as I treated Melissa."

"Do any of your family know the truth?"

He shook his head. "No. Mainly because I didn't go home much, and when I did I always looked after her." He looked straight at Faye. "Don't get me wrong. It wasn't physical abuse, she wasn't frightened of me or anything like that."

"What was it, then?"

"Emotional abuse, I suppose." He winced. "I went from treating her like a goddess to virtually ignoring her as I threw myself into work. On the rare occasions I gave her any attention—like during visits to parents—she was pitifully grateful." He looked close to tears. "Whenever I think about it now, I feel sick. No one deserves to be treated like that, but particularly not her. I hate myself for it."

"Don't," said Faye. Overwhelmed by Tony's transformation from inquisitor to penitent she couldn't think of anything else to say. She wasn't sure if he'd even heard her.

"I almost willed her to take me to task over my behavior, but she never did," he added, as if conducting a conversation with himself. "And she shouldn't have had to, either. Just because I behaved childishly doesn't mean she should have stooped to that level too—"

He was interrupted by the sound of tapping on the door. Faye leapt up from the sofa and motioned for him to remain quiet. She crept to the door, anxious not to tread on any creaky floorboards, and placed her eye to the peephole. There was more tapping and another minute passed. Eventually, she peered out again to check that the corridor was empty, then walked back to the window and looked out. The guests had all disappeared.

"That was Adam and my mother," she said, keeping her voice low. "I was worried about Mum, because I haven't managed to speak to her since I called the wedding off. But I feel better now I know she's with him."

She went back to the sofa and sat down. "Going back to what you were saying about you and Melissa, Mark and I weren't as bad as that." She took a sip from a glass of water. "But I already recognize *parts* of what you're saying in how Mark and I interact with each other."

He gestured for her to continue.

"For example, if I want my own way over something, then I withdraw affection until I get it."

This time Tony nodded in recognition. "And does Mark always end up apologizing after an argument, even though it's not his fault?"

Faye nodded silently and a tear fell down her cheek. She brushed it away, but he'd seen it. "Faye, don't worry about crying in front of me," he said gently. "I barely know you and already I've worked out you're not the tough cookie you pretend to be." He gave her a rueful smile. "By the way, I shouldn't admit this but as we're being so frank—"

"Admit what?"

"I asked Nat for his version of events over the locker room incident, and it was just like you said."

"Wow. I'm so relieved," she said, with heavy sarcasm.

He sighed heavily. "Now, don't get all tough again. What I'm saying is, knowing that the Nat thing was harmless, and knowing that we didn't actually have sex last weekend, then maybe you're not as unscrupulous as I first thought."

Faye looked at him as if he was one floor short of the penthouse. "What's all this leading to?"

He sighed heavily. "I'm saying that if you can convince me you could make this marriage work, I will go back down there and make everyone return to their places." He paused. "Mind you, finding Mark could be a problem. I've already tried his mobile and it's switched off."

She gave a moment's thought to what he'd said, then shook her head. "No. They've all been told now, so the hard bit is done." She removed a sneaker and scratched her foot. "As I said, I almost feel relieved that I don't have to pretend anymore." She took off the other sneaker and tucked her legs back onto the sofa, then let her hair out of the ponytail. "People always tell you their wedding day was the happiest of their lives, and I kept waiting for that feeling to start. But it didn't . . ." She trailed off. "Last night, when you said I just loved the idea of getting married, well, maybe you were right. Perhaps I was trying to prove something."

"I'm sorry. With hindsight, that was harsh." He bared his teeth in a grimace. "You're an intelligent and beautiful woman and there are a million men out there you could have married if you just wanted to prove something. But you chose Mark, and that's because you have genuine feelings for him." He paused for a couple of beats. "But they're just not strong enough to sustain a marriage . . . in my view, anyway."

Faye was irritated by his arrogance, but decided to let it go. She'd had enough drama for one day. "I doubt I'll ever get married now."

Tony made a face that left her in no doubt he found her statement overdramatic.

"No, seriously. Because I didn't have a dad, I don't think I *need* men in the way they like to be needed." Tony seemed thrown by this apparent non sequitur.

"What I mean is," she continued, "I never had one to lean on as a child, so why start now?"

"It depends what you *don't* need them for," he said. "If you're financially independent, then no secure man would feel threatened by that. But if he felt you *never* leaned on him, I can understand why that would be a problem."

"I lean occasionally, but not very often." She smiled ruefully. "I guess I'm just not the leaning kind."

"Me neither," he said. "Maybe that's where we're both going wrong . . . although in your case, may I humbly suggest you just haven't met the right man yet. Forgive me, but Rich and Nat are hardly ideal specimens, and Mark . . . Well, we've been over that already." He suddenly looked tired. "But there's someone out there for you, believe me."

She was doubtful. "The thought of starting again is so depressing. I don't know if I could be bothered."

"Such defeatism," he tutted.

"Have you had another girlfriend since Melissa?"

"A couple, nothing serious. American women can be a little intense for me." He gave her a quick smile, then his face became serious. "But never mind all that. What are you going to do now? As in today. Do you need my help in tying up any loose ends?"

Her face clouded as she remembered how "helpful" he'd been up to now. "No, I think you've done enough for one day."

He had the grace to look ashamed.

"If you don't mind, I'd like a little time to myself now," she said, "just to get my head round things. I suspect my mother will be back soon."

He inclined his head in a silent bow of agreement, stood up and started to walk towards the door.

"Tony?"

He turned. "Yes?"

"I probably won't see you again, so I'd like to ask you a favor."

His hand was resting on the door handle as he waited for her to carry on.

"Don't tell Mark about what happened in the wine bar that night. I don't want him hurt any more than he already is."

Tony looked at her strangely for a moment, then said, "I give you my word I won't."

Seconds later, he was gone.

Saturday, November 30
10:30 a.m.

❦

"So, there's this newly married couple, right?" Brian swung round in his chair to face Mark.

"Uh-huh." Mark didn't look up from his newspaper.

"And he says he wants to try out a new sexual position . . ."

"Uh-huh."

"Well, she's not sure, so he explains it to her. He says it's the wheelbarrow position, and that all they have to do is put her hands on the floor while he grabs hold of her legs, and—hey presto!" He stood up and made thrusting motions with his groin.

Mark's face wore a pitying expression at his friend's miming abilities.

"And do you know what she said?"

"No, what?"

"She said, 'OK, but promise we won't go past me mum's house!' " Brian fell back into his chair in paroxysms of laughter.

Mark went back to reading the paper.

"Oh, lighten up, for fuck's sake!" said Brian, his grin vanishing. "I honestly don't know what's got into you lately."

"Probably a marriage that failed before it even started, and a distinct lack of any personal life since," he said glumly.

Brian rolled his eyes. "Well, you know what they say, if at first you don't succeed, then skydiving is not for you."

Mark glared at him.

"Look, mate," said Brian, adopting a serious tone, "the near-marriage was nearly six months ago, and as for the lack of personal life, try going without one for as long as Muggins here. The last time I had a shag was the Queen's jubilee. The *silver* one."

"Very funny." Mark gave up on the newspaper, folded it and dropped it on the table beside him. "It's not just that."

Brian looked worried. "There's nothing wrong with you, is there? You know . . . medically?"

"No, nothing like that."

"What, then? If it's work, join the bloody club. I'm so bored of dealing with people's bloody divorces." He shifted in his seat. "I forgot to tell you. The other day, I had to write a letter from a client to her ex-husband, asking him to return a Bruce Springsteen CD that was hers. The cost of writing the letter was greater than the value of the CD, but she's so bitter she can't let anything go." He shook his head in despair. "No wonder I can't be bothered to look for a relationship—I see how most of them end up."

Mark got up and walked into the kitchen. He returned seconds later with a packet of cookies and offered one to Brian.

"I'll admit my job could be better at the moment, but it's not that bad."

"OK," said Brian. "I'm stumped. Work's fine, you haven't got six months to live, and it's not the lack of sex. Why *are* you so fucking miserable?"

Mark crunched a cookie and looked thoughtful. "I just can't get it out of my head that I have made one Grade A fuck-up."

Brian looked baffled. "I do that every day. It's hardly worth fretting over."

"No." He helped himself to another biscuit. "This fuck-up concerns my future."

"So, you put the wrong topping on a pizza, big fucking deal."

Mark scowled. "Not my career, my personal life."

Brian snorted. "Just in case you've forgotten, the French débâcle wasn't your fault. *She* dumped you, so how can it be your fuck-up?"

Mark was staring into space, only half listening. By any yardstick, it had been a rough time since his split from Faye.

The first two months had been the worst, mainly because he'd had to face so many pitying expressions as he told people that, no, the wedding hadn't gone ahead and, if they didn't mind, he'd like to keep the reasons to himself. Once the initial fuss had died down, he had finally been able to give some proper thought to what had happened on that beautifully sunny June day. His conclusion was that, from Faye's point of view, he still wasn't sure. From his, all he knew was that he'd survived it and life was returning to normality, whatever that was.

But something nagged at the back of his mind, something that told him his life would take a more satisfactory turn if he could just work out what was troubling him and act on it.

Suddenly, Mark's mind was whirring with the chemical rush of knowing he was about to do something completely out of character. "What time is it?" he asked.

"Ten-thirty," said Brian, peering at the digital clock on the video machine.

Mark stood up. "Do you know what?"

"Er, what?"

"Instead of sitting around here whining about feeling miserable, I'm going to do something about it."

"Great," said Brian, evidently thinking that his friend had lost his marbles. "Let's be really wacky and go rollerblading in Hyde Park."

His sarcasm was lost on Mark, who was now pacing up and down in front of him. Then he stood stock still. "I can't believe that, of all people, I'm asking *you* this question, but as you're the only one here . . ." He looked directly at Brian to make sure he was concentrating. "If you really, really loved someone and thought you could be happy with them for the rest of your life, but you weren't with them anymore, what would you do?"

"Kill myself?" said Brian hopefully. He scratched his groin. "Do I win ten pounds?"

"Brian! I want some advice."

"Er, never kick a dog turd on a hot day?"

Mark fixed him with a steely glare. "This is serious. Just for once, will you drop the comedy routine?"

"Sorry."

Mark waited to establish that his friend was listening, then continued. "What I want to know is, would you tell them how you feel in the hope that it could get back on track?"

Brian stared at the carpet for a moment. "Yes, I would. I'd figure I had nothing to lose and I'd rather know one way or the other. Even if I got rejected, at least I'd be able to get on with my life."

"That's exactly what *I* think," said Mark, triumphantly. "And that's why I'm going to sort it out this morning, once and for all."

He went to the overcrowded hat rack by the door and grabbed his coat, a heavy-duty jacket that had barely been off his back the past few wintry weeks.

"Mark," Brian looked apprehensive, "just be careful, eh? Remember what happened in France."

Mark didn't answer. With a dismissive wave, he walked out of the door.

Paying the cab driver, he turned to the vast red-brick building and looked up at her first-floor window. The curtains were open. He stared up at it for a few moments, but there was no sign of movement inside and he mentally crossed his fingers that she was in.

On the journey over, Mark had run through several opening gambits, but instinct had told him he should just wing it and speak straight from the heart. After all, as Brian had said, he had nothing to lose. If she agreed to give their relationship another try, he'd be the happiest man on earth. If she rejected him, at least he'd know and could attempt to get on with his life.

He realized now that it had been troubling him for some time, but he'd put it down to other things like money or work. She popped into his head first thing every morning, and when he drifted off to sleep each night, his mind was full of dreams about her. She was definitely unfinished business.

He knew there was every chance she'd knock him back, but he *had* to know.

"Here goes," he muttered, and walked into the entrance hall. He noticed two letters addressed to her lying on the hall table and picked them up. Clutching them in his left hand, he climbed the first flight of stairs and stopped outside the bright-red door with brass numbers that said "45." He wondered what lay behind it: future happiness or . . . He dismissed the alternative, determined to be positive.

Then another doubt crept in. What if someone was there with her? After all, it was the weekend. He felt nauseous at the thought, but there was only one way to find out.

He pressed the bell.

Saturday, November 30
11:20 a.m.

A few seconds later, he heard a door open inside the flat and footsteps clattering on a hard floor. Then he saw her outline through the frosted-glass panel and his heart leapt.

"Who is it?" she shouted.

"It's Mark."

She opened the door immediately, looking startled. "My God, it *is* you. What are you doing here?"

She hadn't said it antagonistically, more in a slightly bemused way and he hung on to this as a good sign. "Are you alone?" he asked.

Her expression changed to one of mild irritation. "Is that any of your business?"

"No, I don't mean it like that," he said quietly. "I merely ask because I want to come in and talk to you."

"About what?" Her body was blocking the door.

"About us."

"Mark, the last time I looked, there was no *us*."

He stood there for a few seconds, unsure what to do or say. The old Mark would have muttered, "Sorry to trouble you," and left, but he was determined to get a definitive answer to his question of whether they had a future together.

"I want to come in," he said firmly.

"Oh, do you?" Her eyes were mocking. Then she was serious. "In that case, you better had." She stepped out of his way. "Go into the kitchen. I'll make coffee."

Ten minutes later, nursing a mug of packet cappuccino, Mark had filled her in on how things were going at work, the welfare of his family, and even commented on how lovely the weather was for the time of year. Anything but what he'd come to talk about. Eventually he ventured into the unknown.

"Kate . . ."

"That's my name, don't wear it out," she quipped.

"I said I wanted to talk to you."

"You did indeed." It was clear she wasn't going to make it easy for him.

"There's no point beating about the bush . . . I've come here because I wanted to suggest that we give things another go."

"Things?" Her voice was hard.

"I mean us," he mumbled.

At first, her expression betrayed nothing. A minute or two passed and neither of them spoke. Then she let out an impatient sigh. "Is that it?"

"Um . . . yes." He felt horribly awkward. "There's not much else to say."

She stood up and pointed towards the door. "Goodbye, Mark."

He stayed where he was. "What did I say?"

"It's more a case of what you *didn't* say." She looked furious now.

"Sorry, you've lost me. I've just said I want us to get back together, and you're reacting like this . . . I don't get it." His forehead creased with worry lines. "Unless, of course, the idea repulses you."

She rubbed the frown furrow between her eyes. "Do you seriously think that after everything that's happened you can just swan in here, say you want us to get back together, and I'm going to fall into your arms?"

He looked suitably humble. "No, of course not. I know we have have a long way to go, but I thought we could at least discuss it."

She sat down and stared at him intently across the table. "Tell me why you want me back."

Mark was thrown by this, but he realized that it was a crucial moment. Whatever he said now would undoubtedly determine what happened next.

"I want you back because you're the best thing that ever happened to me."

She said nothing and he deduced that it would take a lot more than that to convince her.

"I want you back because I haven't stopped thinking about you for the past six months, ever since what happened in France." He let out a small sigh. "Sure, I felt like shit at the time, but I soon saw that most of it was humiliation rather than heartbreak."

Her expression had softened. "Go on."

"I worked out that the misery I felt had nothing to do with the aftermath of the non-wedding, and everything to do with not being with you. When I looked back, it struck me that the moment I saw you step out of that car with Ted I knew I was still in love with you. But I denied it to myself, particularly as we were so far down the line with everything . . . and then *she* called it off anyway."

Kate chewed her lip. "I'd love to believe all this, Mark, but the cynical devil on my shoulder is telling me that you've reinvented history somewhat because you're feeling sorry for yourself and want to get back with me because there's no one else on the horizon."

"Kate, that's so not true," he implored.

She raised a hand to stop him interrupting. "In France, I was desperate for a sign, *any* sign, that you still had feelings for me. But there wasn't one. You just looked like a man desperately in love with his wife-to-be."

"I thought I *was* in love with her at the time," he said miserably. "Afterwards, I realized I wasn't. It was lust, really."

"Very convenient," said Kate, drily.

Mark leaned across the table and took her hand, comforted that she didn't pull away. "Look, I can't rewind to that time, so you *have* to trust me on this. There's nothing like making the biggest mistake of your life—or almost, in my case—to teach you what you really want."

"What was I wearing?" she asked suddenly.

"Sorry?"

"When I got out of the car with Ted, what was I wearing?"

Mark closed his eyes. "You had on a denim jacket, with a blue-and-white polka-dot top underneath that showed a glimpse of your stomach . . . and white jeans with blue-and-white sneakers. Your hair was slightly shorter than it is now, with little curls in the nape of the neck, and you were wearing your favorite perfume, Knowing by Estée Lauder . . . Oh, and you were wearing a necklace I hadn't seen before, with a little heart on it.'

He opened his eyes to see that Kate had tears in hers. "Very good." She smiled.

"And in the evening, you wore a black silk dress with—"

"Yes, yes." She laughed joyfully. "I believe you."

"Good." He squeezed her hand a little tighter.

"But I still don't understand why you didn't say something. I can't tell you how it broke my heart to come to your wedding and pretend how happy I was for you."

He smiled. "You did such a good job of pretending you were happy that I believed you. And, as I said, I didn't work out what I was feeling until afterwards, when all the fuss had died down. I just put it down to nostalgia."

She turned her head away and stared at the stripped-wood floor. "I came to find you, you know, but you'd gone."

He looked sheepish. "I just couldn't face anyone . . . I couldn't bear the inevitable questions, particularly from Mum and Dad, so I took the coward's way out and left immediately."

She nodded to indicate that she understood. "Have you seen her since?"

"Nope. She called me a couple of times in the following month, probably through guilt." He took a sip of his coffee, which had gone tepid. "She left a message on my mobile asking if I was OK, but I didn't bother calling back. I didn't need her concern. All I could think about was calling you, but I was convinced you wouldn't want to hear from me."

They sat quietly for a few moments, the only sound that of a pigeon cooing outside the window. Mark was acutely aware of how content he felt, just sitting with her, saying nothing. Then a thought struck him and he stiffened. "Are you still with Ted?" He managed to sound matter-of-fact, but inside he felt uncomfortably apprehensive.

She looked at him curiously. "You don't know, do you?"

"Know what?" His mind raced with possibilities. Perhaps they'd secretly got married. Perhaps he'd died.

"Ted's gay," she said, with a grin. "He just came to the wedding as a favor, so I could pretend he was my boyfriend. There was no way I was going to watch you marry someone else while I looked like a sad singleton."

Mark burst out laughing, more from relief than anything else. "I didn't have a bloody clue!" he spluttered. "And I was so jealous of him!"

"I thought Tony would have told you by now."

"Tony?" She nodded.

He looked baffled. "Yes, he knew. We had a long chat at the wedding, and I told him then, but asked him not to say anything."

"Well, to his credit, he didn't," said Mark. He thought about it some more and smiled. "He's always been a secretive sod."

"He'd say discreet."

Now that things were more friendly between them, Mark felt himself relax a little. Then Kate withdrew her hand and he tensed again.

"There's no one serious in my life," she said, putting both hands round her coffee cup. "There hasn't been since you and I split up. But that doesn't mean I'm going to walk straight back into this." She pointed at him.

Getting up, she put her mug into the sink and turned to face him, leaning against the drain board. "Mark, do you have *any* idea how much you hurt me when you left here to go and live with Brian?"

He shook his head slowly. "I'm so sorry. I was a complete idiot." He didn't know what else to say.

"I'm not sure I can trust you not to hurt me again," she said quietly.

Instinctively, he stood up and took two steps towards her. Grabbing both her hands, he looked her straight in the eye. "Kate, I *swear* I will never, ever hurt you again."

"There's no guarantee of that."

"Maybe not, but as close as dammit. I'm a different person now. That whole France business made me grow up rather rapidly."

She said nothing.

"Being jilted on your wedding day has to be one of the most humiliating experiences of life, but you know what? I'm glad it happened, because it made me realize what I want in life . . . and that's you."

She was openly crying now, though silently. "I don't know, Mark, I—"

"*Please* give me another chance. Then, say in a month or two, if you still think you'll never be able to trust me again, I'll take no for an answer. I promise." He placed his hand on his heart.

"I'll do you a deal."

"Anything," he said, sensing a chink in her armor.

"Let's take it a day at a time, and I reserve my right to drop you at a moment's notice if I think it's not going to work." She pulled one of her hands out of his and gave him a warning tap in the middle of the chest. "The ball is very much in my court, you owe me that."

"I certainly do," he grinned.

"Good," she said. "In that case, we'll start with dinner this week, and take it slowly from there."

Suddenly, he was serious. "I promise you won't regret this, Kate."

"Hmm, we'll see. As I said, you're on probation."

"Oh, and one other thing . . ." He tightened his hold on her hands.

"What? Don't push it . . ."

"Do I have to wait until next week to snog your face off?"

She burst out laughing, wrapped her arms around his neck and pulled him closer. "I thought you'd never bloody ask."

Saturday, December 7
11 a.m.

❧

"If I bend my leg any more it's going to bloody snap in half," muttered Faye.

She was lying on a cold concrete floor with a twenty-five-year-old male model sprawled across her. One of her legs was outstretched, the other curled round him.

"Well, frankly, you look a bit deformed at the moment, dear. So either bend it round a bit more, or move it further down his thigh." Adam was standing about three feet away, his head cocked to one side as he surveyed the scene.

"And wouldn't the budget stretch to a carpet?" she whined. "This floor is arse-clenchingly cold."

Adam looked at the male model. "Women! I'm getting such déjà-moo here."

"Sorry?" The young lad looked confused.

"Déjà-moo. The feeling that you've heard all this bullshit before." He turned to Faye. "Darling, the theme of the shoot is concrete chic. A bit of shag pile would just ruin the effect."

"Whatever you say, Mr. Stylist." She gave him a fake smile. "But could I just make an impassioned plea that we get this over with before I lose the use of my legs altogether?"

"Oh, I don't know. I'm quite enjoying myself," said the male model, peering down the front of her gray gypsy top. It was the longest and most lucid sentence he'd uttered in the past two hours.

"Really?" Faye looked at him disparagingly. "Well, while we're having these intimate moments together, may I humbly request that if we ever work together again, you forgo the particularly strong pickled onion you've just enjoyed with your plowman's lunch? It's making me want to heave."

Adam tapped his watch. "Come on, come on. The quicker we get these next few shots out of the way, the quicker we can all bugger off home."

The shot was for *Couture*, where Adam was now the *senior* stylist after seeing off the aging stick insect who'd been doing it for ten years previously. She'd hung on for as long as she could, but when she'd suggested something last-season as a fashion idea, the owner had decided it was time to get rid of her. Of course Adam had doctored the story somewhat and had told everyone it was because she'd suggested a feature on support tights.

Immediately after the French farrago, Faye had returned home and wallowed in self-pity. Despite Adam's overtures, she had flatly refused to leave her home on anything other than work assignments, and had lost herself in the twilight world of takeout and late-night television. Consequently, she put on about ten pounds.

Then, almost a month after it had started, she had banished the self-pity and adopted a whole new lifestyle in a bid to shed the excess weight and dig herself out of the emotional trough. She'd started attending evening yoga classes three times a week, which mellowed her to the extent that she found it a lot easier to get to sleep at night. She still treated herself to junk food every so often, but for the most part she was making a concerted effort to eat sensibly. After reading a magazine article about healthy cooking, she'd gone straight out and bought a juicer and a steamer, and they were now a daily part of her life. She still couldn't get used to drinking two liters of water a day, but forced herself to do it. Within weeks, her complexion was glowing and her usually fine hair seemed thicker and shinier.

Luckily for her, her new regime had coincided with the demise of the extra-thin model, seen off after a particularly ferocious newspaper campaign that had castigated it as a poor example to impressionable teenagers. The healthy, sun-kissed look was back in, and Faye found herself in great demand, specifically by Adam and the trend-leading *Couture*.

After she had appeared on the magazine's cover, an article in the *Daily Mail* singled her out as a positive role model for the nation's young, and her profile went through the roof. Invitations to the latest film première or club opening poured into her agency, but for the most part she stayed away. If there was a specific reason to go—to help out a favorite charity, perhaps—she put on her best bib and tucker and turned out. But if it was just the social merry-go-round, Faye preferred not to get on board. She'd crossed her boredom threshold on the showbiz circuit years ago.

"It's the same people every single time," she said to Adam, on one recent, rare occasion when they'd attended a restaurant opening. They were squashed together in a corner, clutching neon-blue cocktails and peering into the gloom as the latest It girl air-kissed her way round the room. "I mean, look at her. Doesn't she have anything else to do with her life?"

"They're probably saying the same about us," Adam had retorted.

He was still quite partial to high-profile parties, mainly because he hoped he might meet Mr. Right there, or at least Mr. Will Do for Tonight. He wanted Faye to be his permanent party buddy; he liked her company and he also knew she could look after herself if he suddenly met Mr. WDFT, unlike some of his other friends who were like a sack of potatoes round his neck at such glittering functions. But it took all his persuasive powers to drag her out.

Tonight, post-shoot, Adam wanted her to attend the launch of a new boy band's début single, but she was having none of it. As she changed out of her concrete chic and back into a sweatshirt and cord jeans, he pushed back the cubicle curtain. "If you really loved me, you'd come." He pouted.

"Well, that answers the question, doesn't it?" she said, fastening her fly button.

He jutted out his bottom lip, so that he resembled a small child. "I might find a new man and you should want to see me happy."

"I do, darling, but you're just as capable of finding one of your own. It'll be full of people you know anyway."

"Not the same," he said, in a toddler voice, and stamped his cork-soled sandal on the floor.

"Sorry, I'm not changing my mind."

"So selfish . . ." he muttered, and bent down to pick up a belt that had fallen on to the floor.

Faye was brushing her hair while simultaneously ramming her feet into a pair of slip-on sneakers with no backs. "I've got a late lunch with Mum in a minute, but I'll be home by five, so give me a call and we'll go through our usual rigmarole of you deciding what to wear."

"Will do." Adam turned as he heard footsteps approaching them. It was Troy, the male model.

"Um, hi," he said, looking straight at Faye.

"Yes, hi. I haven't seen you since . . . oooh, two minutes ago."

"Listen, I was wondering if you fancied getting a drink with me?" He shuffled from one foot to another, but looked gorgeous nonetheless.

Faye tutted to feign disappointment, then said, "Sorry, I can't. I'm meeting my mother for lunch." She picked up her handbag and threw it over her shoulder.

He seemed unperturbed. "How about another time, then?"

She gave him a quick smile. "Thanks, but I don't think so. Let's just keep things professional, shall we?"

Adam had remained uncharacteristically silent throughout this little exchange, but suddenly saw his chance. "I'm free right now if you fancy a drink." He gave him one of his sincere smiles.

Troy's lip curled in distaste. "No, thanks. I'm straight."

"A drink, I said, not a shag!" Adam retorted, to his retreating back. "Bloody hell, models are so fucking arrogant."

"Yes, darling. I'm sure you've changed and were only interested in his fascinating conversational skills." Faye punched his shoulder playfully.

"Talking of change," he said, in a singsong voice, "get you."

"What?"

"Turning down Troy-boy there. In the old days, you'd have used him as a rather cute time-waster until someone better came along."

She smiled "True, but I'm a new woman. I'm kinda happy with my own company, these days. Besides, dating one male model is quite enough grief in a girl's life."

"Dear, dear Nat," said Adam, in mock-Shakespearean tones. "I had him in on a shoot last week, but thought better of booking you at the same time."

She smiled fondly. "How is the old rogue?"

"Looking a bit frayed at the edges, actually. It must be all the partying he does."

"Is he still with McLaren?" she asked, out of nosiness rather than real interest.

"Nah, he says he hit the buffers shortly after you-know-what." This was the phrase Adam used now to refer to the wedding, mainly because Faye had banned any mention of it. "He's going out with some up-and-coming It girl."

Faye yawned dramatically. "It exhausts me even to think about it." She glanced at her watch. "Must go, I'm late."

Adam gave her a hug. "Speak to you later. If you change your mind about coming along, let me know."

"I won't. Unlike *some*, I'm way past the boy-band thing."

Alice, as usual, was early. She'd already read the complimentary copy of the *Evening Standard* by the time Faye arrived at the small café in a Covent Garden side street.

"Hello, love." She pointed to the glass in front of her. "I've already ordered your champagne. I hope that's OK."

"Great, thanks." Only Mum could look for reassurance over ordering a glass of champagne, Faye thought.

But Alice's nervousness no longer irritated her. In fact, since her leveling—not to mention humbling—experience in France, Faye had been making a concerted effort to understand her mother, to figure out what made her tick.

Modeling assignments allowing, it had become their routine to meet for lunch every Saturday, and they invariably chose the same café where the accommodating staff always found them a table without needing to book.

Here, the simple act of spending a little more time together had led to them speaking far more freely to each other.

"You know," said Faye, tapping her glass against her mother's cranberry juice, "I've been looking forward to this all week."

"Does that surprise you?" said Alice quietly.

She shook her head. "I didn't mean it like that. It's just that we seem so much easier with each other these days. Something has settled down between us."

Alice looked at her daughter affectionately. "That, if you don't mind me saying so, is because you've changed so much."

"Have I?" She was surprised. "In what way?"

Sipping her juice, Alice narrowed her eyes in thought. "It's difficult to put my finger on it, but you seem to have calmed down a lot. You're not as hard as you were . . ." She paused. "You don't seem to have as much to prove."

Faye considered this for a few moments then nodded in agreement. "That's probably true. There's nothing like a major embarrassment to bring you down to earth with a crash."

"Did you feel embarrassed by what happened?" asked Alice, breaking off a piece of her bread roll.

"What? Dozens of guests schlepping over to France and gathering on the lawn to see me get married, only to be told the wedding was off?" Faye took a gulp of champagne at the mere thought of it. "Yes, it was pretty embarrassing."

When the wedding had been canceled so suddenly, Alice's main concern as a mother had been to check that her daughter was all right. When she had eventually tracked her down in the château, Faye had assured her she was fine. She hadn't elaborated further and, unassuming as ever, Alice hadn't asked. Instead, she had kept a close, motherly eye on her daughter over the next few months, biding her time until the moment felt right to ask more.

That time was now.

She coughed. "So . . . why *did* you . . . call it off, then?"

Faye pursed her lips and thought for a moment. She knew she could fudge the issue by saying she had just panicked and bottled out, but she decided to give her mother a watered-down version of the truth. She propped her elbows on the table. "Because the weekend before the wedding I met a man in a wine bar and found myself very attracted to him. I *didn't* actually do anything, but I wanted to."

"So?"

"So . . . I figured that if I was ogling other men just a week before my wedding . . ." Faye looked at her questioningly.

"Darling, it tells you that you're normal," said Alice. "The important thing to remember is that you *didn't* do anything, presumably because your feelings for Mark stopped you."

It crossed Faye's mind fleetingly to tell her mother everything, but something stopped her. "I know what you're saying, but there's more to it than that," she said vaguely. "I suppose it just made me face up to what I'd been burying for a while . . ."

"Which was?"

"That I was marrying Mark because I wanted to prove to everyone that I could sustain a relationship."

"Everyone?"

"Well, myself, I suppose. I was always acutely aware that certain people thought I was this selfish, high-maintenance woman who put her own feelings before anyone else's . . ." she stared at the far wall ". . . which was true, to some extent."

"What certain people?"

"Oh, just people in the trade, really, no one you know."

Alice looked disbelieving. "I know I'm one of life's worriers, but you never struck me as someone who would fret about what people think of you."

"I did, but not anymore. After all the commotion, I did a lot of thinking and realized it's only the opinion of people you care about that matters. Everyone else can go to hell." She held her glass aloft to toast what she'd just said.

"Hear! hear! Want to know what I think?" said Alice, raising her glass too.

"Of course."

"I think you did absolutely the right thing. Mark was a lovely boy, but not right for you."

Faye raised her eyebrows. "Why didn't you say anything?"

Alice laughed. "And you would have taken notice, would you? I don't think so."

"You're probably right. Adam said it, Mark's friend Brian wasn't keen, and even Mark's brother made it clear in no uncertain terms that he thought it had 'disaster' written all over it." She paused, almost imperceptibly, as she thought about the showdown with Tony. "He told me he was against it not long after he met me for the first time."

Alice gestured to the waiter for another drink. "He touched on the subject with me on the Saturday morning over breakfast."

"Oh?" Faye turned pale. "What did he say?"

"Not much, except that he thought you were an odd couple. He asked me my opinion, but I was diplomatic because I didn't know him." She wasn't lying: she just didn't realize *quite* how much she'd revealed to Tony over their shared breakfast.

Faye waved her hand dismissively. "Anyway, thankfully it's all in the past now. Onwards and upwards, as they say."

"Indeed," agreed Alice. "So, tell me to mind my own business if you like, but is there anyone new on the horizon?"

"No, not really. I've been on a couple of first dates, but realized they weren't going to be a permanent fixture so knocked it on the head." She stopped talking as the waiter placed Alice's drink on the table. "I'm much happier with my own company, these days, and I don't feel the need to fill my time with people who don't mean anything to me."

"Gosh." Alice looked impressed. "You really have grown up."

"Oh, I still have my moments, believe me. I'm not an easy person to have a relationship with—but, then, you know that." She looked out of the window on to the street. It was packed with people, some strolling, some rushing along self-importantly with mobile phones pressed to their ears. A fresh glass of champagne had arrived at the table, and Faye took a sip. It tasted delicious, and suddenly she was overwhelmed by a feeling of contentment, sitting here with her mother, watching the world go by.

"I'm so sorry, Mum." The words just slipped out.

Alice looked taken aback. "For what?"

"For being a cow to you so many times, and for putting you through that wedding business. I really don't know how you put up with me."

Alice pushed her salad around her plate, blinking rapidly as if she was trying to hold back tears. "You were never a cow, darling, just a little demanding sometimes. And as for me putting up with you, well, I should have disciplined you much more from an early age, but I couldn't bear to."

"Did motherly love get in the way?" smiled Faye.

"No. It was more that I had such a miserable childhood myself." Her mother's voice wobbled. "I was determined you weren't going to endure the same. Trouble is, I went too far the other way and let you get away with murder. That's not good for a child either."

Faye knew Alice's childhood had been less than idyllic, but although she'd touched on the subject a couple of times before, they'd never talked about it in depth. If she was honest, Faye, hadn't been that interested because she wasn't the subject. But now she was keen to know more.

"How was it miserable?" she said quietly, stealing one of Alice's french fries and dunking it in a ramekin of mayonnaise.

Alice pulled a "now you've asked" expression. "Oh, mainly because my mother and sister left me in no doubt that they found me irrelevant and irritating. I spent most of my childhood feeling like I was in the way."

"God, no wonder you went for the first man who showed an interest in you," said Faye. That was all she knew about her father.

"Yes," said Alice. "There was an element of that in it. I'd never really been shown any love before, so David bowled me over . . ." She stared at her plate. "I was besotted by him. Of course, I now know it had nothing to do with love. It was just sex, as far as he was concerned."

Faye rolled her eyes. "Oh, don't worry, you don't hold exclusivity on that scenario. But it's a little easier on the soul to have meaningless sex these days."

Her mother shrugged. "That was half the trouble, though. It wasn't meaningless to me, just him. To me, it was the best thing that had ever happened. I was finally the center of someone's attention, albeit fleetingly."

Faye lit a cigarette, ignoring Alice's disapproving look. "So, did you just . . . you know . . . have sex once?' She could hardly believe she was discussing sex with her mother.

"A few times." She popped a chip into her mouth. "Well, for as long as it took me to realize I was pregnant anyway."

"How did he react when you told him?"

"He didn't say much at all, really, which I took to mean he was OK about it. We slept together that night, then he got up to leave and said he'd call me the next day. I never heard from him again." Alice leveled the sugar bowl with her teaspoon.

"What, never?" She had asked her mother the question before, but she still didn't quite believe the answer. "Not even a message through friends?"

"No. Nothing. Someone once gave me a forwarding address for him in Portsmouth, and I wrote to him a few times there, but I never received a reply."

"So, when you realized he'd disappeared, did you contemplate getting rid of it?"

"Getting rid of *you*, you mean?" said Alice softly. "No, not for a second. I knew that I had someone I could pour all my love into, someone who was all mine and no one could tell me what to do." She leaned across the table and took her daughter's hand. "You were the making of me."

"But it must have been difficult for you, bringing up a child alone in those days."

"We did have electricity, you know," said Alice, mockingly.

"You know what I mean."

"It wasn't easy, that's for sure, but the rewards far outweighed the drawbacks. As I said, you transformed my life. I finally had someone who needed me."

"And still needs you." Faye withdrew her hand and sat back in her chair. "On behalf of Faye Parker, former selfish little madam of this parish, may I thank you profusely for all you've done for me." She clinked her glass against her mother's.

While Alice perused the dessert menu, Faye stared out of the window again at the Saturday-afternoon shoppers. It was at times like this that she felt totally insignificant. Until recently it had bothered her: she would have wanted to run outside and make them all take notice of her. Now she relished being freed from the constraints of social expectation.

So *what* if she wasn't at the latest première or wearing the new collection from Gucci? Was her life going to fall apart? Since France she'd grasped that if she wasn't happy in herself, the latest Jimmy Choo or Alexander McQueen creation wouldn't change anything.

Alice's voice cut through her thoughts. "Do you ever think about him?"

"Who?" Faye was puzzled.

"Your father."

"No, never."

"You've never thought about trying to trace him?"

"No. What on earth would be the point?" She lit another cigarette.

"Well, curiosity I suppose. If you think about it, there's half of you biologically that you know absolutely nothing about."

"I've never thought of it like that." Faye took a drag of her cigarette. "I suppose if I needed a life-saving bone-marrow transplant, I'd try to find him. But apart from that, I have no desire to do so. He's never been part of my life."

Alice stared at her for a few seconds, her brow furrowed. "Would you like me to tell you a bit more about him?"

"We talked about him before, and you said all you knew was that he was twenty-three, tall with blond hair and blue eyes, and that his family came from outside Reading."

"There's a bit more to it than that."

"Go on, then."

For the next half-hour, Faye sipped her coffee and smoked while Alice talked her through the brief relationship that spawned her. She described her father as handsome and charming, someone who could light up a room with his presence. It was abundantly clear that she still couldn't believe such an interesting, vivacious man could be interested in the little church mouse she had been. "I was not the type of girl he would have taken home or made a future with. I was far too ordinary," she murmured. "I was probably one of several quiet ones whose life he lit up briefly before moving on."

"Don't do yourself down, Mum. I'm sure it wasn't like that at all," said Faye, not masking her disapproval.

"Oh, I can assure you it was. I stopped kidding myself about that years ago." She looked straight at her daughter. "The weird thing is, they talk about nurture rather than nature, but you are so like him. It's uncanny."

"In looks?" There was no denying that Faye didn't resemble Alice, and she'd always assumed her looks came from her father.

"You certainly look like him, but I meant your personality too. He was gregarious like you, very take me or leave me." He wouldn't take any nonsense from anyone. In a way, it's a shame you don't know him, I'm sure you'd get on well."

"Hmm." Faye was doubtful. "We'll never know, because I'm not looking for him. It crossed my mind recently that if I had a relationship with my father it might stop me being so difficult with men, but then I realized there was too much ground to make up. Instead I decided to embark on a little self-therapy and instigate the change myself." She waved at the waiter to bring the bill.

"So what are you up to tonight?" said Alice, picking up one of her gloves from the floor.

"Absolutely nothing, my favorite pastime." In the old days, I would have felt I was missing out if I wasn't at the latest party. Now I couldn't care less."

"But you won't meet Mr. Right sitting at home," said Alice.

"True, but it's not the be-all and end-all, is it? If I meet someone, then great, if not, so what?" She grinned.

They parted company with a hug, and Faye watched Alice walk off towards the bus stop on the Strand. It struck her that although her mother seemed happy with her life, it *wasn't* what Faye wanted for herself—despite her own claim to be happy sitting home alone at night.

To her, the ideal was to have a child or children in a loving relationship with a man who was your equal, one who could help you take the strain occasionally. She knew there were no guarantees, but since her near miss with Mark, she felt better equipped than ever to make the right choice.

Friday, July 18
8 p.m.

✣

"Hmm, that smells good." Derek leaned forward and dipped a teaspoon into the saucepan.

With a mock scowl, Jean watched as he tasted her homemade Bolognese sauce. "Is it up to my usual standard?" she inquired.

"Of course." He planted a peck on her cheek. "And may I also say that you look rather beautiful tonight?"

"Oh, nonsense." She blushed, clearly delighted by his remark. Taking off her apron, she smoothed down her skirt, then glanced at the kitchen clock. "They'll be here in a minute." She let out a long sigh of contentment. "You know what, darling? I have a good feeling about tonight."

Derek tutted. "Now don't start all that again. Let's just have a pleasant evening without any pressure about you-know-what."

"A mother can dream." She pouted, and dried her hands on a tea towel that had been hanging over the Aga rail.

"Yes," he said, ominously, "but sometimes that dream can turn into a nightmare, as we know to our immense cost."

Jean raised her eyes to the ceiling. "Oh, God, you're not going on about that fifteen thousand pounds again, are you? I refuse to listen." She put her hands over her ears and started humming loudly.

Derek grabbed one of her wrists and pulled her hand down. "Oh, go on. Please listen."

"Absolutely not," she said firmly. "That was then, this is now. And I don't want *anything* to spoil this evening." Hearing the crunch of car tires on the gravel, she turned to look out of the latticed window. "They're here, so that's enough of your negative nonsense!" A car door slammed and, seconds later, Mark burst in through the backdoor. "Hi, folks!" He had a deep suntan and was grinning from ear to ear. Dropping two overnight bags on the floor, he enveloped his mother in a bear hug.

"You look so well, darling!" said Jean. "Good holiday?" Her face glowed with pleasure at the sight of her younger son.

"Fantastic, thanks." Mark brushed his hair off his face. "We did absolutely nothing for the first week, then rested for the second."

Jean took a step back to study him more closely. After a few seconds, she looked over his shoulder. "So where is she, then?"

"Just popped into the loo." He grimaced. "It was a long journey."

The sound of flushing could be heard down the hallway, followed by rapid footsteps. Kate walked into the kitchen, her mid-brown hair streaked dark blond by the sun.

"Hi!" She walked across to Jean and kissed her warmly on both cheeks, then repeated the process with Derek.

"You look utterly gorgeous, darling," enthused Jean, admiring Kate's clinging black dress.

"Yes, she dresses to kill and cooks the same way." Mark grinned.

Kate punched him playfully. "Talking of cooking, something smells good."

Jean went to the Aga and gave the sauce a final stir. "It's Mark's favorite."

"Baked beans on toast?" said Kate, straight-faced. "Because that's all he ever cooks for me at home. It's only paying customers who get the benefit of his culinary skills." She reached over and tweaked his cheek.

"Ah, yes," said Derek, looking at his son. "I was going to ask you, how *is* the restaurant going?"

Mark was thrilled that his father had brought up the subject first, rather than him. It was a major breakthrough in that he had accepted his younger son was never going to get "a proper job."

He gave Derek a thumbs-up. "Good, so far. But if you don't mind, I'll give the full update over dinner when Tony's here. That way, I don't have to go through it twice."

Derek glanced at his watch. "He should be here at any moment. He called from the car about twenty minutes ago. Glass of wine, anyone?"

Five minutes later, they were all standing in the middle of the room, with glasses of a particularly fine Chablis *premier cru* that Derek had been keeping for a special occasion.

"Lovely to see you both." Jean smiled. "I can't *tell* you how pleased I am that you're back together."

Mark looked at Kate, and they both laughed. "We know, Mum, you told us that at Christmas, and all the visits since then."

"Try being me," muttered Derek. "I hear it a hundred times a day."

A horn sounded outside. "Aha, it's big bruv," said Mark.

Tony burst in through the door looking unusually flustered. "Sorry, the traffic was murderous. Have I kept you all waiting?" He kissed Jean and slapped Derek's shoulder.

"No, we haven't been here long," said Mark.

Tony gave him a hug, then walked across the kitchen to give Kate a loud smacker. "How's my favorite girlfriend-in-law?"

"You mean your *only* one." She laughed, blushing. "I'm just dandy, thank you for asking."

"Dinner's ready!" trilled Jean and lifted the pan from the hob. "Go and sit yourselves down."

They trooped through to the dining room where Jean had laid the table as if it were Christmas. Two vast silver candelabra dominated each end of the table, which had been covered in a Stuart tartan cloth with matching napkins, and the best china was on full display. Keeping up appearances was important to Jean. Until he'd gone to college, Mark had never seen a milk carton on the table, always a Wedgwood china jug.

"This looks wonderful . . . as usual," said Tony, loosening his tie and taking the seat next to his father's usual place at the head of the table.

"Oh, it's nothing special," said Jean. It was so rare to have both her boys at home that she had wanted to make it a memorable evening. "It may look grand, but it's rather thrown together actually."

She began to serve the spaghetti and pour over the sauce. "So, darling, have you got over the shock of being back in the UK yet?"

"Ask me again in the winter," said Tony, taking a swig of his wine, "but it's nice to get a decent pint again."

"It sounds like the traffic's driving you mad, though," said his father. Like most middle-aged men, Derek could talk for hours on the intricacies of any car journey.

Tony had moved back to London the previous month. His

company, Jam, had wanted him to head up its New York division, but he was adamant that he should return home. Rather than lose him to a rival, they had created a powerful new role for him in London.

He'd been anxious to return for some time, but since the non-wedding in France he'd found himself unable to settle back into his work routine in New York, let alone any semblance of social life. He had kidded himself that he was worried about Mark and how he was coping in the aftermath, but in fact he was tired of the ruthless commercialism of corporate America and needed an excuse to give it up.

To Tony, just throwing up his hands and admitting he didn't want to do it anymore would have seemed weakness. He'd learned many lessons in the past few months, but he was still working on being able to show vulnerability.

The relocation negotiations had taken a few months and then he'd had to wait for his New York replacement to bed in. By June, he had been on his way to his new flat in Mayfair, one of London's most exclusive areas. A penthouse, it occupied the entire top floor of a newly constructed building with floor-to-ceiling windows, underfloor heating, and an integral stereo system in every room.

Tony had little or no interest in interior design, so he'd employed a specialist to furnish the flat from scratch in time for his arrival. She'd done a good job, equipping the place with state-of-the-art lighting, modern paintings, and lots of stone-colored suede furniture with dark gray throws and rugs. It was masculine but warm.

He hadn't established much of a social life yet, but felt good to be back—not least because he could spend some time with his family. When he was younger, he couldn't wait to get away from home and stretch his legs in the world, but now he had mellowed a little and enjoyed being with them.

On his return, one of the first projects he'd set in motion was a business idea he'd been mulling over for some time: to invest in a restaurant with Mark. In other words, Tony would put up the capital, and Mark would do all the hard work. He had probably made the offer partly through guilt, but he rapidly dismissed the thought, telling himself it was merely a shrewd business decision.

Looking across the table at Mark now, he'd never seen him look so content. The business was up and running, and it clearly suited him to be his own boss. So did being back with Kate.

Mark caught his eye. "I know what you're thinking." He smiled.

"You do?"

"Yes, you're thinking, How are Mark's profit margins?"

"Er, something like that." Tony blew out cigarette smoke. He had resumed the habit full-time since returning from health-obsessed New York.

"Well, the good news is that they're great." Mark stood up and adjusted the position of his chair.

"And the bad news?"

Mark looked puzzled by his brother's pessimism. "There isn't any. The place is pretty much packed out every night, and I've now installed another chef so I can take the occasional night off—and the well-deserved holiday I've just had."

"Good." Tony nodded. "But don't take your eye off the ball too much. Staff will always take the piss when the boss is away." Even now, he couldn't resist preaching to his brother.

"They're very loyal, and they won't take the piss," said Mark, firmly.

"Mark!" admonished Jean. "Don't swear!" She was too intimidated by Tony to chastise him, but she'd never had any such inhibitions with her younger son.

Mark ignored her and gave Kate a small smile. "Now we've got the business bit out of the way, I think it's time, don't you?"

Kate's eyes were shining.

"Listen up, everyone." Mark knocked on the table. "We've got some news." He leant over and clasped Kate's hand.

Jean glanced at Derek. "Oooh, what is it?"

"Well . . ." Mark paused for a few beats ". . . we've decided to get married!"

For a couple of seconds, the only sound was the grandfather clock ticking in the corner, then chaos erupted.

"Darlings! I knew it!" Jean leapt up and enveloped Mark in a hug. "I said to your father I had a good feeling about tonight, didn't I, dear?"

"You did indeed." Derek kissed Kate. "Congratulations! That's fantastic news." He paused. "And what's even better is that it spares me having to listen to Jean going on about it all the time."

Tony stood back and let his parents enjoy the moment, then once the initial buzz had subsided, he walked round the table and hugged Mark and Kate. "Congratulations to both of you," he said. "I can't think of two people better suited."

They all sat down again, except Derek, who left the room, returning with a bottle of Laurent Perrier rosé champagne and five flutes. The cork popped and ricocheted off an oil painting of Jean's grandfather, Albert, looking particularly stern and statesmanlike.

"So," Derek started pouring, "let me guess. You're going to sneak away to some far-flung desert island, get married, then come back and tell us all about it."

Mark and Kate looked at each other. "Well, it crossed our minds to do that," she said.

Jean looked as if she'd just been told the family puppy had been run over.

"But," Kate continued, "we decided that because Jean had been deprived of a big wedding in France, we might as well push the boat out and go the whole hog in England. Big hair, big gowns, big church number. Late September, we thought."

It took a couple of seconds for it to sink in, then Jean's face lit up. "Seriously?"

Mark nodded. "Yes, Mum, and we'd like you to grant us the honor of being our wedding planner."

"Oh, God." Derek slapped a palm against his forehead. "You have just sentenced me to the next three months of napkin and place-card purgatory." He groaned. "That's it, I'm booking a long golfing holiday."

Mark turned to Tony. "And as we've decided to go the more traditional route this time, I'd like you to be my best man."

His brother looked taken aback. "Are you sure? What about Brian?"

"I've already spoken to him and he's fine about it. He says it's not really his thing anyway. He'd rather just get pissed and have no responsibility."

"Mark, what did I say about swearing?" Jean gave him a mock frown.

"Mum, if you think *that*'s swearing, don't ever visit me in the restaurant kitchens."

Kate spluttered. "God, yes, I made the mistake of doing that once."

Tony tapped a finger on the table. "Now that we have the wonderfully good news out of the way, I was hoping someone might bring the conversation back to business," he said, and Mark groaned. "Give me the finer detail on how my investment is doing."

Jean took Kate's arm. "Come on, dear, let's adjourn to the living room. We want to hear all about the proposal, don't we, Derek?"

Derek, who had planned to stay behind and listen to the business talk, knew a whip when he heard one. "Yes, dear, we certainly do," he said wearily. He followed them out of the room, and Mark brought Tony up to speed on the restaurant.

Hawkins Bar and Grill occupied a corner site in Mayfair, which

Tony said was ideal because people could park outside in the evenings rather than competing for spaces in the more over-crowded Soho and Covent Garden areas nearby. Its proximity to his new flat also meant he could use it as an evening canteen. When they took it over, it already had kitchens and the general layout of a restaurant, but they had gutted and refitted it in modern, mini-malist style with beige suede banquettes and teardrop ceiling lights. They wanted it to be a popular hangout known for its great food, but not too stuffy or élitist, so monosyllabic doormen in trench coats and wraparound shades had been ruled out from the start.

Every restaurant can do with a lucky break, and theirs came when the hot new singing star Burgundy Brown had brought her latest boyfriend there for a romantic dinner. Shortly afterwards, the *Sunday Times*'s notoriously fickle A. A. Gill had given it an above-average review, and they were away.

It was packed most nights, but particularly at weekends, and although another new restaurant had opened nearby, the busi-ness was still ticking over nicely.

"So, your investment is safe and sound." Mark stretched across his parents' dining table and picked up a piece of bread from Kate's side plate. "Now, shall we stop being so antisocial and go and join the others?"

"In a minute." Tony poured them each a large brandy from the cut-glass decanter in the center of the table. "First, I want to hear the inside track on the proposal while Kate's not in earshot." He prodded Mark in the chest. "You're bloody lucky to have got a second chance with such a great girl."

"I know." Mark's face had brightened at the gear change from business to his new fiancée. He made a good job of running the restaurant because he loved cooking, but the business side of things left him cold. "There's not much to tell, really. Once we got back together, there seemed little point in hanging around. I'd fucked it up once, and I certainly wasn't going to let her go again."

"Why did you split up in the first place?" asked Tony. "You've never really gone into detail before." He didn't let on that Kate had filled him in during the wedding weekend in France.

"I was a total idiot, that's why." Mark took a mouthful of brandy. "We'd started arguing a lot, which anyone sensible would have put down to work pressures and a bit of a rough patch, but I took it to mean we were unsuited." He slapped his face. "Duh! What an arsehole."

"Can't dispute that," said Tony, with a grin. "So you stuck your head into the sand for a few months, and then you met Faye?"

"Yep."

"Have you had any contact with her since?"

"Faye?" Mark glanced at the door, anxious that Kate might hear.

Tony nodded.

"Just a couple of phone calls early on," he replied. "She wanted to meet up to check that I was OK and explain herself further, but I didn't see the point. The relationship was off and I didn't see that talking about it was going to change that. She left a couple more messages, but when she didn't hear back she gave up."

"So you didn't think you could be friends with her?"

"Not really. We hadn't been mates before we got together, so it wasn't like I missed her friendship or anything. It wasn't like it was with Kate or Jenna." His eyes widened. "God, I *knew* there was something else I meant to tell you!"

"What?" Tony was intrigued.

"Guess who Jenna's started seeing?"

"I give up."

"Rich! You know, the policeman. They met at the wedding," said Mark, smiling. "He rang her up afterwards and they've been seeing quite a lot of each other at weekends. She's even talking about moving to London to be closer to him."

"Great. Well, at least the French weekend spawned one happy ending," said Tony, a touch sarcastically.

Mark rolled his brandy around the glass. "Two, if you count Kate and me. The whole experience made me see sense." He took a swig and screwed up his face as the liquid burned the back of his throat. "Now that I'm back with Kate I could probably see Faye as a friend and not be bothered by it, but I couldn't say the same for my fiancée so I think things are better left as they are."

"You're probably right," agreed Tony. "So you really haven't seen her at all? That's impressive willpower."

Mark shrugged. "Not really. I barely think about her, these days. I've seen her in a few magazines and, hand on heart, I felt nothing. It's as if it never happened now, particularly as I've been so wrapped up in the restaurant and Kate."

"Ah, yes, Kate." Tony gave his brother a warm smile. "So how did you two get back together? I got an overexcited, garbled version from Mum, but I want the man-to-man details."

His brother looked wistful. "God, I love her so much—*real* love, you know?"

"Kind of." Tony gestured for him to continue.

"I didn't get a chance to talk to her in France because I left rather quickly . . ."

"I noticed." He gave him a reproachful look.

"Yeah, sorry about that. I just wanted to go away and hide for a while." He brushed a speck from his shirt sleeve. "Anyway, I didn't get to talk to her there, and when I came back here I got rather bogged down with the drama of making endless explanations to everyone . . ."

Although he didn't usually smoke, he helped himself to one of Tony's cigarettes "Once the initial humiliation of the wedding had died down, I *still* felt like shit. Then it dawned on me why."

Tony said nothing.

"It was because I was missing Kate. It had nothing to do with Faye." He took a long drag and blew the smoke into the air.

"Then, one Saturday morning, I was lolling about the flat as usual with Brian, and I decided to do something about it."

"So you got on your white charger?"

"Into a black cab, actually," smiled Mark, "and luckily, she was at home." He took a drag of the cigarette, with another nervous glance towards the door. "She took a bit of convincing to give me another chance, but here we are."

"Bloody great." Tony clinked his glass against Mark's. "Well, all I can say is, you're lucky someone else didn't snap her up in the meantime."

Mark had just taken another mouthful of brandy, and almost choked. He swallowed hard, then said, "That reminds me, you never told me Ted was gay! She says she told you in France."

Tony had the grace to look sheepish. "Yes, she did."

"Why the fuck didn't you tell me?"

"Because she asked me not to, and because you were supposed to be marrying someone else the next morning, so I didn't think you'd be that interested."

They lapsed into silence for a few moments.

"You really are a bloody dark horse," said Mark, finally.

"It's called discretion." Tony waved his hand to indicate that was enough about him: he'd never been comfortable as the subject matter of a conversation.

"That's exactly what Kate said you'd say."

"When did she tell you the truth?"

"While I was trying to persuade her to give it another go," said Mark. "*As you already seem to know*, it turned out she had brought Ted to the wedding because she didn't want to come on her own and he was the most handsome man she knew. Also, she could share a bedroom with him safe in the knowledge that there wouldn't be any lunges."

Tony blew a smoke ring into the air. "I suppose she also hoped you might feel a teensy-weensy bit jealous?"

Mark laughed. "Probably. And, if I'm honest, I was. Very. But when she told me he was gay and I realized she was single, I thought It's now or never, and told her how I felt."

"Which was?"

"That I still loved her, that I should never have behaved like such an immature idiot in the first place, and that, if she'd have me, I'd like us to get back together."

"Bloody hell. Don't beat around the bush, do you?"

He shrugged "No point. I knew that she knew everything there is to know about me, so it was going to be a simple case of yes or no."

"And obviously it was yes."

Mark made a face. "Not quite. After leaving me in no doubt what she felt about my overall fuckwittery, she agreed to go out for dinner with me and said we'd take it a day at a time."

His brother pursed his lips. "Can't argue with that."

"That was in November and, as you also know, we've been dating ever since. I wanted to ask her to marry me much sooner, but decided I'd wait until after the restaurant opened. I thought if we could survive the launch, we could survive anything."

"Regardless of that, she's the girl for you," said Tony. "I've always known it."

"So why didn't you say something?"

"Well, for the reason I was talking about earlier. I haven't been part of your life for a while and didn't feel you'd take much notice anyway."

Mark looked unsure. "I might have."

"Well, you didn't take much notice when I told you Faye was the wrong woman for you!" Tony cuffed him.

"True," Mark mused. "And, God, you were right."

He made a little bowing action with his head. "Thank you. And don't call me God, Tony will do."

"*Anyway*—will I *ever* get to the end of this story? I proposed to Kate in Antigua last week. I had organized a table for just the two of us on the beach, so I think she kind of suspected what was coming. She did a good job of looking surprised, though."

"Were you sure she'd say yes?"

"Pretty much. We always used to have quite an unpredictable relationship, but it's different this time. Although we're both still quite independent, we don't play as many stupid games with each other. It's much nicer."

Tony sighed. "Glad to hear it. And, once again, I'm thrilled to bits for both of you."

"Thanks, bruv. Now let's go through and join the others." He stood up.

"Hang on." Tony's expression had become serious. "There's just one other thing I need to talk to you about."

Friday, September 19
11:25 a.m.

Adam arrived back at her flat and threw the spare keys into the china bowl by the door. "Fuck me sideways, you're really famous!" he said, with typical under-statement.

"Is it in, then?" she said, feeling a flutter of excitement in her stomach.

He walked over to the living-room table and threw down the big pile of newspapers he was carrying. "You're in practically every one of them, except the stuffy old *FT. And* . . ." he paused for dramatic effect, ". . . you're on the *front* of the *Mail.*"

Faye flipped it over and, sure enough, there was a

large color photograph of her with the caption: "Faye Parker, the new face of Visage makeup, see page 7." "Bloody hell." She looked at Adam wide-eyed. "I knew getting the Visage contract was a big deal, but I didn't realize it would get *this* much coverage."

Adam sipped the coffee she'd made while he was out at the newsagent's. "Two things in your favor, love." He held up a finger. "One, there's fuck-all else happening in the world." He held up another. "And two, it means they can pour piss all over Bonnie Wallis for losing the contract because of her drug problem."

Faye started to flick through the other papers. They had all used variations of the same picture, taken at yesterday's press conference to announce her as the new face of Visage, a makeup company that rivaled Revlon and Estée Lauder.

"You know what this means, don't you?" she said.

"That you'll make shitloads of money and have even more gorgeous men throwing themselves at you?" replied Adam, his face deadpan. A drip of coffee fell from the base of his cup and onto his T-shirt, which was emblazoned with the words "My sexual preference is not you."

"No," she said. "It means I can never leave the house without makeup in case there are some paparazzi lurking outside, waiting to get a picture of me looking dreadful."

"Darling, apart from the piggy-eyed moment not long after Nat dumped you, I have *never* seen you look dreadful. In fact, come to think of it, I hate you."

"I hate you too," she said, blowing him a kiss. "Now, the big question is, what have you got for me to wear tonight?"

That evening, there was going to be a huge party to celebrate twenty-five years of Visage, and the powers-that-be had made it abundantly clear that Faye was to be there, wearing something that ensured them the maximum possible coverage in the next day's newspapers. Adam would accompany her, but before that he had to secure her a drop-dead gorgeous dress for the occasion.

Luckily, his job with *Couture* meant that his ancient Filofax was stuffed with the home numbers of every important fashionista you could think of. Faye had tried to drag him kicking and screaming into the new millennium by buying him a Psion, but he'd let the battery die and it had junked all his numbers.

"I've got you four options, but I think the one you should go for is from Gucci's new collection," he said, munching a croissant. "Everyone goes for black at these things, so I think you should wear a brighter color to make you stand out."

Faye nodded her agreement. "So what color is it?"

"It's greeny-blue. I thought it would bring out the color of your eyes. There's not much of it, but I've brought lots of toupee tape with me so you won't fall out." A thought struck him. "Mind you, maybe you *should* fall out. It's a great way to get into the papers."

"Very funny."

Although she had posed in lots of scanty outfits in the studio, Faye was quite prudish when it came to going out in one. The studio was work and she had to wear what she was told to, but what you chose to wear to a party was your own business and said so much more about you.

"It can only be a matter of time before someone wears a couple of Dairylea Triangles and a bottle top to a party," she said, "but it's not going to be me."

"Spoilsport." Adam stood up and stretched his arms above his head. "Mind if I have a quick bath before lunch?"

"*Quick?*" She raised her eyebrows. "In your case, that means about two hours."

He feigned a hurt expression. "I can't be that long. It's eleven-thirty now and I've booked us into the little French place down the road for one o'clock. Then we can come back here and start getting you ready."

"They're picking me up at six bloody thirty because there's a private reception first and I have to do lots of handshaking with Visage executives."

"Oooh, you're a girl who knows how to have fun." Taking one of the color supplements with him, he headed for the bathroom.

Faye sat there for another half an hour, scanning the papers. Although she'd been in column items before, she'd never experienced blanket coverage like this, and it felt weird to read about herself. Across the articles, her age changed three times, and one even referred to her having dated a male model she'd never met. In truth, the man she spent most of her time with now was Adam. They'd always got on, but their relationship had undoubtedly strengthened in recent months.

Before, she'd always compartmentalized him as a fun friend, but not necessarily someone deep or discreet enough to confide in. Equally, she had never really been the confessional type, preferring instead to bottle things up and work "stuff" out for herself.

But after the events in France, Faye had learned the valuable lesson that, if you admit you occasionally have problems in life, the world doesn't suddenly end. It took her a while, but gradually, she had begun to talk to Adam about her childhood, her relationship with Alice, and how she felt it affected the way she responded to the men in her life.

He had proved a fantastic listener, offering surprisingly insightful pieces of advice here and there, and being incredibly supportive. He still loved going to parties and he would end up staying at Faye's more central flat, creeping in at all hours and using the spare key she'd given him weeks ago. She liked having him there to talk to.

Down the hall, she heard the bathroom door open. Seconds later, Adam emerged pink-faced. "Forty minutes!" he said triumphantly. "That's a bathtime record for me."

Faye smiled. "Yes, but you still have to get dressed, and we all know how long *that* takes."

By 7.30 p.m., Faye felt like she'd shaken the hand of every Visage sales rep this side of the Atlantic. Her face was rigid from smiling, and she had to keep it up for several more hours at the anniversary party.

The event was held at London's Natural History Museum in the vast room dominated by the skeleton of a dinosaur. The empty walls had been decorated with drapes in the distinctive Visage orange, and strategically placed colored lighting gave the room a vibrancy.

It was packed with representatives of the fashion industry and the media, as well as dozens of celebrities and influential business types from other fields. A networker's dream but, to Faye, it was something she could have done without.

Judging by the clamor of photographers as she stepped out of the limo, the dress was an unmitigated success. Adam, standing to one side while she posed this way and that, had done her proud. Slit to the thigh, it showed off her long legs, and the tight bodice emphasized her ample chest. Unlike most couture models, Faye actually had one.

Her hair had been straightened to form a sleek curtain that framed her face, and her all-over St. Tropez bottle tan gave her a healthy glow.

"God, how much longer?" she muttered to Adam, taking care to keep her smile in place as they walked into the main throng.

"Remember, darling, if the world didn't suck, we'd all fall off." He looked at his watch. "Another three hours, then you can make your excuses and leave. You OK?" he asked, knowing how much she hated these things.

"Yes, kind of."

"Come on, lovey, just think of the money."

Indeed, the three-year deal Faye had secured with Visage meant that, invested wisely, she would never again have money worries. The first thing she planned to do was pay off her mother's mortgage, then buy herself the Mercedes sports car she'd always dreamed of. But the remaining money would be put in a high-interest account for the rainy day when she was inevitably usurped by the next new young thing.

Two hours later, she had been dragged around the room by the Visage chairman and introduced to everyone except the waiters. She was utterly exhausted from small talk. Yes, I'm thrilled to be the new Visage girl. Yes, it was totally unexpected. Yes, I do have to watch what I eat. Yes, I do a little bit of yoga. The questions were all the same; only the faces changed.

"Do you mind if I head off now? It's been a frightfully long day," she said, briefly resorting to her old flirting ways and using a little-girl voice. She followed it up by giving the Visage chairman a coquettish smile.

Five minutes later, she was queuing at the cloakroom for her coat, having politely brushed off all offers of help from various Visage flunkys. She was PR'd out, and desperately wanted to be left alone.

"Darling, I'm off. Call me tomorrow." She kissed Adam on both cheeks and left him engrossed in conversation with someone she recognized as a fashion columnist on one of the Sunday supplements. It was full of people like that, who greeted you effusively while looking over your shoulder to see if anyone more important was in view. Adam reveled in the shallowness, but Faye found it horribly wearing.

She was weaving her way back through the crowded room towards the exit, when she saw him. Her breath caught in her throat. Ducking behind a large woman she prayed he hadn't spotted her and, keeping her head low, she set off the long way round the room so she wouldn't have to walk through the danger zone he occupied.

As she reached the edge of the crowd, the heady scent of a nearby exit in her nostrils, she felt a hand pulling her back. "Your pathetically obvious bid to avoid me has failed," said Tony, mockingly. "Nice try, though."

He was looking incredibly smart in a gray pinstriped suit, white shirt, and bright-blue tie. His chin was starting to show the signs of a five o'clock shadow and small beads of sweat peppered his forehead.

"I don't know what you're talking about. I didn't even see you," she lied.

"Whatever." He smiled. "Anyway, congratulations."

"What for?" She looked at him blankly.

"Becoming the new Visage girl." He looked around the over-crowded, hot room. "Unless all this is an elaborate hoax . . ."

"No, no . . ." She closed her eyes for an instant. "Sorry, it's been a long couple of days. I just want to get home."

"I'll take you." He took her arm and started walking her towards the exit.

Stopping dead in her tracks, Faye pulled away from him. "No, really, I'd rather just get a cab on my own."

"A black cab round here at this time of night? You'll be lucky. Come on, I've got a nice warm Jag just outside."

She knew that he was right, but her pride raised its ugly head and she considered rebuffing his offer. In the end, the combination of his persuasion and her exhaustion made her fall into step with him. "OK, thanks."

"My car is just outside, but I'll go and get in first, then you come out on your own. That way, we won't get photographed to-gether."

She shook her head in amazement. "You really do think of everything, don't you?"

"*You* need to start thinking that way now you're well known."

Sure enough, when she stepped outside a few minutes after him, the flashbulbs exploded and she dredged up one last smile. His sleek black Jaguar was waiting at the bottom of the steps, and she hopped in gratefully.

"Home, James." She kicked off her shoes. "Head for Clerken-well and I'll direct you from there."

"Yes, ma'am." He doffed an imaginary cap.

"So what were you doing there?" she asked, jerking her head back towards the museum. "I wouldn't imagine it was your scene."

"It isn't, really, but Visage is one of my clients at Jam. They do a sporty makeup line, so we occasionally merge on ad campaigns targeted at young women," he said, edging slowly into the traffic. "I also hoped I might see you."

"Oh." She'd thought she'd have been the last person he'd want to see, but she didn't say so.

"So, how are you?"

"How am I?" She pondered the question. "Better than the last time you saw me, I suppose. But, then, I couldn't have been worse . . ."

The car stopped at traffic lights and they sat in silence, watching a young couple cross the road in front of them. His arm was slung casually round her shoulders, and she was laughing. They seemed completely at ease with each other.

"Are you over for long?" asked Faye, unsure what else to say.

"I live here now."

"Oh." More silence.

The lights changed and Tony drove on slowly, ignoring a boy racer revving up next to him.

"Mark and I have opened a restaurant together," he said.

"Oh. I knew Mark had, I read a story about it. I just didn't realize you were involved." She paused for a couple of seconds. "Is it going well?"

"Very. He's doing a great job."

"Good, I'm pleased for him. It's what he always wanted to do." She stared out of the side window. "How is he?"

"On very good form. He seems really happy." Tony glanced at her. "By the way, did you know he's engaged to Kate?"

She raised her eyebrows in surprise. "No, I didn't." She

smiled, but it didn't quite reach her eyes. "So, you finally got what you wanted. You always liked her."

He continued to stare at the road. "Yes, I did. She and Mark suit each other very well." Indicating, he turned left. "Are you seeing anyone?"

"None of your damned business."

"Nice to see you've lost none of your feminine charm," he said. "And I'll take that as a no."

"It's quicker if you go straight on here," she said, changing the subject and pointing ahead.

They were about two miles away from her apartment, and she couldn't wait to get there. Her head was pounding from small talk and the shock of bumping into the man who had destroyed her wedding day.

"Faye . . ."

Oh, God, she thought. That sounds loaded. "Yes?"

"I know this is going to seem out of left field," he reached forward and turned down the radio, "but I haven't been able to stop thinking about you since France."

"Guilt is a terrible thing," she said sarcastically.

"It's not guilt. I've never regretted what I did, and seeing Mark as happy as he is now just confirms that I was right."

"I'm thrilled for you all," she said, in a monotone.

Suddenly, he took his foot off the accelerator and let the car grind to a halt at the side of the road.

"What the . . . ?"

He turned to face her, his right arm curled round the steering wheel. "I haven't been able to stop thinking about you for the simple reason that I find you incredibly attractive." He delivered the sentence with a gravitas that suggested he'd just announced the latest initiative in the war on global terrorism.

Faye sat stock still, just blinking in the half-darkness. It was clear from the way he was looking at her that he expected an answer. And, looking at him now, just inches away in the half-light, he looked every bit as sexy as he had when she'd spotted him in the wine bar all those months ago.

She yawned. "Tony, I'm flattered, really I am, but I'm horribly tired and, if you don't mind, I'd like to get home."

He ignored that and remained facing her, the car engine idling. "Have you thought about me at all since then?" he asked.

"Nope."

His face dropped.

"Actually, I tell a lie," she said enthusiastically, and his face lit up with expectation. "I was watching a wildlife program about snakes the other day and your face popped into my head."

He curled his lip. "Ha bloody ha." He straightened in his seat, but showed no signs of driving off.

It was now ten-thirty and a shopkeeper opposite was starting to pack up the magazine racks outside his premises. A slight drizzle had started to fall.

"Tony . . ." she leaned forward, trying to make eye contact with him. "I don't know how you expected me to react to what you've just said, but I'm afraid I'm going to disappoint you." She rummaged in her handbag for her door keys. "I behaved out of character and picked you up in a wine bar. Then you used that to force me to call off my marriage to your brother. Did you seriously think, in your wildest imagination, that I'd be pleased to see you?"

He paused a moment before replying. "Even someone as pigheaded as you must now admit that it was for the best."

She nodded. "Yes, I do, but that's not the point, is it? For all you knew when you interfered, Mark was the love of my life."

"If he *was*, I would never have seen the inside of your flat," he retorted. "You'd have given me the brush-off, plain and simple."

"True, but again not the point. What I'm *trying* to say is that . . . forgive me, but after all that I don't feel you're my kind of person."

Tony snorted. "Oh, come on, don't start taking the moral high ground. I'm *exactly* your kind of person. And, anyway, you've been out with much bigger dickheads than me."

She stared at him. "Are you saying that you think we should go out together—attempt some kind of relationship?"

"Um, yes." He looked extremely uncomfortable. "Well, dinner at least."

She laughed long and hard. With amateur-dramatic flair, she took out a tissue and dabbed the corners of her eyes. "Oh, that's priceless, it really is," she gasped. "You truly are a scream."

His expression changed to that of an adult tolerating the behavior of a toddler. He turned off the radio now, and said absolutely nothing.

Before long, the silence became too much for Faye to bear. "Tony, tell me you're not serious," she said.

"I'm deadly serious."

She looked stunned at first, then annoyed. "You know, I thought you were quite bright, for all your shortcomings. In fact, a couple of the things you said in France even made me think you understood me a little . . ." She pressed the electric window and threw her tissue onto the pavement. "But clearly you don't. Do you *really* think I'm so desperate that I'd start dating the man who ruined my wedding day?"

"Oh, stop being so bloody dramatic," he said. "It wasn't personal, I didn't really know you then."

"And you don't know me now!"

He sighed, but she couldn't tell whether it was through irritation or melancholy.

"Look, Faye, if you mean what you say, then after tonight we'll probably never see each other again." He waited for her to disagree, but she didn't. "If so, then I have nothing to lose in telling you how I feel."

He took a deep breath. "As I said, I haven't been able to stop thinking about you. At first I assumed it was guilt, as you say, but then I realized that had nothing to do with it. You had excited me, stimulated me, in a way no other woman ever has. Yes, you're beautiful, and I fancied you from the moment I saw you in the wine bar. But it's so much more than that. You're feisty, funny, and you stand up to me when I show my control-freak tendencies . . ." He trailed off and looked at her.

She held up her hands. "Hey, don't let me to talk you out of the last one. You make Mussolini look like a nursery school teacher."

He ignored her poor attempt at humor. "It's a failing of mine that I rarely consider women my equal. I love them, but I always want to play the macho role and look after them on every level," he said. "I ate poor Melissa whole because she didn't have the strength of character to stand up to me. But you *do*, and I've never encountered that before."

Faye stifled a genuine yawn as a wave of fatigue swept over her. "So why don't you just chill out a bit, and then your girl-friends wouldn't have to stand up to you? Then you'd all be happy."

He shook his head. "It doesn't work like that, as you well know. I've chilled out an awful lot lately, but it still doesn't stop me from wanting a woman who can curb my excesses."

"I see." She massaged her earlobe. "And you think *I* might be that woman?"

He nodded.

"Sorry," she said irritably. "But I'm not interested in being your glorified therapist, the horse whisperer who blows up your nostrils and tames the wild stud. You need a woman with the rescue mentality and that's not me."

Scowling, he tapped the steering wheel. "Don't be facetious. That's not what I'm saying at all and you bloody well know it. I just think we have a strong chemistry, and I think that's important."

Faye started to play with the cigarette lighter. "Setting aside for a moment the ludicrousness of your suggestion, even if I *were* interested in having dinner with you, how on earth do you think Mark would react when he found out?"

"He knows."

Her head jerked round to face him. "Knows what?"

"He knows that I'm here tonight and suggesting it to you."

Faye spluttered. "Hang on—so you cleared it with Mark before you even knew what my response would be? Fuck, you're arrogant."

"It's not that. I just wanted to be honest with him from the outset."

"Yeah, right. Tell him about our previous liaison, did you?"

"No, of course I didn't. We agreed we'd never tell, didn't we?"

"Yes, we did," she acquiesced. "But cut the crap about your honest relationship with Mark. I still think you should have waited until there was something to tell him about us, and there isn't going to be."

"You're adamant, then?"

"Tony," she said wearily, "as I said . . . you behaved appallingly towards me on the evening before my wedding, then insisted I call it off just a couple of hours before the ceremony—"

"And now you admit it was just as well the wedding didn't go ahead," he interjected.

"Yes, but there's a world of difference between admitting that and actually *dating* the man who did all that to you."

He sniffed. "As I said, I was just protecting Mark. It wasn't personal, and I certainly didn't know how compatible you and I would turn out to be."

"You mean we're both stubborn, opinionated, and always right?" she asked, with a small smile.

"Yeah, something like that."

There was silence for a few more seconds, the only sound the metallic clink of Faye's keys as she turned them over in her hand.

"So what exactly did you say to Mark?" she asked.

Tony took out his cigarettes and offered her one. "I told him the truth. I said that I hadn't been able to stop thinking about you since the wedding and asked if he had a problem with me asking you out for dinner."

"And did he?"

"Didn't seem to. He made some remark about your tentacles sucking me in like they had him."

Faye laughed. "Charming! Besides, the only way I'd use a tentacle with you is to bloody strangle you." She took a drag of her cigarette. "What else did he say?"

Tony blew smoke out of the window. "He said that as long as I thought I could handle you, I was welcome to you. He's so happy with Kate, I don't think he cares either way."

"And to think I've gone and spoiled your little plan by knocking you back," she said.

"Never mind. Plenty more fish in the sea."

"Hello?" She feigned indignation. "A minute ago you were claiming I was the only woman for you, now I'm just one of a thousand minnows."

"Well, we all get setbacks, but life goes on, doesn't it?" He threw his unfinished cigarette out of the window and started the engine. "Come on, let's get you home."

As they drove the final mile back to her flat, Faye's mind went into overdrive, replaying their conversation. His suggestion of dinner had taken her by surprise, but his subsequent declaration of deep feelings had stunned her.

She could see Tony glancing at her occasionally out of the corner of his eye.

"Penny for them?" he said eventually, clearly hoping she were considering what he'd said.

"I was just thinking what I need to get at Waitrose tomorrow," she lied.

"I'm flattered that my company inspires you so much."

He pulled up outside her apartment building, left the engine running, and walked round the car to open her door. She stepped out and gave him a warm smile. "Thanks for the lift."

"No problem."

"You're right, it was much nicer than getting a cab."

"Good."

They stood there awkwardly, her making conversation and him being monosyllabic in return. She wondered if she should give him a goodbye peck on the cheek, but he solved the problem for her.

Glancing at his watch, he took two steps backwards. "Must go. I have a breakfast meeting at seven." He opened the car door. "Nice to see you, and I hope you keep well."

Then he was gone.

Faye stayed on the pavement for a few more seconds, watching as his taillights faded into the distance.

Saturday, September 20
11 a.m.

❦

Faye kicked the door closed behind her, threw the newspapers onto the sofa, and flopped down beside them. Starting with that morning's *Sun*, she flicked through it rapidly, looking to see if the frock had worked its magic. The Middle East flaring up again, Prince William and his girlfriend. She read the headlines, but didn't dwell. Then, on page seventeen, there she was.

"Whey-Faye!" read the headline, with a picture of her stepping out of the limo and revealing quite a bit of leg. Similar pictures with elongated captions were also in the *Mirror*, the *Mail*, the *Star*, and the *Express*.

Good, she thought, the Visage bosses will be pleased with the attention their new signing has attracted.

She made herself a strong black coffee and started to run a bath. She was supposed to be meeting her agent for lunch, but she'd already made up her mind to cancel. Instead she fancied a quiet day at home, giving her wardrobe the spring-cleaning she had been meaning to do for ages. She poured in a generous helping of Penhaligon's Lily-of-the-Valley, swished it around, and watched the bubbles rise. With the latest issues of *Glamour* and *Cosmopolitan* on the side, she was ready for a long soak.

The doorbell rang.

"Damn!" She pulled her trousers back on, walked through to the hallway and peered through the spyhole. It was the concierge to her building, so she opened the door.

"Good morning, Miss Parker." He was a middle-aged man with graying hair and kind eyes, always friendly without being too familiar. "This has just been delivered for you by courier."

"Thank you, Mr. Harris." She took the small package from him and closed the door.

About to throw it on the table to open later, she suddenly realized she didn't recognize the writing and became curious. She tore off the brown paper and a slim book fell to the floor, facedown. Picking it up and turning it over, she noted it was *The Little Prince* by Antoine de Saint-Exupéry. She frowned and opened it, her heart skipped a beat when she saw an inscription signed "Tony."

It read: "Just to let you know, you're never alone . . ."

Sitting down, she started to flick through the pages. She had never read this story, but she remembered her mother telling her about it a few years ago. Although primarily aimed at children, many adults loved it for its simplistic style and touching message.

Her bath forgotten for the time being, she had just begun to read the first page when she was distracted by a door opening. Adam suddenly appeared in the living room, his hair standing on end. He was wearing a pair of white Calvin Kleins and a baggy blue T-shirt with a large hole in the front.

"Hello," she said. "I wasn't sure if you made it back here or not. How was the rest of the party?"

"Shite." He yawned, revealing several old-style silver fillings. "I spent an hour chatting up a gorgeous man, only to find his girlfriend was at the party too." He plonked himself on a chair at the other end of the table.

"You look like you need some coffee," she said. "I'll make you one."

A couple of minutes later, she placed a steaming mug of decaf in front of him and sat down opposite.

"Thanks, honey." He blew her a kiss. "What's that?" He pointed towards *The Little Prince*, which was lying in the middle of the table.

"It's a present . . . There's also a long story behind it."

Adam stretched his legs out in front of him. "Well, I have the whole day free, so do tell."

Faye stared at her hands, deep in thought. She still hadn't told Adam that her prewedding "night of shame" had been with Tony, fearful he might spill the beans to someone else. But since their friendship had become more confessional, she had discovered that he could be discreet when necessary.

"I have a feeling you're going to love this story," she said.

"Ooh, goody," he said, in his best camp voice.

"You know the man I almost slept with the weekend before I was supposed to marry Mark?"

"Yeees," he said distractedly, playing with the front of his hair.

"Well, it was Mark's brother, Tony."

It took a couple of seconds to sink in, then Adam's hand dropped into his lap and his expression transformed from one of serenity to total shock. His eyes widened and his jaw fell open, then his hand rose again to cover his mouth. "Oh, my God." His voice sounded muffled through his fingers.

"Yes, that's pretty much what I felt when I found out."

"What are the *chances* of unwittingly getting off with your fiancé's brother? It's almost a bad miracle, if there is such a thing."

Faye nodded.

"Hang on, let me get a ciggy." Adam darted out of the room and returned a few seconds later with a pack of Camels. "Right, I'm ready. Tell me *everything*."

Saturday, September 20
10 p.m.

Jean's eyes were red from crying, the mascara-stained tears running in rivulets down the side of her nose. Derek passed her a napkin, gave her a "there, there" pat on the back, then looked over at his sons and rolled his eyes.

"Oh, gawd, Mum's off again," laughed Mark. "It must have been your speech."

"I'm flattered you should think so," said Tony, taking another gulp of red wine, "but I think it's more likely that she's crying with relief that you've finally got married without a hitch. She hasn't stopped since the 'do you take this woman' bit in church."

"I know. Poor old Dad, he looks really pissed off at having to deal with it. I'll bet he'd rather be sitting here with us, getting hammered."

They were sitting at one of the fifteen tables for ten set up for Mark and Kate's wedding reception at Claridges in Mayfair. They had all been delivered there on coaches from the vast St. Bride's church in Fleet Street, where the ecstatically happy couple had made their vows in a traditional service.

The dinner and speeches over, the guests were now mingling in the elegant art-deco ballroom. Some were dancing to the band, others were slumped at their tables, unable to move due to an excess of food and fine wine.

Tony had been fairly abstemious before his speech, but afterwards he had sunk several glasses of red wine in swift succession. Unusually for him, he felt drunk. Finding himself an empty table away from the small talk, he sat down to try to compose himself. Within minutes, an equally weary and inebriated Mark had joined him. "God, these things are wearing," he muttered. "All these relatives I haven't seen in ages wanting to know what I've been up to for the past five years."

"Yes, I've had all that too," slurred Tony. "Except that I've had the added pain-in-the-arse questions about whether or not I'm seeing anyone special at the moment."

Mark looked over to the dance floor where their aunt Lydia was being helped back up after doing the twist and falling over. "At least they all seem to be having a good time."

"Aha! So this is where you're hiding!" Kate fell into the chair next to Mark and flung her arms round his neck. She gave him a lingering kiss. "Hello, husband," she murmured.

"Hello, wife." He nuzzled her neck.

"Hello, husband *and* wife." Tony raised his glass towards them, nearly spilling it as his elbow slipped off the table.

"You're pissed!" squealed Kate. "I don't think I've ever seen you pissed before."

"Come to think of it, me neither." Mark frowned. "Except maybe that Christmas when you were about eighteen and drank too much of Dad's brandy."

Tony adjusted his tie unnecessarily. "I'm drinking to your health!" he said. "I can't tell you how thrilled I am to be at your wedding."

"Thanks," said Kate. She was wearing a long white dress with a lace, bias-cut skirt and satin bodice covered in tiny pearls. She had grown her hair into a softer style, and it was decorated with tiny pink roses that matched those in her bouquet.

A makeup artist with whom she worked regularly at the magazine had offered to help her on the day, and consequently she looked stunning, with a natural-looking foundation, smoldering eyes, and a pale-pink glossy lipstick. But it was her joy at being with Mark that gave her an extraradiant beauty.

She watched Tony refill his glass and Mark's. "Right!" she said brightly, getting to her feet. "I can see you two are happy here for the time being, so I'm going to have that dance I promised Uncle Simon. See you later." She gave Mark a quick kiss and wandered off.

"Great girl," said Tony. "Great, great girl. Bloody great."

"Yeah, she is." Mark's eyes followed her across the room. "This all feels entirely natural," he said, with a sweeping gesture, "whereas France didn't. I felt I was bit player in someone else's drama."

"It certainly was a drama," mumbled Tony, staring into space.

Mark stood up and moved a couple of chairs closer to his brother. He was now just inches away from him, a devilish look on his face. "Which reminds me, did you ever do anything about you-know-who?"

Tony struggled to focus on him. "Sorry? I'm not with you."

"Faye." Mark's eyes were gleaming with intrigue. "Did you ever get round to asking her out for dinner?"

"Oh, that." Tony's face had clouded. "Yes, I saw her at the Visage party the other night."

"And?"

"And she let me know in no uncertain terms that she would rather spend an evening with a serial killer than with me."

Mark threw back his head and laughed. "Did she really say that?"

"No, but that was the sentiment." He looked glummer with each passing second.

"She's probably just playing hard to get," said Mark. "She always was one for games." Curiosity got the better of him. "Did she ask after me?"

Tony pursed his lips. "Yep. She asked how you were and said she'd seen a piece about you opening a restaurant."

"Did you tell her about Kate and me?"

"Yep."

"And?" Mark said irritably. "Bloody hell, Tony, it's like getting blood from a stone."

His brother shrugged. "Sorry, I didn't think you were interested in her anymore."

"I'm *not*, but like most men I have a gigantic ego, and I want to know if she tried to end her life when you told her."

"No, she didn't. I think she was genuinely happy for you. She seems to be getting on with life, just like you."

"Is she seeing anyone?"

"She says not, and there's certainly been no mention of a significant other in the newspaper coverage about the Visage deal." This was the closest Tony had come to admitting he had read every word of it all.

Mark had another swig of wine, and wiped away a droplet that ran down his chin. "Well, in that case, how come she was so averse to having dinner with you?"

"I think she probably remembers that I was rather unpleasant to her in France," replied Tony, his heart racing at the thought of quite *how* unpleasant he'd been.

"True, but it was for the best in the end," said Mark.

"I said that too, but she didn't seem convinced."

For a minute they were quiet, watching Kate attempting to last the course of "Disco Inferno" with Uncle Simon, who was bright red in the face and clearly struggling for breath.

"So is that it?" said Mark, after a while. "Are you just going to give up on her?"

His brother shrugged. "She doesn't strike me as someone who says something unless she means it. I doubt I could talk her into it."

"So prove it by your actions."

"I've done a little of that already."

"Let me guess. You turned up naked with a rose between your teeth." Mark grinned.

"Bit cold for that. No, I sent her *The Little Prince* with a message inside." The book had been one of Tony's favorites when he was a child, and he'd passed on his copy to Mark, who also loved it.

"Nice one." Mark didn't ask the content of the message. "Have you heard anything?"

"No, but I only sent it this morning. I doubt she'll call anyway. After all, it's only a book."

"Well, I think you should at least give it one more try in person." Mark had noticed that "Disco Inferno" had finished and was scanning the room for Kate. "If she knocks you back again, *then* you'll know for sure."

"I think I already do," said Tony, suddenly overwhelmed by depression. Unused to discussing his feelings with anyone, the alcohol was loosening his tongue. "I just wish I could forget about it and move on, but I can't."

Mark turned back to him. "You always did like a challenge."

"No, it's more than that. As soon as I wake up in the morning, she pops into my head, and I can't stop thinking about her."

"Blimey, you have got it bad. You sound like me a couple of years ago, and look what happened."

His brother said nothing.

"Mind you, if anyone can handle her, it's you," said Mark, painfully aware that he was now casting around for something, *anything*, to say. Apart from those weeks and months after Melissa's departure, he'd never seen Tony look so despondent. He was usually so positive: nothing was ever a problem—there were only solutions. "Failing that, there are plenty of other women out there."

Tony looked unconvinced. "My wild oats have turned to All-Bran and, besides, I don't want anyone else." He caught sight of Kate heading in their direction again. "Anyway, let's drop the subject. Kate's on her way back."

"That's OK, I told her," said Mark, as she sat down next to them.

"Told me what?" Her face was flushed pink with the exertion of dancing.

"About Tony wanting to ask Faye out on a date." He stroked her leg. "I tell my wife everything," he added.

"Oh, that." She grabbed Mark's glass and took a few sips.

Tony looked at her. "So, what do you think?"

"About you and Faye?" She was clearly surprised that the usually secretive Tony was asking her advice about a woman. "Um, I suppose I think it's a good idea."

"You do?" Now it was Tony's turn to be surprised. "I thought you'd hate her."

She frowned a little. "No, I don't. After all, it's not as if she stole Mark away from me or anything like that." She gave Mark a reassuring kiss. "She's not my kind of person, but I can see that she would probably suit you very well."

Tony smiled for the first time in an hour. "You mean we're both totally spoiled bastards?"

Kate winked at him. "Something like that. Although nice ones."

Mark pulled her on to his lap, and wrapped his arms round her waist. "Anyway, it's all irrelevant, because she told him where to get off."

"Did she?" Kate grinned at Tony.

He nodded, with a rueful smile. "Yep, 'fraid so."

"Wow. How does it feel to be treated like us mere mortals?" she said, prodding his arm.

"Like shit, actually. But life goes on," he replied, looking as if life would do anything but.

Kate leaped up, walked round to his chair, and grabbed him under the armpit. "Come and dance with your new sister-in-law."

"I don't do dancing," he said gruffly.

"You do now." She gave him a firm hoist and he stood up reluctantly. "Life's too short to just sit and watch everyone else having a good time. You need to join in."

"It depends what your idea of a good time is," he said, leading her on to the dance floor as the familiar intro of George McCrae's "Rock Your Baby" blasted out.

Moving in time to the music, Kate took a couple of steps away from him, then a couple of steps back, holding his waist and circling him. Every so often, she shouted something in his ear. "Do you really like her, then?"

He nodded.

"You didn't seem too keen on her in France," she screeched above the music.

"That was because she was marrying Mark," he shouted back. "But I like her a lot. She seems really tough, but she's not."

Kate said nothing for a while, executing a few more circling maneuvers, and raising her arms in the air. "Well, all I can say is . . ." the music rose to a crescendo then died away again ". . . it's not like you to give up easily. If she was a business deal, you'd keep on trying until you got what you wanted."

The record finished and Tony started to leave the dance floor, indicating for her to follow. "But that's just it . . . I've always treated relationships like business deals in the past, seeing something and getting it without even considering the possibility that I might fail . . ." He stopped halfway back to the table. "But this is different. When I asked her out, I felt really nervous. And when she said no, well . . ." He was lost for words.

Kate broke into a huge grin. "Well, well, well . . . I don't believe it!" she exclaimed.

"What?"

"At long last Tony Hawkins is truly, madly, deeply in love! *Properly* in love," she emphasized with a smile. "About bloody time too."

Saturday, October 11
8 a.m.

Tony opened his eyes and rolled over to look at the clock. It was early on Saturday morning and he was wide awake. Despite having a blissfully free day ahead of him, he couldn't get back to sleep, his head already filled with thoughts of ongoing business deals, tasks to be done around the flat, and . . . there she was again . . . *her*.

It had been three weeks since Mark and Kate's wedding and he'd done nothing about Faye. If it had been anyone else, Tony wouldn't have hesitated in calling again and again until she agreed to have dinner. But this was different: not only did she stir unusual feelings of apprehension in him, he also knew he had to make up a lot of ground after France.

He swung his legs out of bed and sat on the edge for a few moments, staring out of the window at the impressive view of London. His flat was in a spectacular location and stuffed with fine art and expensive furniture, but on this clear autumnal morning, it all felt meaningless and empty.

During the week, he could throw himself headfirst into his work schedule, barely raising his eyes to look at the time before he flopped into bed and started again the next day. But weekends were different, and he missed having someone to share them with. Throwing on a cotton robe, he wandered into the kitchen and started to cut up oranges for the juicer. When the phone rang his fingers were covered in the sticky liquid and he cursed. Cupping the receiver between shoulder and ear, he ran his hands under the tap. "Hello?"

"Hi, it's me. We're back." It was Mark, newly returned from his honeymoon.

"How was Mahé?"

"Fan-bloody-tastic, I wanted to stay there forever. Thanks again, by the way." The trip to the Seychelles had been Tony's wedding present to them.

"Don't mention it." He dried his hands on a tea towel, then folded it and placed it neatly in a drawer.

"Listen, I'm not due back in the restaurant until tomorrow lunchtime and Kate's off out with some girlfriends tonight, so I was wondering whether you're free for dinner?"

Tony gave his empty wall calendar a quick glance. "I am indeed. That'd be nice."

"Great," enthused Mark. "I'll bring the honeymoon snaps along."

Tony groaned. "On second thoughts, there's a documentary on tonight about the intestinal workings of the fruit bat—"

"Very funny. Zilli Fish at eight-thirty. Be there."

The phone went dead and Tony put the receiver back on the cradle. Oh, well, he thought, that's filled up some of my rather empty weekend.

Zilli Fish was a popular hangout on the corner of Brewer Street and Lexington Street in London's vibrant Soho. It was walking distance from Tony's flat and he left a little early so that he could enjoy a leisurely stroll and stop at a cash machine on the way. He arrived at the restaurant ten minutes early and settled into a chair by one of the huge plate-glass windows. It was perfect for watching the world go by but, typically, Tony chose to bury his head in a newspaper. Untypically, he ordered a glass of champagne to kick-start the evening.

He was looking forward to seeing Mark and hearing all about the honeymoon. Ever since he'd returned from New York and they'd gone into business together, their relationship had improved no end and regained some balance. They were still close, but it was no longer a case of Mark hero-worshipping him while he played the protective older brother. They were more like equals now.

Mark had learned to stand up to Tony and, in turn, Tony had found that the business didn't fall apart if he wasn't involved in every single decision. He made a silent vow to himself that tonight he wouldn't mention the restaurant at all, sticking to Mark and Kate and the wonders of the Seychelles.

Sensing someone approaching his table, he looked up from the newspaper and his heart leaped into his mouth.

"Hello." It was Faye.

He half stood up, but she gestured for him to sit down. "Fancy seeing you here," he said, inwardly kicking himself for such a hackneyed remark.

"Fancy." She looked down at him and smiled enigmatically.

She looked stunning in a simple white shirt and black trousers, with a jeweled belt resting loosely on her hips.

Tony was about to ask how she was when a thought struck him and he went cold. "By the way, I'm meeting Mark . . ." He glanced nervously over her shoulder at the door. "He's due here at any moment, so if that would be awkward for you—"

"He's not coming," she interrupted.

"Sorry?" Tony prided himself on his astuteness, but he was flummoxed and looked it.

"Mark's not coming. He never was." She sat, down in the chair opposite him. "It's just you and me."

He absorbed what she'd said, and his pulse began to race. "How come?" He was careful to keep his tone friendly rather than confrontational.

"Because he phoned me and asked me to have dinner with you instead," she said matter-of-factly.

Unusually, Tony felt his face flush with embarrassment. "What *exactly* did he say?"

"Exactly?" She thought for a moment. "Let's see now, his verbatim comment was, 'Please will you go out for dinner with Tony as I can't stand seeing him so miserable for much longer?' " She gave him a quick smile.

"I see." Tony's voice was clipped. "And he thought having dinner with you might cheer me up?"

She gave him a mildly mocking look. "He told me everything."

"Everything," he said flatly, not wanting to give anything away. "And what exactly *is* everything?"

She beckoned to a waiter who was pouring wine at another table. "He told me that you can't stop thinking about me."

Tony let out a long sigh. "Faye, as I recall, *I* told you that after the Visage party. You seemed incredibly underwhelmed by the declaration."

"That's because I thought it was just a line to try to get me into bed," she said, taking a cigarette out of her pack and offering him one. "When I found out you'd told Mark the same thing, I realized you were serious."

Tony lit her cigarette, then his, and blew smoke into the air. "So, Mark asked you to come along tonight?"

"Yep."

"Well, please don't feel you have to stay."

Faye, scowled at him. "Stop being so bloody pious. It doesn't suit you." The waiter appeared at their table. "A gin and tonic, please. We'll order wine in a minute." She turned back to Tony. "I'm here for the simple reason that I want to be."

"You do?" Tony felt like a child who'd just been told his school had been closed for repairs.

"Yes. I wanted to say thank you for the book and the lovely inscription."

"Oh." He looked disappointed. "That's it, is it?"

She laughed. "You're such a child. No, that's not *just* it."

Tony sensed a slight change in her attitude towards him. He might be mistaken, but he thought she was being mildly flirtatious. With nothing to lose, he leaned a little closer to her. "So what else has brought you here?" he murmured. He noticed she was wearing meticulously applied makeup that enhanced her striking eyes.

She stared back at him, clearly editing what she was about to say. "I've been doing a lot of thinking," she said cautiously, "about you."

"I'm flattered."

"Don't be. Most of it was about what an arrogant control freak you are."

Placing a hand against his chest, he pulled a wounded expression. "How you misjudge me."

"Oh, I think I've got your measure perfectly," she said, blowing smoke sideways from her mouth. "It amazes me that you and Mark are brothers because you're so different."

"Very true. He's a much nicer person than me."

Her mouth turned down at the corners "Oh, I don't know. There's a nice person lurking inside you too, but it's buried under a pile of crap."

"So poetic." He drained his glass.

"I'm the same," she continued. "But I've been doing a lot of self-analysis since France."

"And what have you concluded?"

"It's a long story and one that requires my tongue to be loosened by alcohol. Let's order and I'll tell you later."

Two courses and two bottles of Chablis later, Tony had filled her in on Mark and Kate's wedding, the restaurant, and the ups and downs of the sportswear trade. When he had gone into too much detail on the latter, she had crossed her eyes and pretended to fall off her chair with boredom. As he was used to women looking endlessly fascinated by his business talk, Tony found this rather refreshing.

She, in turn, filled him in on the buildup to the Visage contract, Adam's love life, and how her relationship with her mother was better than ever. Then they moved on to the subject of her father and Tony asked if she was curious to find him.

"I have no desire to trace him whatsoever," she said quietly, and smiled at the waiter as he took her empty main-course plate.

"Do you think you'll change your mind?"

She shook her head. "No, not while Mum is alive anyway. She's done so much for me, I wouldn't want to upset her."

Tony noticed that her left eye looked watery. Instinctively, he reached across the table and held her hand. She made no attempt to pull away.

"Does she ever talk about him?" he asked her.

"Not often, but yes. In fact, we talked about him at one of our Saturday lunches recently. She told me I was very like him."

"In what way?"

"Looks and personality. Apparently, he was very outgoing and confident too." She shifted in her seat. "Anyway, I hate talking about him. Tell me more about Mark and Kate."

Tony wrinkled his forehead. "Well, it's early days, but you just know with those two that they'll be together forever."

"I remember when you said to me that if Mark was marrying Kate, you would never interfere."

"And I didn't. Don't meddle with perfection, that's what I say." He smiled.

"Where are they living?"

"She's been promoted again, and the restaurant is ticking over nicely, so they've scraped enough together for a two-bedroom flat in Clapham. They move in at the end of the month."

She let out an almost imperceptible sigh. "France seems like a lifetime ago now. I never think about it, unless of course someone mentions it to me."

"You weren't right for each other."

"I know," she said softly. "And I'm thrilled he and Kate are so happy, I really am. It's just . . ." She trailed off.

"Just what?" He squeezed her hand reassuringly.

"Oh, I don't know," she murmured. "It sounds so selfish, but I just hope that I can achieve that level of happiness one day." A tear ran down the side of her nose and plopped onto the tablecloth. She used a finger to wipe under each of her eyes. "God, sorry, I sound so self-indulgent. Alcohol always makes me rather maudlin, I'm afraid."

"Don't be sorry," said Tony. "We all need a little weep now and then." He took a sip of his wine. "Anyway, it's nice to see you're not such an independent, obstructive so-and-so as I thought."

She stuck out her tongue at him and smiled. "I'm trying hard to be less of an island."

Tony refilled their glasses. "Is that part of the self-analysis you were talking about before?"

She took a sip of wine and stared out of the window. It was

dark now, but the street outside was still crowded with people walking to and from bars and clubs. "I spent all my life watching my mother manage on her own, abandoned by the man she loved," she said. "I guess I grew up thinking that the way forward in life is to do everything for yourself, then no one can let you down.'

Tony gave her hand another squeeze. "That makes sense."

"Yes, but it's not very good for finding a balanced relationship. I always ended up with either men like Rich, who were intimidated by me, or men like Nat, who were so selfish they attempted to do little for me in the first place."

"And what about Mark?" said Tony quietly. "Where does he fit into this self-analysis?"

"He was the man who would never leave me. The dead cert, if you like."

"Unlike your father?"

"Correct. My impression of my father was that he was this charismatic, handsome live wire, an emotional flibbertigibbet, as my mother once described him." She smiled. "He was the kind of man who you had fun with, but who would never settle down."

"So when it came to settling down, you decided to play it safe?"

She looked sad again and stared at the table. "Yes, without thinking too deeply about the consequences of spending the rest of my life with a man who I found a little dull." She looked up. "Sorry, I shouldn't say that about your brother."

He shrugged. "This is just between us. Besides, Kate doesn't feel that way about him and that's what's important now."

"True." She perked up. "And he sounded so happy when we spoke on the phone."

"As I said, he is." Tony was anxious to get off the subject of Mark and back on to Faye. "So, what's the longest relationship you've had?"

She looked taken aback by the question and pondered it. "Um, Mark, I suppose. It was nearly a year. The others were a matter of months, sometimes weeks." She withdrew her hand from his and stretched her arms behind her head. "The trouble is, I never witnessed a long relationship when I was a child, so I'm not sure I know how to handle one."

"I think you've probably just chosen badly." He grinned.

"Let's hope that's all it is. But it terrifies me that I might allow myself to really fall in love with someone—then they might leave me."

"No pain, no gain," he said, and regretted sounding so flip. "I'm exactly the same because of the control-freak tendencies you spoke of earlier. I married Melissa because I thought I'd always be in control of the situation. I thought she'd never leave me."

"And then she did exactly that," interrupted Faye. "It just goes to show that nothing is ever completely in our control."

Tony felt his insides churn and shivered. He placed his elbows on the table and rubbed his temples. "I've never told anyone this before . . ." He stopped and stared at her, trying to assess whether to carry on.

"Told anyone what?" This time, it was she who took one of his hands, placing it flat on the table and entwining it with hers.

"I forced her to leave me." He screwed his eyes up with the pain of what he'd just admitted.

"What? But I thought she left you for another man . . ."

"No, I threw her out. When I discovered her at the gym, having a drink with that man . . ." he chewed the side of his thumbnail ". . . it turned out that they had shared a couple of kisses but nothing else."

"And?"

"And when I confronted her about it, she said he meant little to her and that she wanted to stay with me. She said she only spent time with him because she felt so alone all the time." He looked desperately sad. "But my ego was so bruised because she'd even looked at another man that I told her to get out. I was so pathetic."

He looked up at the ceiling, trying to compose himself. "For good measure," he added quietly, "I told her that I'd never loved her and regretted marrying her. No wonder she ran to him."

Faye cupped his chin in her other hand, tugging him to face her. "Tony, listen to me. We all say things we don't mean in the heat of an argument. It's human nature. Do you wish now that you'd asked her to stay?"

He shook his head. "No, the marriage had long been dead. I just wish it had ended in a less acrimonious fashion, but it was my fault that it didn't."

Faye sat back in her chair. "God, what a pair of fuck-ups we are."

Tony picked up his glass. "Here's to my mirror image," he said, taking a swig. "And thanks for listening to me drone on."

"Any time." She smiled. "That's a hell of a burden you've carried around for all these years. Have you seriously never told anyone?"

"Not a soul. They might have thought I wasn't perfect."

"Well, in that case, I'm honored." She tickled the inside of his palm. "But you do know what this means, don't you?"

"What?"

"You know all about my fears of a fatherless upbringing . . . and I know yours about how you treated Melissa."

"Er, yeeeesss." He was puzzled about where this was going. "So?"

"So . . ." She stroked the side of his face. "We can't ever fall out again. We know too much."

He smiled, and some of the old twinkle returned to his eyes. "I have many things I plan to do with you, but falling out isn't one of them," he said, brushing his face against her hand.

"Tony?"

"Yes?"

"After the Visage party, when you said you wanted us to go out together properly, did you really mean it?"

He frowned. "Of course. Why?"

"I'm sorry. It's just that all this unnerves me. On the one hand, it feels deliciously exciting to be with someone who interests me as much as you do, but on the other, it terrifies me because you might break my heart."

"I feel exactly the same way," he said. "There's a great Billy Bragg lyric where he says that love is like a scary ride at the funfair—when you're on it you want to get off, and when you're off you want to get straight back on again."

"That figures." Faye tightened her grip on his hand. "Well, I'm ready to board it if you are."

"Of course. But first there's something I've been dying to do . . ." Standing up, he dragged her chair round until it stood beside his. He sat down, interlaced her knees with his and looked into her eyes, his face just an inch from hers. As their lips made contact, he closed his eyes and breathed in her scent. If he was honest with himself, he'd wanted to do this from the moment he'd seen her in France, but now it was sensual not sexual.

He wanted nothing more than to love and protect her, but not in the same, overpowering, one-sided way he had with Melissa. Faye was his equal, capable of verbally slapping him down when he stepped out of line. He, in turn, had the strength of character to convince her that relying on him occasionally wasn't weakness. Together, he felt sure, they had found the right balance.

Drawing away from her, he held her face in his hands. "God, you're beautiful," he murmured and kissed the end of her nose. Suddenly, the romantic moment was spoiled as a thought struck him and he guffawed.

"What?" She cuffed the side of his head in mock-annoyance. "What's so bloody funny?"

He grinned. "I can't wait for you to meet my mother."

© Brian Aris

Jane Moore is the author of the internationally best-selling novel *Fourplay*, and is a columnist for Britain's bestselling newspaper the *Sun*. She writes regularly for the *Sunday Times* (London), cohosts the acclaimed British version of *The View* (*Loose Women*), and presents the daily breakfast talk show on LBC radio. She lives in London.